VIRGINIA DUIGAN is an author, journalist and
screenwriter who has lived and worked in
Australia, Britain and the United States. She has
freelanced for newspapers and magazines and
written for TV, cinema and radio. Born in
Cambridge and educated in England and
Australia, she now lives in Sydney with her
husband and daughter.

VIRGINIA DUIGAN

Days Like These

VINTAGE

A Vintage Book
Published by
Random House Australia Pty Ltd
20 Alfred Street, Milsons Point, NSW 2061
http://www.randomhouse.com.au

Sydney New York Toronto
London Auckland Johannesburg

First published in Australia by Vintage 2001

National Library of Australia
Cataloguing-in-Publication Entry

Duigan, Virginia.
Days like these.

ISBN 1 74051 013 5.

I. Title.

A823.4

Cover painting by Margaret Olley
Design by Gayna Murphy, Greendot Design
Typeset in 12/14.5 pt Bembo by Midland Typesetters, Maryborough, Victoria
Printed and bound by Griffin Press, Netley, South Australia

10 9 8 7 6 5 4 3 2

The author and publishers are grateful to the following copyright
owners for permission to reproduce extracts of lyrics:

'Days Like This', words and music by Van Morrison © *Exile Publishing Ltd*.
Reproduced by kind permission of Universal Music Publishing.
'Mama Said', Luther Dixon/Willie Denson © *1961 EMI Longitude Music Co.*
Used by permission of EMI Music Publishing Australia Pty Limited. All rights reserved.
'Nobody Told Me', John Lennon © *1980 Lenono Music. Used by permission
of EMI Music Publishing Australia Pty Limited. All rights reserved.*

ACKNOWLEDGEMENTS

I AM VERY GRATEFUL to many friends who have read work in progress or helped with research. Particular thanks to Margaret Olley for her cover painting. To Robin de Crespigny, Jane McLennan, Sophia Turkiewicz, Robyn Vines and Kristin Williamson in Sydney; to Jennifer Bryce in Melbourne; and to Sara Colquhoun, Anne Chisolm and Michael Davie in London. To Simon Bedak for the wager. To Hooked on Fish and Logue's Eating House for always welcoming a lone writer. And to that trio con brio – my agent Rose Creswell, Random House's head of publishing Jane Palfreyman and editor Roberta Ivers – much appreciation.

For Bruce and Trilby

When no-one steps on my dreams there'll be days like this
When people understand what I mean there'll be days like this
When you ring out the changes of how everything is
Well, my mama told me there'll be days like this

'Days Like This', Van Morrison

Nobody told me there'd be days like these,
Strange days indeed.

'Nobody Told Me', John Lennon

1

NINETEEN EIGHTY-FOUR. The year I returned to London with my life in a shambles. Of rather more import to the world at large, it was also the title of George Orwell's cautionary novel about a totalitarian state presided over by Big Brother and his thought police.

Perhaps because I had first read it there in Mim's house at the age of twenty-two, London was always linked in my mind with Orwell's book. At that time, 1984 had seemed an insanely far-off date, associated with age and its inevitable accoutrements: dullness, caution, irrelevance, decay. And conformity, the supreme original sin of the sixties catechism. *Nineteen Eighty-four*, the novel, had a lot to say about that.

And now I was thirty-nine years old and the year 1984 had indeed come to pass. In the twinkling of an eye, it seemed, I had reached that grim and faraway date. The various ironies swanning around it were not lost on me. They would have been hard to lose, since the bookstore at La Guardia was shoving

Nineteen Eighty-four into everyone's face. Sam drove me to the airport, and we'd had plenty of waiting time to fake an interest in other people's bleak futures and doomed love affairs.

The London flight was full of soberly uniformed business-men and a few less sober career women like myself. Someone had concealed a booklet in front of me, between the safety leaflet and the sick bag. It was headlined: Link Between Alcohol Intake and Alzheimers in Females. I studied it while knocking back Bloody Marys drowned in Tabasco. This was one habit I'd picked up from Sam. There were others. Some-times it felt as if he had seized my old personality – nonchalant, cool, composed – and burnt it, and written me a new character full of fever and fire.

I was reasonably anaesthetised when I opened *Time* and saw the photograph of Australian playwright Sam Tinker at his Broadway debut. I had accompanied Sam to this event, but I wasn't in the picture. That was something to be thankful for, I thought. The ability to see silver linings invisible to the naked eye has always stood me in good stead.

It was EEC and Others at passport control now instead of British and Commonwealth, which made me feel old and alien as well as tired and disillusioned. It seemed I'd felt tired and disillusioned for years, but that could have been just the linger-ing aftertaste of New York. New York, there were no two ways about it, had been a disaster.

In the cluster of faces at the arrivals gate I saw Miriam. She looked older and anxious, wore a crumpled red felt hat and a grubby raincoat, and was squinting into the middle distance. I hadn't seen her for ten years, but it was unmistakeably Mim, the girl I'd known since she and I were eighteen, as green as grass and keen to dip our toes in the water. Our toes and much more besides, in quick succession.

To be young in the sixties was bliss, but to be young and in London was very heaven. At least, that was how it seemed, in retrospect, and partially.

'You never would wear your glasses in public.'

'Lou? Oh, Lou!' We embraced emotionally.

Her voice dropped. 'Did you forget to bring any luggage?'

'Eric's got it on his trolley.' I turned to the man I'd sat next to. 'Thanks, Eric, I'm fine after all. I've been met.'

'Well, I'll see you in Manchester soon, then.'

'Manchester. Absolutely.'

He seemed reluctant to go. Mim opened her mouth. I saw that she, incorrigibly well mannered, was about to offer him a lift. I moved her on. I knew she was disturbed by this incident but she forbore to say anything. In the car she chastised me gently.

'We should have given that poor man a lift, Lou. You never would stand up to a man and say no.'

I was gratified to find that my ability to interpret Miriam's distinctive thought patterns remained intact. 'What do you mean?' I said. 'I spend my life saying no. It's the only possible answer, since it's always the wrong men who ask.'

Mim's driving, I noted, had not changed. She suspected all machines, because they were inanimate and thus untrustworthy, and she looked on driving as something you did more or less accidentally while doing something else. In this case the other thing was talking, to which she gave her undivided attention. We slewed all over the road changing lanes at whim, and I sat with my hands tensed ready to grab the wheel. Fortunately it was a Monday night and the North Circular was nearly deserted.

Mim turned and looked at me. 'I know you don't mean to, but you tend to encourage them, out of kindness. Then

3

you vanish from their life.' Almost as an afterthought she avoided the left bank that had been advancing on us at eighty miles an hour.

She was right, of course. At the age of thirty-nine I still wanted men to like me. To Mim's way of thinking I was acutely sensitive to other people's feelings. Mim could always be relied on to view my behaviour in the best of all possible lights. A less charitable person might have seen it as cowardice. I was uncomfortably aware that there were other, even less palatable explanations.

I saw that Miriam, who had never in her life said anything bad about anyone, was worried that I might have construed her remarks as criticism. She turned ninety degrees to her left and the car rocked violently.

'It's not that you intend to do it – anything but. You encourage them for the best of motives. You're so interested in people, and that's the basis of true charm. It's just that they sense your interest, which is a platonic one, and sort of misinterpret it.' She removed her left hand from the wheel and touched my cold fingers. Fat drops of rain were sluicing across the windscreen. She shook her overgrown fringe out of her eyes and peered at the road.

'You can't see because it's started to pour with rain, Mim. Turn on the windscreen wipers.'

We had spent four years together at Sydney University, first in college and then in a variety of shared slums. I knew her very well indeed, but there were lines on her face I hadn't seen before and something – sadness, apprehension – that kept settling itself into her expression, in spite of her efforts to smile at me. I guessed it had everything to do with her marriage.

Miriam Bottom was the first of our year to marry. She was unique among us in coming from a very wealthy family. Her

4

father was a property magnate with interests in publishing and transport. At the age of eighteen, politically ignorant and with no experience of the world, Mim felt an instinctive guilt at her plutocratic background. She was always determinedly proletarian, one of us, choosing dresses from op shops and spending frugally. In the long vacations she took jobs cutting sandwiches, sorting mail, and sweeping floors in psychiatric hospitals. In a deep and fundamental sense she was ashamed of being more equal than others, and we loved her for it.

Not that the rest of us, with mostly middle class parents and comfortable homes, were strangers to privilege. Miriam's advantages were simply on a different scale. Our fathers drove old cars, bottled their own wine and mortgaged their houses in order to educate their children. Miriam's dad drove old cars too, but they were vintage Bentleys and Rolls Royces.

I think none of us was surprised when Mim married, at twenty-one, a communist whose mother cleaned houses. John Black (or Black Jack, as he was known as a student) had an air about him that declared the inevitability of success. Physically he was a big and imposing young man with a deceptively indolent handsomeness. In fact he possessed the most single-minded drive – a combination of ambition, energy and greed, and absolute certainty of his goals – that I have ever come across.

Jack also had a self-deprecating humour and social diffidence very much at odds with his other qualities, which made him very attractive. He was certainly the catch of his year. And he married Miriam Bottom, who was stocky and untidy, who if not plain was equally no beauty, but who was the heiress to a fortune. Jack, of course, may have started off a penniless nobody but he was undoubtedly not going to end up that way. Still, when anyone dirt poor gets hitched to someone as potentially rich as Miriam, there are bound to be rumours and innuendoes.

A few minutes earlier in the car, I could have said to Mim: sometimes I do manage to say no. I said no to Jack. Because the focal point of Jack's character, the fulcrum on which his personality revolved, was an insatiable womanising. The rest of us, sexually naive as we nearly all were in those days, knew this. Around the campus he had the reputation, assiduously cultivated, we suspected, of a summa cum laude Casanova. Only Mim, blissfully and blindly in love, seemed unaware of it.

On cloud nine, over the moon, all her Christmases come at once – such clichés were inadequate to describe Mim in the months leading up to her wedding. And how do you tell someone who is happier than she has ever been, and perhaps ever will be, that her fiancé was guilty of the utmost disloyalty on the night of their engagement?

Faced with a similar dilemma today, I suspect, I would not hesitate. But at twenty the responsibility seemed awesome. Among ourselves we preached a code of rigid non-interference. It seemed then a self-evident truth that you did not tell a friend something that would destroy her. Especially something that might affect the course of her life. Such things were none of your business. Today, even without the benefit of hindsight, I might do things differently. But then, I think I would do quite a few things differently, given a re-run. If I had known five years before that I was going to run into Sam there, and the momentous consequences thereof, maybe I wouldn't have jumped so eagerly when my editor suggested I cover that literary festival in Stockholm. Maybe I wouldn't have. Just possibly.

Typically, Miriam had turned down her parents' offer of a slap-up engagement party and opted for a rort in the Glebe cottage she, Jack and I were sharing. There was an established pattern to our student parties. A few token plates of cheddar, French bread and maybe, if we were feeling sophisticated, some olives would be put out on a table in a corner. Bags of ice were emptied into the bath. A disproportionately large number of people would arrive, dump bottles in the bath, and cram into two small rooms. Cheap but potent music played deafeningly on rudimentary equipment. Guests danced and drank with single-minded dedication, punctuated by brief dashes out the back to be sick in the yard, and continued with stamina unabated until they passed out or staggered home. This decorative sequence of activities was rated highly by all of us.

Mim and Jack announced their engagement after the third year exams, a year before they were due to graduate. Miriam had high passes; Jack, anticipating his finals, topped his year with a string of firsts. The rort we threw in celebration of their impending nuptials didn't differ greatly from its predecessors. The quality of the booze was better: people brought champagne instead of beer and flagon wine, and most guests had made an effort to dress up for the occasion. But generally it unfolded much as usual – reckless drinking, advanced petting in back rooms, and dancing that was alternately frenzied, sentimental and sensuous.

We hadn't planned on any speeches but at midnight Jack leapt on a chair and delivered an impromptu oration about life, love, the universe and other loosely related subjects. The next day I could only recall that it seemed madly witty, was laced with aphorisms apparently pulled out of the air, and that everyone laughed loudly. Later another significance struck me. Jack's habitual cloak of social unease had been nowhere in evidence. It was as if his engagement had given him a charge of sophistication, a finishing course in poise.

It was soon after this that Miriam became ill and the party

broke up. I found her on her knees vomiting into the outside lavatory, and wouldn't have thought anything of it but for the fact that when she tried to stand up she doubled over. She was white-faced and her hands felt clammy, and she complained of stomach pain. I dropped some aspirins in a glass of brandy, fetched Jack and we put her to bed. This necessitated evicting several couples from the pitch-black room and tossing handbags, straw hats (hats were in that year) and academic gowns into the corridor. Mim insisted it was only migraine combined with an upset stomach so we didn't call a doctor, but it was impossible to dance the night away with the guest of honour indisposed. People melted into the darkness, concerned and regretful.

Jack and I tossed saucers of cigarette butts into the garbage bin then tiptoed in to see the patient. She was asleep, breathing heavily, and we crept out again. After that the sequence of events is confused. I remember sprawling on the sofa while Jack popped another cork, then trying to talk normally while the room rotated, first slowly, then with alarming speed. Jack pouring the last of the bottle into my glass, and laughing. Jack reaching up to turn off the light. Jack's arms around me, and the dim but definite conviction that this couldn't be allowed to continue. Struggling to my feet, tripping over them and lurching into the door.

Then Jack's arm tightly around my shoulders, steadying me, steering me towards my bedroom at the back of the house. A wrestling match on the bed and Jack murmuring over and over again, 'She'll never know, why worry? I'm crazy about you, Lou, you know that. Why not? It won't hurt her. She'll never know.'

He wasn't drunk. Black Jack was almost unique among the student fraternity for his abstinence in one area, just as he was notorious for excess in another. I had polished off the last bottle of champagne. Jack was stone cold sober.

8

Nearly twenty years later I glanced at Miriam's profile. She was talking animatedly about the children, Susanna and Timothy. Hers and Jack's. Jack and I had never referred to the incident after the party, although I was always aware that he regarded me as unfinished business. He didn't like to be thwarted and he hated failure with a passion. I was unsure whether this also extended to the object of his failure, and didn't stick around to find out. Miriam spent her first week as a fiancée in hospital having her appendix removed, and I dropped in on my father, stepmother and their young family in the country until she came home. I had no desire to see any of them, but a strong urge to put a substantial distance between myself and Jack.

Sam was an undergraduate at Sydney University too. He wasn't in our group, although Jack knew him. Soon after we met, Sam recounted a story about their first encounter at a sparsely attended lecture by a visiting Finnish linguist. Afterwards Jack had made a sustained attempt on Sam's girlfriend.

'Was it successful?' I'd asked with interest. I'd been aware of her, a glamorous Danish girl with long silvery hair.

'Fair go,' Sam protested with a bashful grin. He and Jack had subsequently become friends, which I thought reflected well on Sam's good nature. When I eventually saw photos of his wife, Ingrid, I was unsurprised to see that she was striking, golden and Nordic. The complete opposite of what my friends teasingly said was my gypsy colouring.

'It's particularly affected Susanna,' Mim was saying, her brows creased. Her forehead, when she pushed her hair away, was scored with deep lines of worry and she looked, I realised with shock, middle aged. 'Jack's hardly ever here, you see, it's got worse and worse. She's at the age where she needs a father figure, she tends to be a bit ... well, you'll see all that.'

We swung off the motorway, causing a car on our left to brake abruptly and sound its horn for a good thirty seconds.

'Must be an Australian,' Mim said absently. 'They're so impatient, they don't realise how thoughtless it is, all those poor people in bed who've got to get up early.'

'But where does Jack go? I mean when —'

'He's got his own mews house in South Ken. He's had it for years. He used to come and see us sometimes, often, at weekends . . . well, till a couple of years ago. Then it got less. And then last week he moved all his clothes out of the house. He's got another place too, you see, in Italy.'

'Does he visit the children?'

'Oh yes, he does try, he's very good like that, but it's difficult, you know, he's such a celebrity now. There are millions of calls on his time. He can't do as much as he'd like. But he *is* devoted to them, Lou. He's always been a conscientious father.'

Like hell, I thought. My knowledge of Jack over the past decade had been sketchy, but the only area I had ever known him to be conscientious about was the pursuit of his own interests.

We were in the dark streets of north London now, weaving intricately among the secret back roads of Mim's special short-cut. She was good at those. She always had her own way of getting somewhere, much, I suppose, as she had her own way of doing things. It wasn't usually the fastest or the most efficient, but it had its own logic.

We slowed to a crawl and Mim wound down the window. 'That's the Buddhist temple. I particularly brought you this way because I wanted you to see it. I think it's so beautiful, standing all by itself here.'

The exotic outlines of an Eastern dome took shape in the midst of suburban terraces. 'Are you a Buddhist now, Mim?'

She stepped on the accelerator and I surged backwards. 'I go in there sometimes. When I'm very . . . you know, when you feel a bit pressed. By things. It's very peaceful. I know quite a lot of Buddhists, I'll introduce you. They're lovely people.'

Her expression changed abruptly. She wrenched her glasses off in a gesture I knew well. 'Oh, Lou. I've been going on about myself when your situation's far worse, and I haven't asked you a thing about it. I'm sorry, how appalling of me. You must be dying to talk, and all I can do is complain.'

I always thought Mim would have made a marvellous actress. She experienced emotions, usually, it is true, the un-selfish ones of distress, sympathy and compassion on another's behalf, with the intensity of physical pain. But at the same time she was incapable of simulation and the least mendacious person I have ever known, so she probably would have been a failure on the stage.

'Put your glasses back on, Mim,' I commanded in panic. She replaced them while watching me with concern.

'Now start from the beginning, Lou.'

She broke off. We shuddered to a halt outside a big, three-storey Victorian house whose emanation came at me like a wave of forgotten perfume, full of the sweet sadness of the past. I felt giddy for a moment, as if I were drowning in a sense of loss, of the old as well as the new. Mim's troubled eyes were on me.

'Oh look, we're here already. You'd rather wait and talk over a strong drink. Or fall into a hot bath. Or – oh, what about a slug of hot chocolate and whisky?'

That remedy, together with the protracted, soul-searching confessionals of the very young, had been the panacea we used for all ills. I hadn't thought of it, let alone tasted it, for years.

'The old cure-all. You know, I think I could wrap myself round a mug of that.'

We heaved my suitcases through an overgrown front garden. In the morning it would dazzle with colour; now it was a tangle of competing shapes and scents. Mim's approach to growing things was like her attitude to people; she liked almost everything, and everything she liked she wanted to plant and bring up. Under her eye they all seemed to grow and flourish and reproduce with supernatural fecundity.

A clear English moon raced between clouds and lit the uneven path periodically, like a searchlight. I breathed in the remembered air of London. It was slightly sooty, still and cold, spiked with faint drifts of fragrance. There was a sense of silence and space, of things growing in damp earth, that was never present in Manhattan.

In the centre of the front door was a large knocker in the shape of a lion's head. The words BLACK INC were inscribed whimsically below.

'Do you remember, Lou? You gave it to us as a house-warming present. Seventeen years ago.'

I remembered. Our student years had seen the publication of *The Feminine Mystique*, but we were feminists well before its crusading impetus. Before her wedding Mim had gone through agonies of guilt over the decision to take Jack's surname. The dilemma was less clear cut than it might have been because of the undeniable disadvantage of being called Miriam Bottom.

'If I had been Miriam Nightingale, or even Miriam Smith,' Mim used to say, distraught, 'there wouldn't be any decision. Of course I'd keep my name. But Bottom. People find it amusing.' She omitted to add that the name Bottom, thanks to her father's activities, was a household name in Australia. Lesser women than Miriam might have regarded this as an

12

advantage; for Mim it was a mortification to be concealed. The rest of us, who had not neglected to persecute her in the past on this sensitive subject, were righteously stern.

'Of course you can't be so supine as to change your name, Mim.'

'It's an outmoded, subservient custom. You'd be going back into the dark ages.'

'You'd lose your identity.'

'What's wrong with Bottom, for Christ's sake? An earthy old-fashioned Anglo-Saxon name with Shakespearian echoes. You could've been called Smellie or Freake. Or Botti.'

'Breasted or Titworthy.'

'Cock or Organ.'

These names were the product of a wet Sunday Bess and I had once spent going through the Sydney telephone directory for vulgar surnames. It had afforded us much innocent amusement. An artistic friend copied the list in medieval script, with Bottom decorated and glowing like an illuminated manuscript, and we stuck it on Miriam's door. That, together with student parties, is a recreational activity I might now, in incipient middle age, avoid.

In the end the decision was made for Miriam, because Jack wanted it. When Mim was out of earshot we sniggered that if Jack had insisted she change her name to Smellie, Freake or Botti, she would have done it without a murmur.

2

AT TWENTY-TWO, I HAD thought of this house as home. Not that I ever lived here – I shared various flats around the frayed fringes of London – but the newlyweds functioned as a kind of surrogate family, not only for me but for the growing number of friends who made the long sea journey from Australia to England. Mim and Jack ran, with unfailing patience and generosity, a combined boarding house, soup kitchen and sanctuary for the homeless and the spiritually adrift.

There was a big, flagstoned kitchen and an infinite supply of sofa beds and inflatable mattresses. Sleeping bags were stored along with wine in the cellar. You could always be sure of a welcome, a hot meal and a bed at Mim and Jack's. Most of us were hard up and coping with the rigours of what appeared in those days to be endless youth – mostly, it seemed in retrospect, affairs of the heart gone wrong, or briefly and gloriously right before the recurrent catastrophe.

Mim's marriage, as well as her temperament, qualified her

as a mother confessor to her peers. Jack saw himself somewhat more fancifully as a paterfamilias. But if we chose not to confide in Jack we had no qualms about sitting down at his groaning board, where his impersonation of a middle class mine host became daily more detailed and convincing.

Jack had agreed to accept the house, his father-in-law's wedding present, largely because it contained a cellar. Although he drank very little he had expensive visions, and the idea of a wine cellar stocked with rare vintages was compelling. The more perceptive of Jack's friends had detected cracks in the edifice of his radicalism; before long they would become chasms. Like others before him, he found affluence and Marxism increasingly hard to reconcile.

Reg Bottom hadn't been to London since the Second World War, and he readily accepted his daughter's description of the delights of Kilburn. Reg probably thought he was buying a house in Belgravia. This showed how little he knew his daughter. Jack, as a proclaimed communist enrolled at the London School of Economics, had rather undercut his own bargaining power. But if a student had to admit to owning a house it was ideologically permissible, if not strictly correct, to own one in a working class suburb. Preferably a house with a leaking roof, rising damp and immigrants living next door.

These requirements were triumphantly fulfilled by the Kilburn establishment, with a few enhancements thrown in. The house had been hard to sell, and by the time Jack and Mim got to see it there was a blocked lavatory, several broken windows and a pathetic family of squatters in the cellar. Miriam invited them to stay on free of charge, but they disappeared mysteriously the day before she and Jack moved in. Lilian next door said the squatters had gone off with a couple of large men who'd come round in the evening. The visitors seemed to have their own key. I asked if one of them had a broad Australian accent, but as Lilian was still at the stage where all white people looked and sounded the same, she couldn't help there.

We did up the house with amateurish enthusiasm. Truck-loads of rubbish were carted away and a few painting parties followed, including the one that had decorated the big room Mim and I were now sitting in. It hadn't been painted since, I guessed, and Classic Magnolia, the dernier cri of the sixties, had turned the colour of putty. The room looked like the rest of the house, comfortably shabby. The fact that it looked very much as it had when I'd last seen it, when the children were toddlers, made the intervening years melt away like an irrelevant interlude.

Mim had reacted, as we all did, against her parents' standards of cleanliness. We regarded our mothers as obsessively house-proud, making a career out of trivial and unnecessary tasks. As students our habit was to avoid housework altogether. When we came to move out of a flat we would spend an energetic morning wielding rusty carpet sweepers and mops stiff with disuse. The furniture, we observed, had not suffered for going without polish. Layers of dust act as a preservative, proclaimed the First Bottom Law of Housework. The second stated that dust-coloured carpets do not show the dirt. If one had the misfortune to own a carpet that was not already dust-coloured, the remedy was simple: avoid vacuuming.

Over the years my attitude to the Bottom Laws of Housework had undergone modifications. Miriam, I concluded, was still a fairly solid supporter.

'I do have help these days, a cleaning student. The babysitter, Gayle, actually.' She moved a tray of eyeshadows, a ginger cat and a mug of cold coffee from an armchair.

'She's studying cleaning?'

16

'No, well, she's a schoolgirl. Although she doesn't necessarily look like one. Unfortunately she's not frightfully thorough, but she desperately needs the money to stay at school. She's just like we were, really – at that age you don't notice dirt.'

Miriam confided that Gayle was having trouble with her boyfriend, who was an older man of sixteen. 'Darren wants sex and Gayle's terrified he's going to give her up if she doesn't come across. She's Irish, you see, and the Pope forbids it. It's all such a worry for the young these days, Lou.' She was, I knew, referring to her thirteen-year-old daughter Susanna.

Susanna and her younger brother Timothy attended a local independent school, Kilburn Old Barn, run on experimental free-range lines. The choice of school had been Mim's. English public schools were obviously out of the question ('you and I know what a ghastly creation they produce, Lou') besides being fee-paying and therefore inequitable. Kilburn Barn had an admirable system, Mim explained, with high fees for those who could afford them, such as the Blacks, and considerably lesser ones for those who couldn't.

This, admittedly, led to 'certain problems at times' (some parents, I gathered, tended to take a more modest view of their resources than that optimistically held by the school) but it did mean there was a wide cross-section of students.

The Black children were in a racial minority, being heavily outnumbered by Jamaicans, Pakistanis and Indians. They were growing up, Mim told me, surrounded by friends from inter-esting and/or disadvantaged backgrounds. This did mean that Timmy, who was an impressionable boy, was mixing with kids who liked having a bit of fun after school, and that Susanna was tending to grow up rather more quickly than one might have wished, but on the whole it worked well.

Reading between the lines I deduced that the Black family

were supporting Kilburn Barn more or less single-handedly, Timmy's eleven-year-old chums were latchkey kids whose creative attitudes to leisure led to frequent appearances in the Children's Court, and Susanna was likely to engender a carnal knowledge charge. Miriam did not know whether her daughter had experimented with sex.

'But, Mim, haven't you talked to her about it?'

'She's only thirteen, Lou. She's not yet fourteen.'

'Conception is no respecter of tender age,' I said sanctimoniously. 'I know you and I were reading *Five Have Plenty of Fun* at that age, but . . .'

'Weren't we innocent? I didn't read chapter four of *The Group* until second year university. I know I'm terribly remiss in not talking to her, especially about crabs and herpes and things, but I find it hard to . . . she's a little difficult to . . . well, you'll see.'

Mim downed the rest of her mug in a hurry and poured two more slugs. 'Let's not talk about the children for a moment. I need your advice on a number of things to do with them, particularly about Timmy and the kennel, but we can come back to that.' She paused. 'Lou, you are staying, aren't you, for a long time? You're not just going to rush off?'

'I've had the nomadic life for a bit. I think I'll stay put.'

She came over and gave me a hug. I saw that her eyes were glistening.

'You've been having a tough time, Mim.'

'Haven't we all?'

Mim was looking at a photograph on the mantelpiece. It was a big silver-framed shot of Jack being presented with a gold statuette by a voluptuous blonde. He had acquired a prosperous girth but he still had a full head of hair, and even in the fixed image he exuded victory. His grin had the old combination of artless charm and rapacious carnality. The latter was directed quite flagrantly at the blonde.

'Margaux Fremlin,' Mim said without expression. I recognised the name. 'That lasted a while, but I don't think he sees her now. He thinks he's in love at first but then he moves on very quickly. The trouble is, he's so famous it gets around. Susanna and Timmy get flak at school. And the other kids' parents read things in *Private Eye*. Thinly veiled references – you know the routine.'

I had just come from New York. I knew the routine. For the past three months I had been living with an Australian playwright who, if not the household word Jack Black had become in the Western world, was already a glittering prize. I hoped the last three months were the last gasp of a five-year problem that had terminated yesterday. That particular problem had been around so long I felt lost and lonely without it.

'Other women were never the trouble with Sam, were they?'

'I was the other women. That was the trouble.'

'It was his children.'

'Yes.'

It was Sam's children. It was also Sam's wife Ingrid, who had commanded her battalion with its frontline troops (twins Fergus and Hannah, fourteen) with masterly finesse. Ingrid Tinker had employed impeccable military tactics, massing on Sam's vulnerable flank and then beating a strategic retreat to Australia, where she ordered the children to cut off the lines of communication.

It was, in its way, a heroic performance. Even I, with my more than mildly jaundiced view of Ingrid, had to admire it. She had kept her marriage intact, in name anyway, by disregarding the Geneva Convention.

But I was in no position to judge what constitutes squeaky-clean motherhood. It doesn't take much observation of marital breakdown to see that a few centuries of civilisation are a pretty thin veneer when the chips are down. Perhaps anything is permissible when your house is suddenly revealed to be founded in sand, and there is a cyclone blowing up outside.

I had endlessly wondered whether, in Ingrid Tinker's position, I would have resorted to the same manoeuvres. Did she lie in bed at night with her toes curling as she replayed some desperate and humiliating incident? Probably not. Probably she just stretched her toes out and encountered Sam's.

'At least you never did anything dishonourable, Lou.' Besides being charitable to a fault, Miriam was often disconcertingly psychic. 'It's not much comfort, I know, but it must make you feel morally above reproach. And that's something to have come out of it all with.'

I almost laughed, but she wasn't joking. She really believed you could derive some deep moral consolation from having clean hands, in spite of having lost the love of your life. Conceivably she was right. It was her devout belief in my virtue that was amusing.

'Many would say it is morally indefensible to take up with someone else's husband and father. Many, if not most.'

'But you fell in love with each other. You didn't intend to hurt anyone else. That was the last thing you intended.'

The classic excuse of our age, I thought wryly. We trot it out on demand and it has a way of covering every eventuality, from a fatality caused by drunk driving to a marriage breakup. I knew all about it, because I had used it to dismiss a suicidal abandoned wife and fatherless children at the end of a telephone. Clean hands was stretching it a bit, I thought.

I said, 'Mim, what are you and Jack going to do?'

Mim reached for a cigarette, lit it and threw me the packet. Her hands were trembling fractionally. 'I simply must give up smoking, it's such a bad example for the kids. Although Susanna never follows my example in anything, sensible girl, so with luck she'll never take it up ... Jack took his clothes away, Lou. And all his files.'

I glanced at the wooden plank bookshelves that lined the room. They were still full of Jack's first editions. 'Even the press cutting books I kept – all the articles and interviews. It seems so final, yet I can't believe – I always thought he'd come out of this ... this phase.'

'But it's been going on for years, Mim,' I said with gentleness.

'Yes. And I thought it would always go on like that. Stupid of me, wasn't it?'

The situation struck me as ominously clear cut. Mim's good nature had been there to take advantage of, and for years Jack had stuck around with one foot in the marriage and the rest of himself outside, taking advantage of it. Miriam's money and devotion, together with his own talent and energy, had enabled Jack to live English life on his own terms. Now he had no more need of Miriam's money and none, I guessed, of Mim herself.

Jack had risen spectacularly, writing revue sketches, becoming a political commentator, finally hosting his own television show, *Black and White in Colour*. This was the BBC's first big attempt to reflect Britain's multiracial character. It had its own format of heavy interviews, light chat, humour and variety. It broke new ground and it was, from the start, a sensation. In the United States it had become a cult program, starting with regular trans-Atlantic link-ups and, in recent months, evolving into a multinational enterprise with weekly editions alternating between London and New York.

Sam and I watched it on the huge TV in the bedroom of Sam's apartment overlooking Central Park. This was a favourite occupation of ours, but the location of the set meant that we watched a lot of beginnings of programs, and not too many endings.

Black and White in Colour was one of the few shows we watched to the end. We admired without reservation Jack's dynamism, professionalism and abrasive wit. If you hadn't been subjected to Jack's particular style of zany and unorthodox interviewing, you hadn't arrived. The program was so successful it could afford the best supporting acts, but the secret of the phenomenal appeal of *Black and White in Colour* was its unpredictability. Guests might be subjected to a merciless interrogation, made palatable by Jack Black's transparent interest in them. They might be asked about their sex lives, they might find themselves made fall guy, stool-pigeon or straight man to one of Jack's impromptu performances. He played off the cuff and he created a feeling of danger.

The show went over live and completely unedited. There was always the possibility that guests might be confronted by some unsavoury revelation from their past, or even by an embittered former lover out to settle old scores publicly. Jack regarded the program as a game and he played with it, much, I suspected, as he played with the people in his life.

The other quality that made the show compulsive viewing was its high and not always merely implicit erotic content. Jack, on the box as well as in life, radiated lechery rampant. Particularly if his interviewees were young, nubile and female. He had taken Freud to heart; his questions implied a passionate belief that sexual experience, proclivity and desire lay at the foundation of every personality and every action.

Others, it is true, hold to this conviction, but they generally make some effort to conceal it from the people they meet, at least in the early stages of social intercourse. Jack, for whom the early stage of an intimate relationship was often the first five minutes with a person, held no such scruple.

He had the rare ability on screen to make every woman feel that she might be the soul mate for whom Jack Black had been restlessly and diligently searching all these years. As a woman and, moreover, one who had glimpsed Jack's technique in its imperfect, embryonic form, I could appreciate that other women tended to respond by feeling unusually feminine and desirable. This was not infrequently followed by a tendency to speak freely. More freely, perhaps, than their managers had advised in the privacy of the dressing room.

The publicity value of the program was so immense that it was never short of candidates. To date Jack had not been sued, although there were rumours of out-of-court settlements. In any event, since his guests had spoken freely of their own volition, one assumed that the show was reasonably impregnable. But American law was tantalisingly vague on the subject of coercion. Sam and I once dined with a Californian lawyer who had made his name in palimony actions. He admitted to watching the program with growing interest. Sam and I perceived that his interest was not altogether unprofessional.

'Would you have married Jack if you'd known? You know, about his womanising?' This was a question we had all wanted to ask Miriam when we were twenty. I couldn't now recall why we hadn't. Misplaced adolescent sensitivity, I suppose, added to that article of immature faith: Thou shalt not interfere. It occurred to me that a lot of misery might have been averted if I had summoned the courage to ask that question when youth and idealism were still dewy on the ground.

Miriam inclined her head. 'Cyn told me, you know, when she was drunk once, but I didn't believe it.'

'*Cyn*thia told you?' I was astounded.

'Yes, but I just put it down to the fact that she was plastered. And – oh, you know dear old Cynthia.'

I did know. I also knew what Mim had the delicacy not to mention, and what had probably been uppermost in her mind at the time: Cyn's jealousy. Cynthia Whicker, plain, studious, clever, large, as gangling and clumsy as an ill-bred donkey. Cynthia, who was desperately in love with Jack and hating herself for it, who was tactless and well-meaning and jealous of Miriam and loathing herself for it. Cynthia trying to hide these two facts from everybody and fooling, maybe, only herself.

'When did she tell you?'

'When I came out of hospital. Do you remember, I had my appendix out? She said that Jack was sex mad and had even tried to get her into bed after some party. I discounted the whole thing.'

'No wonder.' I asked myself if it could conceivably be true, and decided it just could. Cyn's tactlessness derived, as I remembered, from a scrupulous honesty. My opinion of Cynthia Whicker rose. If the story were true and not just a figment of her inflamed imagination, it meant she had displayed both courage and discretion. Not only had she told the person it directly concerned, Miriam, she had also refrained from spreading the story among the rest of us, Mim's cronies. We would have seized on it with prurient fascination. Faced with a precisely similar dilemma, I myself had chosen the opposite two courses of action.

Mim said, 'It seems unkind to say it, but one of the reasons I knew it was all in her imagination was that if Jack had gone for anyone at the time it would have been you, not poor Cyn.'

I felt chilled. But nothing would be gained by confessing now. There is a season for things, and the time for that little titbit was long past.

'Would it have made any difference, Mim? If you had known?' I felt the question was deeply important.

'Oh, none at all. I'm sure I would have married Jack even if I'd known everything.'

I should have guessed that Miriam would always let me off the hook, but I found her answer deeply depressing. Mim must have regretted it too because she immediately added, 'You mustn't think I'm sorry, Lou. There were – there are wonderful times. And I've got the children, you see. I've been very lucky really.'

For a moment we were lost in different reveries. Mim poured more whisky and provided another milder revelation. 'I shouldn't say "poor" Cyn, it's so patronising. Anyway, she's coming to dinner on Sunday, and she's dying to see you again.'

'*Cyn* is?'

I shouldn't have been surprised. Cyn had come over to London at the same time as the rest of us, and had featured now and again in Mim's letters. Mim was a bad correspondent and I, being a journalist, was worse, but when she did write once or twice a year a sprawling stream of consciousness screed compelled me to put all work aside. Embellished with Mim's unique voice, it would transport me from wherever I happened to be in the world, straight back into this house.

'Good Lord, Mim. Is she still the same?'

'Well, she hasn't married. I suppose she is sort of the same, only if anything she's become more so . . .' Mim trailed off with a curious gesture.

'More so? In what way, exactly?'

'Oh, she's a dear, really, and she can be terribly funny –'

'In what *way*, Mim?'

Miriam waved her hands in a series of disconnected shapes. 'Do you remember, she had that thing about sex?'

'She never got any. Of course I remember. It was her defining feature. And?'

'Well, if anything, it's become even more of an obsession. She talks about it a great deal, the dear old thing.'

I drank some more whisky. 'I'm not sure I feel capable of Cynthia, in my present weakened condition.'

'I shouldn't have inflicted her on you, it's just that she heard you were coming and she needs cheering up at the moment. Well, I know we all do, and I thought this would be an opportunity to dilute her a little and have an Open Dinner.'

There had been passing references to Open Dinners in Miriam's letters. They were a monthly institution in the Black household, designed, I understood, to prevent anyone from becoming smug, middle class or narrow minded. Anybody knowing Mim would have felt there was little danger of that, but she was always one to make sure. Each member of the family was expected to invite one guest to an Open Dinner. Mim emphasised that the preferred type of guest was someone rather out of the ordinary in an offbeat, stimulating fashion – a type, perhaps, not normally encountered in the mundane daily round. Anarchists, emirs, laundromat attendants and bag ladies had featured in her letters, each one described with vivid interest and empathy.

'I'm sure you don't feel like meeting a whole collection of new people right now, so I thought we'd make this a modified occasion. Only one guest, a black American teacher Susanna keeps talking about. Then there'll just be you and me and Cyn. I'd have asked Bess and Roland, but they're away. Oh, and there'll be Jack too, of course.'

This last name was tossed off in a casual manner, rather as an afterthought. I jerked to attention.

'Jack's coming?'

'Yes. Well, he knew you'd be here, you see, and I know he wants to see you, so I thought this would be a good opportunity to have him – you know – with other people around . . .'

I considered objecting, saw Mim's face and dropped the idea. I didn't in the least want to see Jack, and I dreaded Jack's hearty questions about Sam. There were very few people in the world I could bear to talk to about Sam. Mim was one of them. Jack, emphatically, was not. Nor, for that matter, was Cynthia. Another thought struck me.

'But – what about Cynthia?'

Mim looked puzzled.

I said lamely, 'Well, you know, Jack and Cyn . . .' and trailed off. Mim looked completely uncomprehending. Lodged in my mind was an image of Jack as I had last seen him, at a party for New York glitterati, surrounded by an admiring, adoring throng, holding court with effortless ease and boundless charm. Then Jack a few hours later, at supper with Sam and me, demolishing with cheerful and sadistic venom the people who had lionised him.

There was no reason to assume that Cynthia's pomposity and clumsiness had mellowed with the passage of years. It occurred to me that she might be the kind of pathetically vulnerable target Jack would find irresistible. Such a thought was clearly heresy in Mim's scheme of things. Always believing the best of everyone, she was invariably bewildered when people behaved, as they frequently did, in ways that were other than entirely civilised. I had always believed that Mim was too nice for Jack. Without in any way revising this opinion,

I surmised that someone as worldly as Jack Black might, on occasion, have had justifiable grounds for exasperation.

With hindsight I saw Jack's attendance at the Open Dinner as the trigger in a chain of events that ended in disaster for one person, and crises, growth and enlightenment, perhaps, for others. On the other hand, just possibly these things would have happened as they did, regardless.

In my philosophy course at university I had studied cause and effect. This had left me with the philosophy student's aversion to absolutes and a reluctance to assign blame. A reluctance that I had enjoyed to the full on my own behalf. It had also bestowed on me an almost neurotic determination not to see things in black and white. Both of these ingrained tendencies, however, flew out of the window when Jack stepped into a room. I could assign blame to Jack, nothing easier, and no shades of grey either. Jack was the kind of person who makes others jettison the habits of a lifetime.

I could have pursued the matter of Cynthia and Jack and conceivably averted a great deal of subsequent pain and suffering, if the sitting room door had not opened at that moment. A woebegone little boy clutching a plastic shotgun and a mangy khaki blanket strode purposefully into the room. It was now nearly 1 am but Mim looked unsurprised.

'Timmy, darling, come and meet Lou, who hasn't seen you since you were . . .?'

'Two, I think,' I said feebly. Without glancing in my direction the small boy marched up to Miriam and hissed something fiercely in her ear. Miriam looked chagrined.

'I'm so sorry, sweetheart, I always forget.' She looked at me meaningfully and enunciated slowly and loudly. 'This is Jake, Lou.'

'Hi, Jake.'

He ignored me and addressed his mother, tugging his blanket tightly around him. He was shivering and appeared to have nothing on underneath. 'I'm starving. I want something to eat.'

Mim jumped up looking concerned. 'What do you want, darling?'

'Froot Loops.'

'There's only muesli, love, but it's very good for you and all the soldiers eat it.'

Jake spoke slowly and patiently in what was almost a parody of his mother's earlier tone. 'I'm not training to be a soldier, Mum, how many times do I have to tell you?'

Mim led him to the door. She turned and spoke seriously to me. 'Jake sleeps outside sometimes at the moment, he's toughening himself up, and he tends to get hungry in the middle of the night.' I followed them into the kitchen, which was littered with plates and crockery and what looked like the remains of several meals.

'Susanna didn't wash up,' Jake said in a surly tone. 'If I do it tomorrow can I have her two pounds?'

'One pound, darling,' said Miriam automatically. 'Well, it's sweet of you to offer, love, but Gayle's coming tomorrow and I think we can get her to do it for free.'

'It's not free, you have to pay her.'

'Yes, lovey, but we're paying her anyway, you see, and Gayle's quite good at washing up.'

I took the implication that Gayle was not especially good at other things. This was confirmed the next day, when I was able to observe a disconsolate teenager pushing a broom in random circles around the kitchen.

'Shit, that's not fair. When I offered.' He mashed his muesli with a savage spoon, then poured half an inch of brown sugar over it. 'I'm going to toast this.' He dragged out a small electric griller.

I watched mesmerised as Mim's half-hearted gesture of dissent was overruled with transparent contempt. While the sugar was bubbling under the grill Jake found a radio and turned on a raucous pop station. 'Did you watch all-night movies on American TV?'

As he was not looking at me I took a moment to realise I was being addressed. A picture of Sam and me lying on the bed oblivious to the flickering screen flashed unbidden into my mind. I thrust it aside painfully. 'Sometimes, Jake. But we thought American TV was pretty awful on the whole.'

'My dad's got the best show on American or British TV.'

'It's amazing,' I said truthfully. Jake busied himself turning off the griller, wrapping a tea towel round his hand and removing the hot plate. He had obviously done this before. He trotted off, holding the blanket and the gun in his free hand.

Miriam suggested anxiously, 'Wouldn't you like to eat it in your warm bedroom, darling?'

'No, I want it outside.'

'Say goodnight to Lou, lovey.'

There was a banged door and silence. Mim turned to me apologetically. 'He insists on being called Jake at the moment. I think it's a stage they go through.'

'Has he got a tent out there?'

Mim looked worried. 'He won't have a tent, he's sleeping in the kennel.'

'What, with Ché?' I remembered a portly black mongrel.

'With the cats. Poor Ché died of old age.'

I started to feel jet-lagged. 'Mim, it's late and I'm probably being obtuse, but why is he sleeping in the kennel?'

'It's a long story, Lou, but basically because he's training to be a soldier, you know, one of those SAS commando things. He thinks it'll make him tough. It's quite a big kennel, actually, it's not one of those tiny little ones.'

'Good God.' I felt a wild urge to laugh, but at the last minute managed to turn it into a yawn.

Miriam saw me and sprang to life. 'Poor Lou, you're exhausted. It's way past your bedtime.'

The guest room was high up in the attic at the top of the house overlooking the garden. It was friendly and cavernous. On the bedside table Mim had placed a pottery jug overflowing with winter flowers – lavender, yellow and white daisies and early jasmine. The walls were covered with posters and photos, most of them dating back to the sixties: David Hockney and Bridget Riley exhibitions, a Gilbert and George Happening, Ché Guevara and Bobby Seale, Manet, Gauguin, Frida Kahlo. There was a blown-up photograph of Danny Cohn-Bendit linking arms with Tariq Ali at the head of a student demonstration.

They looked like familiar, forgotten objects viewed from the wrong end of a telescope, these icons of a former life. The effect was unarranged, spontaneous and inherently youthful, like Mim herself. It was also evocative of thoughts and feelings I didn't want to be reminded of.

The room was full of Mim's touches. It was faintly scented with bowls of dried rose petals, the air warmed by a sputtering gas fire that looked antique. Hooks on the door were jammed with op shop hats – an old weakness of Mim's – and she had covered a Victorian screen with dozens of lacquered postcards. Most were picture side up but a few showed the inscription. I recognised my signature on a jaunty note from Beirut, posted fifteen years earlier.

A pine chest of drawers was crowded with framed photos.

All seemed to have been chosen for their connection with me; all, inevitably, were filled with laughing youthful faces. Together with the posters and other relics, I found them yearningly sad. One picture, the colour already fading, showed a bunch of young people dressed in outlandish outfits and striking preposterous poses. Bess's wedding, at a tiny stone church in a Suffolk village she knew nothing of but had chosen for its romantic appeal.

Bess and Roland were at the centre of a rollicking group that included Mim and Jack, Cynthia and myself. I was wearing a floral trouser suit with flared legs and an orange boater dripping with geraniums. Like the others, my face was lit by a soft evening sun.

These gilded youngsters looked in their dated clothes and attitudes like puppets from a silent film. They seemed to be happy in a way that was now out of reach, with an uncomplicated, wholehearted joyousness. I felt a tearing envy for them, frozen in the days before real feelings, and I meant love, had moved in and altered the course of our lives. Thereafter, or so it seemed to me, happiness would always be elusive and, when it came, fragmented and equivocal.

I stared at my old, and paradoxically young, face. Was this what it was like to grow old, perpetually reminded of the past in an acccelerating process of regret? It was as if having once been young had ceased to have any meaning, or that whatever meaning it had could be reduced to a paper image to be picked up and scrutinised, a curiosity with no connection to the present. There was no interest for me in that former self, beyond a fierce covetousness I recognised as futile and destructive.

There was a tap on the door and Mim rushed in, carrying a hot water bottle and a mauve chenille dressing gown. 'I thought you might like these. Hot water bottles are so comforting. I think it's because they're so old fashioned. No dreadful modes and switches. I've been overtaken by the new technology, Lou. Soon I won't be able to turn on a light.'

Her eyes dropped to the photo in my hand. 'Ah, Bess and Roland's wedding. I love that one too – weren't we so young? And we thought we were so old and experienced.'

'Did we?'

'Oh, we knew everything, Lou. Everything. Sometimes I think life's just a process of unknowing. What is it the Masons say? You progress towards The Knowledge. To me it's the opposite. You start off with The Knowledge and lose more and more of it as you grow older, till it's gone completely, and you die in the true knowledge of your ignorance.'

'I've always thought you were intermittently capable of wisdom, Mim, and this is one of those moments.'

She squeezed my hand and tucked the hot water bottle under the bedclothes. 'Now go to bed, Lou. I should never have kept you up so long. You'll be seeing double.'

I wondered if that was what I was doing. But there were more than two of them here, there was a whole legion of uninvited ghosts. In the corner of the room was a settee in faded navy corduroy. It had once been in the sitting room downstairs, and I remembered lounging on it and kissing various young men, sometimes, but not always, imagining myself in love.

Over the bed was a shelf of books, mostly Penguin Modern Classics with frayed spines. They looked like Mim's English Lit. novels from university. *The Voyage Out*, *The Golden Notebook*, *Women in Love*, *Nineteen Eighty-four*, *Decline and Fall*. I hoped the arrangement was an irony and not an omen.

I sank down under a hand-sewn patchwork quilt against a

heap of pillows. They were soft and well-worn. The mattress was squashy with a steep dip in the middle and it needed someone else in it. It was the first time for many weeks that I had tried to sleep outside Sam's arms, and it felt like being adrift on a wild and lonely sea.

I remembered this feeling well because it was a carbon copy of the one I had when they told me my mother was never coming home again. She'd been seriously ill all through my childhood. There would be brief home visits, when I was enveloped in her frail embraces, and then the ambulance and the stretcher. I was only nine when she died, but the memory was as sharp and sombre to me now as it had ever been.

Soon after her death my father married the secretary in his small country law firm, and as if to make up for lost time they had three children in quick succession. He never spoke to me of my mother, and even now I was unsure of the exact nature of her illness. I distanced myself from this new family by pressuring my father to send me to boarding school, where I protected myself by trying not to think of her.

I wondered if the same strategy would work with thoughts of Sam. At least I was an adult now, and Mim's house was a lifebelt. When I closed my eyes I could imagine for a moment that the high waves were my mother's enfolding arms, holding me close.

3

THE IMPRESSION OF HAVING stepped back in time intensified in the week before the Open Dinner. I spent hours beside the fire, wrapped in rugs, brooding over novels. It was as if the intervening years had never been, and I was in the bosom of Mim and Jack's surrogate family, twenty-two again and being nursed through some crisis. Only now the family was Mim, whose maternal qualities were indestructible, and her children, for whom traditional mothering was something to be scorned. Mim had more success babying the cleaning student, Gayle, whom I identified as one of the tribe of lame ducks Mim habitually took under her wing. Gayle's heart was not in her work, and I suspected she needed the money to finance her hairstyle, a strident confection of spikes in shades of orange and mauve.

Both Jake and Susanna appeared to be formidably independent, using the house in the way one treats a hostel, as somewhere to eat and sleep. The important business of life, they made clear, was carried on elsewhere, and well out of Mim's earshot. Occasionally the thud of army boots would advertise the presence of Jake and one or two friends, as dishevelled and unkempt as Naples street urchins. And occasionally a group of long-haired, sylph-like waifs, whose elaborately disordered garments testified to the expenditure of dedicated thought, would waft along the corridor and into Susanna's bedroom. When they emerged hours later, significant rituals had clearly been wrought on one or other of them. Hair had been streaked or coloured, eyelashes curled, eyebrows plucked, fingernails treated as miniature canvases.

I was looking at my own face through new eyes now, since Susanna had patiently explained how, with a minimum of effort, it could be improved. My eye sockets could be smudged, the illusion of interesting hollows might be achieved in the cheeks. The eyebrows, plucked from below, could be endowed with a disarming arch instead of their present horizontal dullness.

'I can't understand how you could have got to your age without knowing all this,' Susanna told me as she redrew the contours of my face with casual expertise. 'The trouble with you is, you haven't changed your makeup for twenty years.'

I had to admit the truth of that.

'Mum's the same. She's a sixties refugee. Only she's unregenerate. A touch of blue eyeshadow and she thinks she's something out of the Arabian Nights. Blue eyeshadow! That went out with foot-binding.'

My own blue eyeshadow was consigned to the garbage, and replaced by an artist's palette of colours, most of which I had never associated with eyes. I submitted to Susanna's ministrations passively one afternoon, finding it soothing to be in someone else's capable hands. In just such a manner, I realised, had generations of unhappy women used the hairdresser or the beautician's touch as a substitute for sexual attention.

Susanna's self-assurance was daunting enough. But her attitude to her mother, a combination of the exasperated solicitude one feels for an overgrown child, and her brother's open indifference, I found unnerving. She was undeniably an extremely pretty child. Glossy chestnut hair, thick, curling eyelashes, a flawless skin. Until recently I might have attributed the shine, the arresting auburn hue, the curl and the alabaster complexion entirely to nature, and youth. Now I knew they were only largely responsible. Unfortunately Susanna was all too aware of her attributes. As her mother observed, she seemed to have sidestepped childhood. Having her around was like sharing the house with a disdainful and deeply self-absorbed young person of around thirty. One, moreover, who was preoccupied by the ticking of her biological clock.

As far as I could see, everything in Susanna's private universe was organised with one objective: boys. Or more accurately, young men. Sixteen seemed to be the cut-off point below which a male was dismissed as unreconstructible. Between Susanna and her mother I could detect no similarity, no common ground whatever. Her father's input, however, was all too evident. Jack's looks, confidence and sex appeal she had in abundance. All evidence indicated she had also inherited his one-track mind. His charm was not yet apparent, and I had to hope that his ruthlessness and associated defects of character might have been similarly bypassed. Surely Miriam had made some contribution to the genetic makeup of her offspring? But perhaps Jack's seminal fluids, like Jack, just overpowered everything in their path.

Still, it remained inconceivable to me that Mim could have lived in the same house as her children, brought them up more or less unassisted, and yet handed on little or nothing of herself. Jake was too young and too one-dimensional to pass final judgement on, although his obsession with military manoeuvres did not augur well. But Susanna? In some ways both children seemed untouched by the violent disturbances in attitude and behaviour that had so indelibly imprinted itself on our generation.

Yet when I thought about it, perhaps the brazen self-confidence I found so alien in Susanna was a direct legacy of just that upheaval. She was more at ease with herself, more satisfied with her position as a female in society, than Mim or I could ever be. The idea that men and women started the race from the same baseline, and were equally well equipped for the running of it, was taken for granted. The freedom – social, mental and physical – that such a conviction brought in its wake was surely revolutionary.

It was one thing, however, to be free in the unrestricted environment of home and school. Quite another out in the convention-ridden confines of the world.

Mim stirred chilli con carne in a Le Creuset pot that had been a wedding present. Once orange, it was blackened with use. 'It's the best freedom, I think, that attitudinal kind. I just hope it's not illusory.' Coming from someone else, coming from myself, this would have testified to a degree of worldly cynicism. From Mim it was hope shining eternal.

'It's funny, you know, Lou, all that time they spend on their clothes and appearance. Our idea that they might be pandering to a male view of themselves as sex objects doesn't seem to worry them.'

'I don't suppose it even enters their mind.'

'No. Well, it's probably best they don't have that additional worry. It certainly tied us up in knots.'

'It still does. It was solely responsible for me not changing my eyeshadow all these years.'

We were preparing for the Open Dinner. My apprehensions about this event had worn off slightly as it loomed closer, and had been replaced by guarded anticipation. I had always enjoyed parties. I was even looking forward to seeing Cynthia again, with a feeling of curiosity and misgiving in roughly equal parts. The thought of seeing Jack aroused in me, as it always did, a warring brew of emotions. On the one hand I had known him for too long not to feel affection. On the other, I knew him too well for that affection to be absolutely pure and unsullied.

At times, particularly where his treatment of Mim was concerned, he was capable of arousing me to a pitch of outrage. At other times his ebullience and warmth made people, myself included, happily overlook his excesses of hubristic selfishness. It was frequently said of Jack that he could charm the pants off people, and it wasn't said figuratively. The fact that he had not succeeded in charming them off me was a source of profound relief that the passage of years had left undimmed in intensity.

I resented Jack's effortless charm. I resented my own susceptibility to it, and I had a nasty suspicion that my attitude to Jack these days was not entirely free from jealousy. That I could be even slightly resentful of an old friend's success was an unpleasant blow to my self-image, particularly as I knew very well that Mim harboured no such feelings.

Miriam Black had always shown an ungrudging delight in her husband's achievements. Indeed, she had voluntarily submerged any career ambitions of her own in wholehearted support of Jack's activities. In that respect, I reflected, she had been a traditional wife, a helpmate, and now she found herself reaping the equally traditional unjust desserts. It wasn't that she had surrendered her own identity in the process. Mim was a genuine individualist, far too evolved a personality to lose it to another, even to such a demanding and controlling character as Jack. Nonetheless she had always placed herself discreetly in the background, in full agreement with whatever Jack proposed to do with their lives. In Mim's book Jack was always right and she automatically put him first. Which, perhaps, remained their strongest common denominator.

For the past ten years and in a voluntary capacity, I knew, Mim had worked in a local housing co-operative. She was one of the prime movers in establishing this organisation, which had begun in a modest way by finding temporary shelter for homeless families in empty houses marked for demolition. Later it had developed and expanded, working in conjunction with the local council, and now boasted a paid staff of five. While it was non profit-making and mainly interested in accommodating homeless and low-income people, it raised handy funds by releasing some of the better renovated properties onto the mainstream rental market. Mim, naturally, had sought neither status nor salary, and while her work was nominally part-time, Susanna told me she put in more hours than anyone.

'Mum's such a patsy. Working without pay. Can you imagine? They just ride all over her. She's always in the office – it would totally fall apart without her.'

After the wedding gift of the Kilburn house, Mim had steadfastly refused any further money from her family. She now found herself dependent on Jack, who certainly was a very wealthy man but who, I had no doubt, was soon to become her ex-husband. She felt herself morally ineligible to be paid by the housing co-op, almost equally reluctant to accept Jack's continued support, and adamant that she would not call on her family. It was a triple bind of a kind, I felt, that only Mim could have contrived for herself.

Susanna had assured me the co-op was healthy and flourishing.

'Sometimes old people die and leave them things too, like really cool flats and stuff. They get more dough by flogging them off.'

Wouldn't it be best all round, I proposed tentatively, if Mim went on the payroll?

'I know I'd be independent of Jack,' Mim conceded. 'But really, Lou, I couldn't. They rely on the surplus for the running costs, building fund, repairs, cash advances, new housing stock. For people who have nothing, Lou, in the world. It's not as if I have to have the money to survive.'

'Well, I can see nothing for it but to accept it from Jack gracefully.' I pointed out that Mim and the children were but flesh and blood, and that they too needed the wherewithal to exist. But I could see from her expression that she was unconvinced, while reluctant to disappoint me over something I clearly felt strongly about.

I cast around for the most persuasive argument, and led up to it cunningly. 'If nothing else, you owe it to the children. They're Jack's too. And after all, that kind of money's nothing to Jack. It's a drop in the bucket. Isn't it better that he continues to support you and the kids, and has the moral satisfaction of knowing he's doing his duty by you? I mean to say, wouldn't it be very undermining to his masculinity if he wasn't supporting his own family?' I could see I was making some headway and I paused before delivering the coup de grâce. 'And, Mim, think what the gutter press, what *Private Eye* would do, if they found out he was paying nothing!'

Her reaction was pleasing, and instantaneous. 'Lord! They'd pillory him as a Scrooge. When he's really so generous. His reputation would be completely besmirched.'

There wasn't a great deal of Jack's reputation left to smirch, I thought. They had already seen to that, and I couldn't in honesty say that I blamed them. If I pushed the honesty far enough, I had to admit that reading luridly embellished accounts of Jack's perfidy had afforded Sam and me considerable entertainment.

The resolution of the financial dilemma was a victory to me, but I knew Mim too well to suppose it would be complete, or permanent. She was tormented by the injustice of the situation. Why should she be entitled to automatic upkeep when the husbands of countless other unfortunate divorcees defaulted shamelessly?

'It all seems terribly unfair, Lou. There are so many poor women who get nothing, who are struggling to bring up children on welfare – four, five and six children – completely alone. With only the most basic, depressing accommodation. Overcrowded, filthy –'

'You could take Jack to court and get a vast settlement, and give most of it away . . .' I knew this was an unwise tack when I perceived Mim's eyes take on a wandering look. 'Maybe Jack will default too,' I said feebly, but she would have none of that. I marvelled anew how after nearly twenty years of his sustained treachery, Mim still carried a blazing torch for Jack. Was this a peculiarly feminine aberration, I wondered. Or was it simply the province of certain innocent natures, the gentlefolk of the earth, trusting, always believing the best of everyone? And, too often, ending up trampled underfoot by the ravening hordes.

While out shopping that morning, I'd casually asked Mim

if she had warned Jack about Cynthia's presence at the dinner. She had not, it transpired, spoken to him at all.

'I left the dinner invitation with his secretary – she's extremely helpful.' I gathered that Jack had declined to come to the phone. 'It was a bad day to ring, his worst day, with the show being lined up and everything.'

'Did he call back the next day?'

'His secretary called to confirm it. He's so busy, you know, he just doesn't have time for normal chitchat.' Unlike normal people, I thought.

'So he doesn't know Cyn's coming?' I felt a compulsion to rub it in.

'I thought it was best not to mention it, in case you were right.' On anyone else's face I would have described Mim's expression as disingenuous. On Miriam it was truly guileless. She had been married to Jack for seventeen years. I couldn't blame her for wanting to see him, but I hadn't realised, until that moment, quite how much she wanted it.

A blast of cold air filled the kitchen as the back door swung open and a lumpy figure lurched in, dark hair straggling over a sodden, dun-coloured oilskin. Even though her face was blurred by the rain and nearly concealed by a shapeless sou'- wester, I knew immediately that this was Cynthia. I felt I'd have recognised Cynthia Whicker fifty years hence if she was coming at me in impenetrable darkness disguised as the Invis- ible Man. There was something peculiar about Cyn, something obscurely physical and intrusive, which had always discomfited me. Now, as she charged straight at me, motorbike helmet under one arm, swinging a wine bottle, I fought the urge to retreat. She had always come too close, invading one's personal space with a rapacious homing instinct.

'Lou, is that really you? You look so different!' She kissed me on both cheeks, her icy skin radiating an inner, unrestrained warmth, shaming me. 'What is it, how many years? Mim and I always see each other, we're practically sisters, so we don't notice the ravages of time, but we must look like strangers to you.'

'No, Cyn, you really haven't changed at all,' I said wonderingly. It was substantially true. As she struggled out of her coat and shook the rain off her hair onto the floor – rather like a shaggy water spaniel, I thought – her features took recognisable shape. The same watery, protuberant eyes, the same aggressive nose and wide, thick-lipped mouth heavily emphasised by a dark purplish lipstick that looked heavily old-fashioned to my newly tutored eye. Everything about Cynthia was large and loud, even more so now as she had gained weight and lost a certain youthful bounce.

Mim regarded her with uncritical affection. It was clear that Cyn felt completely at home here, knew where every small household item lived, felt, like me, an essential part of Mim's family. The fact that we were both refugees in Mim's house, bound by the indissoluble ties of a shared youth, gave me a sudden surge of fellow feeling for Cyn. But it was short-lived, overtaken almost at once by the suppressed irritation I recognised as endemic to this relationship.

'Lou, you must tell me all about Sam. What's it like, living with a celebrity? And in New York too. Is it really as dangerous as they say? I lead such a dull life, the only excitement I ever have is hearing about your activities. The number of times I've told my students that I know someone who lives with the playwright Sam Tinker, or *lived* with him I suppose I should say now. Almost equal to the number of times I've dined out on the fact that I went to university with Jack Black. Not that I dine out very often, don't get the wrong idea.'

'Cyn, dear, could you possibly lay the table?' Mim said

hastily, but it was too late. Cyn was peering over my shoulder, her dripping hair obstructing my vision.

'Lou, that's not the way you grate cheese! Here, let me show you how.'

One of Cyn's least endearing qualities was her conviction of superiority, practical as well as intellectual. This was made much worse by the suspicion, once voiced by Mim and never referred to again by the rest of us, that it was not entirely unjustified. It took several forms, most often a compulsion to do things Cyn's way, in what she saw as the most efficient scientific manner. We called it the indiscriminate job takeover. The fact that her way was indeed faster and more effective endeared her to us even less. She was especially intolerant of illogicality, and absolutely merciless with stupidity. She had been a dedicated student with a rigorous academic mind, took a double first in English and went on to a doctorate at Cambridge. The rest of us consoled ourselves sourly by saying we would have done as well or better if we had worked as hard. And we asserted our moral superiority by awarding her, in private, an F for human relations.

I surrendered the cheese to Cynthia and obeyed her order to open the red wine and let it breathe. Having surveyed the remaining tasks, Cynthia assigned them with a sergeant major's precision, even co-opting a manifestly reluctant Susanna. She drew the line at Jake, who had announced his intention of cooking baked beans on a primus and eating outside, while watching TV on a portable set with an extension cord.

The assembly line was such that we finished a good half hour before the remaining guests, Jack and Susanna's teacher, an American named Dave Benwell, were due to arrive.

Cyn's curiosity about Sam was insatiable, but she suspended her interrogation whenever Susanna was in earshot out of some kind of misguided scrupulousness. I could only be thankful for this, although I was convinced that nothing in my heavily censored account would shake Susanna's awesome knowingness.

In her relentless desire to hear every detail, Cyn was very like Jack. But their attitudes and motives were poles apart: where Jack's interest would be predominantly prurient, Cynthia's came from a disinterested spirit of inquiry, a desire to amass all the facts of the case in order to arrive at an informed opinion. Whatever the cause, however, the visible effect on me was such that Mim intervened frequently, first with diversionary tactics and then confronting the issue head-on.

'Cyn, dear, I don't think Lou really wants to talk about Sam. It's all a bit recent and upsetting.'

Cynthia's expression of genuinely innocent surprise almost disarmed me. But the respite was brief. I could see her dealing with the impulse to query this, and she had begun to frame the question when Jack appeared, closely followed by a staggeringly good-looking young black man who had to be Dave. Since Dave's skin was only marginally darker than Jack's leathery Australian hide, I would have described him as white had Susanna not lectured Mim and me on this sensitive subject. It was a political issue. Dave's paternal grandfather was black; he liked to be called black; he *was* black.

He was also, I recognised straightaway, a New Yorker born and bred, a savvy Bronx kid made good whose street-smart upbringing was apparent from his coiled muscular frame and barely controlled energy. Instead of walking, he came sideways on the balls of his feet, his eyes alert and wary.

It was evident from the moment he entered the house, surrounded by an invisible electrically charged field of pheromones, that Susanna was completely besotted with him. I observed as the evening progressed that Cynthia and Mim were becoming equally and unwittingly smitten.

Jack Black was not in the market to be overshadowed by any young male, black or white; he was far too consummate a performer. The gust of his presence was like a tornado. He did a quick visual inventory of the assembled company, bussed Mim on the cheek and staged a theatrical double-take when he saw me laying the table in the dining room. In a second he had tossed his wet raincoat at Mim, crushed me in a bear hug, kissed me passionately on the lips and gazed into my eyes.

'Lou! Darling heart, light of my life! As gorgeous as ever, you desirable woman, you. Where has she been all these years, this deserter? Adventuress extraordinaire and intrepid foreign correspondent! Well, you're back in Blighty, sweetheart, cradle of civilisation, sanctum of sanity. Where's that ne'er-do-well pillar of domesticity, the cad? Upholder of family values, the bounder! Given him the elbow at last, have you? Given him the Big E?'

It was only a few months since I'd seen Jack, but I was always caught off balance by the sheer raw power he injected into any gathering. He acted as a superconductor, the magnetic epicentre of a circuit that energised every bystander in his path. What he said was often unremarkable or patently ridiculous, but he delivered it with such force and zest it was invariably, momentarily, convincing. Afterwards, of course, one either cursed oneself for a fool, or mentally saluted a master player. It all depended on how much you recognised and surrendered to the enjoyment of the game.

Some personalities were particularly ill-suited for this. Cynthia's was one. Cyn's dogged, hectoring earnestness could almost have been designed with one objective: to provoke Jack. At the best of times Jack was scarcely tolerant; at times like this, when the air was heavy with undefined tensions, Jack's patience was like a snake's used skin – just waiting to be sloughed off.

He acknowledged Cyn's presence with a wave and blown kiss, which by Jack's standards were barely cursory. I saw the hurt register in Cyn's eyes. Then, in a seamless transition of roles, he switched from guest to host. He charged the fridge. 'Pre-prandial apéritifs, everybody! Mim, where's the bubbly? You know I can never tolerate dinner without first lining the stomach with the nectar of Monsieur Cliquot's widow.'

Mim looked crestfallen.

'Christ, Mim, a fridge without champers is like sex without orgasm. A contradiction in terms. Go to the bottom of the class. Here, Dave – is it Dave? – come down to the cellar with me and flex your youthful rippling biceps on a worthy object.'

Dave sloped off after Jack looking rather like a press-ganged recruit, but when he returned minutes later, heaving a crate, with Jack in tow, the two were grinning and chaffing like old hands. Another convert, I thought, although the guarded look in Dave's eyes was never entirely absent. They stacked champagne in the freezer, then disappeared outside and returned with a load of cardboard boxes which they dumped in the sitting room. I guessed Jack was using this opportunity to do some stocktaking. Mim's face crumpled in alarm.

'Sit down, everybody! Compulsory relaxation and stimulating intellectual discourse, until the champagne's cold and we all get drunk and are allowed to be frivolous. Improving topics will be nominated in turn. Topic the first is life, morality and existence.'

The mischief on his face was all too familiar. During the brief pause that followed I watched him survey the room, his eyes alighting first on Susanna, whom he had so far ignored, then on Dave, whose eyebrows were raised in humorous appeal, on me with a conspiratorial wink, and finally coming to rest on his chosen target – Cynthia.

'Cyn, you're our resident intellectual. What is your considered opinion?'

'My doctorate's in English literature, not life, Jack,' Cyn said with a grim smile. 'Let alone virtue or ontology.'

'English lit, bless its heart! And is English lit not a reflection of life?'

'It's drawn from observation of life. Teaching it doesn't qualify one to pontificate about morality. Any more,' Cyn added slyly, 'than inducing people to make fools of themselves in front of millions on a popular TV show qualifies you, Jack.'

'Touché! But I think you protesteth too much. They be lusty bedfellows, literature and morality, forsooth. The mighty Dr F.R. Leavis knew what he was on about!'

'Dr Leavis has been superseded, Jack. Purged. Didn't you know that? Your age is showing.' The triumphant light in Cyn's eyes was, I feared, premature.

'So, are we to surmise that you live a blameless, contemplative life in your sequestered ivory tower of academe?'

'You can surmise whatever silly rubbish you like.'

A dreamy look came over Jack's face. It was the look, I'd always thought, of the predator preparing to pounce. 'Is this, or *is* this, question-dodging of the most nefarious kind? The kind induced by a lifetime of ingesting intellectual fudge? Let's have the plain answer: where is the contemporary convent to be found?'

I watched Mim's face. The desire to intervene on Cyn's behalf battled openly with her reluctance to cut short Jack's entertainment. And if he had shouted 'Tally ho!' Jack's enjoyment could not have been more palpable. Cyn's smile was taut.

'I'm sure you've already decided that, Jack, so I won't attempt to steal your thunder.'

Well done, Cyn, I thought. But unless you were one of his favourites, which usually meant sexual objectives, it was always unwise to goad Jack. He dropped his voice and leaned forward, towards the exposed jugular. 'Weren't you, just between ourselves – I promise it will go no further than these four walls – weren't you, in your heart of hearts, attracted to the academic life because it is the modern equivalent of a nunnery? Because it allowed you to opt out of the sexual circus without making that explicit in the eyes of the world?'

Someone – Mim? – drew a breath sharply. Help, however, came swiftly from an unexpected quarter.

'Hey, guys, this is too heavy on an empty stomach. If we're gonna have a vintage Jack Black interview right here in the living room, I have to defend my student Susanna. She's under age. And I need a drink, man, I don't care if the champagne's on heat!' His grin at Susanna was apologetic and also, I thought, flatteringly conspiratorial.

Jack took the reverse with an equanimity that declared it was only temporary. 'Chivalry lives! Off the streets of Eve's Big Apple, no less! Okay, parfit gentil knight, come and lend me your hand. Mim, are any of those champagne flutes still functional? You know, the ones I got –'

'When the program went into its second year!' In her relief Mim sounded like a schoolgirl who had just discovered she wasn't pregnant after all.

'Yeah. Did they all get broken?'

Mim headed for the kitchen. 'Oh no, I'm sure there's three at least.'

'Out of twenty-four. Well, that's something, I guess.'

'You have to stand up to Dad,' Susanna said sagely to Cyn

when he was safely out of the room. 'Otherwise he just bullies you into the ground.'

'I know how to behave with your father, I've known him since before you were born!' Cyn looked about to break into angry tears.

Susanna turned to me animatedly. 'Dave's something, isn't he?' Cynthia forestalled me with fervid agreement. Within seconds, she and Susanna were deep in a sotto voce discussion of Dave's physical attributes, apparent and imagined. It was an improbable conversation, the young girl – not yet fourteen, Mim had said, untouched and ardent – swapping lurid speculation with the gauche 39-year-old. Linking them was the bond of sexual inexperience and a mutual thirst for enlightenment. This bond would be of brief duration, I thought, looking at Susanna.

Mim had confirmed that most of Cyn's life was spent in a reluctant, yearning celibacy. Jack's taunts could not have been further off the mark, or more calculated to wound. It was a cameo of his television technique: the wilfully apposite slander that propelled a victim to tell all.

Cyn, I was glad to see, seemed to have put it behind her, spurred by her interest in the subject at hand. Its appeal for me was resoundingly negative. I was still at the stage where the world held no men of any interest other than Sam; Sam for me also embodied the whole notion of sex. And Sam was unattainable.

I got up and went into the kitchen, where Jack and Dave were bickering over the correct method of opening champagne. As I watched, Jack grabbed a bottle, took aim and popped the cork. There was a loud explosion and the kitchen went dark. It was a freshman trick Jack had never grown out of, and it usually backfired. This time was no exception; out of the ensuing confusion of laughter and broken glass it emerged that Mim had run out of light bulbs and the two cats, Sheila and Bazza, were somewhere in the house.

In the past, Mim had always been the one to clean up after Jack's practical jokes, an equation of cause and effect that was rather a neat metaphor for their lives. As she swept the floor without resentment, I wondered who was going to take on the task in future. I hoped Jack would have the residual decency to get right out of Mim's life and cut the umbilical cord. Even as it came and went, it felt suspiciously like a vain and forlorn hope.

He grumbled loudly as he came down the stairs carrying lamps for the kitchen. 'How in heaven can one prepare gourmet cuisine under such archaic conditions? Exposed light bulbs under Chinaman's hats are there to be shot at, Mim. Why on earth don't you invest in something a bit more *Tatler*-esque? And if not, at least splurge on a few spare bulbs.'

Whenever he visited his family Jack assumed the mantle as head of the household. When anything went wrong, it was always Mim's house and her fault. Why did those around him, why did we all, go along with it? To my mind, Mim's love for Jack was heroically selfless, but for the rest of us the answer was writ large and plain: because it was easier. To stand up to Jack, let alone try to thwart his selfishness, required such expenditure of effort and energy that most people didn't even make an attempt. I was running with the best of them. Basking in the privileged glow of Jack's approval, I was more craven than most.

He put his arm round me as he proposed a toast. 'To our guests! They're the ones with the best glasses, the only champagne flutes this crumbling, third world household can run to! To Lou, intrepid globetrotter, foreign co-respondent extra-ordinaire' (with a sly glance at me) – 'aspiring president-elect,

Home Wreckers Anonymous! To Dave, who clawed his way out of the rotting apple, specifically to open the eyes of our sheltered children! To Cynthia, the very model of a modern career woman, pure and undefiled! To . . .' (another sideways glance) 'absent friends who don't deserve it. Let's drink to their absence! No – let's drink to their replacements – come on, Lou, down the hatch!'

Jack was still an abstemious drinker but he did enjoy champagne, and he derived some sort of pleasure from pressing expensive drinks on other people. As a result his dinner parties were invariably merry affairs. By the time we all sat down to eat, the mood was decidedly upbeat. Jack had left Cynthia alone, swapping New York stories with Dave and me. Jake was nowhere to be seen, but Susanna had been served champagne and was now, pink and excited, embarking on a glass of Pouilly-Fuissé. Both Mim and Jack believed in educating their children for life by letting them make their own decisions and more or less look after themselves. As a theory expounded to the reprise of the babies' gentle breathing in their cots, this had appeared pretty sound to me. Now I was less sure.

As I watched Mim ladle soup from a homely earthenware tureen into the mellow cobalt-blue bowls I had picked up on a trip to Florence, the convivial familiarity of the scene suddenly threatened to overwhelm me. Jack at one end of the table, holding forth in his powerful hypnotic baritone, Mim at the other serving minestrone, a hearty peasant brew I must have eaten a hundred times. The clatter of spoons and plates and wine glasses, the same dusty pictures on the walls – trivial domestic elements inextricably linked by the spiderweb of memory.

More than just the building blocks of my past, they seemed unnervingly to have become part of myself. In the interplay of these people, Mim and Jack and Cyn and me, I saw invisible connections, linking our identities in an intricate scaffolding.

Later, and in another context, Cynthia would write to me: 'I was always at my best with Mim and Jack and Bess and Roland. Always my funniest and cleverest and most at ease. Although I knew Jack didn't like me, the point was we all reinforced our ideas of ourselves. We were second nature to each other, we recognised each other's leitmotifs and generously indulged them.'

At the table in the candlelight, as she leaned avidly towards Dave, lank hair brushing her soup, I would never have credited Cyn with such insight. But at that stage I still nursed a vision of myself as an island of perception in a largely oblivious world.

I could have charted from memory every groove and indentation of Mim and Jack's table. The way I put my glass down, moving it over the ridges to find a flat surface, was learned behaviour that had become automatic. In this elegiac haze, we even looked the same.

Yet I was aware that it was all a trick of the light. More things had altered than had remained the same. The candles were too kind to us, smoothing lines and airbrushing uncertainties. It was only to each other that we would ever be as we once were. This was the source of our interdependence. I thought: we're each other's fountain of youth.

But the equation had shifted irrevocably. There were children now, who would view Mim and Jack inevitably as parents, not people. And Jack, presiding over the table, was only preserving the illusion of permanence. In recent years his presence in Mim's life was like that of a conjuror's pigeon: now you see him, now you don't. Soon the bird would have flown, and although I knew that the evening's deceptive surface was the product of a mutual conspiracy, for a second it dissolved and I fancied I was touched by the feather of Mim's dread.

I wanted the impossible – to hang on to the things I knew, and make them immutable by force of will. Some crucial elements – Mim herself, the house – were there still. But I couldn't help feeling the infrastructure was foundering, and I was a child again, watching the ebb tide of my mother's life surge around my ankles and slowly recede. I wanted to cling to Jack and beseech him, don't go. It's not just Mim you're leaving, it's all of us, and it's more than that, it's our youth, our stories, our selves. Then I looked at Mim, steadfast and uncomplaining, and I was shamed.

Jack's refusal to talk shop was one of his most likeable characteristics. Most people who have achieved some celebrity give out signals to ensure that their status is not lost on the most casual acquaintance. Jack, on the other hand, never name-dropped and only discussed his professional life with reluctance. 'I'm not interesting,' he would say, grinning disarmingly, 'let's talk about you.' It was the oldest ploy in the world but it worked, perhaps because it was, at least for that point in time, completely sincere. It was only after some energetic probing that Sam and I had uncovered the kind of gossipy details we craved to hear about *Black and White in Colour*. Not that Jack was averse to gossip. He simply preferred the process of getting it out of other people. He wasn't particularly interested in passing it on.

'I'm a whore, a professional confidant, Lou,' he had once told me. 'My program is a modern-day public confessional. People tell me things because I don't disapprove. There are no Hail Marys on my show, kiddo!'

His nature was undoubtedly manipulative and voyeuristic, but it had its discreet side. Sam, who was fascinated by Jack and was writing a character based on him in his next play, said the clue to Jack's personality was bloodlust. 'The thrill of the chase, that's what Jack loves. It's all he's really interested in.

He's quite consistent – what appear to be opposite traits in his character are actually manifestations of the same basic impulse.'

Strangers were always charmed by Jack's lack of side. Dave was responding to his fascinated questions about his childhood with an unexpectedly free dissertation on the underside of New York. In a moment, I thought, they will get onto sex.

Jack's pyrotechnics, so familiar from the television, were just as dazzling in the flesh. They put me uneasily in mind of Sam's new play. The typist had delivered the first draft one evening while Sam was out, not long before I left. The temptation to sneak a look was irresistible. So was the temptation to go on to the end. I discovered that the Jack character had metamorphosed into a fortyish female divorce lawyer who was strenuously pursuing a very married client. Her relentlessness was fuelled by a romantic belief that love alters, excuses and transforms all. I read on eagerly as she lassoed and brought down her quarry. Then she lost interest, became bored and switched her blazing energies back to her work, leaving a trail of devastation in her wake.

I had closed the manuscript feeling rather sick. Even an amateur analyst could see there were some very murky waters here, but I held back from grilling Sam about the ramifications. I have a highly developed sense of self-preservation, and the last things I wanted on the eve of walking out of his life were apocalyptic revelations. Never mind that encoded versions of these would soon be declaimed for the delectation of theatre goers around the world.

As Jack homed in on Dave, laughing appreciatively, gasping extravagantly, I was beset by demons. I had a vision of my face transposed over his. Only where he was full of life, enthusiasm spilling over, I was sniggering and mugging. Could I really be as predatory, as single-minded, as Jack? Did others beside Sam see us as kindred souls? Or was it a flight of Sam's fancy, pure fantasy?

I had refused to go to bed with Sam after our first meeting. For all I knew then, he might have engaged in little seductions whenever he was away from his family, and I had no intention of being another notch in his belt. But until he met me, he confided after our second meeting, he had never been unfaithful to Ingrid.

I had always prided myself on being impervious to other people's opinions. But that, I recognised, was largely because until fairly recently I had been satisfied with myself. Satisfied to the point of complacency, which now appeared to be common delusion. It was ironic to be sitting at dinner in the company of old friends who loved me, suffering stabs of self-doubt, all the sharper for their unfamiliarity. Was I perhaps a deeply unappealing person, comparable to Cynthia? No, worse. Cynthia was painfully honest, whereas I was versed in the theory and practice of deceit.

'Lou. *Lou!* Wake up!' Jack's boisterous voice sliced into this unpleasant reverie. 'Absolutely no-one, not even you, is permitted to sleep while I'm talking. It makes me nervous – I must be losing my touch, getting – God forbid the blasphemy – boring!'

'I wasn't asleep –'

'You were looking down. Your eyes were downcast. Definitely downcast! When they should have been fixed on me. Fixed adoringly on me.'

'They had been fixed on you, Jack, worshipfully, for some time, but the unexpected profundity of your discourse impelled me to look down, overcome as I was by an unaccustomed rush of humility.'

Jack shouted with laughter. 'Ah, Lou, it's good to have you

back. Now, before anyone else's eyes dare to wander, and in my own house – not that it's my house any more, I suppose, but it's hard to break the habit – let's get on to something more esoteric and of interest to everybody, like sex –'

'What do you mean, it's not your house any more?'

The staccato interruption came from Cynthia. My heart sank, and I avoided Mim's eye. Jack was unfazed.

'We're having a thoroughly modern, thoroughly civilised divorce, in which our deep mutual affection is never in doubt. Didn't Mim tell you? That's right, isn't it, Mim? Modern, mutual and merry! Let's drink to it!'

Swept along by Jack's persuasive torrent the rest of us, even Mim, even Susanna, raised our glasses like automatons. Only Cyn sat rigid, her eyes, moving between Jack and Mim, wide and beseeching like those of a drowning woman.

'You aren't – you can't be serious . . .'

'Of course I'm not serious, that's the point. This is not a serious occasion. It's a celebration, of new directions, new lives, new freedom. A celebration of the future! Shaking hands with the past, and – hey, Cyn, hey!'

Tears had welled in Cyn's eyes and her face was coming out in large red blotches. I had a vivid and uncomfortable memory of Cyn's youthful crying fits. Some girls, and Bess was a prime example, could sob in a way that aroused instant protective chivalry from any male within earshot. Cyn, at the opposite extreme, was an ugly, crumpled and noisy weeper. Mim grasped her hand hastily.

'Cyn, please don't be upset. It's not – it's not a shock or anything. You're a darling to be so concerned but there's nothing really to worry about. I mean, well, we'll still see each other, we'll still be great friends. Loving friends . . .' Her voice petered out unsteadily.

'Nothing to worry about? You and Jack breaking up, nothing to worry about? The poor children – oh, Susanna!' To my dismay, and patently Susanna's, Cyn scrunched the girl in a muggy embrace. I could see Susanna's look of fastidious horror as she wriggled to detach herself with a discretion I wouldn't have credited her with.

Dave was shaking his head. 'You guys are something else,' he said to Jack, in a low voice. 'Is it always as crazy as this here?'

'Always!' Jack said heartily. 'Mim, why don't you take Cyn out for a good lie-down, give her a brandy? That'll pick her up.'

'I don't think she needs another brandy –' I started to object but half-heartedly. Mim had extricated her daughter and was pouring cognac into a large balloon. I could see beads of Cyn's tears on Susanna's hair. The girl's face was closed and blank.

'I don't need picking up, thank you, Jack.' Cyn's voice was shakily angry. 'And I don't want a lie-down. What good would it do? It won't change anything.'

'But you will have a brandy!' It was a matter of conjecture whether Jack's irrepressible buoyancy was born of insensitivity or optimism. Colossal doses of both, probably. Either way, his manner had a useful way of defusing situations which threatened to become nasty or impossibly embarrassing. It was difficult to go on displaying deep feeling in the face of such unrelenting banter. That was the plus side. On the negative side it meant that Jack neatly sidestepped any real engagement with life, or the more complex emotions he was instrumental in provoking.

It also meant that everyone in Jack's orbit followed his lead in avoiding confrontation. As if the situation had never happened, we now set about recreating the illusion of conviviality.

Cyn, bent over her plate, forked chilli con carne between mouthfuls of brandy. Her eyes were swollen, her cheeks red and shiny. Every now and then a dewdrop fell from the tip of her nose onto her plate. In my head, acute distaste competed with sympathy; as always, distaste came out ahead. Mim, for whom another's distress was infinitely more upsetting than her own, enveloped Cyn and the outsider Dave in a warm conversational blanket. Her efforts to include her daughter were thwarted by Susanna's own attempts to monopolise Dave, who showed a marked aptitude for maintaining two conversations at once.

'Dave's spreading himself around pretty well,' I observed.

Jack grunted. 'Those street kids have eyes in the back of their head. They can fuck and wank at the same time.' His eye was on Susanna and I thought I detected a vestige of censure. The idea of Jack harbouring anything as mundane as a parental qualm was diverting in its novelty.

I said, 'Susanna's certainly growing up fast.'

'Too fast.'

'Isn't Dave a bit on the raunchy side for a teacher? Those little nymphets'll be all over him like a rash.'

'Don't rub it in.'

'Wouldn't have happened in my day. In my day they barricaded the door against studs like him. The only males allowed to penetrate our chaste portals were hand-picked for their repellent aspect.'

'Very sound. I agree with that.'

'Jack. I never thought I'd hear you say anything so bourgeois.'

'Parenthood makes reactionaries of us all.' He leaned closer. 'Talking of which, Lou, what are you doing in this region? I mean in the vague general area of close personal relationships, significant others, progeny —'

'Yes, I get your drift.'

'Well? You and Sam. Is it really splitsville? He's run back to the bosom of the famille, the skunk?'

I took a deep breath. 'That's about it.'

'He'll never leave la casa domestica, Lou. He's not the type. I told you that years ago. Remember? I told you Ingrid was strong, smart and ruthless when cornered. Very strong, very smart, very ruthless. Which is not to say I don't like her. She's an impressive bloody woman and I wouldn't want her as an enemy. Remember all that?'

I remembered all that, all too well, and I didn't like being reminded. I had never found mortification productive, and in my present state it was perilously undermining.

'You didn't have to get all dressed up and come out of your way to tell me I told you so, Jack. But I sure do appreciate it.'

He reached out and stroked my hand. 'There, there. You can't help it that you were born with a shithouse taste in men. But I can help you change it.'

He was about to look deeply into my eyes. I jumped up, clattering my chair. I was responsible for the dessert course, which allowed me a sporting chance of nipping this conversation in the bud.

Jack followed me into the kitchen. 'Lou, you know I've always been mad about you.'

'You've just suppressed it all these years.'

A grin. 'I've just suppressed it for Mim's sake.'

'But now you've dumped Mim — well, there's still a few odds and ends to tie up — but basically she's in the other room and now you can come out into the open.'

'Lou, don't be like this. We're fated. I've always known it and so have you, if you're honest.'

In a moment he would kiss me. 'Jack, we're not fated and

I've never known it and neither have you. Look, I've got to get the pudding out of the oven –'

He put his arms round me, and I hit him quite hard on the cheek. It was a reflex action and rather clumsily executed. I had never slapped anyone before, apart from a recalcitrant cousin. From his reaction, however, Jack had clearly been on the receiving end before. He looked extravagantly taken aback, but he did take a step away. To cover my confusion I put a towel underneath the hot apple pie and handed it to him. 'Take that in, will you?'

'Lou, you shocked me.'

'Oh come on, Jack. Being assaulted by a woman is routine for you.'

He considered this. 'I haven't been slugged since, let's see, since I became intergalactically acclaimed.'

'You have now.'

'Well, you didn't mean it, sweetheart, and you're a bit over-wrought.' He dodged my extended foot, and I seized the pudding from him.

'I'm going to give you a particularly small helping, Jack. I know it's your favourite.'

I was depressed by the encounter and my inept handling of it. I reflected, not for the first time, that Jack could on occasion, and effortlessly, bring out the worst in me. The best method of dealing with him, of keeping him at arm's length, was an ironic stance of coolly detached amusement. With other men I was quite adept at sophisticated fencing. Jack made me too hot under the collar.

Was this an inescapable consequence of having grown up together, behaving as one had always and was always expected to behave? Perhaps the truth was that we were the same, only more so, like Cynthia. Like Jack. The mature Jack, if that were not a contradiction in terms, was simply a more pronounced and developed version of the youthful model. Given a degree of worldly achievement, perhaps maturity just conferred on one the confidence to explore and be more emphatically oneself. Like I was with Sam, I thought. Always, right from that first electrifying encounter at the writers' festival in Stockholm. Crushed together, the only two Australians at the crowded welcoming reception, we joked that it was all our badges' fault. Our name badges adorned with our country's flag had zoomed in on each other and we were powerless to stop them.

With Sam I had experienced an expanded, intensified sense of self. Greater self-esteem, awareness, fulfilment. Where were those heady feelings now? As if I wasn't there, Sheila the tabby cat wound herself around my feet and I almost dropped the pie. For a brief, nerve-wracking moment I felt amorphous. I had never had a panic attack, and I wondered if this could be a variation on the theme.

What I later identified as the starting point in a catastrophic chain of events was already underway in the dining room. Cynthia had slumped sideways, interposing herself between Dave and the table. One hand clutched his upper arm, the other was draped across his thigh. She was slurring intimately into his ear. Dave's stance, I noted, was a model of polite detachment. Susanna, on his other side, looked thunderous. I ladled apple pie into a bowl and Mim whisked it in front of Cynthia with desperate urgency.

Cyn's voice rose and fell in a parody of drunken confidentiality. She was telling Dave all about Mim and Jack's wonderful long-term marriage and the significance of their presence in her youthful life and mine.

'We would have fallen apart if it hadn't been for them. They loved us. Rescued us. They put all the pieces together, so many times. Lou's romances were always going wrong. She was so unstable, everything always had to be her way. She always fell on her feet, though, or Mim and Jack helped her to. I don't know how we're going to survive now they're breaking up. It's dreadful. It's the worst thing that's ever happened, the worst thing . . .'

Mim looked helplessly at me.

'Can't you do something, Mum?' Susanna hissed. 'It's revolting. Why do you ask her? You knew this would happen, she's always like this. You did it deliberately to embarrass me! He was my guest, and now he'll hate me and never come back here.'

She rushed out of the room in a flood of tears. Mim followed, looking stricken. Jack made a ghoulish clown's face at me.

'Quite right. She asked for it. Misguided kindness, that's Mim's raison d'être. Indiscriminate, impulsive, simple, childlike. And verging on stupid.'

His easy assumption of my complicity stung me.

'So is the habit of reducing complexities to a series of facile, crass, simplistic judgements.'

'Wait on. You omitted jejune.'

'I was saving it up for the coup de grâce.'

Jack leaned back with his arms behind his head, regarding me quizzically. It was an expression familiar from the television screen, and usually preceded a creative analysis of his victim's repressed libido.

'Why d'you suppose it is, Lou, that our intercourse always degenerates into an adolescent slinging match?'

I had been wondering the same thing. 'That's easy. Because one of us is still an adolescent.'

He grinned and patted my hand. 'Maybe we're trying to convince ourselves we're still young and foolish.'

'When only one of those is the case.'

'Oh, we're foolish too. Lou? Let's be foolish together. Take my hand and let us go forth into the woods, the forests of recklessness. Who knows what wanton desires may descend and intoxicate us!'

'That way madness lies.'

'Divine madness. Capable of obliterating all that's gone before. A present beyond imagination and a future beyond dreams.'

I had never been quite so aware of how blue Jack's eyes were, or how mesmerising his gaze. While half of me was standing back in a habitual cynical appraisal of his performance, the other half was floating languidly in a velvet lagoon. I braced myself to stride out of these treacherous waters while the two halves were still fairly evenly matched. My susceptibility appalled me. Had Sam's defection left me so demoralised that I was vulnerable to such a glaring sensual conman as Jack? Even now, part of me was protesting that I was being too hard on Jack, that perhaps for once he really, genuinely . . .

I drank a large glass of water and sat up straight. With Jack's eyes safely out of the way, the rest of the room lurched into focus. Cyn had opened the connecting doors to the sitting room and was leaning over the hi-fi. She seemed to be rummaging through a shelf of ancient LPs in dusty sleeves.

'Come on, everyone, we're going to dance! Just like we always used to, like old times.'

She lurched heavily against the bookshelf and put an arm out. A stack of cassettes and Jack's precious new compact discs crashed to the floor, and the record she was holding thudded onto the turntable.

'Fuck, Cyn, for God's sake!'

Jack was out of his chair with the speed of light. Music – classical, opera, jazz – was his second greatest passion. On his knees, he sorted through the debris, an expression of outrage on his face as Cyn clanged the arm of the record player sideways onto a record. The needle juddered between several grooves before the Beatles' 'Help!', a simple song I had once known so well, soldiered gamely over two decades of grime and static.

Jack, his face screwed up in real pain, found himself seized by the arm.

'Jack, dance with Mim. Come on, for the good times. Dance with your wife!'

He shook her off with such contempt that I flinched.

'You're plastered, Cyn. It's deeply unattractive, and I'm sure you've been warned that it's ageing. Don't minimise your already slender chances still further.'

With some idea of sparing Cyn the additional humiliation of another witness I went in search of Mim's steadying influence. I had the feeling that things – particularly Jack and Cynthia, and maybe even a frisson of myself – were getting out of hand.

Mim was in the kitchen putting a coffee pot and mugs on a tray. She looked exhausted. She was also, I saw with misgiving, putting out fresh glasses and a bottle of port.

'We'll need this, Lou. It's all getting a bit much tonight, isn't it? She's locked herself in her room and won't come out. Is Cyn all right?'

'Not really. In fact not at all. And she put on that.'

Mim listened. 'Oh. The one we always used to bring out after dinner. Happy memories can be awfully sad in another context, can't they? It's as if their whole nature has changed.'

'It has. Time's ground its dread heel into them. Or something.'

Her eyes returned from far away and looked at me.

'The last thing I want is to spoil all those memories for you, Lou.'

'Don't worry, they were ruined years ago. I'm not sure I ever liked looking back. It's like old photos. Guaranteed to induce melancholia.'

'That was always one of your strongest points. I always admired it.'

'What was?'

'Living in the present. Never in the past, or even in the future like so many people. You were always concerned to get the most out of the present, live it to the full. It's a delightfully attractive characteristic.'

I wondered if it was a delightful characteristic or unattractive opportunism.

Mim said, 'On the other hand, if one negates all one's memories, blots them out because they're so painful, what do you have left? A person with no history, constantly starting again. A shell without any substance. Don't you think that could be very threatening to one's whole self-image? I mean, if you can't in a way come to terms with your past, how can you have any idea, any real idea, where you've got to? What kind of a person you are?'

The amorphous feeling returned. I seemed to be feeling increasingly confused, and the nagging problem of Cynthia was on my mind.

'I'm sure you're right, and we're all headed for a mass identity crisis. But one thing's certain, Mim – you'll never be a shell without substance.'

We laughed together – I think from memory it was the last

laugh of the evening – and returned to face the music. Dave and Cyn were in the middle of the floor engaged in a shuffling activity. He was supporting her semi-recumbent weight. Her eyes were shut, her arms had his neck in an encircling vice. The Beatles were singing 'You've got to hide your love away'. As Mim and I watched, the dancers reached the settee and subsided on it in slow motion. Dave was uppermost, visibly straining to keep Cynthia's vital airway open and them both from spiralling vertically into the upholstery. I caught his eye.

He removed some of Cynthia's hair from his mouth and gesticulated downwards with five fingers up, nodding his head.

'What does he mean?' Mim whispered anxiously.

'I think he means Cyn's on the way out. He'll stay there till it's safe to get up.'

There was an irritated throat-clearing noise from the direction of the bookshelves. Jack was still on his hands and knees surrounded by piles of books. He was loading them busily into cardboard boxes.

I looked at Mim. Her face was unnaturally pale. I poured her a large port and a small black coffee, hesitated, and gave myself a small port and large white to keep her company. Dave's prone posture I judged too hazardous for a hot beverage just then.

Jack's voice cut in like a buzzsaw.

'Mim, where the hell's my *Prater Violet*?'

'Prater Violet . . .'

'You know, my autographed copy. First edition. Signed by Isherwood. It's not here. What have you done with it?'

'Oh dear. It should be there.' Mim looked stricken.

'It should be there. Like so many other things in this house. You can't be reading it. You haven't given it to a jumble sale for your no-hoper friends?' His voice changed. 'Hey, is that coffee I see before me? Ripper. Long black, thanks, Lou.'

'Get it yourself.'

Mim half rose, in a reflex action, and I pushed her down. Jack loped over and chucked me under the chin. Jerking my head away, I was just in time to see Susanna come in. She took in Dave's couchant position astride Cynthia and went back out quickly, banging the door. I judged Mim was about to break into tears and shoved Jack away, spilling his coffee on his trousers.

'What the *fuck* are you doing, Jack?'

He looked surprised and injured.

'Careful, Lou, these are my best moleskins. What do you mean what the fuck am I doing? Not fucking enough, that's for sure!'

He roared with laughter. Behind us Dave levered himself gingerly off Cynthia. Cyn remained motionless, her limbs splayed at an unfortunate angle. I caught a reluctant glimpse of frilly Marks and Spencer's underwear. She was breathing in a noisy, snorting fashion that drowned out the music.

Jack's face took on a preoccupied look.

'Listen, Mim, I'm taking the CDs. There's no point in leaving them, you never play my highbrow stuff and the kids only like pop rubbish. That's fair, isn't it? I'll leave all the old tapes and records. Although, hell, you let them get into such a state . . .'

He was blowing dust fastidiously off one of his new acquisitions. Dave was putting a lighted cigarette in Mim's mouth with one hand. He was pouring them both another port with the other. I kicked Jack's shin and he jumped backwards, hitting his head on the corner of the bookcase. Another pile of teetering cassette tapes toppled onto the floor.

'Jesus, Lou, what's the matter with you tonight? It's like having a Sumo wrestler in the house.'

'How can you be so bloody insensitive?'

'You're the one who's hypersensitive. It was only a figure of speech. God, you never used to be so –'

'Jack.' I took a deep breath and tried to steady my voice. 'You can't just blithely stand here and pack your things in front of Mim. Can't you see the state she's in? You could at least have the grace to come back when she's out of the house.'

He considered this.

'All right, if it'll make you happy. Your happiness being a condition devoutly to be wished. But aren't you really saying I shouldn't be taking anything? I'm a mean grasping bastard, isn't that the subtext?'

'You can read that into it too, if you like. Suits me.'

Jack got down on his haunches and picked up the top volume from the nearest carton. It was *Sacred and Profane Love* by Sacheverell Sitwell.

'Look at this. First edition, signed, very rare. Look at the dust jacket – in tatters. When I bought it, at an obscure book-shop in an even more obscure Tasmanian country town in 1965, it was pristine, in mint condition. Now look at it. It's criminal, Lou. Everything falls to pieces in this house. Books like these are treasures, and I'll treasure them. Mim never will.' He lowered his voice. 'I'm not mean. I'll make sure they're well provided for. There's no need to be righteously buckling on your breastplate and spurs on that score. Although it's a bloody battle to get Mim to accept anything, you know that.'

I had to acknowledge the truth of this. Now that he had considerable wealth in his own right, Jack got a kick out of being generous with it. He was supporting his elderly mother in style, and after being a domestic servant for most of her life she now had a live-in housekeeper. I knew of two friends who had fallen on bad times, to whom he'd sent, unsolicited, large sums of money. And it was also true that Mim, with her disregard for material possessions, was the last person to be impressed with priceless chattels. Her attitude to these was that they were very nice, unique perhaps, but that they were, above all, just things. What mattered to Mim were people. She found it hard to understand how anyone could become besotted with inanimate objects.

Jack, on the other hand, was a collector by nature. As a struggling student he was always coming forward with some triumphant find he had unearthed in a junk shop or school fete. A first edition, a rare recording, occasionally a piece of bric-a-brac that had caught his eye. And even then his eye for a rarity or a bargain was discerning and acute. It was true that, for him, these books were pearls beyond price. Mim could lose the lot without a second thought.

'You mustn't worry, Lou, about all that.'

I hadn't seen Mim get up. Dave hovered behind her. I fancied his expression was protective.

'I'd really much rather Jack had them. I know how important they are to him. Also they would . . . they would always remind me of him, seeing them there, and I couldn't play the music, not his favourites, for the same reason. He bought them all anyway, not me . . .'

Her voice trailed away and she fumbled for a handkerchief. I suggested to Jack in a whisper that his imminent departure might be a sound idea. He straightened up, brushing his hands together and raising a small cloud of dust. 'I may as well take the boxes I've packed,' he said in a conciliatory tone. 'No point in leaving them to clutter up the room, is there?' He raised his voice. 'Hey, Muscles, give us a hand with these crates, will you, sport?'

I looked at Mim as she watched the two men lug the cartons out to Jack's car. She was lighting another cigarette, but what she was really doing was absorbing Jack's departure from her life. That it was another stage in a professional marathon that had been underway for some time didn't seem to make it any easier to bear.

Our silence was punctuated by Cyn's regular trumpeting snores. They heightened the unreality that Jack's casual playing down had left hanging in the air. To me suddenly the whole room swam with the artificiality of a stage set, and the cardboard boxes, the gaps in the bookshelves, the disordered dining table, Cynthia, all became movable props in our small domestic tragi-comedy.

'Do you think it's always like this, Lou? When something happens in one's life that is cataclysmic?' Mim had put her hand up to her eyes as if to shade them from the light. 'I feel disconnected, as though I'm watching this happen to someone else, in a film, perhaps, or a play. I suppose it's a defence mechanism. Of course it could just be alcohol.'

'That natural anaesthetic. Yes, I feel the same.'

'What should we do about Cyn?'

I was startled. 'Do we have to do anything?'

'Oh, she couldn't possibly go home in that condition, riding on a motorbike. I think we'd better try and help her upstairs. We can't just leave her there all night. She'd get awfully cold.'

I thought we could very well leave her there all night, but realised that in Mim's eyes this would be tantamount to abandonment on a Spartan hillside.

'We'll need reinforcements. She's a helluva weight. I'll get Dave.'

I found Jack and Dave in a jocular tête-à-tête outside the

front door. Jack's car, an old Sunbeam convertible in immaculate condition, stood by with the engine purring softly.

'Excuse me. We need help in the lifting Cynthia upstairs department.'

Jack groaned.

'Not you, Sunshine,' I said hastily. 'You're going. Goodbye.'

He shot me a pained glance.

'You can be cruelty transmogrified, Lou. But be warned, it'll take more than this feeble token resistance to put me off.'

Before I could sidestep him, he had kissed me with considerable force and the added weight of skill and experience. To my mortification I found myself responding for a split second before pulling out in some disarray. This involuntary capitulation, brief as it was, was noted and filed away by my opponent. His eyes as he batted a hand through the car roof had a wolfish gleam that dissected the dark like a laser.

Dave's grin lit up his eyes and had irksome male-bonding overtones. He took an assessing look at Cyn, and waved Mim and me away. Then he scooped up Cyn's inert body as if she were a slip of a ballet dancer. 'Lead on,' he said to Mim, who was looking at him with her 'Rise, Sir Galahad' expression, one that I had hitherto only seen bestowed on Jack. They trundled upstairs in convoy, and I turned back to the dining room with the virtuous idea of clearing the debris.

I scraped leftovers, emptied glasses and stacked plates on automatic pilot for some time before becoming aware that I was the only one around. I looked in the sitting room and listened at the foot of the stairs. There was no sound. I returned to the kitchen, finished rinsing and stacking and went upstairs with a flicker of disquiet.

Muffled artillery from Jake's room testified to Cyn's occupancy. She was tucked up in bed, outer garments folded over the back of a chair, boots stacked below. Two other bedrooms and a bathroom opened off the landing. Susanna's room had a shut and locked look. The door to Mim and Jack's old bedroom, recently occupied by Mim alone, was also closed. I looked at it for some time, trying to see through it, standing still and breathing silently. There was no sound.

But Mim and Jack's house, with its heavy doors and substantial walls, was pretty soundproof. It was a house that kept its secrets. That had been one of its strongest points, in our uninhibited youth.

4

I WOKE EARLY WITH the feeling that I hadn't slept at all, and a question nagging at the back of my mind. It moved rapidly to the forefront and wrestled briefly with the powerful inclination to remain under cover in a darkened room. But it was an unequal struggle, and I emerged on the landing disguised in Mim's chenille dressing gown, feeling like a morals inspector from the social welfare.

Another bedroom door was now open: Susanna's. The bird had flown, but raised childish voices floating up the stairwell from the kitchen against a heavy metal backdrop established her and Jake's location. Mim's door was still firmly closed. An anonymous body was slumbering in Jake's room with the blankets over its head. I assumed it was still Cynthia and felt a twinge of envy.

Downstairs Susanna and Jake were engaged in one of their running quarrels. Both were dressed for school, Susanna in an extremely short skirt and a combination of layered garments that managed to look stylishly disordered, Jake in dirty jeans and climbing boots and a flying jacket that was much too big for him.

'Be quiet, you two, and turn that thing down. I'm feeling fragile and dangerously bad-tempered.'

'I'm just telling him he's got to put something on underneath, a shirt or something. He's so dumb and stupid, it's not true.'

'Shut up and fuck yourself.'

I kept well out of it. If Jake wanted to wear a leather jacket over his bare skin it was fine with me. He was eating his usual meal of grilled caramelised muesli, and dipping into what looked like an army survival pack of chocolate and raisins. An open tin of condensed milk stood next to his bowl. For him to eat inside at the kitchen table was unusual enough to be remarkable in itself, and beyond suppressing a rising gorge I was indifferent to his eating habits.

I filled a teapot from the kettle on the hob. Mim had resisted change in the form of classy high-tech stoves and hung on to her old briquette-burning Aga cooker. What it lacked in humdrum precision, she claimed, it more than made up for in caprice and theatricality. She was right. The stove had a mind of its own, with which Mim was completely in tune. She enjoyed assessing the strength and longevity of her fires, the relative heat of different parts of the oven. Things that would have driven Jack, with his sharp practical mind, mad.

More than anything else, I thought, she liked the fact that the cooker was animate, a source of living, breathing energy. For the same reason she had opposed Jack's wish to replace the open fires in the house with lookalike gas models. Real fires were inconvenient, time-wasting, dirty and inefficient, Jack said, and entirely inappropriate for city life. Mim had agreed but the fires remained, as I knew they would. Where convenience was pitched against romance there was never, for Mim, any real contest.

The kitchen was the nerve centre of the house. Always verging on the overheated, it conjured tribal memories of a kinder, gentler era, of being bathed in warmth and safety. Looking back I couldn't identify any period of my life that had been notably warm and safe, not even babyhood, when my mother's illness meant I was often looked after by strangers. But Mim's house did funny atavistic things to the mind. The ever-present muddle and mess ruled out any identification with the twee country kitchens of glossy magazine fiction. Nevertheless it was always full of the inviting, spicy smells of home-baked bread and fresh herbs on the sill, and an authentically blackened kettle perpetually simmered. On most mornings I found it a soothing balm to the spirit, but on this one I was in no mood to linger.

'Has Mim been down?' I inquired casually.

'No. Probably hopelessly hungover. That nauseating Whicker female is still asleep too, in *Jake*'s room.' She turned to her sibling and crowed. 'Ha *ha!* Yuk! You'll have to change the sheets! Just as well you were in the kennel – she might've jumped on you. Nothing in trousers is safe with her around, even smelly little brats like you.'

She rumpled his hair with a kind of residual, grudging affection. He went on eating impassively. Susanna switched back to me.

'Could you believe what she was doing last night? The way she was all over Dave, in that drunken stupor? God, it was so repulsive I could puke. That's what happens to sex-starved spinsters, Dad says. He's actually right for once, even if it is sexist.'

I made a noncommittal noise. 'Maybe I'd better take her a cup of tea. She's tutoring this morning.'

'You should let her miss it. Serve her right. She'll still be too drunk to make any sense anyway.'

I made some toast and laid a tea tray with two mugs. They started arguing again before I was halfway up the stairs.

'Cyn. *Cyn!* Wake up!'

The top of Cyn's head was now visible. I touched gingerly what I judged to be her shoulder, got no response and shook it. Cyn emerged like a groggy mole.

'You look pale and deeply wan. Much as I feel. Wrap yourself around some tea and toast.'

Cyn groaned. 'Why are you rudely waking me up?'

'Well, partly because it's Monday, and you have a tutorial. And I thought it was time for a fresh new start.'

'That's not the reason. Why else?'

Cyn may have been pale, wan and rudely awakened, but she was still on the ball. She looked at me keenly through bloodshot eyes.

'Well, it's Mim and the kids. Or Susanna, specifically. I rather think we may have to mount a decoy operation.'

Cyn surprised me by leaping out of bed and sprinting from the room. A noise that indicated incipient illness was cut short by the bathroom door slamming. She returned with her vital signs looking even more depleted. I offered tea but she waved it away with a strangled sound. I drank mine anyway, turning away considerately, and ate some toast with peanut butter and Marmite mixed. Cyn lay back on the pillow, holding a wet flannel over her eyes and forehead. I wondered if she would be more of a liability in the forthcoming manoeuvre.

After an interval she said in a faint voice: 'I'm waiting for you to explain yourself. Do you mean a man stayed the night with Mim?'

'There was only one man. Apart from Jack.'

'Be specific. Are you saying it was David who stayed?'

'Well, I don't have any concrete evidence. I didn't actually see them. But this is my cautious conclusion.'

'What do you mean, you didn't actually see them? What *did* you see?'

'Well, they went upstairs and didn't come down. Not that I saw.'

'How long were you watching? All night?'

I was getting tired of talking to a wet flannel, and moved sideways on the bed so I could monitor Mim's bedroom door.

'No, of course I wasn't watching all night. But Mim's door was shut when I went to bed, and it's still shut now. And she always sleeps with her door open.'

'That doesn't mean he didn't come out while she was still asleep, and shut it behind him. Or that she didn't shut it herself for a change. Or that it wasn't open and blew shut during the night. There was a wind last night. I heard the trees creaking.'

I felt a mounting impatience and said rapidly: 'Look. I know there are infinite logical possibilities standing in the way of concrete certainty, and the wind is undoubtedly one of them, but on the balance of probabilities my tentative hypothesis remains that Dave stayed the night in Mim's room.'

There was a pause. Cyn moved her head experimentally from side to side.

'I think I could try aspirin now. It might stay down.'

I dropped three tablets in a glass of water and she sipped it slowly.

'There's no need to be so circuitous, Lou. We must shield the children. Is that what you're saying?'

'Not exactly, or not in any moral sense. It's Susanna. I think it could cause a major rift between her and Mim, or a violent row at the very least. You saw how she was about Dave. And

I don't think Mim is in any state to cope with more trauma just now.'

Cyn said slowly, 'But it's so unlike Mim. It's so out of character.'

Unlike the wind, this objection got to the heart of the matter.

'People do uncharacteristic things when they're traumatised. The balance of her mind is disturbed.'

I recalled my involuntary response to Jack's kiss.

'And he *is* terribly sexy.' Cyn's tone was wistful. 'And probably incredibly virile. Don't tell Mim,' she leaned forward confidentially and I could feel her breath on my face, 'but I actually thought he was about to seduce me last night. I was all ready to succumb. But I think I must have gone to sleep. I was dreadfully tired, and upset of course about Mim and Jack.'

I was anxious to avoid giving an opinion on any of these topics, and was both reprieved and galvanised by the sight of Mim's door inching open and the cautious emergence of Mim herself. She closed the door behind her, confirming my hypothesis.

'Mim's come out and shut her door,' I said complacently to Cynthia, whose field of vision was still limited. She whipped the flannel off in time to see Mim dart into the room and sit heavily on the bed next to me. Her hair was dishevelled, her face shiny and rosy. The expression on it, a mixture of embarrassment, guilt, disbelief and apprehension, made her look almost girlish.

There was a pregnant pause.

'Have some aspirins,' I invited.

She took them obediently, with automatic movements. I felt rather than saw Cyn's personal battle.

At last she burst out: 'Mim, is it true? Lou has a theory, on very flimsy evidence, that David stayed the night in your room. I've pointed out to her that there are a number of alternative explanations that would fit the facts.'

Mim put one hand over her mouth and her eyes met mine in what used to be called a speaking glance. Only in this case it was more beseeching than conversational.

'Take it as read, Cyn,' I said briskly. 'Now, Mim, should we try and hide him or smuggle him out? He's got classes, presumably, this morning. My feeling is that Susanna wouldn't take kindly to his presence here. What it implies, that is.'

Cyn leaned forward, instantly absorbed in the problem at hand. 'On the other hand it might be better to keep David here until they're safely out of the house. But then there's still the problem of his clothes.'

'His clothes?'

'At school. He'd still be wearing the same clothes,' Cyn said patiently. 'Susanna's an observant girl, she'd notice, and draw conclusions.'

'Why can't he go home and change?'

'He can't go home and change, Lou, because he lives in Cricklewood and he hasn't got a car. He has early football coaching this morning, too.'

'You know a lot about him,' I said nastily.

'We talked a lot, before I fell asleep. I told you we got on well.' This was delivered in a low, meaningful tone which was clearly not intended for Mim's ears. I felt unreasonably irritated.

Mim ran a hand distractedly through her hair. 'I must have gone mad. We went upstairs to put you to bed, Cyn – you see, you'd been asleep – and then we went into my bedroom for some reason I can't remember. What could it have been? And I remember being dreadfully tired all of a sudden, and him starting to kiss me, and say things – and then I think I sort of gave up . . .'

Her voice, which had started off in rigorous self-flagellation, finished in a wondering, dreamy tone.

'I've never done anything like that before. Not even as a student, you know, when the pill had just come in and everyone was so promiscuous. I never quite fancied one-night stands or sleeping with someone on a first date. I suppose the reason was, I only ever wanted Jack . . .' Her voice faded again.

'What was it like? Was he a good lover? What did he do?'

Cyn was the only person I could think of who could put such questions and sound as if she were asking about the demographic composition of Nigeria. Who could ask them, moreover, as if she was entitled to receive full and frank answers. Mim, too, was one of the few people renowned for taking things in their intended spirit, just as she always gave others the benefit of the doubt. She would have thought it rude or demeaning to do otherwise. But her natural delicacy made these hard deliveries to field.

She said carefully, 'He was very considerate, I think. But I was so confused, you know, about what I was doing, and why. I'd drunk too much, that was part of the problem. I wasn't quite sure how I'd got there, and once it had reached a certain stage I couldn't seem to stop things without being impossibly churlish and, well, ill-mannered. Doesn't that sound ridiculous, like a teenager? I think I must be regressing. I'm dreadfully sorry, Cyn. I know how much you liked him, and Susanna too. I think I became painfully aware of that when it passed the point of no return. That's the worst part of it, isn't it? The selfishness.'

I would have liked to tell her that they were both free agents, that this kind of breast-beating was the legacy of a double standard long gone, even that a therapeutic fling might be just what she needed, but I knew none of it would wash with Mim. Cynthia, though, was seriously concerned with misunderstandings and resolutions.

'Mim, you must believe that I have no resentment whatsoever over this. On the contrary, I think it's a positive development. I'm sure sexual experimentation – or diversification, in your case – is very healthy at our age, and invigorating. You don't know where it could lead.'

Mim's rather diffident smile suggested that she had no desire for her life to be invigorated or transformed. Watching her, and admiring her forbearance, I glimpsed Dave emerging from her bedroom. He spotted us and advanced across the landing. In the hard light of morning he looked even younger, taller and tighter-jeaned than the night before. His hair was becomingly tangled and he was naked from the waist up.

'David!' Cyn managed to inject breathless sexual admiration into the two syllables. Her eyes travelled from his bare chest and definitely admirable muscles downwards to the unmistakeable, rivetting bulge. Mim jumped.

'Oh, Dave, I'm so sorry, the loo! He was wanting to go to the bathroom –'

'Wait!' I pushed him behind the bedroom door and reconnoitred. The coast was, thus far, still clear.

'Do you have a shower? I could really use a wash.'

'Too risky. The kids'll be up any second.'

'He can't go to school and teach all day without a proper wash.' Cyn's voice rose in partisan indignation. 'Americans are used to showering every day, you know, Lou.'

'Not like us, is that it? Well, he can shower after football practice.'

'Nonsense. Let him go into the bathroom with Mim.'

'With Mim?'

Cyn sighed noisily. 'It's like dealing with a child, isn't it? I'd forgotten how you have to have everything explained in words of one syllable, Lou. With Mim, so that if the children come upstairs, needing the bathroom, Mim can call out and say she's in there.'

I had a feeling there was a fatal flaw in this reasoning, but was strongly disinclined to enter into a protracted quarrel with Cynthia over it. Mim looked doubtful but allowed herself to be hustled into the bathroom with Dave. It was a commodious chamber with original Victorian fixtures – claw-footed bath, lavatory with ball and chain, tiled shower recess and pedestal wash basin – and the Black family had tended to use it in tandem. There were crowded times, I recalled, when it had been used in concert.

Early in the marriage, at Jack's behest, Mim had replaced the outdoor dunny with a shed and storeroom. He had nagged at her to put in an en suite bathroom for years but the words en suite set up fearful reverberations of gentility in Mim's mind. It had never been done, and with Jack's departure now never would.

Where her principles were engaged, Mim was capable of surprising stubbornness, even against Jack's bullying and blandishments. She had given in over the plumbing, which was swiftly upgraded to his severe Australian standards. I remembered him furiously ripping out the prehistoric gas water heater after yet another explosion. Even that was to Mim's background protests. She was firmly of the school that anything old should be preserved and cherished. In the area of bathroom fittings, as in the wider domestic arena, the taste-makers had come round to her view, and the house's once despised Victoriana would now be its principal selling point.

Not, I felt sure, that Mim would ever part with it.

While she and Dave were safely locked away I appraised Cyn of Susanna's early morning body count.

'She thought it would have been me David stayed with,' Cyn explained. 'That would have been the reasonable assumption.'

'Thanks for elucidating.'

Cyn sat up in bed. Someone, I hoped it was Mim, had draped her in an oversized T-shirt. It slipped down low over one shoulder, and I averted my eyes.

'You should try not to be so wearingly sarcastic, Lou. It's not an endearing habit and it should be eschewed along with your other behavioural juvenilia.'

'I have the grace to look abashed.'

'David is an extremely amorous boy, you know. Very hot-blooded. And he obviously likes older women. I think he finds us exciting. He didn't make any overtures to you, though, did he?'

'None. He unaccountably missed me out.'

'I'm a bit worried about Mim, however. It's a big step to embark on your first affair the very night your husband leaves you. And she's still rather naively idealistic, don't you think?'

The clear and ominous sound of girls' laughter floated up from downstairs. I froze, and Cyn's jaw jutted with Churchillian determination. 'You run down and stop them coming up. I'll alert Mim and get her out.'

'It's too late.' Feet were pounding up the stairs. I looked out to see Susanna and her friend Ruth, an ethereal Indian girl, fan out onto the landing.

'*Mum!*'

I improvised loudly. 'She's in the bathroom. She's not well.'

Cyn was right behind me. 'Not well at all. She's very ill.'

Susanna ignored this and rattled the door. 'Mum, open up. I need things in there.' She turned to Ruth. 'God, she's always deaf when she's in the shower. And she stays in for hours. *Mum!*'

'Better wait. She'll be out soon. Listen, could you be a paragon and get your mother's elderly friends some more tea?'

'No can do, we're running late, sorry.' She started banging on the door with rising intensity. 'This is unreal, she knows I've got a breakfast meeting, she's so effing thoughtless.'

'I thought you'd had breakfast.'

'I've had my main breakfast, this is just social – coffee and croissants. It's every Monday. Mum knows it's crucial. Ruth and I only just got into the club – we can't be late.'

Ruth was backing her up with vigorous nods. 'It's an honour to be invited.'

Susanna's pounding surged against the thunderous roar of the shower. Jack's obsession with state of the art plumbing had its uses, I reflected.

'*Susanna!*' Cyn's outraged tone was worthy of a boarding school matron. 'Leave your mother in peace for a minute and go downstairs at once!'

Susanna's face set in an obstinate pout. 'For goodness' sake! All I want to do is get into my own bathroom. What *is* this, some kind of –'

She was cut short by Cynthia's formidable frame coming at the door in an unstoppable charge. Cyn's voice rose in a bellow that would have sliced through the roar of Niagara Falls. 'Get out of my way! I'm going to be sick! Mim – open this door at once!'

I watched mesmerised as the door crept open obediently and Cyn, T-shirt billowing over mottled limbs, almost fell inside. The door slammed again, leaving behind a good six inches of T-shirt trapped outside. As if in slow motion it opened an inch and the offending material vanished inside. I was aware of the abrupt termination of the shower, followed by the unmistakeable sound of violent retching. Aware also of Susanna's and Ruth's theatrical groans, and Ruth's cartoonishly exaggerated face as she asked, 'What was *that*?'

'Oh God, don't ask. The revolting one I told you about. The ancient university chum.' She flashed a glance that was largely mischievous and only a little apologetic in my direction.

'The one who was monstering Dave?'

'Yeah. He'll be impossible today. It'll be all over the school. He'll never leave it alone. Being slobbered over by a witch with cellulite thighs. An Australian witch, too – sorry, Lou. I know you can't help being one. Australian, I mean, not necessarily witch.'

They dissolved in giggles. The decibel level from the bathroom had risen to a pictorial pitch, then subsided into a spasm of coughs and moans.

I made a last-ditch attempt to deflect disaster. 'Listen, Susie. I really think you should both pop downstairs for a minute or two, or go into your room and shut the door.'

Susanna said incredulously, 'Pop downstairs? Shut the door? What *is* this?'

'I mean that Mim and Cynthia need a bit of privacy. To straighten themselves up.'

They wore identical expressions of amused exasperation. 'Oh, Mum won't mind Ruth. She's seen her with a hangover a million times, haven't you? It's no big deal.'

'Well, maybe, but Cyn's upset now and she'll need to pull herself together. I think it's only tactful to make yourselves scarce.' Covert shuffling and murmurs from within testified to a council of war.

Susanna shrugged mulishly and resumed her tattoo on the door. 'I'm not going to make myself scarce for that old bag. She should've thought of that last night.'

The door yielded a fraction and Mim's head came round it. She looked as if she was up on a murder charge, about to hear the jury's verdict.

'Mum!' Susanna surged forward.

Mim stayed her ground gamely. 'Darling, can you just tell me what it is you want and I'll pass it out? Cynthia's a bit – she's not very well.'

'Mum, it can't be passed out, I have to do things in there.'

'There's the downstairs cloakroom, darling.'

'Mum, I don't want the *loo*! We've got a breakfast meeting, remember, and we're late. I promise not to even *look* at Cynthia!'

With that, as I relayed the sequence of events later to Jack, she stormed the door. 'Nothing would have stopped her. It burst open and Mim nearly went flying. Inside it was like a Feydeau farce. Cyn was heaving over the basin, white as a sheet. Dave was crouching naked in the shower trying to hide behind a towel. All hell broke loose. The catastrophe at its fullest.'

This was embroidered mildly for Jack's benefit. In fact Susanna's reaction was disturbingly muted. If she had staged a tantrum, shouted and screamed or thrown something at her mother, it might have been rather easier to deal with. Instead she seemed to retreat into herself in some kind of shock. She said nothing, but it was apparent from a stiffening of her face that she grasped the basic premise and drew the necessary conclusion.

'But surely you could have said he stayed on the bloody couch!' Jack had expostulated. 'You could've said something, for Christ's sake. Why did she have to assume the awful truth? Where were your fabled inventive powers? You've never been a slouch at creative dissembling.'

I let this pass. 'Jack, you weren't there. Not a chance. Susanna's definitely not stupid. She's mature. Awesomely. Besides, you know Mim as well as I do. She couldn't be party to a direct lie. She'd had enough trouble with her conscience as it was.'

Jack grunted. 'Mim's conscience is overworked and underpaid. She's in the Guinness Book of Records for the world's longest conscience. Not a fault you suffer from.'

'Nor, emphatically, you.'

'Don't get nasty.' The conversation petered out into the usual aimless bickering. But I could see Jack's customary aplomb had slipped a degree or two. His insight into human nature might have its limits, but he didn't need a psychology doctorate to grasp that an element of discord had been introduced into the Black household. A household, moreover, where harmony had been at best precarious. The fact that the tensions were entirely one-sided, emanating from the children towards Mim, didn't make things easier. Her apparent obliviousness and refusal to be roused probably exacerbated the situation.

I was no expert, but the problems on display seemed more than just normal friction of child against parent. I had no qualms about laying the man-sized portion of the blame at Jack's door. Mim's faults were the generous ones of blind, uncritical love and tolerance. Jack's were the more heinous ones of irresponsibility and indifference.

5

STILL, THE ATMOSPHERE Before Cynthia, as I thought of it retrospectively, was positively jovial compared with the glacial standoff that set in After Dave. To be forced at thirteen to adjust your view of your mother from comfortably asexual being to functioning woman is one thing. To perceive yourself as being erotically upstaged by her in a public contest is quite another. It was only too obvious that Susanna's burgeoning sexual identity, which Mim and I had both regarded as rock solid, was reeling from a mortal body blow. She was also, she made it plain, engaged in a painful process of re-evaluation.

'She's reinventing her maternal image from mother as selfless doormat to mother as wanton party girl,' I told Cynthia unwisely a few days later. 'She sees Mim as the complete scarlet woman. That's an image so bizarre I suppose it could only be entertained by Mim's daughter.'

We were having tea in Cyn's flat in the Barbican. It was a public holiday, but Mim of course was working, keeping the office open for emergencies while the paid staff took the day off. I had always found the Barbican a cheerless place, and Cyn's cramped and crowded eyrie depressed me. She had bought the one-bedroom apartment on the thirteenth floor of a tower block a few years earlier during a market slump. It faced towards the cold north with views of scudding clouds and rooftops, and it felt both stuffy and oppressive.

It was also a monument to Cyn's lack of expertise in interior decor. She had tried; everywhere one looked was evidence of strenuous efforts. There were struggling pot plants and straggling dried flower arrangements, and a profusion of objets, arty or whimsical, arranged on shiny black plastic shelving. A collection of ceramic toad musicians stood on a lacquered oriental sideboard, overlit by badly made leadlight lamps and strewn with peacock feathers. Clashing cushions in brocade and needlepoint sat stiffly on a leatherette sofa.

I thought of Mim's house, which without really trying and against all odds managed to combine chronic mess with welcome and comfort. Cyn's flat leant over backwards to impress the visitor with its owner's laid-back eclecticism and succeeded only in conveying loneliness. All this hectic informality was desiccated and contrived, suggesting the hand of a much older person.

But the sitting room was a model of sophistication and taste compared with the bedroom. Cyn insisted on the complete guided tour and I trudged in her wake, muttering insincere compliments. My first glimpse of the bedroom must have elicited an involuntary catch of breath, as Cyn turned to me with an expectant look.

'It's quite something, isn't it?'

'Quite something, yes. Definitely.'

She clearly wanted more. I remembered Mim telling me

that the bedroom was Cyn's pride and joy and I must be sure to admire it. Pressed for further details, Mim had merely said that it was rather like a Parisian boudoir and I must see it for myself.

'It's very feminine.' I groped for an appropriate elaboration. 'Very fin de siècle.' Cyn seemed pleased. I pressed on. 'Bella figura? Yes, and somewhat, ah, demi-monde.'

'It's interesting you should use those words, Lou. I wanted something sophisticated and un-English. Not that a room, strictly speaking, can be fin de siècle, bella figura *and* demi-mondaine. But I know what you were trying to say.'

'Oh, but it can be all those things.' I was warming to the theme. 'It's making a big extravagant statement, and at the same time it suggests the debauchery of the bordello. Lascivious, Cyn. I think I'm shocked.'

Cyn was gratified. 'Allowing for your natural hyperbole – which has its charms – yes, that's what I was trying to achieve. A fantasy. Sensuality with a hint of naughtiness.'

'An Arabian Nights caprice?'

'Les mots justes.'

I felt I had humoured Cyn well beyond the call of duty, and my eyes were beginning to ache from the riot of tints and textures on display. The room was small, and made even smaller by striped red Regency wallpaper and a king-sized four poster bed covered with a ruffled purple quilt. It was piled with carefully arranged cushions in white, lilac and mauve. A lacy negligee disported itself across the bed in an attitude of abandon, and one edge of the bedcover was carelessly turned back, revealing what looked suspiciously like satin sheets.

Cyn caught me staring.

'I had to send to the States for those. They're hardly stocked here, people are too conventional. Frightened of appearing brazen. In America they go in for exotic luxuries, but doubtless you know all that.'

I ignored the hopeful carrot and turned away. But I wasn't going to escape that easily. Cyn grasped my arm in the intrusively physical way she had.

'You haven't seen the little girls' room yet. Come!'

We squeezed in single file between the end of the bed and the wall, brushing past feather boas dangling from lookalike candle sconces. Cyn opened a door concealed in the wallpaper.

'This is my bijou en suite.'

A triangular sunken bath, hand basin, lavatory and bidet were crammed together, reminding me of the bathrooms on a sleeper train. The walls were lilac, the fittings pink with grey veining.

'I had the bath put in.' She looked at me sideways. 'Big enough for two. And would you credit it, there was no bidet? I really believe the English still consider the bidet a rather blush-inducing affectation, when it's a necessity of civilised life. Or rather, civilised sex.'

She looked into my face searchingly. Apart from inside the bath there was scarcely room for two people to stand, and I was aware of a faint body odour emanating from Cyn. She had always sweated heavily; at university balls I remembered dark underarm stains on the satin or taffeta gowns that had always seemed too tight and too revealing. We had dealt with this matter-of-factly, giving Cyn items of personal hygiene for birthdays and Christmas, and slipping advertisements for anti-perspirants and vaginal deodorants under her door. Nothing had helped and we concluded it was a medical problem. I was deputised to suggest to Cyn that she consult a specialist, and was on the brink of discharging this errand when Mim, distressed, talked me out of it.

My lack of response seemed to strike Cyn as particularly irritating.

'Most people think they can wash themselves quite adequately in two minutes under the shower. You may be one of those people, Lou, for all I know. In point of fact, clean genitals are quite hard to achieve in a shower – you really have to make an effort. Whereas the bidet is efficient, quick and to the point.'

I was reminded of Jack and the gas fires.

'You're right, Cyn, it's a smashing invention. When I come to power I'll make bidets compulsory. Unclean genitals will be a thing of the past.'

'Sometimes I think you have only aged superficially, Lou,' Cyn said, frowning. 'You were always embarrassed by plain speaking.'

'Embarrassed by plain speaking?' I was stung. 'What absolute rot.'

'When you're uncomfortable you always lapse into obsolete adolescent jargon. Like absolute rot, and smashing. Face it, you're embarrassed by the subject of bidets.'

'That's ludicrous, Cyn. Why should I be?'

'Because they involve the washing of private parts, I should imagine. I can't think of any other reason.' She put her head back and regarded me quizzically. I was half amused and more than half annoyed. I sat on the bidet to put some space between us and looked up at Cyn.

'I'm quite prepared to analyse the philosophical and social significance of the bidet and the washing of private parts, in exhaustive detail, if that's what turns you on.'

Cyn frowned.

'It's impossible to discuss anything sensible with you when you're in one of your provoking, showing-off moods. Quite pointless.'

'Showing off to a vast audience of one? And you, at that? Why would I bother?'

'You show off to yourself, Lou. You're your own best audience.'

We grinned at each other in mutual resigned exasperation. There was grudging affection in our friendship, but there was also some barely acknowledged dislike. I wondered which was uppermost on either side, and if the word friendship was even appropriate. If Cyn and I had met at this point in our lives, it was inconceivable that we would ever have become friends.

But as we walked back through her preposterous boudoir I felt a rush of compassion. The parade of longing was too exposed, too naked. Had any male person actually penetrated this sanctuary? There was something expectant about it, something untouched, and desperate. In the less highly charged but overheated atmosphere of the sitting room, even the vinyl armchairs were a relief.

'All that work must have cost you a fortune,' I said. I knew she was hard up. In spite of her undergraduate promise Cyn had never cracked the academic big-time. She was still a senior tutor, Mim told me, her brow wrinkled in puzzlement. For me, the reasons were self-evident. Cyn rubbed people up the wrong way. Jack had summed it up brutally. Cyn was bolshie, pompous, Australian and a woman. She was also over the hill.

'She'll never get any further. It's amazing she got this far. These days you have to have good tits and a bit of style to be a lecturer. They'd be chucking paper darts and rolling the Jaffas. Any interview panel could see that before she got her foot in the door.'

Crude and sexist he might be, but he had a knack of pinpointing the harsh realities of life that for others were too unfair, or too unpalatable, to contemplate.

Cyn needed no encouragement to talk about her renovations. The sunken bath alone had taken years off her life. The mess and disruption, the delays and let-downs. Dealing with incompetent British plumbers had sorely tested her lifelong Labour convictions.

'But it was all worth it. It's an investment. It's put up the market value of the apartment. And not only that, I've got something nice to bring people – bring men – back to. Something special, that shows another aspect of myself.'

It was plain, I thought treacherously, that along with the flat Cyn believed she had raised her own market value. At her age it wasn't only the academic world that was increasingly competitive, it was what Jack called the meat market. 'It's Sundays in the park for Cyn,' he said. 'The meat market's closed. It won't be reopening.'

My skin crawled. I contemplated us both with as much detachment as I could muster. Did we have more in common than I liked to think? Two women with their feet up drinking PG Tips. Both no longer in the first flush of youth, both no longer happy, and drowning their sorrows with slabs of chocolate mud cake. Both unattached. No, that wasn't quite right. One was unattached. The other was still hanging on to – how did Jack put it? – a relationship with a black hole at the end of a tunnel. Sam was like a lead lifejacket thrown to a drowning woman.

'Get the hell out before he pulls you under, Lou. That's my advice.' He had said this to me in New York once, when Sam was out of the room. It was good advice and I had taken it. Eventually. A couple of years down the track. But it wasn't as simple as he made it sound. It was a struggle to throw off that lead vest. I was aware that, if not a life and death struggle, it was a choice of freedom versus a form of penal servitude. Well, I had got the hell out and I had my head above water. That felt like quite an achievement, and I was proud of it.

'. . . don't you think?' It dawned on me that Cyn had asked a question. Possibly more than one. She was staring at me, leaning across with an accusing, fixated expression.

'What?'

'Lou, it's rude to ignore people. Especially people who kindly ask you to tea and give you cake. I suppose we have to make allowances for you, as Mim insists, you being lovesick and so forth, although I must say it seems rather ersatz to be heartbroken at your age. I'd have thought you'd got it all over with during your extended post-adolescence.'

'It's your age too,' I said pettishly.

'That's got nothing to do with it. I'm not mooning over someone else's husband.'

'Christ, Cyn, if you're going to moralise –'

'I'm only teasing. You always did have trouble with jokes at your own expense. No such worries about dishing them out.'

One thing about being with Cyn, I reflected. You were guaranteed not to emerge with inflated self-esteem. 'If I ever become famous, I must remember to take you with me to keep the adulation from going to my head.'

'You always used to say, *when* I become famous. Not *if*. What's happened to the vaunted ambition and renowned self-confidence?'

'Sort of temporarily underwater, I guess. Pulled down by a lead lifejacket.'

'What do you mean?' Cyn looked immediately interested.

'Nothing. Just a throwaway line.' But it wasn't easy to deflect Cyn when she scented something meaty. She was temperamentally inclined toward intense, up-all-night soul-searching.

The rest of us had been an ongoing disappointment in this regard, particularly as she must have known that we luxuriated in self-revelations the moment she left the room. I knew that the main reason she was now being unusually aggressive with me was my frustrating refusal to talk about Sam.

Her eyes rounded speculatively. 'Throwaway lines are often the most revealing. My analyst always picks them up. Is it that you feel your personality is being submerged by your feelings? The strength of them is pulling you down?'

I was startled. 'Are you having analysis, Cyn?'

'Of course. So should you be. Every sensible single woman I know is in analysis. It would do you a power of good. Answer my question.'

'When did you start?'

'About three years ago. Tell me more about this lead whatsit pulling you down. Is it your alter ego? Is it another person? Sam, for instance?' She peered at me, thirsting for confidences I was determined not to confide.

'It was only a clumsy metaphor for life in general. Nothing deep and meaningful. Rather maladroit, actually.'

'You know, Lou, you should really think about shedding your resolutely vacant veneer. What can be charming at twenty is tiresome at forty. You should get things off your chest. It's not good to bottle up your feelings. It can be positively harmful.'

'You mean it can cause cancer in rats?'

'Sneer if you will but this is pretty much received wisdom these days. I'm not talking quackery.' She got up and went to the kitchenette. It was separated from the room we were in by a melamine counter on which I noticed an array of small containers, the kind stocked by chemists and health food shops. Vitamin and mineral supplements with names like St John's

Wort, and what looked like homeopathic remedies in little brown jars.

'Cyn, could it be that your hypochondria is showing?'

Cyn selected two containers and put them on the coffee table beside my chair. 'In your situation, one of these capsules each day would really help.'

'What is "my situation"?'

She ignored this. 'Negative thoughts and hostility are very depleting to the system. The beleaguered body makes increased demands and quickly exhausts its resources of essential nutrients. Resistance is lowered and you become more susceptible to illness – at first minor assaults then, if the imbalance is not righted, major assaults and major disease.'

She didn't have to tell me about the minor assaults. During the last year in New York I had experienced a series of them, one after another. First a recurrence of the eczema I hadn't had since childhood, then falling hair, then a shutdown of the healing mechanism so that everyday cuts and scratches remained as permanent tiny scars. There was a lull at the moment. I guessed my beleaguered body must be standing back and debating which area to deplete next. None of this did I wish to share with Cynthia, and I had no desire to indulge her by taking the proffered pills and capsules.

'Just for you, Cyn, I'll see the doctor and get a tonic.'

'That's the equivalent of going home to mummy for a dose of cod liver oil. Comforting, but you should have grown out of it. Orthodox medicine is notoriously inadequate in the field of stress management, you know. Still, I can't help you if you won't be helped.'

My relationship with Cynthia and Jack had certain key elements in common, I reflected. They were unlike those I had with anyone else. Cyn was frowning at me and I was reminded of a matron at boarding school whose face had settled into the same lines of thwarted helpfulness.

'Well, we still haven't worked out what to do about the Susanna situation.' I wasn't aware that this had been on the agenda, but the change of topic was welcome. Cyn settled back with another slice of cake. 'Something has to be done. Has Dave been round again, or was it just a one-night stand?'

Unlikely as it had seemed, I thought there was more between the two of them than that. In their farewell in the strangled aftermath of discovery, I had glimpsed a graphic meeting of eyes.

'He's been to the co-op. They've had lunch together twice. Sandwiches in the office.'

'Sandwiches. Not bed?'

'They couldn't go to bed at the co-op. Not in front of everybody. Well, Dave might be willing but Mim's definitely too inhibited.'

'You realise this is extremely unsatisfactory for them, Lou. They must be dying of frustration. It's probably harmful too, all that pent-up sexual tension unreleased.'

'I hadn't thought of that. Does it get absorbed back into the body? Is it toxic?'

Cyn looked at me with unrestrained mistrust. After a moment's internal debate she said, 'Do you think it's possible that Mim initiated David? I'm inclined to think not.'

'Cyn, you astound me. No, I'm sure not. The other way round, if anything.'

'You mean he would be more experienced?'

'Almost anyone would be more experienced than Mim.' Possibly even you, I thought, and made a mental note to grill Mim about Cynthia's sexual history.

'Of course Mim and Jack have probably had very little sex

100

lately,' Cyn said meditatively, 'if any. Whereas someone of David's age needs it a lot. How often, would you say?'

'On the hour?'

'Every other hour is probably not overstating his capacity. Young males are notoriously obsessed by it. It's well known that they have a sexual thought every twenty-three seconds. How often do you have them, Lou?'

'Oh, about once a year.'

Cyn's assessing gaze was discomfiting. 'Anyway, something must be done about Mim and David. Couldn't you suggest they rush over to the house at lunchtime for a quick one?'

'I'm sure it's occurred to them, but Mim won't leave the office when she's officially on duty. And after work she's too – anxious about the effect on Susanna.'

'Surely the girl goes out sometimes?'

'Actually she hasn't been out after school since that fateful night. She watches Mim like a hawk. Won't let her out of her sight. Won't say a word to her either.'

'But this is dreadful. Mim must be distraught.'

'Pretty much, I'm afraid.'

Cyn ran sticky, agitated fingers through her hair. A crumb of chocolate icing caught in one of her heavy eyebrows and hung there. 'There's nothing for it. One of us will have to speak to Susanna.'

My heart sank. 'I don't see –'

'It's the only possibility of getting some sense into her. She looks up to us, strange as it may seem in your case, and we're in the fortunate position of not being related to her so we have the kind of influence a mother can never have.'

This struck me as less than axiomatic. 'I'm not sure we have any kind of influence over anyone. Least of all Susanna.'

'No, Lou, that's where you're wrong. We're older, wiser,

and she sees us as women of the world. You see, we're career women, unlike her mother. And it may come as a surprise to you but I, too, have some experience of the opposite sex.'

'I never doubted it, Cyn.'

'I may not be able to compete in the rarefied femme fatale stratosphere you like to claim as your own, but I've had relationships. More than you might think. And I, too, know what it's like to be brokenhearted. Possibly rather better than you.' She looked down, and I saw the crumb of icing fall on her nose then lodge itself on her jumper.

'That's very touching but it won't cut any ice with Susanna. She's not in the business of being consoled or reasoned with by experienced or brokenhearted career women. She's part of the brave new generation of emotional robots. Alarmingly self-sufficient.'

'That's exactly what she's not, and moreover it's cowardly. You're just frightened of confrontation. It's you all over, if I may say so. Take the easy way out and avoid the issue. That's the way things get out of hand. The girl desperately needs help. Her father just abandoned her and she's lost the man she loves to her mother. And she's only fourteen.'

'Not yet fourteen,' I said automatically. 'Good God, Cyn, it sounds like the plot of a sub-standard Mills and Boon. Let's not get all sanctimonious and drama queen about this. In point of fact her dad abandoned her at birth and she wasn't remotely in love with Dave. He's her teacher. He's just another in the endless list of crushes you have at that age.'

Cyn sat up straight and glared at me. Her eyes bulged with strong emotion. 'What do you know about anything? My father divorced us when I was about Susanna's age and I don't care how long it had been coming – when it finally happened I was devastated. Nobody talked to me. Everyone was concerned with my mother, as if the fact that she was grown up meant she was the only one to have feelings. And if you think that puppy love is any less desolating than the real thing, you're sadly mistaken.'

I was silent. I realised I had not even been aware that Cyn's parents were divorced. I had no memory of ever meeting either of them; perhaps they had never visited her at university. Cyn's strictures were getting to me. I felt chastened. It had been an unaccustomed sensation, but it seemed to be coming home to roost rather often lately. I thought, I hardly know anything about Cynthia. I was never interested enough to ask.

Cyn said, 'I'm going to see Susanna tonight.'

'*No!*' This sounded explosively negative, and I repeated it more gently. 'No, I'll do it. I'm staying there after all, it's easier for me. I can wait until the right moment presents itself. Until she's in a receptive frame of mind.'

Cyn looked sceptical. 'I'm not sure you're the right person for this, Lou. Not sure at all. You might stir her up and make things worse.'

'I can show rare qualities of empathy when roused. It's my journalistic training. Countless hours spent wheedling confidences out of recalcitrant recluses and drunken celebrities.'

'You and Jack both,' Cyn said slyly.

6

THERE WAS TRUTH IN WHAT I had said to Cynthia. I was a practised and skilful interviewer. I prided myself on my ability to put people at their ease and draw them out. Disparate characters whose politics might be anathema to me, whose personalities might be incompatible with mine, who in any other context I would find uncongenial.

Nevertheless I had no intention of speaking to Susanna. But when I relayed the conversation to Mim I found her unexpectedly keen on the idea. We were talking in her bedroom, almost the only place we could go to avoid the girl's accusing eyes. Even my suggestion of a retreat to the Indian restaurant round the corner had been rejected.

'She's making you a prisoner in your own home, Mim.' I knew there was no point in expressing my view that this penance was completely unwarranted.

'I know, but it won't go on forever. I just don't want to do anything else to upset her. It might help, I think – your talking to her, if you could possibly think of something to say. I mean, Cyn's right, you know – she does rather look up to you.'

'Surely not, Mim. She has a thoroughly healthy attitude to me – to any of our generation. She sees us as irrelevant.'

'Me, yes, but then I'm her mother. You have to expect that with teenagers, don't you? And she's a bit negative about poor Cyn, too, I'm afraid, although I hope she'll grow out of that. But you see, you're a glamorous figure to her, you know, having wild affairs and grand passions – well, *a* grand passion – and living a kind of free-spirited life with bylines and expense accounts and no responsibilities. Well, no-one has no responsibilities, of course, but you are chiefly accountable to yourself, as she sees it, and that's very attractive to the young.'

This was how Mim saw me, I realised, and it struck me how rarely other people's impressions of one's life conform to one's own. Mim added hastily, 'That's a silly oversimplification, don't think it's intended to accurately describe your life. Other people always tell one's biography through rose-coloured images, don't they?'

She pushed her fringe out of her eyes, where it stayed less than a second before falling back. Mim's hair was always over-grown, her brown eyes peering through the undergrowth like those of an Old English sheepdog. She claimed it was because she feared hairdressers, but I thought it provided a filter between her and a frequently harsh world. Cyn's hair was the same, but it straggled in lank rats' tails where Mim's was fluffy and flyaway.

'I never knew Cyn's parents were divorced. And she's having analysis – God, imagine having to endure Cyn droning on about herself for hours every week of the year.'

'It's only three hours a week now, two one-and-a-half-hour sessions. It was five a week last year. And it costs a dreadful

105

lot — all her surplus salary. After she did her bedroom and bathroom she went on to the analysis.'

'No amount of money would make me sit through that.'

'Actually it's done her a lot of good. I think she understands herself better now. And it's helped get her resentment about her father out of her system. It had been fermenting inside for years. She never saw him again, you know, after he left. And then he died when she was twenty-one.'

'While we were at college?' I had no memory of this.

'Just before her finals. She didn't want anyone to know. It was very painful for her, as you can imagine. She wore her academic gown to the funeral. It was the only black thing she had.'

'How do you know — were you there?'

Mim said almost apologetically, 'She needed a bit of support. But she didn't want to talk about it to anyone, so I thought it better not to mention it at the time.'

'She talked about it to you?'

'Yes, well, a bit, over the weekend. I suppose she had to confide in someone. Anyone would have done.'

Diligent questioning elicited the fact that Mim had taken Cynthia to the Blue Mountains the weekend after his death, to an old Polish guesthouse called Green Gables. Neither of them had achieved any work as Cyn had been in floods of tears for the entire two days. They had returned on Monday morning, and Mim admitted when pressed that her own final art history paper had been that afternoon.

'It didn't make any difference to me, and Cyn did brilliantly anyway. Her mother died too, not very long after that, one of those terrible cancer deaths. Poor Cyn, nothing's gone right for her. Time's running out and she's desperate to have a child, that's why she's always been so attached to Susie and Jake. I

106

often think of that sumptuous bedroom of hers and how it's waiting for a man to come and romp with her in it. And it never happens. She just doesn't seem to meet a feasible man.'

'She told me she had had rampant sex. More than I might think, she said.'

'Yes, well, that's true, she has. But still . . .'

I waited, but Mim appeared disinclined to elaborate. 'Whoever with, Mim? When?'

'Oh, there've been one or two affairs. You know.'

I said disingenuously, 'Cyn wanted to tell me. She was waiting for me to ask, only we got sidetracked onto the subject of Susanna.'

Mim brightened. 'I do think it would be wonderful if you could try speaking to her. Really, it's the only thing I can think of that might help. Break the deadlock. Otherwise I thought we should consider therapy, separately or together.'

'Oh, anything but that.' Years of living in America, where everyone had a private therapist, had left me violently opposed to the practice.

Mim looked close to tears. 'I've tried and tried to sit down with her but she . . . well, I don't have to tell you how poisonous I am to her at the moment. I feel like a viper in her house. Why did I ever do such a thing, Lou? How could I have been so heartless? When she's so disturbed about Jack and everything.'

I told her yes, I would certainly try speaking to Susanna, if she thought it might achieve anything. Privately I thought it hadn't a chance in hell of achieving anything much, except widening the catchment area of resentment to include me.

Susanna was never going to be in a receptive mood and I didn't bother waiting for the right moment to present itself. I buttonholed her after dinner, which had been a cheerless meal with the four of us sitting around the table, Susanna silent, Jake listening to music through headphones and Mim and I making bright, stilted conversation. It had been exactly like that, I remembered, on the rare occasions that Sam and I had eaten with his children. Seeing me accost the girl, Mim bolted upstairs murmuring something about sewing on a button.

Susanna sat stiffly in an armchair and I parked myself opposite. I had selected a bottle of spumante for the occasion, judging it to be about right for the thirteen-year-old taste and conceding that a level of self-sacrifice was in order. 'Let's have a drink,' I invited chummily.

Surprise temporarily felled Susanna's habitual expression of sullenness. 'What's there to celebrate?'

'Your becoming an adult.' She looked at me as if I was mad, but accepted the proffered glass, one of the three remaining champagne flutes Jack had made such a song and dance about. We sipped. After a judicious pause I said, 'Welcome to the world. It's a painful process, entering adulthood. You're finding that out, rather earlier than most.'

She said nothing, her eyes fixed over my shoulder.

'It's a world where there's no make-believe any more. Things are for real. There's heartbreak and there's disillusionment. Everyone grows up thinking their parents are perfect, if they're lucky.'

'If they're lucky!' The bitterness was savage.

'Yes, if they're lucky. Lucky kids are the ones born into families where they're cared about. Where they have the luxury of being angry with their parents. Where they have enough to eat and a roof over their heads.' I risked a joke. 'Even if the roof's a kennel.' She didn't smile. 'Unlucky kids die before their first birthday, of hunger or disease, or they're abused or born with AIDS. I've seen kids like that. Believe it, you were privileged to be able to believe in your parents. However briefly it lasted.'

'Not long, that's for sure.'

'Okay, there's a price to pay. The lucky ones don't have it all their own way. The more you believe in your parents, the greater the outrage when the penny drops: hey, they're not perfect after all. The best most people can hope for is that their parents turn out to be ordinary, halfway decent human beings.'

I took a big gulp of the sweet fizzy liquid. The slight figure opposite me sat tensely. Her shining, straight hair hung like a storm cloud across half her face, obscuring her eyes. 'If these imperfect, full of holes, normal human beings love you, you're pretty damned fortunate.'

She jerked her head up, her eyes dark and shadowed. 'What makes you think that? Dad only loves himself. Mum hates me.'

A surge of cold rage jolted me like a jab from an icepick. 'Susanna, you bloody know that's not true. No-one could love you more than Mim.'

'She's got a pretty funny way of showing it. Fucking the guy she knew I really really liked. Right here in my own house. A teacher, who I have to see every day.' Her face flooded with angry tears, making her look childish and vulnerable. My voice softened.

'Your mother has the most nearly angelic nature I've ever encountered in the world. She's also a fallible person, not the Virgin Mary. She's been under appalling strain with your dad. Yes – ' forestalling the interruption, 'so have you, I know that. It's been pretty damn tough for both of you. But look, in the twenty years I've known Mim, this is the first major lapse I've ever seen from her. Just one out-of-character move. She's entitled to that, wouldn't you say?'

'Well, there's billions of old farts she could've chosen from.

Why did she have to deliberately choose him?' The voice was muffled again, and the mouth trembling. Tears squeezed out. 'He's much too young for her. He's half her age. She's making herself look ridiculous. Everyone at school is just laughing at her.'

I wondered if this was the nub of the problem. Susanna's friend Ruth, the witness, must have had no qualms about spilling the beans. This choice item would have raced through the Old Barn School like wildfire. I marshalled my forces.

'Listen to me, and don't ever repeat this to Mim.' I had her attention and I towed in the big guns I'd been holding in reserve. 'When I said you were lucky, earlier,' she shook her head obdurately, 'I only said half of it. You're someone with things going for you that other girls would kill for. You're bright, you're beautiful and you're young. You have a famous father. Yes –' seeing the expression, 'maybe that's a mixed blessing but believe me, it gives you a whole bunch of inbuilt advantages.' This tack was a mistake, I realised. Her mouth was set in a line of irony and disdain.

'Having a famous father just means you don't have a father at all.'

I judged it preferable to overlook the accuracy of this. 'Like it or not, Susanna, you're one of life's golden girls. Now look at your mother. I don't want to be disloyal to Mim but the hard truth is, her youth's behind her, she's a bit overweight, her looks are going and she's lost the only man she's ever been crazy about.'

'Bring on the violins.'

I was tempted to seize her by the shoulders and shake her violently. 'There's a limit to how much people can take. I'm not sure Mim can take too much more right now. She needs her kids, she needs you, rather badly.'

'She should've thought of that before.'

'It's asking a hell of a lot, I know. It's asking you to respond not with the reflexes of a young girl who's been thwarted, but as the young woman you're becoming. Once you have found out what it's like to care deeply about a man, you've learnt something about yourself, and about the world. Painful, but all worthwhile experience involves some pain. Right now I think you could afford to be a little generous, a little understanding. Unlike Mim you have your life ahead of you. Infinite possibilities.'

'They've ruined my life. She and Dad.'

I thought I had lost her and I felt drained with the effort of getting through. I thought I had been putting it rather well, but I seemed to be getting nowhere. Even the toughest interview was never such a struggle for the right words. She emptied her glass. I poured a drop more for both of us.

'You can decide to let your life be ruined. It's a decision you're entitled to make. It's your life.'

'It's got nothing to do with me. They've done it.'

I put my glass down. This was easier. This was something I felt passionate about.

'Oh no. That's the child in you talking. No-one ruins your life, unless you let them. The decision is in your own hands.'

I looked at my own hands, outspread in a theatrical gesture. A ring Sam had given me, and which I always wore, two elegantly interlocking bands of solid silver, was on the fourth finger of my right hand. Our initials were engraved inside the connecting circles.

'You can resolve to let something like this – your parents' divorce, a disappointment in love – destroy you, or you can determine to rise above it. It's up to you, no-one else. This is what, when the chips are down, separates the winners from

111

the losers, the women of character from the emotional cripples who remain prisoners of their childhood. I want to emphasise this as strongly as I can. This was unnecessary, as I heard my voice rising and vibrating with conviction. 'Do you want to be stunted forever, consumed with resentment over things that happened to you long ago? Or do you want to seize life with both hands and have a say in your own destiny?'

I willed her to look at me. We watched each other silently for a full minute. There were tears now in my eyes, too.

'Be nicer to your mother, okay?' I said finally. The corners of her mouth moved fractionally but I couldn't tell whether they had moved up or down. 'I worked all this out rather late,' I went on conversationally, in what I hoped was a woman-to-woman tone. 'I didn't even meet Sam until I was thirty-four.' I hadn't intended to invoke Sam's name, let alone further details, but I had a confused idea Susanna was due for a bit of quid pro quo. I had the impression that everything I'd said could be related to what had occurred between Sam and me. Without it, I suspected, I would have lacked the impetus to say anything to her at all.

I told her about our first meeting, when I had been sent from Washington to cover a Swedish literary festival. I was to interview that year's Nobel Laureate, the keynote speaker in a programme that also included a relatively unknown Australian playwright. Told her how, up to that time, I had believed that passionate love was a social convention, fuelled by romantic novelists, designed to give lust and infatuation a respectable moral tone. And how, half an hour after Sam and I had bumped into each other, in a blinding Pauline conversion I had realised I knew nothing about anything.

From my present position, just downstream of the seething rapids that had swept me along for the past five years, the complacent emptiness of that ignorance, its tranquillity, had a fleeting appeal. I didn't tell Susanna that occasionally I found myself wishing I had never met Sam, that I could go back to those innocent, peaceful days. Even now, that wish felt suspiciously like treachery, not so much to him as to experience. In spite of its attractions, it was a denial of the riches of life itself.

She listened to my account of the affair expressionlessly but with concentration, and I was surprised to find a curious cathartic release in this straightforward telling to a much younger person. The attempt to make a coherent picture from the jigsaw of meetings and partings, joy and anguish that had formed the pattern of Sam's and my relationship was a big challenge. It was the first time I had made the effort, even to myself.

But it was time to move on. What we needed now was therapy, I told Susanna with more assurance than I felt, and the best therapy for both of us was work. For me that meant rejoining the mainstream, reviving old contacts.

'Hitting editors with groovy story ideas and scoffing double martinis in pubs, in short,' I said, conscious of my image. Not quite yet, I thought, but soon.

Thousands of miles removed from the epicentre, I was still unsure of Sam's part in my life story. I was certain of only one imperative: to get on with my life as if he had never inhabited it. I hoped it wasn't being too fanciful to suppose that Susanna might scrape some residual relevance from it all.

'Have you met Dad's girlfriend?'

She put the question casually, but it dropped like a stone into the ensuing pause. It was an effort to emerge from the world I had just re-entered, dense with a remembered reality that seemed a universe away from this one.

'His girlfriend? Is there one? That is, any particular one?'

'Of course there is.' She looked derisive, but her voice sounded more scoffing than contemptuous. 'There must be, mustn't there? Otherwise he'd never have got to the point of leaving Mum. I mean, really leaving. Do you want another glass of champagne?'

The bottle was less than half full. I moved it out of her reach. 'No, I won't have any more and you'd better not either. It tastes like lolly water but it's deceptive stuff, and I don't want you going to school tomorrow with your first hangover. I still have the remnants of a sense of responsibility. More importantly, I wouldn't want your father to accuse me of corrupting your palate. In answer to your question, no, I haven't heard of anyone special in his life. I'd say it's unlikely. I don't think Jack is the type to tie himself down to one person.'

After a pause I added hurriedly, 'Not again, anyhow,' but I could see she wasn't fooled.

She said, 'I know what Dad's like, you don't have to whitewash him to me. His idea of being faithful is to stay overnight.' I thought this was a trifle hard, even on Jack. Then she said, 'What was he like when you first knew him?'

I considered. 'Pretty much as he is now. Younger.' She looked impatient. 'Very attractive, very noisy, thinner, and with much longer hair. And quite political – he was more left-wing in those days.'

'Always chasing girls?'

'Yep, 'fraid so.'

'Did you ever sleep with him?' She gave a small smile, which instantly transformed her face. 'The delicacy is for your benefit.'

'Thanks. No, I didn't.'

'Why not?'

114

'Well, he was Mim's friend.'

'Would you have, if he wasn't?'

'I don't know. Perhaps. Probably.' I wondered what lay behind this line of questioning.

'Would you now?'

'The same thing applies. Besides, he's not really my type.'

'But you said you would have, before. How was it different?'

'I said I probably would. Well, we were both much younger, for a start. I wasn't so discriminating and I was very inexperienced.'

'But you must've been eighteen or nineteen.'

'Yes, but it wasn't like it is today. We were far more innocent than you lot.'

She looked unconvinced. 'Why did Mum marry him?'

'Oh Jesus, why does anyone do anything? It's a big question. Maybe you should ask her.'

Her face reverted smartly to its usual scornful cast. 'I can't talk to Mum. She'd only waffle on about how lovely he was, and still is. I mean, she's let him trample on her all her life and now she's getting dumped for it. Ruth's mother says it'd be poetic justice if it wasn't so pathetic, and she's right.'

'Ruth's mother?' I found it alarming to think of Mim's plight being discussed so outspokenly among the parents of her daughter's friends.

'She's a feminist writer. Her name's Daria Webster, you might have heard of her. She's written a book called *The Male Monopoly: How Men Take Over Women's Lives*. You might've read it. Mum's in it.'

'In it?' I echoed dazedly.

Susanna looked irritably patient. She was practised at investing any expression, however workaday, with a contrary

115

subtext. 'In a chapter. There's a whole chapter on her and Dad, how she let him take over her life. She's one of six people Daria uses as examples.'

'Did she interview Mim?'

'No, she didn't need to, she's known her for years. There are other mothers in it too, from school.' I thought Daria must be fortunately placed. All her primary sources evidently lay close at hand, among the exploited female parents of the Old Barn. Had Mim read it? Was she even aware that she had been used as research fodder?

Susanna dismissed my fears without compunction. 'Sure, she doesn't care. It's all disguised, anyway. Daria couldn't use their real names or Dad would've sued. He's a German singer in the book and Mum does charity work. Dad's called Carl and Mum's Constance.'

'Constance? She's not above labouring a point, this Daria.'

'Oh, they've all got pseudonyms like that. There's Patience, Prudence and Constance, Faith, Hope and Charity. I know Hope and Prudence too. They're the other mothers. It's really clever, the way the names sort of pick out the main personality point of each person.'

'And she shows how that particular characteristic was responsible for each person being taken over?'

'That's right.' She looked surprised at my perspicacity. 'You can read it if you want. There's a copy somewhere. I'll go and find it.' She ambled off, looking almost amenable. There was nothing like the prospect of showing her mother in a bad light to cheer her up, I guessed.

That night in bed I opened *The Male Monopoly: How Men Take Over Women's Lives*, feeling furtive. Susanna had tucked it into my bed, in a rare display of tact. I hoped Mim wouldn't notice its absence from the bookshelf. The flyleaf was inscribed

'To Miriam, with love and squalor, Daria'. It was written in violet ink in an oversized, dashing hand. The dedication was 'To Ruth, my daughter, without whom this could not have been written'.

Daria Webster must be quite a formidable customer, I concluded after devouring the pertinent chapter with disloyal gusto. It was keenly observed and rather well written. Constance was unmistakeably Miriam, sketched in fluent, telling strokes. The sad story of her marriage to Carl, a famous singer of popular songs, was told with the kind of detail that testified to a close familiarity with the subject. What I hadn't expected was the sincerity of the portrait of Mim, whose very human faults and generous excesses were described with affection.

The picture of the Germanic Carl bristled with malice. Daria had taken a few judicious liberties with him, no doubt at the prompting of the publisher's lawyer. Carl was now, enjoyably, stout and bald, with a vain posturing format that suggested a caricatured operatic tenor. I warmed to the unknown Daria when I learnt that he sang middle of the road, soupy ballads to a swooning legion of housewives. To portray Jack as a corpulent crooner was inspired. It also revealed an insider's grasp of precisely how to deliver maximum unactionable offence.

I passed an idle minute ruminating on a comparable literary metamorphosis for Sam. Sam shared with Jack a puritanical distaste for indolence and a violent distrust of drugs. He would be a lazy tabloid hack, I decided, newly sacked for heroin addiction. I returned to Daria feeling slightly ashamed of myself and considerably cheered.

Daria's summation carried few surprises but managed some neat barbs along the way. The lecherous Carl, whose appeal to women was inexplicable in terms other than the lubricating intoxicant of fame, had earmarked Constance with the wolf's unerring eye. She was the type of woman who was unfailingly loyal and forgiving – the only type who would tolerate his blatant philandering. Compulsive womanising of this order, Daria maintained, was invariably pathological in origin and probably indicated suppressed homosexual tendencies, together with fear and hatred of women. Carl was covering these up in the most convincing way available, for himself and his public.

I was deeply entertained by the thought of Jack reading this theory. The theory, too, was engaging, but somehow in Jack's case it seemed to lack the patina of indisputable truth. I stored it up, however, for future use. Constance also came in for her share of clinical evaluation. Women like her, Daria concluded, were plagued by a constitutional niceness that did no-one any good, least of all themselves, and was a magnet for unscrupulous bounders like Carl. They should take a long hard look at where their biddable disposition had landed them. It came from a childhood identification with traditional ideals of femininity that kept women in servitude. Compulsive niceness was rooted in low self-esteem, a reluctance to incur other people's wrath by being assertive. The approval of others was life-giving oxygen to this personality type.

It was here that Daria dropped the ball. No-one, I felt jealously, knew Mim better than I, and there was a fatal flaw in this analysis. There was a fundamental centre to Mim's character that transcended behavioural theories, however glib and plausible. The missing ingredient was goodness. I was convinced that this goodness was innate, unconnected to child-hood influences, impervious to opinion, and quite unrelated to fashion. Mim was not forgiving and generous because of things that had happened to her; she was this way because this was how she was.

I opened the book again. The suspicion that I might find

something distractingly applicable to myself was not to be resisted. It had not escaped me, independent of the hypotheses of Daria Webster, that in the cause of passion I had let Sam dominate my life. I had willingly subordinated my autonomy to his, moving house and even country to be near him and treating my own career with cavalier disregard. It occurred to me that I might fit rather snugly into Daria's scheme of things. Sure enough, I found a recognisable variation on my theme in the chapter titled 'Hope Springs Eternal'.

The woman given the name Hope was younger than me by about a decade and divorced with two children. The object of her affection was a university lecturer called Saul, father of three, including a toddler. They had met when Hope, a nurse, enrolled in one of Saul's tutorials. A steamy affair ensued, initially resisted by each with considerably more scruple than Sam and I had mustered, and leading to the enslavement of both.

From here the account proceeded with depressing familiarity. Saul promised he would leave his already pregnant wife, and finally brought himself to tell her. He actually left home a month before her due date, then returned in a fit of belated compunction after the third child was born. Since then he had been struggling with the same can of worms. It was now two years on, and he was still giving Hope the same fervent assurances, still enmeshed in hearth and home.

Hope meanwhile was banking everything on his eventual extrication, which to the clinical observer such as Daria was a self-evident non-event. Moreover, Saul was contriving to combine work and love life with a great deal more panache than the hapless Hope. She had all but abandoned her studies, lived for Saul's visits and the odd snatched weekend, and was giving herself no chance of meeting other men.

What was especially dispiriting about Hope's story was its

prosaic quality. It seemed scarcely worth the effort of telling. The idea that I, on the same dispassionate page, might be reduced to an identical level of banal self-delusion was galling in the extreme. I lay back on my bank of downy pillows, eyes closed, comparing my own version of events as told to Susanna – a full-blown drama with all the pathos and transcendence of grand opera – with Daria's interpretation, as commonplace and bathetic as a soap opera.

And yet for the protagonists the agony and ecstasy were surely real enough. Too real. Perhaps it was Daria's version, bloodless and objectified as it could only be by someone not involved, that was guilty of trivialising. I had no doubt that Hope would have told it differently, would have slotted it, like me, under tragedy.

I felt curious about Hope, and an urge to meet her. She was, I remembered, one of Susanna's two 'other mothers'. There had been a stage where the only subject I wanted to discuss with anybody, friend or stranger, was myself and Sam. That obsessive, self-indulgent phase was long gone, but there remained a special bond with anyone who had experienced the same baptism of fire. That had been Sam's phrase, and he and I always maintained there was a quality shared by those similarly baptised that set them apart, making them instantly recognisable to each other at some subliminal level.

Those who had really loved, we thought, were the aristocrats of the senses. This elite was privileged to know something about life denied to those whose more pallid affections consigned them to the emotional rank and file. This knowledge they owned was austere and terrible, and it altered their perceptions, not temporarily like a drug, but permanently and profoundly. We were aware how smug we sounded, but we believed our theory utterly. More than that, we *knew* we were right, revelling in the knowledge with the complacent self-absorption of lovers.

At this remove, in my cocoon of isolation, I found that I was still a believer. It was the reason I could not betray myself to Susanna, by admitting the occasional treacherous regret. No member of an elite will willingly surrender her position, even when most of the privileges have been removed.

7

MIM WAS TOUCHINGLY grateful for my intervention with Susanna, insisting that miracles had been wrought. It was flattering, but I could see little improvement. With me Susanna behaved, as before, with what I would have called marginal courtesy, speaking when spoken to in recognisable sentences, occasionally even vouchsafing a smile. She probably thought she was overdoing the exuberance. When Mim hove into view she reverted to her tight-lipped mode, giving monosyllabic replies and scarcely favouring her mother with a glance.

'At least she talks to me now,' Mim said almost gaily. 'You've no idea how demeaning it was to be treated as if one didn't exist.'

I had a good idea, although to me the treatment was more like that dished out to a subspecies. Fortunately there was a diversion. Jake's spartan existence took one of its periodic tolls and he was confined to bed with severe flu. Mim had the rare luxury of mothering him for a few days. He was a horrible patient, sulky and resentful at being confined to barracks, but Dr Tracey Garrett, who was a friend of Mim's, threatened him with hospital if he disobeyed her orders.

'You will be strapped to a stretcher and locked in an isolation ward,' she rapped out. I admired her no-nonsense conjuring of childhood ogres. While Mim had horrified visions of straitjackets and padded cells, her desire to get him over the threshold and under his Rambo duvet narrowly overrode her alarm at Dr Garrett's robust tactics.

Susanna came in as the doctor was leaving and gave me a piercing look, flicking her eyes meaningfully at the broad medical back disappearing down the stairs with Mim. When they were out of earshot she said, 'That's one of the others.'

'The others?'

'The other two mothers. In the book. She's the Hope character.'

I was electrified. 'Hope? Dr Garrett?'

'That's right. The one that's hopelessly stuck on a married man.' As she said this it seemed to dawn on Susanna just what she was saying and she stopped in mid-sentence looking comically dismayed.

'Like me, eh?'

'Oh no, I mean it's not the same, is it? Your situation's totally different.'

I was enthralled to hear that the fearsome Dr Garrett was Hope, and equally struck by Susanna's response. For the first time I had seen her mother in her. The immediate disclaimer, the instinctive chivalrous rush to protect my sensibilities was exactly how Mim would have reacted. I felt a spark of unaccustomed liking for the girl. It went out almost at once, but it had been there, just a glimmer. She tumbled on, sounding almost garrulous.

'No, she's really a pathetic case. Josie, that's her daughter, says she's a disaster at home. Always crying. Her boyfriend's a creep, Josie can't stand him, and he's obviously never going to leave his wife. Nerds like him never do. Anyhow, a guy who could treat his family like that's obviously not worth having . . .'

She trailed off in discernible consternation at the deepening hole she found herself in. I watched amused as the urge to secede from an impossible situation overcame her. She shrugged her shoulders as if to abandon a bad job, threw me a glance that could have been apologetic, and disappeared into her room.

I had imagined Hope as a wan, consumptive figure with a conventional prettiness, the opposite of this young and bossy whirlwind, strong-featured and strongly built. Dr Garrett had swung into the house with impressive authority. The way she dealt with Jake put me in mind of my most respected school teacher. I would have been driven to ask Mim about her if she had not raised the subject herself.

'Tracey's an angel. Fifty carats, or whatever the top diamond is. She's the only person I know who can actually make Jake do something against his will. Apart from Jack, I mean. She's the one tower of strength I always resort to if I'm absolutely at my wit's end.'

'Every family should have one,' I said, thinking it was a pity that this family didn't have Jack. Jack was notably good at throwing his weight around and bending other wills to his own. I decided to seize the nettle.

'Susanna whispered the magic intelligence that Dr Garrett is Hope. She caught me surreptitiously reading that popular tome by Daria Webster, I'm afraid, this morning.' The white lie, I felt, was excusable. 'I'm amazed. I hadn't pictured Hope as an avenging battle-axe.'

'No, well, of course Daria's a master of disguise. But it's funny how love reduces people, even the strongest, to a kind of jelly. In all other areas of her life Tracey's extraordinarily competent. She's a first class doctor, a fine mother. Actually that manner of hers is misleading. She's as gentle as a lamb underneath and children adore her. I think that's why they do what she wants, really, because they like and respect her.' She looked pensive. 'It's an extraordinary talent some people have, isn't it, that ability to combine being lovable and authoritative? The essence of leadership. I've always thought Tracey Garrett would make a wonderful general. People would follow her into battle and die if she said so. Dangerous, of course, in the wrong hands, that quality. But she's true blue.'

I was having trouble fitting Tracey, the true-blue general, tall and broad-shouldered, into lovesick Hope's pinched silhouette. It was my fault for thinking in stereotypes. Hopes obviously came in all shapes and sizes. Mine included.

'The book was published last year. Is the affair still going on?'

'Oh yes. You know how it is, it's like a bushfire in a wind. Once the flame is lit it's blazing out of control and impossible to stop. Not humanly possible, anyway. She tried, because she hates what it's doing to her. But then she finds it's even worse not seeing him, and gives in again. It goes against all her instincts, being the other woman. She's a feminist, of course, and that aspect of it bothers her, what she must be doing to his wife. And as I said, she's a leader, used to being in a dominant position. In this affair she feels subservient, powerless over events.'

'She's got to get out!' I said, surprising myself with my vehemence. Getting out, I knew, had saved me. For the first time in years, it seemed, I was involved in other people's lives. The treadmill of preoccupation with Sam, with our own absorbing world, had been a form of solitary confinement. Leaving it wasn't easy, but it was easier than it had looked. Marginally. Even the thought of a separate future had ceased to be an abyss yawning ahead. I felt the cool brush of the unknown on my cheek, and simultaneously a surge of exhilaration of a kind I had almost forgotten. Like the spark I had felt for Susanna, it was gone almost straightaway, but the familiar emptiness that replaced it didn't seem quite as desolate as before.

Mim was experiencing this with me. 'I was watching the shadows chase across your face,' she said, with the poetic phrasing she sometimes surprised me with. 'I think Tracey would like to do what you've done. But it's hard to move, with two children and a flourishing practice. She used to find it helpful talking to Daria, but I'm afraid they don't see each other now. Tracey took exception to her chapter. It unfortunately caused quite a rift between them.'

I wasn't surprised. 'But what about you, Mim? I mean, I know any similarity to actual personages is purely imaginary, but I found Constance's desperate need for approving pats a little hard to take.'

Mim looked vague. 'Oh, I think Daria mixed a few other people in. You have to marshal the evidence to support your thesis, don't you, in a book like that? Daria's sources were very wide. Look at the picture of Carl – he's light years away from Jack. That's what I always point out, when people ask me if I minded.'

The tantalising name of Daria Webster was going to be made flesh on Saturday night, at a party Mim had organised to celebrate the co-op's tenth birthday. I was keen to meet her. Lots of other neighbourhood notables would be there too, Mim said, looking worried. I gathered she thought there was a strong possibility the party would be gatecrashed by Dave

Benwell, and that Susanna would probably go along in the role of saboteur.

In the event Dave pre-empted matters by turning up at the house on Saturday morning. I had been shopping, and was reaching under the hatch of Mim's station wagon for the groceries when I became aware of a shape looming over me and hands massaging the base of my neck. The hands performing this service were so deft and knowledgeable, the effect so pleasant, that I stayed in this semi-recumbent posture for a good few seconds.

'A lotta tension in those muscles.' It was Dave's laidback drawl. 'You like that a lot, huh? I did it for Mim. She liked it too.'

I straightened up. Dave was standing so close to me that I got an acute whiff of his animal magnetism. Again he was wearing extremely tight jeans, emphasised by a leather bomber jacket that cut off just below the waist. He flashed me a disconcertingly knowing grin and reached under the hatch. His very strong, light tan hands hoisted several overloaded supermarket bags into the air above my head like so many hot air balloons. He strode in front of me, running shoes bouncing off the pavement as if he were made of rubber.

'Dave!' We were at the front door, which was unlocked – a habit of Mim's that disturbed my Manhattan-honed sensibilities. 'Dave, does Mim know you're coming?'

'I figured it was best to surprise her. And if she's not at home, I'm quite happy with the company.' He directed another very unambiguous look at me. I opened the door quickly, feeling unpleasantly rattled.

We found Mim in the garden raking dry leaves into a bonfire. Her hair was tangled, cheeks flushed with the cold, and she wore baggy corduroys and a sweater with darned elbows – did anyone else still darn their sweaters? She looked like a member of the gardening staff of a country estate. Jake, heavily rugged up in a set of Arctic fatigues Mim had found at an Army disposals store, was burying potatoes in the ashes. Susanna was there too. She and her friend Ruth were scurrying about collecting sticks and tossing them on the flames. In gumboots and scarves they looked for once, I thought, misleadingly like real children.

Susanna and Mim saw Dave at the same time. Mim's eyes darted to her daughter for guidance. Susanna flashed Dave a smile of blatantly seductive charm. Mim's relief was palpable.

'I ran into Dave at the door,' I said. I didn't want anyone to think that this was my doing. I watched him shadow-box with Jake, buss each girl lightly on the cheek, then kiss Mim, with the semi-flippant intimacy that informed all his actions. Ruth, who, I remembered, was the natural daughter of Daria Webster, stood on the sideline observing everything with bright-eyed interest. She was probably earning extra pocket money, I thought sourly, researching her mother's next book.

I hung around long enough to reassure myself that I wouldn't be needed to break up any fights, then went inside to unpack the groceries. The kitchen window gave a good view of the garden. I opened it, and the tang of wood smoke drifted in. Later I would recall details of the scene with the sharp contours of an etching. The figures in their heavy jerseys, splashes of colour behind the translucent threads of pale smoke and the bonfire's sparks. Dave's lanky frame weaving easily among the others; snatches of laughter and American slang hanging in the air like a tracery of bullets.

Perhaps it was the autumnal melancholy of skeletal trees and bleak sky, perhaps the effrontery of tensions masquerading as casual informality. Whatever it was, I felt a tingling chill at the back of my neck, where Dave's hands had been. I don't know when I identified it as a foreboding; probably much later. I had always thought of myself as practical rather than psychic, but this urban pastoral idyll made an impression on me out of all proportion.

It was obvious that Dave would be staying to lunch, and I put out a green salad, cheese and a loaf of Mim's wholemeal nut bread, all the time fencing with this vague feeling of unease that wouldn't go away. It was probably indirectly responsible for my drinking too much at the co-op birthday party that night and becoming involved in an unwisely intense conversation with someone a good deal more susceptible, and unstable, than myself.

Dave Benwell had not only stayed for lunch but stayed firmly put all day, making a fire in the sitting room and spreading himself out on the sofa with every appearance of being at home. His arrival was a clever manoeuvre. I guessed it was fortuitous; he didn't know Mim well enough to grasp that she would be incapable of the rudeness, in her eyes, of asking him to leave. Or perhaps he did; a big-city childhood gives you a crash course in sussing people out. It also leaves its alumni, if they get as far as twenty-four years, which I judged to be about Dave's age, with a fine proficiency in the art of self-preservation.

He was careful not to single out Mim for special treatment in the presence of her daughter. He was scrupulously impartial with his attentions, spreading them around between her, me and the two girls. I realised very clearly during the course of the afternoon that he was a primarily physical animal, draping an arm across whoever's shoulders happened to be nearby, holding the nearest hand, casually touching in a way that bordered on the sexual but never quite crossed the line. I was paying much closer attention to him than I had done at the dinner, when he was just a young schoolteacher over for a free meal. His appeal to a young girl like Susanna – and, I could see, to her friend Ruth too – was all too understandable. He treated them quite unselfconsciously as equals, fellow adults. This, I remembered from my own girlhood, was pretty thrilling in itself. His appeal was intensified by his accessibility, the explicit impression he gave of being ready, willing and able. There was the additional bonus of his youthful swagger and rather insolent good looks.

These talents were comprehensive enough, but I recognised another element as the clincher. Like Jack's top-rating television interviews, Dave gave off a charge of danger that was, I knew, irresistible to pubescent girls and often to their mothers as well. Jack had it himself, although by now it seemed to me dulled by constant use. It had undoubtedly been a large part of his appeal to the youthful Miriam, and I wondered if an echo of that risky quality had attracted the older Mim.

It was Dave's offhand, indiscriminate sensuality that enabled him to keep the aspirants for his favour dancing in the palm of his hand. Mim, I could see, was reassured by the affectionate attention he paid Susanna, who in turn was flattered and mollified. He seemed considerably more confident than he had at the dinner. I guessed Jack's dominating presence had inhibited him. The type of competitive man who relaxes in the presence of females, he had the adulation of three out of four of those present to boost his morale. Not to mention his seduction of Mim, for I had no doubt that was at his instigation.

I say three fans out of four, although I was not absolutely sure of Mim's feelings. Our discussions on the subject hadn't advanced much beyond Mim's ritual hand-wringing. While she gave a solid impression of fancying him, I knew that this could merely be good manners. She was treading a classic Miriam tightrope, anxious to behave with sensitivity and politeness, and equally reluctant to further alienate her daughter. Dave had the additional credit in her eyes of being alone in a foreign land, and thus doubly vulnerable to slights and rejection.

While not impervious to his talents I found myself standing outside the charmed circle of Dave's admirers. I was fairly sure that his presence in Mim's life was a bad idea. I didn't altogether trust him, and I was suspicious of his motives. Still, Mim was a big girl now, and if she had to learn to run her life without any interference from Jack, Dave might supply some valuable practice.

We all ended up at the party. Dave had ensured his presence by employing the classic limpet technique. While the rest of us disappeared at intervals to change clothes, shower or wash hair, he remained firmly in situ. We trooped off in the early evening when Gayle, the cleaning student, showed up to babysit. The idea of the spiky-haired teenager babysitting Jake was rather like the blind leading the lame, or the terrorist coaching the anarchist, but Mim was scrupulous about never leaving her feral child alone at night. She had already been to the co-op early in the morning to supervise deliveries of alcohol and hired glasses. She wanted to be first there in the evening, so Dave, Susanna and I turned out too. Ruth had gone home to collect her mother, and no doubt spend a happy hour filling her in on the latest scandal-in-progress.

The party was held in the largely disused upper storey of the house where the co-op had its offices. Once part of a condemned row, the whole terrace had been saved from demolition and renovated by the co-operative's self-trained working parties. The upstairs area now functioned as an emergency shelter for desperate families or women fleeing violent partners, and comprised a bathroom and two sparsely furnished large rooms. There was a small kitchenette downstairs, used by the staff.

I had been impressed by the co-op's professionalism when I visited Mim there. The offices were clean and well organised. Telephones were answered with prompt politeness, and there appeared to be a highly methodical system of administration and referral. Seeing Mim in this environment was to see her from another perspective: as the co-ordinator whose hands-on role was central. I had spent a morning as an observer, listening and taking notes for a projected article, and I had seen how Mim's contribution was not only pivotal but also warmly valued by the staff. I was reminded of Mim the resourceful student whose patent filing system we all plundered. Her nature was such that she also functioned as a mother figure for the other five employees, two of whom were full-time and three casual or part-time. The housing co-operative she had devised and set up had come to take the place of the extended family to which I had belonged in my early twenties.

The party was a bigger deal than I had anticipated. In its decade of operation the co-op had established itself as a pillar of the surrounding community. The number of homeless families who found temporary or long-term housing ran into hundreds. Funding now came from a variety of sources, including the local council, banks and businesses, and the network of contacts included the area MP, doctors, social workers, builders, plumbers and architects – a large percentage of whom dropped by in the course of the evening.

Susanna introduced me to Daria Webster quite early on. I had noticed her arrive, a tiny figure eclipsed by what looked like a peaked bus conductor's cap and a huge air force greatcoat that skimmed the floor. The moment she took these off she blazed, her scarlet and turquoise sari standing out from the surrounding more utilitarian clothes in their sombre wintry hues like a poppy in a field of bracken. She must have been barely five feet, and Ruth, who was also wearing an exquisitely printed sari, was already a good half head taller.

Daria had a serene, unlined face and enormous charcoal eyes, with her daughter's identical expression of vivid, intelligent curiosity. Her hair was her most striking feature, pulled severely off her face by a hairband and hanging below her shoulders, giving her the look of an exotic Alice in Wonderland.

'This is Mum's friend Lou,' Susanna said, and I saw Ruth flash a meaningful glance at her mother. Daria immediately sprang into what I recognised as professional action. She shook my hand with a show of delight and asked me how long I was staying, where I had come from and why I had left. She knew the answers, I didn't doubt, to all these questions, but I found myself supplying the details readily. I had always got a kick out of meeting people who loved their field and were experts in it. When the field was comparable to my own, the pleasure was magnified.

She had a strong musical voice capable of an impressive pitch, volume and velocity. The contrast between her dainty, fragile appearance and this metropolitan, almost New York attack was startling. Her petite frame exuded a vivacious energy that testified to a racing metabolism, a theory confirmed when I saw her making short shrift of a huge pizza later on. The Daria Webster brand of feminism was of the all-encompassing variety, informing her personality and attitudes in a way which particularly incenses many men. She and Ruth were unaccompanied, and something told me that this was not by chance but Daria's permanent and chosen condition.

When you have two seasoned interviewers meeting socially

for the first time you tend to have a brief jockeying for position. When the two sides are well disposed and fairly evenly matched, as in this case, a balance usually sorts itself out very quickly. A certain type of enjoyable, probing conversation results where each elicits a great deal of personal information from the other in a remarkably short time.

Daria, I discovered, was a barrister with the Kilburn legal firm that acted for the co-op at substantially reduced fees. This made sense; I detected a trained legal mind behind the classifications and analyses in her book. She had never married, and viewed the institution as an unvenerable fossil. Ruth's father had been a fellow student at Cambridge, a well-born young man with autocratic tendencies who had sought to marry Daria and whisk her home to a life of closeted luxury in New Delhi. This unwise aim had triggered off warning bells in Daria's youthful consciousness. Male takeover bid imminent, she must have thought, and told the young man where to put his offer. She had had her baby and brought her up, very efficiently it seemed, alone.

Aspects of this story sounded oddly familiar. After some thought I concluded that Daria had tailored it to fit the chapter titled Prudence. The eponymous heroine was so-called because, in making the difficult choice she was actually being wise and sensible, ensuring her own freedom and autonomy in life, secure from the threat of male domination.

Daria confirmed this with a beam of unalloyed pleasure. While I trifled with sour white wine she quaffed beer from a pint tankard that dwarfed her face. We were on our own in a corner near a big trestle table that served as the bar.

Daria leant forward and raised her voice excitedly. 'Now what is Miriam doing with that hunky spunk Mr Benwell? She's not proposing to get serious about him, is it?' She had the distinctive habit of combining a creditable North London pronunciation, glottal stop included, with frequent grammatical oddities. Her book, on the other hand, was written in fluent and unidiosyncratic prose. I guessed she had an adroit editor.

'Oh I don't think so. There's obviously no future in it.'

Daria pursed her lips. 'No future in it, no of course, we can see that, but Miriam is too tender hearted. She will be befriending the boy out of pity and it will end in sorrow.'

I remembered that Daria knew Mim well. 'Casual affairs have certainly never been Mim's forte.'

'More is the pity.' This was said with a dark shade of meaning, and amplified with considerable force. 'More women should dabble with them, and it would do them good. A whole lot of good, Louisa.'

She had found out my full name and used it like a piano trill. 'You speak from experience,' I said, hoping for some revelations.

'From extensive experience, yes. I organise all my male interactions on a temporary basis. It is the only way to have them.'

This, I fancied, was aimed at me. Out of the corner of my eye I saw Cynthia come in and cast her eyes around the rapidly filling room. I looked away hastily. 'Well, I suppose you avoid a lot of hassles that way.'

'Louisa.' She looked at me intently, like a tiny birdlike moral tutor. 'Most of the botheration in this life comes from women's connections with the male of the species. I speak as a woman, you see, and I see it all around me. The secret is to keep the connections tenuous. Frequent unplugging is the secret.'

'Unplugging. You mean –'

'Unplug the connection before the mutation. Or the

atrophy. The women who do this, they own their own lives. They are not in thrall to the men.'

'But not everyone can do that.' Not everyone wants to either, I thought.

'Sadly, no. Although this, I think, is due to poor upbringing of girls. The right education is the key. This brings independence, of mind and emotions, as well as economic, which is the conductor. Women are too often taught that the key to happiness is a man, when the case is the opposite. A man is the key to their discontent.'

Cynthia had joined us during this speech and now kissed us damply on both cheeks. Mim waved from across the crowded room, where she was circulating. She always liked to see her various friends getting on well. Daria greeted Cyn with every appearance of pleasure.

'Cynthia, you see, has been wise enough not to tie herself to a man. She is a free agent, of spirit.'

'Not altogether by choice, Daria,' Cyn said with admirable candour.

Daria turned to me. 'Cynthia thinks she is badly off because she is not having the one best man in her bed every night. But it is sex she is needing instead! Not just one boring man! She must bite the bullet. It is not difficult.'

Daria was overflowing with boisterous verve. Cyn looked sceptical and irritated. I felt an unaccustomed empathy. 'It's not that easy, Daria,' I began.

Cyn interrupted. 'Daria thinks everyone should go and pick sex off the streets like sweetpapers. That might have been all the rage in the sixties, Daria, during your formative years. To carry on like that these days would be not only ridiculous but irresponsible and dangerous.'

'There are ways for a woman to get sex wherever she is

136

and no matter how she looks, and I am not talking about sweetpapers,' Daria said with dignity. 'If she is in touch with her femaleness, these things are not important. Femininity is what I am meaning. It is the very precious pearl and every woman has it, moreover. Only some are hiding it under a bushel.'

The contrast between her own delicate beauty and negative ageing propensities and Cyn, bulky, spotty and dishevelled, made me wonder whether Daria was being deliberately cruel or merely obtuse. Her delivery, on the other hand, had the ring of total conviction. She looked as if she really believed this moonshine.

'Daria always begins by telling you what you need, not what you want, and ends by invoking the eternal feminine,' Cyn said caustically.

Daria smiled. 'Sometimes it takes another person to tell you what you are needing. You are looking out of your own eyes, Cynthia. You cannot be seeing yourself. But Louisa and I are seeing you, in three dimensions.'

'Surely men and women need each other,' I said, in an effort to defuse the personal. 'Interdependency being the natural condition of this benighted species. I mean, we all know men are deeply unsatisfactory but they're all we've got. At least until women take charge of genetic engineering.'

'Men are needing women because women are continuing to perform domestic services without having payment,' Daria said patiently. 'In the cave day women needed men for protection. Then for economic. Now it is only for ego.'

But what about love, I wanted to say. I forbore to say it, because I felt confident that it would be greeted with lively incomprehension. Or derision. Such was the force of Daria's personality that it was already starting to feel like a quaint, olde worlde notion, even to me. Instead I said, 'What about the mutual society, help and comfort one ought to have of the other? Not to mention the little olive branches around the table.'

'The olive branches were round about the man's table, Lou. The woman was just the fruitful vine on his wall.'

Daria beamed. 'Exactly correct, Cynthia.' She turned to me animatedly. 'What man do you know in your experience who does any of the work in the bringing up of the progeny? And any more of the home duties than the washing of the dishes? All he is good for is doubling the work for the woman and halfing the pleasure of the child.'

'*Halving* the pleasure?' Cyn's inflexible vigilance embraced linguistic as well as logical eccentricities.

'Because it is diluted in two, with a mum and dad.' Daria pointed to a loudly chattering group of young people. 'You see my Ruth? I have all of her love and she has all of mine. We are happy and fortunate together. A man galumping round we do not need, I can tell you that! Dropping the clothes and crying to be fed.'

I perceived the futility of buying into this line of reasoning. Cyn had no such qualms. All her combative instincts were up and running. She always loved a good argument, and preferably one with an abstract or recondite theme. I headed for the bar as Cyn's voice rose behind me, shrill with pugnacious relish. 'Daria, you have committed a prime philosophical solecism. You are guilty of basing an entire theory on a series of empirically unverifiable value judgements.'

Apart from Daria, my other significant encounter of the evening was with a man called, harmlessly enough, Stuart Friend. Later it transpired that Mim's relationship with Stuart was purely a business one, although from the warmth of her introduction I had foolishly taken him to be a good friend. He was the information officer for a big civil service union, and his appearance and manner were pleasantly unremarkable. The next day I tried to think what he looked like and could only recall someone in his early thirties with an open, boyish face and a self-effacing, evasive quality that came and went rather mysteriously.

This unassuming ordinariness, it was rapidly borne on me, masked a very real ability to cause trouble. Stuart Friend possessed a refined and potent talent to introduce hassles into the lives of his friends and acquaintances.

We checked each other out with the alert antennae of the single and confirmed that we were both on our own. We then embarked on a playful dialogue which, fuelled by a fast turnover in beer and wine, soon progressed to the mildly flirtatious. I had no particular interest in Stuart, beyond mechanical professional curiosity. But his attitude to me I had no hesitation in interpreting as favourable, and I performed accordingly.

Now and then I felt the cutting edge of Cyn's appraising eye. I had no doubt I was being weighed and found wanting, yet again. With no stake in the outcome it was easy enough to be witty and sparkling. Cyn would have said I was showing off. I told myself instead that I found someone else's interest socially liberating. Ego-stroking, is what Cyn would have called it.

We retreated to a quieter corner as the party ebbed and flowed around us. Stuart had lived in the area all his life and knew most people by sight. He pointed out local identities and dished the dirt on them with an airy indiscretion I found refreshing. Daria Webster, somewhat to my surprise, was given a clean bill of health.

'She was treated badly by men, in my humble opinion, and

it's left her scarred. Once bitten . . .' I didn't argue, though I thought this was manifestly inaccurate. How many men, I wondered, had been wishfully misled by Daria's fragility into casting her as one of her own victims?

Stuart, it turned out, had close links with the co-op. He had done up a derelict basement flat and now leased it on a rent-adjusted basis. It had been unoccupied for years and was full of water when he took it on. 'Not much better now,' he said cheerily. He was, I gathered, fairly cynical about the co-op's celebration. 'Window dressing. Waste of money. Trying to get in with the right people.'

'A good idea, I'd have thought. They need money.'

'Cadging respectability. I've known the co-op since it was born. It was much better when it was a grass-roots thing. Getting by on the smell of an oily rag, locals dropping in for a coffee and chat. I don't want to say anything against Mim, but she's been given a lot of bad advice, and the consequence of that is, it's got all mainstream and impersonal.'

The constrained quality I had noticed earlier had been replaced by a curious vehemence. There was a note of bitter-ness here that seemed disproportionate and caught my attention.

'Surely the bigger it gets the more homeless people it can house and the more effective it is?'

'That's how it may appear on a superficial viewing, if you'll excuse my saying so. But you'll find there's an optimum size for organisations like this. Beyond it they get out of touch, lose the old idealism. Get gentrified. Attract the wrong people.'

'Who are those?'

'People who are in it for the wrong reasons. Middle class do-gooders, if you'll pardon the term. Like those viragos in the office. The co-op should be for the workers and it should be run by working class people who understand each other.'

'But Mim's not working class. Never was, you know, old fruit.'

'Mim's an Aussie, so it doesn't count. Australia's practically classless, isn't it, compared to this fossilised country? We only have to open our mouths and it's a dead giveaway.'

Stuart's accent I judged to be comprehensive rather than public school. I was intrigued by the evident passion in his views, while retaining sufficient journalistic nous to recognise a partial witness when I saw one. Still, he might be a useful counterweight for the article.

I told him I was planning a ruthless exposé of the housing co-op. He promptly offered to help with contacts and information. When I reviewed what I could remember of the conversation later, I realised he had been almost excessively helpful.

He could drive me around and introduce me to anyone I wanted to meet. His office had an excellent supply of stationery and a photocopier that was underused. His secretary was not overworked and she was an excellent typist. Not only that, he thought he could pass some contract jobs my way. He was organising a series of health posters to encourage safer practices in the workplace, and he needed a slogan writer.

'You look as though you could write snappy one-liners.'

'With one hand tied behind my back and the other hand otherwise engaged. Excessively well-paid snappy one-liners, that is. I'm more expensive than I may appear.'

'Oh, you look pricey all right. Way out of my class.'

'Do I? That's encouraging.'

We made a cautious date to discuss work prospects over an Indian meal midweek. There was a tentativeness in his proposal, a bashful hesitation, which made me think he was unused to asking women out. Later I recognised that what I had taken as timidity was more likely to be furtiveness.

Viewing myself as a recovering convalescent – a tautological way of viewing oneself, as Cyn had not hesitated to point out – and beyond toying with the co-op piece, I had been ignoring the pressing need for work. But it was becoming more imperative by the day, and this offer felt like manna falling into my lap. Something of this surge of relief and gratitude must have written itself on my face, because Stuart moved closer and put an arm – experimental, featherlight – across my shoulder. Cheap alcohol was contributing much to my feeling of well-being. Although I knew it was transitory, the novelty of this feeling and the buzz of it was going to my head. I leaned towards him a fraction. There wasn't much difference in our height so I had to bend sideways. Sam, I recalled, had been much better proportioned.

What followed was confusing and happened very fast. I was almost knocked off balance as Stuart's arm jerked backwards and his body cannoned into mine. An expressive face – I had the residual wit to perceive it was young, female and furious – swam like an apparition in front of me and unloaded a stream of incoherent abuse in a sobbing drone. It seemed to be aimed mainly at Stuart but I was included on the periphery. The gist was that he was a heartless devious monstrous bastard.

'You never told me about the party, you hid it from me –'

She looked to be on the verge of collapse, slurring her words in a way that suggested drugs other than – or perhaps as well as – alcohol. Stuart's reaction was quick and to the point. Apart from an initial pithy profanity he said nothing. He grasped her shoulders and propelled her the most direct way through the throng to the nearest exit. She seemed quite passive and unresisting, and something in his response suggested he had done this before. His face as he turned back to me with a mouthed 'sorry' was chalky, and then just as rapidly flooded with scarlet.

The gap closed behind them like water swallowing a stone. I stared after it. The scene had been over in a matter of seconds but it had attracted a lot of interested attention and it left me distinctly unnerved. I thought no-one I knew had witnessed it, but Dr Tracey Garrett's monolithic head loomed above the crowd, advancing purposefully in my direction. Behind her were Mim and Cynthia, Mim looking upset and Cyn accusatory.

'Don't worry,' Dr Garrett patted me on the arm with a vigorous yet oddly soothing motion. 'You couldn't be expected to know.'

'Lou, are you all right?' Mim had arrived. 'What an unfortunate thing to happen. I probably should have warned you —'

Cyn said simultaneously, 'Encroaching on someone else's territory again, Lou? I should have thought this worn-out old habit would be at odds with your avowed feminist principles.'

Mim put a full glass into my hand. It was probably her own but I drank half of it first and then the other half. I was surprised to find my hand shaking. Tracey Garrett grasped it. Her own hand was large, warm and safe, rather like a man's. 'You couldn't be expected to know,' she repeated. It sounded reassuring but obscure.

I was anxious to unravel the obscurity. 'I'm feeling guilty and I don't know why. What was all that about?'

'That poor girl was his drug-addicted live-in lover, Lou —' Cynthia revving for takeoff was overruled by Dr Garrett's authoritative basso-contralto.

'Lou wasn't to know about Gaby, Cynthia, since I'm sure our Stuart neglected to mention her existence. Afraid you have unwittingly blundered into one of our long-running

143

neighbourhood domestics. Stuart's a ninny. Been trying to extricate himself for a year or more, but young Gaby's addicted to heroin, among other substances. Can't or won't accept the reality of the breakup. He should seek professional help, of course, but he's too independent – read pigheaded.'

'He is being the typical male, never seeking help because he is thinking that other people will notice his weakness!'

A flash of turquoise tugged my eye downwards. Daria Webster had joined us unnoticed and stood alongside Tracey Garrett, absurdly miniaturised by the doctor's tall sturdiness.

'Except when he needs the practitioner of medicine – your old man is running to the doctor very fast, I can tell you that, if he thinks he has a cold!'

She glanced slyly upwards. Dr Garrett did not look down. Instead, an expression of marked distaste came over her broad, pleasant face. She turned away and said, 'Men go to the doctor for small ailments, but at the slightest hint of something serious they stay away in droves. They simply don't want to know.'

This was said in a tone of corrective reproof which seemed to be hopelessly lost on Daria, who bubbled on racily. 'Exactly correct, Tracey! Men are cowardy custards, you see, when it comes to facing the nasty music. If they have a suspicious mole their wives are having to drag them along the ground to the clinic. That is the trouble with our friend Stuart.'

Stuart's trouble, in Daria's view, boiled down to the traditional male reluctance to face unpleasant facts, because once faced they might have to be dealt with. I said he seemed to have dealt fairly capably with the situation that presented itself, but Daria would have none of this. I suspected she had a doctrinal ally in Tracey Garrett, but Tracey's reflexive hostility to Daria ruled out any show of public agreement.

It did not surprise me to learn that on several occasions Mim had tried to mediate between Stuart and Gaby in their demarcation dispute, but had been firmly rebuffed. 'Stuart thought I was interfering in a private matter, and I suppose I was. But I think he really needs help. You get told things, you know, working in the co-op . . .'

'What kind of things?'

The customary look of vagueness came over Mim's features. 'Oh well, you know, arguments. Out in the street. Things getting broken. That sort of thing.'

I turned to the doctor in the hope of eliciting more pungent details, but she and Mim were buttonholed by a florid, proprietorial couple who exuded patronage and benefaction. Almost simultaneously a large untidy man stepped backwards almost on top of Daria, whose full glass of red wine spilled down the front of her sari and splashed onto the backside of his corduroy trousers. His annoyance and her loud shriek of indignation dissolved into apologies and chuckles as each examined the other's stains with close attention to the location. They disappeared together in the direction of the cloakrooms.

I was left standing with Cyn. 'That was a neat little exercise,' I said. 'She'll take him to bed now, I don't doubt.'

Cyn's mouth was pursed in an aggrieved pout. 'It was quite accidental, Lou. He couldn't possibly have seen her standing behind him.'

'Right. It's just the use you make of fortuitous incidents, I guess. Plus being in constant touch with your femininity, let us not forget that.'

Cyn remained stony-faced. 'You've only just arrived here and you hardly know anyone.'

There was a longish pause. 'You're right,' I said at last, wondering what was coming. After a further pause it came at me like an avalanche.

Cyn burst out, 'You've only just arrived here and you spend half the evening chatting up an apparently available man. One of the few! And Daria picks up another just by chance, by the crudest of tactics. I haven't spoken to one available man all night. Not to mention available, I haven't spoken to one man all night! Why is it? Why do some people have all the luck?' Her lip trembled. I realised she was drunk. She moved in on me, her eyes protuberant and accusing. I tried to avoid them. 'It's looks, isn't it? If people don't consider you conventionally good-looking you don't have a chance.'

'Come on, Cyn. I've no interest in Stuart. He was just someone to talk to. I'm not attracted to him in the least.' It sounded feeble and evasive, and I knew it was the wrong thing to say as I was saying it.

'That's worse then, isn't it? You've got no interest in someone so you monopolise him and no-one else can get a look in. Doesn't that strike you as selfish?'

I took a step back, having checked there was no-one behind me. 'Let's not make a big thing of this, please, Cyn. Let's try and be sensible and grown-up about this. Mim introduced me to some ordinary guy and I had a perfectly ordinary conversation with him. What else could I do?'

'What else could you do?' Cyn's voice was rising dangerously. I glanced around for Mim but she was nowhere in sight. 'What else could you do? I'll tell you one thing you could do, one small thing. If you had no interest in him you could pass him on to me!'

'Cyn, I would have, like a shot, but he works for a trade union. He's not in your intellectual class. You'd have nothing in common.'

This clumsy attempt at humour produced a visible recoil.

'It's quite an art, Lou, the way you contrive to be at once

snobbish, patronising and smug, apparently without effort. You might think about encapsulating your method and teaching it to an adult education class, to apprentice immigration officers or theatre critics. You've always thought of me, haven't you, as a boring old bluestocking, a pedantic, out-of-touch spinster? While you swan around with the in-crowd? Well, let me tell you, I may not be as adept as you at the frivolous banalities that masquerade in your world as sophisticated small talk, but I am perfectly capable of a polite and genuine interest in another person. And unlike you I don't judge people by their intellectual or social attributes.'

If it had been anyone other than Cyn delivering this manifesto it might have led to a lifelong rift in the relationship. But I felt a lofty indifference to Cyn's attitude to me; whatever she thought struck me as self-evidently immaterial. The words washed over me rather like a mundane marital flare-up between two long-term adversaries who viewed each other most of the time with peevish tolerance. But I was startled and abashed by Cyn's astute insight into my opinion of her.

'Cyn, I'm feeling magnanimous. I'm willing to forget these wounding if well-chosen words were ever uttered, if you are. What say we call it a night, and have a nice drink together next week? I promise to try and find a good working class lad to introduce you to.'

Cyn managed a half smile. I was suddenly very tired and I wanted to go home. One way and another, it had ended up being quite a tough night.

8

CYN OFFERED ME A LIFT home on her motorbike, but I turned it down. The thought of riding pillion behind Cyn, the proximity even for such a short time, was more than I could stomach. Besides, I felt in need of a bracing walk in a cold wind.

'I do carry a spare helmet, Lou, if that's what you're worried about. I always come prepared. You never know who you may encounter at parties like this.'

So Cyn had secretly hoped to encounter a dashing knight and whisk him home, twin-helmeted, on her trusty steed. I even found it in me to mourn, just briefly, the onward march of her disappointment. It was after midnight but the street outside the co-op, dour and deserted during the day, vibrated now with waves of people swarming in unruly surges across the road and in the gutter. They were almost entirely young, male and inebriated, flaunting football ribbons and tartan trophies. Cyn and I found ourselves suddenly surrounded by a riotously chanting throng and borne bodily sixty feet along the pavement. When we escaped, harassed and breathless, Cyn seized my arm.

'Lou, I'm simply not allowing you to walk home by yourself. It's asking for trouble of a kind you emphatically do not need.'

The spirit may have been unwilling but I found the impetus to resist had ebbed. We mounted, buckled on identical white helmets ('White is less aggressive, more feminine than those threatening black masks, don't you think?') and zigzagged among the unpredictably lurching bodies, my reluctant hands about Cyn's waist. Cyn meanwhile utilised the moment to lecture me on the perils of London streets in general and the more specific perils of English football fans. London was not the comforting tea and scones place it used to be, she shouted, her voice dissected into spiky fragments by the wind.

The sitting room lights were on, shining through half-open curtains. There was a car parked right outside the Black house and it was towing a trailer. We pulled up in front of the car. I think it struck us both simultaneously that it was a red Sunbeam convertible. I got off the bike stiffly and unbuckled my helmet with icy fingers.

Cyn pushed up her visor and looked at me. 'What is he doing here? Could he have changed his mind? Regained his sanity?'

'He's packing, isn't he?' My lips felt dry and chapped. Suddenly and unexpectedly I didn't want Cyn to go. She was sitting heavily on the bike, her eyes blank and unfocused. Under the street lamp I fancied they had a bereft and bewildered look, like the one they had worn at the Open Dinner.

'Cyn, could you come in for a bit, please? I think I might be able to use a chaperone.'

Comprehension snapped in her eyes, followed by a gleam of amusement. 'Well, it's a change to see you admitting vulnerability. Are you afraid of Jack making the proverbial pass no female can resist? Or is this eventuality an assumption based on your proven track record?'

I was nettled, but I didn't want to alienate Cyn. 'Let's not get too analytical out here on the pavement. The neighbours might be looking. And besides, it's sub zero. Cyn, my gratitude would be unbounded. Dinner next week, place of your choice. Three courses. Premier cru.'

'I suppose that's the closest to beseeching you're constitutionally able to get,' Cyn said musingly. At that moment the front door swung open and Jack materialised carrying a big box. He saw me first and gave an explosive grin, then saw Cyn. He put the box down and bounded forward. Cyn was still stolidly seated. I said in a low voice, 'Mise en bouteille au chateau.'

Jack was hugging me tightly. He said pointedly to Cyn, 'Chugging off home, are you, honey bunch?' Cyn clambered off the bike at once, throwing me a satirical glance. 'No, Jack. Lou has kindly invited me in for an old-fashioned nightcap.'

Jack looked disappointed, but took it on the chin. 'Well, I guess Mim and the gang'll be showing up soon anyway.'

'I think you should definitely self-destruct before she gets here.'

'Lou, don't start all that again. Look how tactful I've been, stealing in while the cat's away. I've been here for bloody hours and I've just finished the lot. I deserve medals not vile abuse. Obsequious, blandiloquous grovelling. And I came straight from wowing 'em at the studio. Barely took off the pancake. What greater love hath any lisping swain, sweetheart?'

He turned and I saw behind him the small figure of Jake, stumbling under a bulging carton. 'My military detail,' Jack said. He winked. 'Man of iron. SAS trainee. They start 'em young these days, you know.' My immediate unworthy thought was that with the boy around, I needn't have bothered about Cyn.

Inside it was like our forlorn home movie replayed. Jack's crates of papers, books and music, the memorabilia of a well-lived cerebral lifetime to date, were stacked neatly ready to go. The double sitting room looked as if it had been looted, the distinguished books, first editions and leather-bound volumes gone, only the paperbacks remaining in dog-eared heaps. A number of favourite pictures had gone too, romantic pre-Raphaelites and Symbolists that were, rather surprisingly, Jack's taste. The house had a strangely half-made look as a result, symbolic of its disintegration. What it had been, the organic creation of two diametrically opposed people, it could no longer convincingly pretend to be.

The long charade of keeping up appearances had been abandoned. An essential homeliness, comfortable, congenial and loved – Mim's half of the creation – remained. But I now recognised that Jack's contribution, the austere aesthetic of a natural connoisseur, although less pervasive had been very real. With its idiosyncratic flavour it had supplied a vital balance and intellectual life which, in its removal, left a void.

Jack saw my face. 'Lou, you're in your disapproving mother superior mode again, and it's making unattractive lines on your forehead. I thought we'd gone through all this.'

I felt weary and depressed. 'We did. It's just that the outcome's worse than the hypothesis, if you know what I mean. I've always loved this house and now it's as if its whole nature has changed. When you really love something it's an organic part of your life and I guess you feel you own it, you have a vested interest in its perpetuity. When it's changed, by things beyond your control, you feel – robbed, in some way.'

'You feel bereaved.' Cyn was breathing heavily, and I regretted my insistence on her presence. Jack seemed struck by my little speech and peered at me as if I were a biological specimen awaiting dissection.

'Lou, baby, I never knew you cared. I'm touched. Deeply.'

'We feel *bereaved*, Jack!' Cyn interrupted in an explosive charging shout, and Jack visibly started. 'Of course Lou cares. We all care. You might at least have the sensitivity to pretend to take us seriously instead of treating the whole thing as a Whitehall farce. Haven't you even the most elementary human understanding? It's as if we're losing a loved one. That's bad enough, but it's worse when – when what you're losing is one of the central things in your life and there might never be anything to replace it.' She was starting to cry now, with the full repertoire of blotches and heaving sobs I dreaded.

Jack's levity persisted unabated. 'Cyn, you're not losing a loved one, darl. I'll still be around to drive you to drink.'

To my astonishment Cyn charged at him, pummelling her fists into his chest with the ferocious force of pent-up emotion. For the first time I felt a twinge of real unease about her state of mind. Jack's eyes met mine eloquently, above Cyn's head. He mouthed, 'All your fault,' before staggering backwards under the brunt of two especially violent punches. Jake came in to fetch another box and stopped, his mouth falling open in a comic-strip parody of amazement.

I thought about intervening but decided to let Jack deal with his own mess. It was, after all, entirely of his own making. He was a big strong man but Cyn, too, was quite a substantial heavyweight and she had the added fuel of motivation to power her arm. Jack seemed to be taking a long time to marshal his forces, and I realised the opening blows in the surprise attack had winded him. Cyn was pressing home her advantage and giving no quarter. After what seemed an inordinate length of time but was probably only fifteen seconds, Jack pulled himself together and battened Cyn's arms behind her back. She responded by butting him hard with her head. Jack gasped and stepped back, then seized her by the shoulders and held her at arm's length, straining with the effort.

They faced each other like panting animals. Then Cyn seemed to crumple, and only Jack's grasp kept her from pitching forward. With a gentleness remarkable under the circumstances, Jack led her to the nearest couch, the one she and Dave had subsided upon, and deposited her on it. He seemed momentarily lost for words. Jake still stood in the doorway, gaping. The telephone rang, making all of us jump. It was on a table next to Jack, who flopped onto the arm of the settee and picked up the receiver.

I thought, it has to be Sam. At this time of night. He's mistaken the time zones. Jack passed it across to me. 'One of your lovesick admirers.' My heart lurched.

'Lou? Look, I'm really dreadfully sorry about all that.'

'What –?' It wasn't Sam. I had trouble working out who it was. My mind was elsewhere. I realised the caller was waiting for a response. 'Ah . . . yes?' I said feebly. I could feel Jack's quizzical eyes on me. He was making no attempt to move away, and I remained standing. Cynthia was slumped at the other end of the settee. She looked immobile, as if she were in some kind of a trance.

'I'm just appalled to have subjected you to that scene. It's happened before, but I didn't think she would make such a public humiliation of herself. I'm so embarrassed . . .'

Stuart Friend, I thought dully. Stuart and Gaby. 'It's quite all right, really,' I said to cut him short. 'Think nothing of it.'

'It'll never happen again, I've seen to that. I'm just so upset to have caused you so much embarrassment, in front of all those people, it was just unforgivable.' He sounded exhausted and on the verge of tears.

'Stuart, it's all right. I'd quite forgotten about it. Honestly.'

His voice quivered with relief. 'You're so understanding, I can't believe it.'

'Oh, these things happen. Forget it.' Just get off the phone, I thought tiredly.

'So you're still okay for our date?'

'Date —?'

'Dinner. To talk about that work I've got.'

'Oh. Okay.' Please hang up.

'Great. I'll pick you up at eight, then.'

'Cheers, Stuart.'

'Sweet dreams. I'm really glad I met you.'

'Goodbye.'

I replaced the receiver. Jack put his hand over mine. I whisked mine out from underneath and retreated to a distant armchair. Cyn still hadn't moved. Jack was rubbing his chest tenderly. He raised his eyebrows at me and looked over at his son. 'Hey, cobber. Pretty hair-raising stuff, eh?'

Jake came to him. 'You didn't hit back. You could've easily stopped her. Why didn't you sock her one?'

Jack put a hand on his shoulder. 'Because a real man never hits a woman, kiddo. Never under any circumstances. Not done. Message received and understood?'

'But she hit you first.'

'Doesn't matter.'

'But that's not fair.'

'That's life, mate. One of the first important lessons you have to learn. Life's not fair. Or rather,' he glanced at me, 'it's a hell of a lot fairer to some than others. Don't they teach you the basics at your expensive academy of erudition?'

Jake looked sulky and Jack ruffled his hair. 'Cheer up, cobber. Being a man has its compensations. They don't let women into the SAS, remember? Now buzz off and take some more of those boxes out to the trailer for your old dad, there's a good chap. I'm feeling battle-scarred.'

Cyn got to her feet slowly. Jack and I both watched, mesmerised, as she turned and faced him. I could see Jack stiffen and brace himself. Cyn addressed him with dignity, her face puckered in concentration. 'Jack, I owe you an apology. My behaviour was intolerable and uncivilised. I don't know what came over me. I've never done anything like that before in my life.'

I risked a glance at Jack. The expression on his face was located somewhere between the sheepish and the intensely fascinated.

'Mind you,' Cyn continued, 'I doubt very much whether I have ever before been subjected to such a degree of provocation. I am a reasonably self-controlled person, as I think you and Lou would agree. Perhaps you should regard this as an unfortunate lesson to be taken to heart. A timely warning, Jack. When you provoke normally rational women beyond endurance, this is what you can expect. You handled it, if I may say so, in a surprisingly gentlemanly fashion that does you credit.'

She paused. 'Now, if you don't mind, Lou, I'm going home. Goodnight.' She nodded gravely to each of us. At the door she turned. 'Jack, I think Lou and I would deeply appreciate it if you would gather the rest of your belongings and leave before Mim gets home.'

We heard the splutter of her motorcycle engine. Jack expelled a long whistling breath. 'Strewth!' He plumped down on the couch in an attitude of exaggerated prostration, legs splayed, arms dangling limply.

I shook my head. 'Cyn's the only person I know who can turn an apology into a sermon, and end up with a backhanded compliment.'

'Of course, the woman's completely mad. A total raving ratbag.' His eyes were still glazed with wonder, like a child who had just seen a transvestite Santa in a department store. 'She shouldn't be let out, she's a danger to ordinary law-abiding citizens going about their business.' He massaged his abdomen protectively. 'Lou, you wouldn't like to come and caress the upper part of my poor battered body, would you? I'm a mass of bruises. Just the upper torso, nothing below the belt, Scout's honour.'

'Nup. Sorry.'

'God, you're a bloody heartless bitch. You never let up, do you? Even when a fellow's a fainting victim of a deranged fist-flailing Amazon, the president of the – where does she live?'

'The Barbican.'

'President of the Barbican chapter of the Society for Castrating Cut-Up Men, the stuff of one's worst feminist nightmares made solid rampaging flesh, coming at you, avenging bosoms heaving like battering rams – even then, *even then* you do not find it in you to let up.'

He drew breath. Jake had been shuffling in and out during this diatribe. He appeared to be oblivious, but I wondered if any good done by Jack's chivalrous restraint was being undermined.

'Jack, aren't you overdoing the hysterics? Indulging in a bad attack of overreaction?' I flicked my eyes to Jake's retreating

back. 'Be a pity to undo such a sterling job of role modelling.'
Especially, I wanted to add, as it's been in notably short supply
in this house.

'Lou, you have evidently no idea how it feels to have
narrowly escaped genital mutilation at the hands of a frenzied
harpy. You just stood there like a fucking shop window
dummy. Jesus Christ, I wouldn't like to parachute into occupied France with you. Let alone escape in the Wooden Horse.'

I remembered that Jack had been a keen reader of Second
World War heroism stories. 'She's quite safe with me, and vice
versa. You just have a bad effect on her.'

He grunted morosely. 'How's Mim been getting on with
that raunchy black stud?'

'You mean Dave?'

'You know who I mean. Is there another raunchy black
stud hanging round Mim that I should know about?'

'I don't think you should necessarily know about any of Mim's
casual acquaintances. They're getting on all right, I suppose.'

'Come off it, Lou, don't be so tight-arsed. Are they getting
in any regular fucking? What's the current state of Susanna's
envy quotient?'

'It's as high as ever. And no they're not.'

'God, you're prim these days. A gossip columnist's nightmare. D'you know what it is?' He sat up, a familiar gleam in
his eyes. I didn't deign to answer, having a fairly good idea of
his thought processes. He flinched and rubbed his middle. 'It's
sexual frustration, that's what's behind it. The rot's setting in.
You'll be born again, next thing we know.' He looked at his
watch. 'See, when did you get here? Two weeks ago? That's
fourteen days without a solid screw. You must be screaming
for it. There is one infallible remedy and – I know this is
scarcely credible – I happen to have brought it with me. It is,

in point of fact, upon my person. And I am willing to give it to you.'

He looked at me speculatively while I tried to rally my sense of humour. I wanted very much to go up to bed, but this would have been a reckless wish to utter with Jack so restive. With Jack in any mood.

His unrestrained enjoyment of this was boyish. Even at his most obnoxious, I reflected, Jack had a way of reminding you why, in spite of everything, you continued to like him. Knowing full well that his performance was designed expressly for this purpose didn't diminish the fact of his basic good nature. He was watching me with, I was sure, a shrewd idea of what I was thinking. Our eyes met in a moment of perfect understanding.

It was shattered almost immediately by the return of Mim, Susanna and Dave. I could tell from Mim's face that she had seen the car and was nerving herself for the twin encounters with Jack and her depleted house, whereas Susanna's offhand 'Hi Dad' was a model of teenage cool. Dave saluted Jack with a glance I couldn't quite interpret. Jack rose to his feet, giving vent to a prolonged groan that was only partly theatrical.

Mim darted forward. 'What is it, darling?'

'I've been attacked!'

'It was only Cyn,' I started to say, but any idea that Jack might voluntarily foreclose on the subject was of course absurd. Since the Open Dinner Susanna had affected an expression of epicurean distaste whenever Cynthia's name came up. She embroidered this now with some finely tuned contempt. For once father and daughter appeared to be united, although Jack's attitude, when it could be detached from the burlesque, had more of a quality of forensic awe about it.

Halfway through his highly coloured account of Cyn's

bombardment, Mim was ready to rush out to an all-night chemist for therapeutic unguents. Jack would happily have let her go, but my derision overruled them both.

'You will stay the night, then?' The eagerness in Mim's voice pierced me.

'No, no, I'd better get back,' Jack said, to my profound relief. I intercepted another peculiar look between him and Dave. 'My offsider's practically loaded the trailer. Actually I was thinking of taking the kids back for the night. Sabbath tomorrow, we could do a slap-up brunch and a horror movie, hot fudge sundaes at Fortnums and I'll wrap 'em up and post 'em through the letter box in the afternoon.'

This sounded to my ears like the rehearsed parody of a divorced father's weekend treat, and I suspected the motivation behind Jack's show of benevolence might have been to provide himself with a pair of ready-made removalists. Whatever the origin, it clearly had the virtue of novelty. Both Susanna and Jake covered their initial surprise with identical attempts to conceal their joy and delight, and failed. I saw Susanna dart a covert, longing look at Dave, who was helping Jake with the last carton of books. Her shoulders slumped. Jack was on the other side of the room, and in one of the rare displays that proved he could be a lot more empathetic if he tried, he bounded to her side and crushed her to him.

'I'll brook no arguments! I want my gorgeous girl all to myself for once.' He bent his head, but I was near enough to hear him say, 'Nip up and grab some snazzy gear for tomorrow, darling. We're brunching with Jamie Quinn!' I recognised the name of a hot young British actor.

Susanna's desire to go with her father prevailed, but I could see it was a close-run thing. Dave flashed her a grin that managed to convey just the right mix of regret and promise.

Mim's own disappointment was eclipsed by her pleasure for the children, and she rushed around collecting their toothbrushes, night things and clothes for the next day.

Jack's meditative gaze followed Jake and Dave out of the room. 'So you reckon they're not getting much, eh?'

'Sorry?'

'Mim and Dave. Low fucking quotient?'

'Jack, what *is* it to you?'

As I spoke, the various hints and looks I had intercepted coalesced into a sickening suspicion. 'Jesus Christ, Jack, you didn't . . .?' I tailed off. The truth was almost too awful to articulate. His face was like a card-index with three headings: guilt, innocence and guile. Only Jack, I thought, could have arranged his features in this particular configuration. I said wonderingly, 'You set it up, didn't you? You put him up to it. You – complete, unmitigated, barefaced *bum*.'

'Cripes, don't mix your sophisticated anal and oral metaphors on me. I was only trying to help. A good screw never did anyone any harm, you know that better than anyone. Good for the morale.'

I could see he was on the verge of making me another offer. 'Don't even think of saying it, Jack. I'll punch you harder than Cynthia.'

'Talking of punching, you have to admit Mim's morale's been flatter than a boxer's nose lately. Listen, Dave was chuffed to help out. They're making more than enough to go round, these young blokes. He assured me it was a pleasure, not a duty.'

For once Jack's effrontery left me at a loss for words. He caressed his stomach solicitously, looking pleased with himself. When Mim returned with a packed case she had the pleasure of seeing Jack grin happily at her with every semblance of normality.

'I suppose they'll have to leave a supply of clothes at Jack's from now on.' The burst of energy Mim had shown vanished the moment the car and trailer pulled out. She dropped like a rag doll onto the couch, into the precise indentations Jack had left behind. She seemed unnaturally pale, and I thought she looked haggard. Typically, her concern was for anyone but herself. 'Lou, I'm worried about Cyn. Do you think she's –' she hesitated.

'Hurtling off the rails?'

'Well, not that exactly, but is she getting a bit nervously overwrought? You know, about all this.' She gestured at the empty shelves. 'People sometimes don't always realise because of her efficient manner, but underneath she's highly sensitive. She's a very vulnerable person, poor dear, more than one might think, and there she is living on her own with no-one to unburden herself to.'

'She's certainly been hit hard. She certainly *hit* hard.' Mim didn't smile. 'But she'll get over it.'

Mim's hands were clasping and twisting on her lap. It occurred to me that I had never before seen anyone actually wringing her hands.

'I feel responsible. This breakup is not only upsetting me and the children, the immediate family, and the house, too, of course, but it's somehow reaching out and catching other innocent people in its net, like an octopus. Affecting their lives. Your life and Cyn's, and who knows who else?'

Dave came over and sat next to her, putting his arm round her shoulders. He had gone outside to see the others off, and I had glimpsed him laughing with Jack in the headlights. I scowled at him over Mim's head. She had temporarily forgotten his presence, I guessed, because she turned to him with an apologetic smile and snuggled under his arm. I felt angry and superfluous.

'Mim. Cyn is an independent, grown-up woman. You can't take on her problems, it'd be an insult to her. She's resilient, she'll be okay. It probably did her a power of good, getting rid of all that festering angst. She's always going on about how you should give vent to your feelings.' But the memory of Cyn's desperate face as she laid into Jack, her dull comatose state afterwards, did not suggest catharsis. Mim, too, looked unconvinced.

I left them sitting together. Dave had made it clear he planned on staying the night, and I could see from Mim's demeanour that she was not geared up to argue. As I went out he favoured me with another of those unambiguous grins. I glared back. At least Susanna was briefly out of the way, interestingly at Jack's contrivance. I wondered if he thought he was being magnanimous in smoothing Mim's path to dalliance, or whether he was showing unwonted concern for his daughter.

Thinking about Susanna's response to Jack's affection and the machinations of the father–daughter relationship kept me awake for some time. I felt I'd lost my own father when he remarried with such alacrity. From this distance, I saw that I had set about trying to fulfil the prophecy. I had discouraged him from visiting me at university and it was years since I'd even written to him. He would be in his mid-sixties now, still working as a country town solicitor.

I thought of my half brothers and sister. They were called Edward, Henry and Thea, names that I had both refused to help choose and thought hopelessly out of date. Apart from my father, they were my closest relatives. I would have to inquire about them, if I wrote. I began to compose a letter in my mind.

9

THE TELEPHONE WOKE ME before eight the next morning, shrilling up the stairs from Mim's bedroom. It woke me from an uneasy dream in which disembodied voices kept calling my name. Eventually I revived enough to grasp that I was indeed being called. I dragged myself out of the enveloping warmth and stumbled downstairs to the kitchen.

I knew, as soon as I picked it up, who it was. He only had to say one prosaic word, hello, but the timbre of the voice and the pitch were unmistakeable.

'Hello. Hello? Lou, is that you?'

'Yes. It's very early.'

'Thank Christ it's you. I've been trying for days and there's never an answer.'

Sam always exaggerated. He had probably rung once, I told myself. My heart was pounding but my head felt cool and calm. I stood in my thin nightdress shivering, although the kitchen was warm.

'Lou. Talk to me, please.'

'I'm trying.'

'Are you all right?'

'I'm fine.'

'Are you really? I'm not. God, I've missed you. I've been going mad here by myself, drinking triple bourbons, avoiding places we went, seeing you everywhere in the street. There was a girl got into a car yesterday, outside the theatre on 45th Street. I saw her from the back, the same long curly hair, wearing a brown corduroy skirt exactly like yours. I rushed out – my heart lurched and then raced, I thought I was going to keel over right there on 45th Street . . .'

His voice was tense and emotional, the words tumbling over each other. The style of the conversation had a familiar ring. We've been through all this before, too many times, I thought. It's old and stale. I felt oddly apathetic and uninvolved.

'Have you seen the family? Ingrid?'

'Oh, don't. Lou, I know this is the wrong thing. I knew it was wrong at the airport. Before when we've parted it's been terrible, but I always felt it was the right thing to do. This time I knew it was wrong. D'you know what the guy at the passport gate said to me? He said, if that was my girl, I wouldn't be letting her go.'

I said nothing. There was a long silence and I could hear his short, jerky breaths, but I felt detached from his pain and, for the moment, from my own.

'He was right. I shouldn't have let you go. I knew it, so powerfully, even as you were walking away from me. I knew I was standing there and letting the wrong thing happen.'

'Well, it's done now.' I couldn't think of anything to say, and I didn't want to prolong the conversation. There seemed no point.

'I'm going to Australia next week. The kids are so happy. They're talking to me on the phone again now. You remember how they wouldn't talk, how Ingrid stopped them? That was the cleverest thing she did. It just destroyed me.'

'I know.'

'It's torture hearing your voice and being so far away. I just want to put my arms round you. It's torture, darling, being separated from you.'

'Yes. How's the play going?'

'The play? It seems so unimportant. Oh, it's doing well, it's a big hit. But that doesn't matter, does it? Nothing matters, except you and me.'

'And the children. And Ingrid.'

'Ingrid?'

'She's the mother of your kids. Your wife, remember?' The old rush of feeling, primitive and violent, half choked me. But it subsided almost as it came, leaving me numb and stony-hearted.

'Don't do this, Lou. Oh, you've every right. I'm a prize arsehole. I've managed everything so badly, haven't I? I've stuffed everything up.'

I didn't answer. I seemed to have heard this tape before, many times over, and both of us knew the question was rhetorical.

'I'd better go now, Sam.'

'Go?' There was a world of desolation in the single syllable, but I hardened my heart.

'I've got things to do. Goodbye.'

'But it's Sunday, don't hang up yet, please. I love you, Lou. Tell me what you –'

'Goodbye, Sam.'

I stood on the unyielding flagstones next to the phone, as

rigid as a statue. When I finally moved, my feet were stiff with cold. During the past fortnight in London I had done a fairly solid hatchet job on thoughts of Sam. It had used up a lot of willpower, but there was something else at work, urging me on. This was exhaustion, full-dress burnout, a kind of spiritual inertia that was, Mim had told me the previous day, the healthy body's last and best defence against accumulated stress. Whatever it might be, it had a tranquillising effect. And the traditional tonic of a change of scene was helping the rehabilitation process. London might not be all tea and scones any more, but New York in comparison was nonstop feeding time at the zoo.

Now I wondered if one phone call was about to undo this hard-earned progress. I found myself grappling with an old familiar temptation: to snatch up the phone again and dial Sam's number. It would be so easy. Five thousand miles away, I knew, Sam was going through the same struggle. He would ring me again, I felt sure. The prospect attracted and repelled in roughly equal parts. The head and the heart, I thought, the classic dilemma. Except in this case the strong and resolute head was in full possession of the facts. It knew what was good for it, and it would overrule the susceptible heart. Wouldn't it? I turned away in the grip of an old familiar feeling, light in the head, sick in the heart. I despised it. I needed an old-fashioned talking-to, needed it badly.

Of all the names I knew in London, Daria Webster's came forward as the one best qualified to dispense disapproval in a brisk, no-nonsense manner. A few hours later I sat opposite Daria in her kitchen, drinking Indian tea from lacy porcelain cups. Like everything else in her flat they did not belong to a set but co-existed harmoniously.

Daria and Ruth occupied the top floor of a narrow, three-storey Edwardian terrace. Their small immaculate apartment put me in mind of a Japanese doll's house, although it was triumphantly deficient in the associated qualities of minimalism and restraint. Instead it was a wild bazaar of colours and textures: Indian rag rugs on the floors, hessian curtains, Thai silk cushions in tangerine and turquoise, sofa and chairs draped with tartan rugs or material swatches. The walls of the kitchen alcove were hand-painted with a trompe l'oeil mural of misty Italianate ruins. Below it, wallpaper offcuts disguised boring utilitarian cupboards.

The rooms that I could see were painted in clear, very pale pastels – lilac, aqua or lemon – and the cornices navy blue. The furniture was an inexpensive mix of wicker and pine picked up, I guessed, from junk shops and markets and then sanded and varnished.

The end result was unorthodox, verging on the rollicking, and any interior decorator would have disowned it on the spot. But it was all put together with an imagination that struck me as authentically oriental, and which thumbed its nose at stuffy Western notions of good taste. The underlying sense of pattern and colour was faultless. I found the whole production exhilarating, and very revealing of its owner's joie de vivre.

'I would find it hard to be depressed in this flat,' I said. 'Cynthia should hire you to redo her place.'

'Ah, Cynthia.' Daria looked sprightly. 'Yes, I am afraid that woman has none of the physical graces. She is needing someone to take her in hand.'

'Who better than you, Daria?'

'Ah, I am willing, like a shot, but our Cynthia is certainly not having it. She will go her own way, galloping into everything like a blunderbuss, and nothing will stop her.' She paused to sip her tea, managing to perform this task with her head on one side and putting me in mind of a skittish canary. Then she added mysteriously, 'But the waters will not part for her. She will go down over her head.' For some reason these words gave me a pricking sensation on the back of the neck. I waited for some amplification but none was offered.

Daria had seemed unsurprised by my arrival, greeting me effervescently and shooing me upstairs like an old friend. Instead of a sari she was wearing conventional blue jeans and a T-shirt covered with Van Gogh sunflowers, but she looked, if anything, even more exotic. I felt she had a good idea why I had come, and after an interlude of chatting about the party she darted straight to the point.

'You have something in your mind. Is it this man in the United States of America mishmashing your life?'

I told her about the phone call. 'I was a model of indifference while we were talking. After I hung up I had a bit of a relapse.'

Daria put her cup down and leaned forward, intensely involved. 'This is bad news, this is very bad news, Louisa. Here you are, you have come all this expensive way to escape from the clutch of this man.'

I nodded gravely. I felt rather like a naive postulant consulting the oracle at Delphi. Daria went on, 'The telephone is a most unfortunate contraption in many ways. Without having the telephone this man – what is his name?'

'Sam.'

'Samuel?'

'Just Sam.'

'This man, this Sam, would be safely hidden on the moon, out of your reach. There are letters, but they do not stop the heart in the same way as the voice. The voice is bringing him down off the moon, into the – where is the telephone in Miriam's house? The kitchen, isn't it?'

'The kitchen, yes. Yes, that's quite true.'

'So, Louisa, what are you going to do about it?'

'Well, try and resist, I suppose.'

'So. We are all going to be grunting and groaning and saying poor old Louisa. Just like poor old Tracey Garrett, isn't it?'

'Well . . .' I watched admiringly as Daria proceeded to combust. It was as if someone had touched her with a lighted taper and she sprang to life, her eyes blazing spots of passionate conviction.

'No, Louisa, this is definitely not it. You are a full-grown woman, and you are definitely not wanting and not needing our pity. But our pity is what you will be having, as sure as eggs, if you do not stiffen your top lip. You have gone halfway, now you must go the whole hog. Tell this married man to run and jump into the lake. If not, Louisa, you are wasting your life hankering and mooning after him. But it is not necessary I tell you this, because you know already.'

I was impressed by her commitment to the welfare of someone she barely knew. It wasn't often one came across genuinely disinterested fervour, and it was flattering. Equally, most of one's friends, whatever their private opinions of one's conduct, were hesitant to express their views in such a forthright manner. Cyn would not have hesitated. She could have made identical recommendations, and been rewarded with a sneer. Jack was right. Life was unfair. It was grotesquely unjust that two people of the same sex could give the same advice and one be listened to, the other ignored.

Perhaps disinterested was not quite the right word for Daria. She was a crusader for the sisterhood, of whom I was a representative. She quite clearly wished to alert all women to the error of their mating-fixated ways, and this made her not only a reformist but something of a zealot. Her advice had to be regarded as partial; was it therefore entirely suspect?

She was regarding me shrewdly. 'You are thinking I am a man-hating bachelor girl.'

'Not that exactly, no. Just a trifle jaundiced, maybe, about the durability, viability, advisability and general state, temper and condition of male–female relationships.'

'Jaundiced.' Daria repeated the word twice, then bunched her fist emphatically. 'No, I do not think that is an accurate description. I am instead a realist, because I see the evidence of my eyes. Every day I am seeing females who are in a stew over their relationship with the opposite sex. I am seeing females who are severely disordered in their lives by a male electrical field. What I am not seeing, I am afraid, is the happy ever after rose garden.'

'So, you reasonably conclude, who needs it?'

'Who needs it?' She laughed, a tinkling sound like the high notes of a child's xylophone. 'I like men, you see, oh very much indeed, but they are better kept for sex, or fathering. And then,' she glanced slyly sideways, 'recycled. Not left around the place rusting and corroding up.'

'Very environmentally correct, Daria. Very green. But is it possible your ideas are a bit ahead of their time?'

'That is true, I think. In the long run, you see, there will be only one sex. What a pity, but luckily it will not affect us and there is nothing we can do about it. It is nature's clever way out of this pickle.'

In the social chaos she observed around her, I gathered, Daria detected the seedbed of a cataclysmic evolutionary movement. Human beings would eventually evolve into a hermaphroditic species. Daria sketched this process as a kind of inexorable roller coaster. She made it sound as if it was proceeding on a single track in one direction, rather fast.

The philosophy of civilisation together with the emancipation of women had put intolerable strains on traditional male/female commerce. The peaceful coexistence of men and women, Daria asserted, had always been in a fragile equilibrium. It was based entirely on sexual hierarchy and a rigid separation of roles. Once women began to emerge from their primeval straitjacket, once the fundamental inequities were perceived for what they were, the old order was doomed.

Well yes, I could take that. It was fairly unexceptionable. But Daria's conclusion, from which she would not be budged, was her trump card. It possessed a definite shock–horror quality which she clearly cherished. Nature's comeback, her consummate revenge on a recalcitrant species, was to remove the need for sexually conducted reproduction. With this out of the way, having two sexes would become inefficient, not to say old-fashioned. There were no prizes, I assumed, for guessing which one would be shoved down Daria's redundancy chute.

'Well, I suppose it's one way of resolving the differences.'

'Resolving the hostilities, Louisa. Women are angry. The angers are running very deep.'

Women were disappointed, and with their disappointment came a drive for independence and autonomy. Some females, Daria pointed out, had pushed their autonomy to the sticking place. They had already taken the first tentative steps towards dispensing with men. They were conceiving without a man's direct physical invasion. Anonymous sperm donors were commonplace.

I saw an opening and butted in. 'The sperm may be anonymous but it wasn't made in a factory. They haven't dispensed with men entirely.'

Daria had an answer for this. It was now theoretically

possible for a woman to produce a child from the genetic blueprint of her own egg alone. Theories had a way of becoming eventualities. Science was marching on.

'Men are trying hard to get into the act before it is too late. They can now have babies too. They can carry a foetus, implanted in their tummy, to the complete full term, and have it out with a caesarean operation.'

'The procedure might be possible, but they're not trying too hard. Volunteers have been notable for their absence.'

Daria smiled. 'You wait and see, Louisa. Someone, mark my words, probably a poofter, will want to be the guinea pig, sooner or later.'

Even now, women could become surrogate mothers, and mothers could give birth to their own grandchildren. The Virgin Birth, that lynchpin of Christianity, was being routinely upstaged.

This seemed to afford Daria particular enjoyment. 'It is happening all over the place. Young women with intact maidenheads are choosing to have insemination instead of sexual intercourse.' She looked at me with a mischievous purse of the lips. 'They do not even have any Christian faith, half of the time. Well, well, fancy that. Instead of God, perhaps your Jesus' father was a student of medicine at the University of Nazareth.'

'No, it had to be God. Nazareth was too small to have its own university.'

Daria's silvery laugh was as infectious as Jack's, if less robust. She scooped up her material in an ingenious, wide-ranging net, reciting it with the triumphant air of prophecy vindicated. That she would be regarded in many quarters as a prophet of doom did not appear to worry her in the least.

The evidence was all there. Unisex dressing, the burgeoning

homosexual movement, failure of the New Man, production of dildos (rocketing, she said), unstoppable entry of women into traditional male preserves like armed combat, soccer and gentlemen's clubs. Even boxing. After a few minutes I began to feel as if any random statement pertaining to sexual relations could be taken up and brandished to prove her point. It was partly her conviction, but I was also starting to find it all creepily persuasive.

'Women in their thirties and forties cannot find suitable men, we all know that. Why not?' She was expecting an answer.

'Because they're all married, gay or wimps.'

'Correct! The available men are not of their standard. They are not in the same class, and I do not mean social class. So the poor things are turning to women, in very large numbers. I am seeing this every day in my practice and the social worker's.'

I remembered that Daria, beside being a futurologist and behavioural guru, was also an active lawyer for the housing co-op.

'Lesbians are coming out of their cupboards all over the place, Louisa. You would be surprised. All the members of Miriam's co-operative are lesbian, except for Miriam herself.'

'Really?' I recalled several energetic young women typing and taking phone calls, but couldn't picture their faces.

'Oh yes. They are all Friends of – who is it?'

'Dorothy?'

'Friends of Dorothy, yes. They have Friends of Dorothy meetings in the evening at which they show instructional video films.'

'They do? Instructing what exactly?'

Daria looked smug. 'How to give pleasure to each other, in sexual actions.'

'Good God. Have you been present at one of these enticing soirees, Daria?'

'Certainly not. They tell me. They point it out as an example, you see. To show me how much nicer women are to each other. They say, can you imagine men gathered together to discuss how to give women pleasure?' She sipped her tea daintily. I had long ago finished mine. 'And I have to say, no, it is quite true, I cannot imagine it at all.'

'Well –' I felt a staunch desire to stand up for men, but it was hard to know where to start. Disconnected thoughts were buzzing round my head like bees, swift and chaotic. Daria watched me with her attentive, quizzical expression.

'You feel anger, don't you, Louisa, about your Sam?'

I was startled. 'A bit, I suppose. Well, yes I do. Yes, definitely.' As I said this I felt anger bubble up inside me, corrosive as acid. I fought to keep it down. The key turned in the lock and Ruth came in, carrying a bundle of papers. She was wearing identical clothes to her mother, except that her T-shirt featured lilies by Georgia O'Keefe.

She flashed a smile in our direction and set the packet down carefully on a table next to a golf ball typewriter. Daria jumped up with an excited exclamation. 'Thank you, my honey.' She and Ruth bent over the table, murmuring to each other and flicking through the pages, two mantles of dark hair shading their bright eyes. I felt a stab of envy for their closeness. Until Sam, it had never occurred to me to want a child.

Daria straightened up and did some dancing steps on the spot. 'Here are the first chapters of my new book, Louisa! Now it is real for me, it is becoming a professional bit of work. Before it was a child's fiddle-faddle.'

'Daria always gets a big thrill when we see the first pages properly typed,' Ruth said indulgently. 'Neither of us types very well, we have to pay someone. That's silly, isn't it?'

'I don't type properly either, and I'm a journalist, which is not just silly but ridiculous. It's got something to do with not wanting to be perceived as a secretary. Female role paranoia.'

Daria put an arm round Ruth's waist. 'We are saving up for a lovely proper newfangled word processor. Then nobody will be needing to do silly typing ever again. There is all your writing neatly on the little blue screen in front of you, and then it prints it off all by itself. Great fun!'

'You still have to type it – it doesn't get onto the little blue screen by magic!' Ruth dissolved into peals of giggles. 'What shall I do with my funny old mum? I've told her so many times!'

She looked perfectly at ease leaning affectionately against her mother. I thought of Mim and her daughter. If ever Mim touched her with spontaneous affection, Susanna's irritation was so unconcealed that her mother drew back immediately.

'Oh dear. Poor Big Bertha. We must not hurt her feelings.' Daria bent over the squat, toad-like typewriter and kissed it unselfconsciously. 'Big Bertha has been a loyal working horse for us. She is a dreadful hulking old clodjumper, but we love her to bits, don't we, Ruth?'

'Clodhopper, Daria. Old clodhopper, not clodjumper!' Ruth shrieked with laughter. Daria joined in.

'Ruth is my correction fluid, Louisa. It is a jolly good thing I have her. Otherwise my readers would all be laughing fit to bust, don't you think?'

'She helps you a lot?'

'A lot? Oh yes, a very big lot. Everything I have written Ruth composes again in proper Queen Elizabeth English. I could not do it without my Ruth. She is my amanuensis.'

I remembered the dedication in Daria's book: 'To Ruth,

my daughter, without whom this would not have been written.' The book was written in a fluent, rather graceful style. I regarded Ruth with renewed respect. She and her mother were sharing a secretive smile of mutual pride.

'What is your next book about?' I had a moment of unease as I foresaw the possibilities. There was no doubt that Daria was showing a more than casual interest in my personal life.

Daria looked amused. 'Ah, you must guess! I think it is not hard to do.'

'Could it be the advent of single-sex humans? The consignment of the male sex to the evolutionary rubbish bin?'

'You have hit the nail on the head, Louisa. It is rather a good topic, don't you think so? I have a feeling the Americans in particular will be interested. Perhaps it could be the subject of a movie by Steven Spielberg.'

Daria and Ruth sniggered together like a pair of conspiring schoolgirls. I had an impression this whole enterprise might have been conceived as a dig at men, an elaborate practical joke. That it was intended to be playful and provocative rather than a scholarly hypothesis I had no doubt. Shrewdly marketed it also had the potential to be a very big seller indeed. I thought that Daria was well aware of the possibilities.

'In my next book, Ruth's name will appear alongside mine, on the title sheet. We will be shared authors.'

'Joint authors, Daria,' Ruth corrected gently.

Susanna called her mother 'Mum', usually managing to invest the syllable with a halo of disdain. Ruth seemed to view her mother as an equal rather than her natural adversary, and she called her by her own name. I wondered if something as apparently trivial as this had some arcane significance. My stepmother had wanted me to call her Mum. Instead, I had avoided calling her anything. She was kindly, but preoccupied with her three young children. I'd felt indifferent to them and cold towards her.

The visit to Daria powered my arm. Without being quite sure why, I walked away from her flat feeling moderately optimistic about myself, Sam, and my ability to deal with the conjunction of the two. I also felt, for the first time in months, the stirring of a desire to get back to writing. It was a nascent desire, but its very existence took me by surprise. It wasn't just the need to earn money again, which was pressing enough; it was something else.

I remembered the book I had always meant to write. Entitled *Prefaces to Unwritten Novels*, it was to be a story woven from introductions to non-existent books. People seemed to agree that this was rather clever and amusing, and the undeveloped idea had kept me happily entertained for years. Since meeting Sam, though, it had scarcely crossed my mind.

The house was strangely quiet when I returned. For a moment I thought Mim and Dave were still in bed. But I located Mim on her knees behind a rhododendron bush in the garden, weeding strenuously, her breath misting the cold air. She seemed to be locked in her own world, and I watched her silently for several minutes.

She had cooked breakfast for Dave, bacon and eggs. 'It was so strange, Lou. Just him and me in the house. As if – as if we were a young married couple, and yet knowing all the time in the back of your mind there was something terribly wrong. He said he wanted his eggs done over easy. It's an Americanism for turned. Jack always had his the other way.'

'Sunny side up. Has he gone then?'

'He said he had some work to do. I suppose I was a bit relieved. I wasn't sure what we could do with each other, with the morning stretching out. And I didn't want him still here when the children – when Susanna got back. Then he said he would come round again soon.' She dropped her trowel and faced me. 'What am I doing, Lou? I feel that I've somehow found myself in a place I shouldn't be, somewhere terribly out of bounds, and I'm not sure what to . . .'

'How to extricate yourself without hurting his feelings?'

'Well, I'm probably flattering myself. I expect he's thinking exactly the same thing – how can I let the poor old duck down gently?'

'Oh nonsense, Mim. He probably can't believe his luck in pulling a real live mature woman. Let's go inside, it's frigid out here.'

In front of the fire, with a mug of coffee, Mim relaxed slightly. But I sensed there was something she wasn't telling me.

'Why don't you just be honest with him? Come straight out and say it was nice while it lasted, but it's time to move on.' This sounded so unlike Mim that I revised it rapidly. 'Tell him a white lie. He's dishy, but the difference in your ages makes you feel awkward. And you can always use Susanna as a perfect excuse. Say you're sorry, but the relationship with him is causing ghastly problems.' Or rather, I added mentally, wildly exacerbating already existing ghastly problems.

This was so plainly the most painless way to go about it that I couldn't understand why Mim was not more enthusiastic. She twisted a strand of hair around her index finger in a pre-occupied way, not looking at me.

'It's not hard, Mim, really. Just take a deep breath and do it, and you'll be free again. You probably should do it soon, before people start thinking of you as an item.'

That this might happen seemed not to have occurred to

Mim, who looked appalled. 'He was spending a lot of time with me at the party. I hope people didn't think – it would seem so disloyal to Jack.'

'Disloyal to Jack?' I heard my voice rising with indignation, rather like Cynthia's. 'It's about time you took up being disloyal to Jack in a big way, Mim, and made a habit of it. He hasn't exactly been a paragon of loyalty to you.' I paused for breath. 'And anyway, he's left you. You're separated. Loyalty doesn't come into it.'

I realised as I said this that I was speaking as if I didn't know Mim at all. Where Jack was concerned, loyalty would always come into it. She was watching me with the look of a startled and wounded fawn. Perhaps I had never before expressed my feelings about Jack's behaviour with such vehemence. I thought this was probably Daria's influence.

I wanted to get back to the subject of Dave. I didn't know quite what to make of my own attitude, why I was so negative about Mim having what she surely needed and deserved, an innocent little fling. Was that it, that deep down I had some instinctive, visceral feeling that it was not and could never be so innocent? And did Mim sense the same thing?

'Of course you could just go on seeing Dave occasionally. Have him over when Susanna's away. But maybe you're right, there are too many deep feelings at stake. There's a faintly dangerous edge about the whole affair. Or something.'

Mim was looking away again. The hair she had been winding around her finger spiralled in a corkscrew under her chin. She reached for a strand on the other side. I wondered if I had gone too far.

'Look, I'm probably being uncharacteristically melodramatic. At least, I hope it's uncharacteristic.'

'I don't think so. I mean, not melodramatic, exactly. But

it's not quite as straightforward, there's something – there's a little aspect . . .'

'You're mumbling, Mim.'

'Sorry, I'm being silly. It's just that there's a private . . . there's a complication. Only a little bit of one.'

'Of course there is. Everything's complicated where you're concerned. This is because of your natural propensity to see things from everyone else's point of view. Your own gets excluded in the process. What you have to do is discard whole layers of your sensibility in order to function in the wide cruel world.'

She smiled at me, a sad little smile.

'Well?'

'Oh it's nothing, really. I shouldn't have mentioned it.'

'You haven't mentioned it, Mim, that's the trouble.' The coil of hair looked so tightly wound it must have been causing her pain. 'What is it? Is he falling in love with you?'

She shook her head emphatically. An inspiration struck me. 'Has he got a terminal illness? Some sort of dread disease?' Nothing was said, but I could feel that I was getting warm.

'There's something wrong with him, Mim.'

'Not exactly, Lou. Just a minor niggle. A temporary thing, a nuisance more than anything else. Nothing to worry about.'

'Herpes? He thinks his dick's too small?' I could see Mim thought she had said too much already, and was about to clam up seriously. It was that wretched loyalty factor again. I knew I had very little time. A minor niggle. It had to be something sensitive, to explain her diffidence. Almost certainly, something to do with sex. Impotence? Not, surely, a minor niggle, even in Mim's anxious-to-downplay-this canon.

I ran through a mental inventory of sexual irregularities. Bestiality, paedophilia, transvestism, incest, fetishism, necrophilia.

Fairly major niggles, I should have thought, every one.

'He prefers to think of you as a sheep. Or his mother.' Mim flinched. 'He can't ejaculate unless he's wearing a bra and panties.' I was watching her like a hawk, and I detected a small involuntary movement on the third word.

'He's a premature ejaculator!' I delivered this with the triumph it deserved. I felt rather as Professor Higgins had when Eliza finally perfected rain and Spain. Mim looked as if she had been caught in flagrante behind the toilet block.

'Lou, please keep this to yourself. I should never have told you – it's such a betrayal of trust.'

'You didn't tell me, I guessed. Have no fear, Mim, I can't think of anyone it would conceivably interest.' This was a barefaced lie. I knew several people who would be significantly impressed by the news. Cynthia and Jack to name two, plus the entire population of Kilburn Old Barn School.

'I don't quite see how this makes it any more difficult,' I said, keeping my tone casual. 'I mean, it's a nuisance for him and, God knows, a bugger for you, but it's one of those things, isn't it?' All the more reason to dispense with his services, I thought.

'Well, not exactly –' My practised eye could see that Mim was levitating on the horns of a dilemma.

'Have you been trying to deal with it, Mim?' This key question was put with as much delicacy as I could muster. I fought to keep my seething prurience under wraps. The best chance of eliciting information, I knew, was to keep the conversation as relaxed and matter of fact as possible. 'It's a tricky problem for the chaps, isn't it?'

Mim looked up. 'Have you ever come across it, Lou?'

'Oh good heavens, yes – well, not recently, but I did have a brush with it when I was, oh, in my early twenties. Several brushes, actually. Do you remember that classical guitarist –'

'No, don't tell me any names,' Mim said hastily. 'It would – it might affect my memory of them. Do you think it's fairly common, then?'

'I think so. Oh yes. Among young men, especially if they're fairly inexperienced, I'd say it was almost universal. Not that Dave, I imagine, is ...'

'No, he's not really.'

'No. But perhaps his background has tended to, ah, encourage the tendency. You know, frequent short-term encounters, back seats of cars, cinema floors, school classrooms and so forth. Skyscrapers. The urban jungle of New York. Your average youth catastrophe, and all that.' I was rambling a bit, but Mim was looking relieved.

'The problem is, Lou, that he says I'm helping him. He's always had this – this difficulty, and it's badly affected his relationships with girls. Girls these days know all about sex, they've read all those magazines like *Cosmo* that tell you everything, so they seem to expect an immediate wonderful time. They tend to be impatient and rather cruel. I'm sure you weren't like that at all.'

Looking back from this distance, it seemed that I had spent the best part of my youth in a lather of sexual frustration.

'I wish I had been. I was far too well brought up, which meant far too inhibited, shy and retiring to say a word. That was how we saw femininity. Remember how we thought men's egos were so fragile, especially about sex, that the merest whiff of criticism would blow them away? And how we were taught to put their needs way above ours? All that subtle, subliminal, insidious brainwashing. We were brought up to be self-effacing, and bloody hard it is to shake off.'

Cynthia's response to this would have been to offer earnest

reassurance that I didn't have to worry myself about being self-effacing or putting other people's needs first, didn't have to worry at all. Mim just looked sympathetic. If there was a gleam of amusement in her eyes, it was wholly affectionate and guileless.

I cursed myself for getting sidetracked. 'He says you're helping him?'

'Well, perhaps a little. A bit. I'm not sure how, really, but he says it helps. We talk about it too, you see, and he says he's never been able to do that with anyone before. It rather defuses the whole thing, the tension, a bit. We've even been able to laugh about it and sort of start again from scratch.'

I could visualise the set-up. In spite of her numerical inexperience, Mim's innate empathy and patience would make her a natural sex therapist. Dave must indeed have blessed his luck in pulling the perfect real life mature woman who would assist him with his problem without charging him for it. And here Mim was, only two sessions in, saddled with a grateful patient who could already see results. Who could already glimpse the pot of gold, a total cure, not so very far away on the horizon. Just a few months of weekly treatments, maybe twice a week if he was lucky. Nothing to lose and the combined ecstasy of a thousand grateful girls to win.

'You do see the difficulty, Lou?'

'I do see it clearly, yes.'

'On the one hand I feel I ought to move the relationship sideways, into a platonic friendship. On the other I really don't want to let him down. He's got no-one here, in this country, and not even any family he can rely on back home. I just can't see my way clear to doing it, Lou.'

Now she was twisting her hair around both forefingers, and it was up around her ears. The idea of letting anyone down, particularly a young single black man affected with a short sexual attention span and all alone in this country, was more than Mim could bear.

I recognised an impasse when I was stuck in one. I knew Mim well enough to be confident that she was not about to budge on this issue, not without persuasion from another, more authoritative source. And I had thought of a more authoritative source I might tap. It would entail breaking Mim's confidence, but I had a clever idea that this would be in a good cause. As a philosophy undergraduate, I had usually found it hard to argue with real conviction against ends justifying means.

I looked up Tracey Garrett's home number in Mim's address book. We made an appointment to meet in her lunch hour, a couple of days later. The doctor and her two children lived in a small, antiseptically clean and tidy apartment above a greengrocer's shop in the High Street. I was relieved when she suggested she and I repair to the next door cafe, a chummy place full of steamy talk and cigarette smoke, both emanating mainly from groups of Irish and Pakistanis.

I sketched the situation in a few graphic phrases. Dr Garrett (I had difficulty thinking of her as Tracey) loomed opposite me like an Easter Island statue, incongruously biting into a frivolous choux bun. She grasped the nub of the problem readily, although its inherent humour seemed lost on her.

'Once Mim has perceived something as her duty, however disagreeable, nothing I can say will persuade her otherwise,' I said. 'But I thought an expert opinion, coming from a distinguished medical personage such as yourself, might have weight.'

Dr Garrett ruminated for a minute. Froth from her cappuccino had gathered in a moustache on her upper lip. She wiped it off with a paper serviette, then used the same one to scrub at some old coffee rings on the laminex table.

'You know, of course, that I'm a GP. Don't run a sex therapy clinic, as far as I know. Heaven forfend.'

'Yes, quite. But you would be well aware of the dangers of an incompetent amateur such as Mim dabbling in the field, however well-intentioned . . .'

'Dangers? What sort?'

'Well, dangers of, er, inadvertently making the problem worse, or giving rise to a series of other unforeseen associated problems –'

I was disconcerted to hear the doctor give a gruff bark of laughter. Behind her I saw some lewd gestures being bandied around the nearby table of boisterous Irishmen. Their gestures drew clear and unflattering implications about our sexual proclivities. Tracey was wearing a navy polo sweater with a sensible if mannish overcoat and a corduroy cap. She had the opposite of a bedside manner and a crisp shorthand delivery, eschewing where possible definite and indefinite articles.

'Much more advisable to fall back on psychology. So unscientific that you can utter any old hogwash and be immune from prosecution. They like to relate most dysfunctional problems to some sort of early trauma. Mim could be opening up a whole can of worms she would be incompetent to handle. Old chestnut of patient fixating on therapist is another useful approach.'

Dr Garrett spoke in a rapid, firing monotone that had an authoritative resonance. You could tell she was used to being obeyed. I was impressed. 'That's very constructive. How do we explain your being a party to Dave's guilty secret? We needn't tell Mim that I told you, need we?'

'Could have heard a rumour,' Dr Garrett said cautiously.

'Certainly can't say I treated him when I haven't. Dave looks to be an active young fellow. Can we assume that Mim hasn't been the only favoured lady?'

'He certainly doesn't give the impression that he lets his little peccadillo cramp his style. Decidedly the reverse. I think we can safely surmise Mim is not the only recipient of his lightning largesse.'

'Hmm. Hope she made him use a condom.'

'God yes.' I thought it unlikely. Mim would probably construe it as an insult to ask for one.

'Just like old Mim, isn't it, to get herself enmeshed in this particular type of quagmire?'

The doctor grunted. 'Type? More of a one-off, I'd say.'

'I guess sex makes fools of us all . . .' I hovered on an upward inflexion, but she wasn't about to be drawn. I toyed with the idea of divulging my own foolishness in this regard, in the hope of eliciting some juicy details of Tracey's romantic adventures, but I didn't fancy shouting. Two raucous female compatriots had joined the Irish table. Dr Garrett pushed back the sleeve of her overcoat and consulted a bulky diver's watch. She reacted and stood up.

'Best be off. Due for an assignation three minutes ago.' She said this in a coy way quite at odds with her usual delivery. My ears pricked.

'An assignation? Someone nice?' I said before I could stop myself. She beamed, revealing three spectacular dimples, the third, improbably, in the centre of her chin. It was a beam of unalloyed joy.

'Ha. Well. Nice and naughty. The main squeeze, in point of fact.'

This skittish side of the doctor was a revelation. We paused in the alley leading to her front door to fine-tune our strategy.

While I was safely out of the way with Stuart Friend, Tracey would drop by for a drink with Mim.

'Whereupon the subject of Mim's dangerous liaison will just happen to come up. And then, hey presto! you will proceed to skilfully dissuade her with every low, mean weapon in your professional arsenal from this deeply inappropriate venture into erotic mentorship –' Halfway through this fulsome sentence I sensed I was losing Dr Garrett's attention. Before I could finish she turned from me with an eager, inarticulate sound and fell into the arms of a balding man considerably older, stouter and shorter than herself. They kissed unselfconsciously for an extended period while I contemplated making myself scarce. That this was Tracey's notorious married lover there could be no doubt. Curiosity rode roughshod over tact, and I was rewarded with beaming smiles.

'Louisa, Nathan. Nathan, Louisa.' Dr Garrett seemed tongue-tied with girlish shyness. They leaned against each other, fingers entwined.

'I'm a friend of Mim Black's,' I said lamely, at length.

'Aha, a friend of Mim's. Well, well. That's a recommend-ation, indeed, in itself.'

'Not that Mim would describe any acquaintance, however tenuous, as anything other than a close friend.'

Nathan laughed in an unaffectedly appreciative way that made me take to him. The doctor joined in. I saw she had unlocked the street door and had one foot inside, pointing up the stairs. They gazed on me benignly, but I sensed an underlying erotic charge. It distanced the two of them from me as effectively as a barbed wire fence, and I resented and envied it.

'We'd offer you some of Tracey's excellent coffee, but alas, tempus fugit and we must prioritise.' He winked at me quite brazenly, and Tracey made a noise closely approximating a giggle. For an unsettling moment she looked like a large and ungainly schoolgirl in the company of an older seducer.

It was more than I could bear to conceal from Mim the juicy news that I had met Tracey Garrett's Nathan. Rather than admit my appointment with the doctor, I said I had run into the two of them serendipitously in the High Street.

Mim was delighted. 'Isn't he a pet? They're so sweet together – like teenagers in love.' There was an audible snort from behind her back. Susanna had come into the kitchen wrapped in a towel.

'Mum, he's disgusting. He's just a dirty old man, an old fat slug fucking her on the side, because that's all he can get.'

'He's not that old,' Mim objected mildly.

Her daughter made a satirical face. 'But you admit he's a dirty fat slug!' She poured herself a mug of instant coffee and went out again. The towel slid off and lay in the doorway.

'It did sort of scream at one that sex was the prime factor in their equation. Not that there's anything wrong with that . . .'

'Just whether there's a long-term future for Tracey,' Mim mused. 'Well, he has said he'll leave. His, ah, wife. He has tried. It's terribly difficult, of course, or can be for some people, as you –' She bit her lip.

'As I know only too well. Indeed. Daria takes a dim view.'

'Yes, well, of course Daria's using examples to make a point. Idealised case studies, not necessarily corresponding to real life. She might actually think it'll all work out for Tracey. In the long run, that is. They're terribly attached to each other.'

'They couldn't wait to detach themselves from their apparel. Right there in the High Street, in front of all those people. Quite de trop, I felt.'

I paused in the doorway, as if I had just remembered something. 'Oh yes – the good doctor said she might drop by tomorrow night. For a drink.'

Mim looked surprised and pleased. 'Tracey? Did she really? How funny. She's never done that before. She's, you know, not a particularly casual kind of person, and she finds it quite hard to relax with people, I think, unless she feels she really knows them.'

'Well, I think she feels she knows you by now, Mim. What is it – about ten years? Actually, I got the impression she might be wanting to tell you something.' The moment I'd said that, I regretted it. Mim's eyes shone.

'Ah – that explains it. She's got something special to tell me! It must be Nathan. He's done it at last. They're going to live together! Lou, that's such wonderful news – it's what she's wanted for so long.'

'Hang on, hang on, you don't know it's that at all.'

'Oh, but it must be. It's so unlike her, you see, she's not exactly a, well, she's not a drop-in type of person, if you know what I mean. She's a more formal, *invitation* kind.'

'She probably wants to change the relationship ballpark. Crank it up a notch. But Mim, I do think it would be best if you didn't anticipate anything before she –'

'Goodness, I wouldn't dream of it. I'll let her tell me and then react as if it's a bombshell. I can be quite a good actress, you know, when I need to be.'

I experienced a qualm of guilt as I changed for my dinner date with Stuart Friend. The inaccurate prospect of Tracey Garrett's imminent happiness had made Mim herself look more light-hearted than she had since my arrival. Mim specialised in vicarious pleasure, something I was particularly bad at. I hoped the reality of Tracey's news would not be too much of a letdown.

Stuart picked me up, to my surprise, in an MG. I hadn't thought of him as sports car material, more rundown Ford. My mental list of assumptions underwent a rapid revision. In the car I seized on the embarrassing incident at the party. He was vague and evasive. The girl Gaby was an old ex from way back who had fallen on hard times. She had an annoying tendency to seek out his help when her problems got too much for her.

'What kind of problems?' I asked innocently.

'Oh, you know, life in general. She always was a bit of a fragile flower.'

'But doesn't she live with you, Stuart?'

'Oh, that was ages ago. It's ancient history now. Well and truly over.'

He seemed anxious not to elaborate. At the Indian restaurant in a Swiss Cottage back street he was obviously a regular. The bearded, chatty proprietor brought us Singapore slings, an incongruous speciality of the house, and made a fuss of me. As I did, Stuart went for the hot curries, though not as hot as Sam. Sam regularly sent vindaloos back to the kitchen for being too sissy.

'So you're an extrovert too,' Stuart said. The drinks, umbrella-festooned and nicely top heavy on the gin, were going down well. We were on to our second, and I made a mental note to keep track of them.

'Whatever gives you that idea?'

'You're a chilli lover. It's a well-known fact, extroverts like getting their mouths burnt.'

He looked at me innocently. He had a habit of saying things that sounded innocuous and imbuing them with a risque hue. I liked the habit, but I had to remind myself that I didn't find him especially attractive. I decided to steer the conversation into safe, practical shallows. Towards the vital subject of work which, after all, was the object of this particular social exercise. I warmed to Stuart as he took this up with enthusiasm.

He proposed a freelance arrangement. He would give me designs for posters on workplace safety, and I would devise catchy one-line captions. We would start off with four or five samples, and if they approved my slogans, there were more designs in the pipeline. With my dwindling bank balance I would probably have said yes to anything, but the proposed rate of pay sounded generous. The fact that I had never tried anything like it before seemed irrelevant. I had always fancied myself as an advertising copywriter. Cynthia would have said I'd be eminently suited to this line of work, seeing as how it was fundamentally frivolous and trivial.

'Payment will be on a piecework basis. By results. But I'm sure you'd be one to always deliver the goods?'

'Where brilliant one-liners are concerned, invariably.' I preferred not to consider any implications that may have been lurking in the undergrowth. Just then the waiter came over and whispered something in his ear. Stuart changed colour, and darted a furtive look at the restaurant window. He raked the glass with his eyes, then muttered something to the waiter who went outside and stood under the street light. I observed him scanning the horizon. After a while he shook his head at Stuart and came back inside.

'It's okay,' said Stuart, to me.

'What is?'

'Oh, nothing.'

'Stuart, are you being stalked?'

'Hell no, it was probably just someone looking for me. You know, for a chat or something. Anyway, it's all right, they've gone now.'

'They? Or could it conceivably be she?'

He grinned. To my practised eye he looked both sheepish and shifty.

'You said she was looking for you. You mean, like she came looking for you at the party?'

'Oh nothing like that at all, no. In fact she was probably just walking past and happened to look in and see me.'

'Uh huh. Eight million people, and yet it's still basically a village, London, isn't it? Nice of the waiter to take the trouble to tell you.'

I saw he had clammed up, in a way that was becoming familiar. If he wasn't prepared to elaborate I couldn't be bothered pursuing the matter further, and the rest of the meal passed pleasantly enough in a boozy haze of inconsequential banter. He overrode my attempts to pay my share, and insisted on footing the bill. I was unsurprised when he suggested we dispense with coffee and have it at his place instead, although it was not something I had factored into my game plan for the evening.

Before I could reply he added: 'I do a pretty mean espresso, if I say so myself. And we can pick up the poster samples so you can make a start tomorrow.'

'And your flat just happens to be around the corner.'

'Just around the corner, as it so happens.' The cocktails and wine had given him a shot of self-confidence. 'Besides, if you're still thinking of writing about the co-op, you can inspect my humble abode.'

Keen to get my hands on the posters, I dumped my better judgement. I had forgotten Stuart was one of the co-op's tenants. For a flat in a once-condemned building, his abode turned out to be scarcely humble. It was a spacious Victorian basement with French windows opening onto a floodlit garden. I prowled around while Stuart tinkered with the espresso machine in the kitchen. Polished floorboards, smart utilitarian furniture and white walls with framed posters gave the flat an air of masculine functionalism. There appeared to be two bedrooms and a study.

'Do you live here all by yourself? Since Gaby shot through?'

'All by my lonesome.'

I had already noticed a subtle tendency he had to belittle himself. It was disguised as jauntiness, but tendencies such as this had always irritated me.

'It's a pretty nice flat. Is the rest of the house let out?'

'The co-op gets a fortune from it.'

'But not from yours?'

He paid peanuts, I discovered, because he had renovated his basement some years ago. As a long-term sitting tenant who had done the initial hard labour he reckoned he was entitled to stay put, and without an expensive and uncertain court case it seemed the co-op was powerless to evict him.

'They can't get me out and they can't put the rent up either,' he said. I began to see where the wherewithal for the MG and some pricy hi-fi equipment derived.

There was a complacency in the way he divulged the information about his own circumstances, camouflaged by a show of reluctance, which I found unpleasant. Stuart Friend might, I deduced, be something of an ongoing thorn in the side of the Kilburn Housing Co-op.

He put on a record. Marlene Dietrich and 'Lili Marlene'. 'I hope this isn't too much of a cliché for a woman of the world like yourself.'

'Oh, both Marlenes transcend cliché.'

His coffee was good. He had, of his own accord, added a slug of whisky or brandy – I wasn't quite up to telling which.

As I put the cup down he edged closer and put an arm round me. Before I could move I found myself being kissed. Too immediate a show of displeasure might, I decided, be unduly impolite, and I made a working decision to sit it out for a brief but respectable interval. In making it I was well aware that my needy side, the side that was crying out for male body contact, was in the ascendancy.

Wine, spirits and strong cocktails always did have a tendency to influence my behaviour. Particularly a combination of the three, over a shortish period. 'Lili Marlene' was succeeded by Lena Horne's sexy, wistful 'Stormy Weather'. We snuggled back against the sofa's yielding cushions. So long as he doesn't overstep the mark, I thought, I can probably endure a bit more of this.

Set against my most recent kissing experience with Jack, Stuart was a manifestly less effective operator. But his enthusiasm was impressive, and verging on infectious. As his hands began to stray I took belated evasive action. It wasn't quite evasive enough, as he shifted his weight around and over me. I was reminded of Cynthia, prone on the couch at the Open Dinner, with Dave's reluctant body overhead. Stuart was slightly built and less muscular than Dave. Or Sam, for that matter.

I forced my head sideways. 'Stuart – it's pumpkin time. My curfew.' I was piqued to hear that I sounded hoarse. Stuart immediately silenced me with more of the same, revved up to a higher and deeper level. I was distantly aware of his hands toying with the top buttons of my shirt.

It was at about this juncture that there was a piercing sound, somewhere between a howl and a scream. Stuart uttered a graphic oath and rolled off me. Before my unfocused eyes he pitched forward and grappled bravely with the intruder.

Without a word or a pause they went rocketing around the room, reeling into furniture and rebounding off it, all the time accompanied by the jagged noise that swerved at random between low moaning and high keening. As the second figure detached itself from Stuart and hurled itself at me with flailing fists I recognised, belatedly, the girl from the co-op party.

I put my hands up to protect my face, but Stuart dived between us and caught an ugly red weal on the cheek. He failed to grip her and she careered away from him into the kitchen. In another second she was facing us with a carving knife held out in front of her in a shaking hand. I noticed her wide staring eyes and telltale pinpoint pupils.

'You bumhole, you little shit fuck, I'm going to kill you!'

Stuart was standing absolutely still, both arms extended.

'Gaby, Gaby, darling –'

'Don't darling me, you fucking worm!'

She lunged at him. As she moved, I flung a glass ashtray. It caught her on the temple, and a gush of blood spouted into her eye. The ashtray smashed into a thousand pieces. Stuart grabbed at Gaby's wrist and the knife clattered to the floor, spinning among the shards of broken glass around her bare and filthy feet. She and Stuart faced each other, panting.

'You even played her our song – "These Foolish Things" – you foul traitor. You even stooped to that.'

She dived for the knife, but Stuart managed to kick it towards me. I snatched at it and touched it, but she hurtled into me and sent us both crashing backwards onto the hard-wood floor. I took the full impact of her body as it slammed down on top of me. The force of the impact derived more from velocity than substance as she looked dangerously anor-exic, but for a moment I thought I was going to pass out.

As Stuart dragged her off me she seemed to disintegrate

against him, her head lolling forward like an empty glove puppet. All of a sudden Stuart was cursing and swearing and slapping her face. He shook her violently. I picked myself up off the floor, fighting surges of nausea. Drops of Gaby's blood were spattered over the front of my cream silk shirt.

'Is she concussed? That ashtray hit her –' I dabbed at her forehead with a handkerchief. Stuart pushed me away.

'Overdose. Call an ambulance. Now! Quick!'

It took a precious second for my befuddled brain to register that this command was directed at me. I stumbled to the telephone, the back of my head throbbing painfully. As I dialled 999, battling the urge to vomit into the receiver, Ella Fitzgerald calmly reached the end of their song. Even as I stammered out Stuart's address I knew that 'These Foolish Things' would forever afterwards remind me of them.

'Now, get cold water!'

Amazed that my mind was still functioning I ransacked the kitchen for a bowl. Stuart hurled the water into Gaby's face, but she didn't react. He told me to keep slapping her face while he groped for her pulse.

Meanwhile he was muttering to himself, almost inaudibly, 'Oh Jesus oh Jesus bugger bugger bugger Jesus bugger Christ go and open the door so they can come straight in.'

'Shouldn't we carry her up?'

'No, it's too fucking cold on the landing – go now. Quick!'

It occurred to me as I opened the front door that he seemed to know what to do. The ambulance men, when they arrived, also had no need of my instructions. They headed straight down to the basement and had Gaby on a stretcher and up the stairs in seconds. The blood on her forehead seemed to have dried, but there were small cuts on her feet.

'I'd better go with them, I'm sorry –'

'Yes of course, of course you must.'

'I'm sorry, she's — oh, it's just all such a dreadful frigging mess.'

'Yes it is, don't worry, I hope she's okay.'

'I'll call you tomorrow. Or . . .' he hovered at the ambulance door, 'or could you possibly stay, if you feel like it?'

I think he knew that I didn't feel like it. Not in the least like it then, and as certain as night follows day that I would not feel like it with Stuart Friend at any time in the foreseeable future. Under any circumstances, conceivable or otherwise.

I caught a glimpse of myself in the hall mirror. Under the dingy light fitting, black with the bodies of dead moths, my face was stippled with red and white blotches. My hair stuck out like scarecrow straw and the top three buttons of my shirt were undone. The shirt was streaked with scarlet, and there was more blood on my hands.

While I waited for a minicab I sat in Stuart's leather armchair feeling cold and numb. There was a sticky lump on the back of my head, and all around me the room was littered with debris and fallen chairs, like the aftermath of a punch-up in a pub. I didn't feel inclined to straighten things up, any more than I felt like staying the night.

10

CHORAL MUSIC – Fauré's *Requiem*, an old favourite of Mim's – seeped under the front door as I fumbled for my key. I pushed the heavy door open cautiously. It creaked loudly as it always did, and I heard voices. My heart, already less than buoyant, sank further. The last thing I wanted now was contact with another human being, even Mim.

The sitting room door was half open. I tried to make myself invisible as I slipped past it, but a familiar and deeply unwelcome figure bounded out and seized my arm with a whoop of triumph. It was Cynthia. She pulled me inside to the crackling fire. I found I lacked the strength or energy to resist.

'Don't think you can weasel your way in like a thief in the night! We know where you've been!' The accusing anger in her voice was obvious even to my dazed mind. Behind her I could see Mim and Tracey Garrett. Cyn gripped my shoulder and held me at arm's length while she looked me over with goggling eyes.

'Landsakes, Lou, what in heaven's name have you been up to? You look terrible, like something the cat dragged in, not to put too fine a point on it. Un peu déshabillé, shall we say?'

I had done up my buttons, thankfully, but neglected to repair any of the other ravages. Cyn leaned her head myopically into my chest. I recoiled. Too late, I realised I had left my coat in Stuart's flat.

'Is that *blood*? Here –' she yanked a handful of material, 'on your expensive silk shirt. Have you cut yourself?'

'I spilt some tomato sauce.'

'Rubbish. You hate tomato sauce. Your boyfriend phoned while you were out, by the way, from New York. While you were pursuing your libertarian social life, which appears to embrace mysterious pugilistic pursuits. A spot of recreational S and M, perhaps? Whose blood *is* it? Can you recall?'

A spray of her saliva landed on my cheek. Mim was up and out of her chair. 'Are you all right, Lou?'

I backed away from Cyn and landed heavily on the sofa. Bazza, the ginger cat, jumped in my lap, purring.

'Lou, we know you've been with Stuart so you might as well come clean. Not that that's an appropriate phrase, under the circumstances.' She shrieked and snatched at my wrist. 'There's blood on your hands too!' She was temporarily speechless. Her mouth dropped open, exposing two rows of black fillings.

'Are you all right? Can I get you something?' Mim was so patently distressed that I shook myself mentally.

'Yes, yes, I'm really quite okay,' I nodded stupidly, finding I was suddenly cold and shivering. I stroked Bazza's fur. Tracey Garrett's deep voice broke the expectant silence.

'Brandy and a hot cup of tea might be efficacious, Mim.'

Mim flew into relieved action. Cynthia was barely containing herself.

'Come on, Lou, get a grip. Have you been mugged? Should we call the police? Were you in a fight, and if so with whom, and who won?'

Dr Garrett interrupted. 'Cynthia! Your curiosity is understandable, but the poor unfortunate woman has obviously had a shock and needs quiet time to recover. Tact and self-control are the keynotes.'

I sat up slowly. Being called a poor unfortunate woman had a bad effect on my psyche. 'I wouldn't mention Cynthia, tact and self-control in the same breath,' I said. It was an unwise thing to say, and I could see Cyn's nostrils dilate. 'I've just come from ministering to a drug-overdosed girl – woman – and I really don't need –'

'Is that hers? Is it Gaby's blood? What on earth have you been doing? Wherever *were* you?'

'In Stuart's flat, of course,' I said with some dignity.

Mim put a brandy balloon in my hand and whispered, 'Tea's on its way.'

'In Stuart's *flat*, of course. Not at a Lady Macbeth audition. How silly of me.' People always maintained that Cyn could mimic my voice. She managed to inject a lofty, smug note that she knew I particularly resented. Now she had her quarry in her sights, and was up and running in that unstoppable way she had made uniquely her own.

'Well, Lou, since that is Stuart *and Gaby's* flat and has been for quite some time, for four years in fact, and given that Gaby has been in and out of detox and is currently out and about on the streets, it was probably less than astute to make *that* particular little location your lust nest of choice. Why, the dreary old ex might turn up at an awkward moment and make a scene, a wretched *nuisance* of herself! How fortunate that you're used to dealing with such trying situations. I don't suppose anyone's heartbreak would faze you now.'

Cyn took a hefty swig of wine and poured herself some more. I exchanged an eloquent, eyeball-rolling glance with Tracey Garrett, and a second one accidentally with Cyn. But where the doctor's eyes conveyed a liberal measure of fellow feeling, Cyn's glittered with full-on hostility. Unfortunately she intercepted the previous look and leapt to her feet, colliding with Mim as she leaned towards me with a mug of tea. Hot liquid scalded Cyn's hand and she uttered a yelp of pain.

'Well, you'll be relieved to hear I'm going home and I'll take my fuddy-duddy attitudes with me. Then you can all feel free to lavish your sympathy on Lou, without the hindrance of my tedious sententious moralising.'

She rushed out of the room, closely pursued by Mim. Tracey Garrett and I sat in a pregnant silence for a moment, avoiding one another's eyes. She cleared her throat.

'Afraid I couldn't see my way to broaching the sensitive subject.' I looked at her blankly. 'Little matter of Mim and Dave. Thought it best to abstain, with a third party present and all ears, you understand.'

'Cynthia? Oh. Yes, I see.' I found it beyond me to bend my mind to Mim's little problem just then. And Sam's phone call I had banished from my consciousness. It was unnecessary to explain any of this to Tracey, who promptly reverted to the point at issue.

Stuart, she explained in a businesslike precis, had been trying to detach himself from Gaby for some time. The girl refused to accept the end of the relationship and kept returning to the flat. Stuart had been trying unsuccessfully to get the co-op to house her.

'Not their province. They're not in the business of housing

professional basket cases. And their favourite pin-up boy he ain't, needless to say.'

Gaby was eighteen when they'd met, he was her first boyfriend and she was unhealthily dependent on him from the start – neurotic and possessive, no job, low self-esteem. When the affair foundered she took up drugs in a big way. Hogarth could have painted the saga. It was the classic decline and fall, contemporary style.

'Fuck. He might have told me.'

'He's a fool. Coward too. Shouldn't have taken you there. Difficult for him, can't deny that. She's tried to top herself more times than you need to know. He books her into detox, she books herself out. He changes locks, she breaks windows. Could and should have moved, of course, but there you are.'

'He knew when he was onto a good thing.'

It all fell into place. Stuart had been trying to palm Gaby off on the co-op while refusing to budge from his smart, spacious pad which was far too big for one and for which he was paying small change. Mim, with her typical generosity, had told me nothing of this. Meanwhile Stuart's erstwhile lover and flatmate was selling herself on the street, supplementing the takings with welfare and charity payments. Both protagonists were longtime patients of Dr Garrett, hence her familiarity with the story. I drained the dregs of my tea. Something about this scenario was oddly familiar.

'Charity . . . charity . . . Of course. Gaby's the Charity character in Daria's ladies' manual.'

Tracey snorted. I remembered her antipathy to Daria and her book. Mim came back in, looking upset.

'She's ridden off on the bike in a bit of a huff. I couldn't persuade her to stay over, or even come back in. She said she could see when she wasn't wanted.'

'Well, she was spot on there,' I said brutally.

Mim twisted a handkerchief in her hands. 'I tried to tell her of course she was wanted, she'd always be welcome here, but – you know, she'd got herself into a state, and nothing I could say would –'

'Why was she like that, Mim? I mean, I know she's like that all the time, but this was a bit over the top even for Cyn.'

Mim lit a cigarette and looked away. 'Well . . .'

'Mim, I was the target of her venom, and I've had a bad evening. My head's throbbing and I'm bruised and battered all over from where I was wrestled to the concrete floor by a knife-wielding drug addict. My tea's been spilt. I think I deserve to know.'

'I'll get you some more tea –'

'Mim!'

'Well, I'm afraid Cyn's had this – *thing* about Stuart. Ever since they . . .' she ground to a halt. My patience, never a strong point, was close to being exhausted. I made a strangled noise, involuntarily. Mim caved in at once.

'Ever since they had a small fling, you see –'

'Cyn and Stuart? A *fling*?'

'Actually, to tell the truth, just a one-night stand. Although Cyn would have liked –'

'When did this happen? God, and Cyn was being so sanctimonious. When it's not as if I got to the point of even *contemplating* a fling.' Tracey Garrett gave an explosive chuckle. I added hastily, 'Not that I was going to, of course.' I remembered something else. '*And* she had the gall, the frigging mendacity, to berate me for not introducing her to Stuart at the party!'

'Yes, but you know what a private person she is. She likes to keep things to herself. It happened a long time ago, a very long time. Well, years, actually. Before Gaby came on the scene.'

Tracey seemed to find all this amusing. 'And the poor benighted female is still carrying a torch. Ah, welladay, and who are we to talk?' She grinned quite unselfconsciously at Mim and me. I felt the three of us drawn together for an intimate confessional moment. But I was anxious not to extend it. Bed was beckoning with an overwhelming allure. As I hauled myself to my feet the phone rang.

Mim picked it up and, before I could stop her, said brightly, 'Yes, Sam, what good timing, she's just got back, she's right here.' She handed over the phone as if she were bestowing upon me a priceless Dresden figurine.

Sam's voice, urgent, passionate, came down the line as clear as a bell. 'Lou? Darling, thank God you're back. Where have you been? Don't tell me you were out with someone, I couldn't stand it.'

The green phone lay heavily in my hand. I was reminded of a clammy frog.

'Lou? Are you there? Talk to me –'

'Sam, I'm awfully tired . . .' My head was throbbing, an early warning sign of migraine. Behind my back I seemed to hear the door chime. I sensed Mim and Tracey tactfully exiting. A kind of flurry came from the hall, then another deeper, male voice.

'You're too tired to speak to *me*?' There was a world of tragic drama in the tone.

'You know, I really think I am.' I heard myself say this with a sense of disbelief, but found I was too exhausted to care. 'I'm sorry, but I'm just totally knackered. I've had a – a long day. A bad day.' I heard muted goodbyes from the hall and the front door banged.

'But what happened? Tell me. Who were you with? Was it a – another *man*?'

'Yes, it was –'

'Yes. *Yes*?'

'I just can't talk about it any more. I'm going to have to hang up.' Footsteps, heavy and light, and not just Mim's, clumped up the stairs.

'Hang up? On *me*? Just like that? Leaving me wondering what the hell's happened, when you've just been out with someone else, with some other bloke, and I'm in Australia, I'm on the other side of the world. You can't hang up, I'll go mad, sweetheart –'

I knew that the longer he talked, the greater the inevitability of my capitulation. I said gently, 'I'm afraid I must. Sorry, Sam.' I put the phone down, marvelling at my self-control. Almost immediately it rang again. I ignored it and tackled the stairs. They had never seemed so numerous or so steep. After some time, when I reached the landing, the ringing ceased.

Seconds later I was slumped on my bed fully dressed when there was a knock on my door. Mim's dishevelled head appeared. 'Lou, something really rather terrible's happened.' She sat on the bed, hugging one of my pillows. 'There's been one terrible thing after another today, hasn't there, and this must be the worst. I don't know how to tell you . . .'

'Just tell me and get it over with. It can't be that bad.'

'Oh, but it is . . .' She reacted to my face, and spoke faster than normally. 'The phone was ringing in my bedroom, and it went on and on until finally Dave got to it, just before me, and I'm afraid it was Sam again –'

'Dave?'

'Yes, well he just arrived unexpectedly, as Tracey was going.'

'And?'

'Well, I think Sam was put out to hear a male voice, very put out by the sound of it, and a bit hostile. I think he assumed Dave was someone to do with you, you see, the person you'd been out with. Apparently he asked Dave what he was doing here, and Dave said he was sitting on the bed. He meant my bed, of course, but Sam must have assumed it was, well, this is the awful thing – yours.'

Dave in turn had reacted badly to Sam's manner, and rather than clear up the misunderstanding had told Sam to bugger off and fuck himself. Mim was too delicate to say this in so many words, but I inferred it from her tortuous euphemisms.

'And then when Dave was about to hang up, Sam shouted something at him. Understandably.'

'What did he shout?'

'He said that he was coming over here, to see you. Dave was a bit confused about when he meant, but it might be as soon as next week.'

'Oh well.' These two phlegmatic syllables were received by Mim with amazement. She obviously thought that in my shell-shocked state I had failed to grasp the full dramatic import.

'You see, Lou, the awful thing is that now Sam probably thinks that Stuart stayed here with you. Overnight. Well, he thinks someone's here, some man. Of course, he doesn't know Stuart's name.'

'And it's not Stuart, it's Dave. And he's staying with you.' I started to laugh weakly, then stopped as the hammer blows in my head intensified. Mim's face clouded over. I could tell she was dying to say more, but consideration for another's wellbeing, as always, overrode her own desires. I shut my eyes and turned on my side. Mim took the hint. She tiptoed out, closing the door with a considerate, featherlight touch.

In the late morning after a sleepless night, armed with hangover and migraine, both full-blown, I ventured into the kitchen. A tangle of coffee dregs, cereal bowls and cold toast crusts testified to hectic breakfast activity. Bazza and Sheila were sitting among the debris, washing themselves. Fighting waves of nausea, I wondered how Susanna had dealt with the sight of Dave across the table. The doorbell jangled, giving my nerves an unpleasant jolt.

A delivery man stood there with a huge bunch of flowers. Sam, I thought, Sam consumed with jealousy. Then I saw that most of them were carnations, flowers Sam knew I particularly disliked. And they were pink, a colour he knew I hated. In the hall I ripped open the card. It read: 'Darling Lou, so sorry for ruining what had been the most wonderful evening. Can't wait to see you again. With all my love, Stuart.'

There was a sound at the top of the stairs. I jerked round. Through the flowers I made out a white shape at the top of the stairs. My heart gave a painful kick.

'Lou –'

'Mim! Bloody hell, I thought you were a ghost. Aren't you at work?'

'I just couldn't face it. I rang them up and pretended to be you.'

'Be me?' A heady drift of perfume from the flowers caused the contents of my stomach to lurch sickeningly. I dropped the blooms on the hall table. Mim was still standing there, stockstill in her pale nightdress. 'What are you talking about?'

'Well, I put myself in your shoes, and sort of guessed what you might be feeling. I said I had a migraine and a hangover. I've never done it before, not gone in, I mean . . .' Her voice sounded hollow and disembodied.

'You were very prescient. I've rarely felt worse in my life.

And I've got these wretched bloody fronds from that menace Stuart to put in water.'

Mim didn't offer to help, which should have alerted me. I stumbled around the kitchen looking for vases, then gave up and shoved the whole lot in the sink. It struck me then that the kitchen was unnaturally chilly. I laid a cautious finger on the Aga. It was stone cold to the touch, and that felt like an insult. I had never known this to happen; not once in all the tumultuous times I had passed in this house had the Aga ever been left to go out. I gazed resentfully at the blackened stove, which for the first time struck me as insensate and inanimate. I knew it was trying to tell me something but my leaden mind was unable to unravel the clues.

As I headed back upstairs to bed, the spectral sight of Mim on the landing gave me a second, almost identical jolt.

'Mim! You're still here. What on earth are you doing?' She had not moved, but her head was down, I now saw, buried in an open newspaper. I peered at the headline. It was a full-page article on the famine in the Sudan, from the previous Friday's *Guardian*. Mim's eyes weren't moving, but she was staring fixedly at a distressing photo of children with the familiar distended bellies and stick limbs.

'It's so terrible . . .' Her voice, barely a whisper, trailed off into a long shuddering sigh. The newspaper rattled in her hands.

'You're shivering, Mim. Get something on, for heaven's sake.' But she was also crying, I realised belatedly, crying quite silently and unnervingly, and seemed unable to move. I fetched a dressing gown from her room. It was impossible to avoid seeing the bed, which looked like the aftermath of a tornado. Sheets and doona were jumbled up on the floor, and there was a sweet, musky scent hanging in the air. It was a private scent with which I was retrospectively intimate, and it head-butted me in the guts.

I parked Mim in front of the Aga while I scrunched up balls of newspaper and struggled to get the thing alight with a few twigs. Concern for Mim, I was surprised to find, had a palliative effect on the migraine. She had stopped crying, but her eyes still had a dull, vacant look that troubled me. It wasn't hard to winkle out the cause. As I had already guessed, the conjunction of Susanna, Mim and Dave at breakfast had everything to do with Mim's present state of agitation.

Susanna had gone off to school with Dave and Jake, but not before she had swiped Mim with a belt of invective, a studded, chain-mail belt chosen, as only a mother's daughter can choose, for maximum disabling effect. The vituperation was unloaded, I understood, while Dave was safely out of earshot.

'It's her fourteenth birthday tomorrow,' Mim said tonelessly. I knew she had organised a special dinner out for all of us, including Jack, as well as a separate celebration Susanna was planning with her own friends. 'She said she didn't want to be here for it. She won't be at home for her birthday for the first time in her life. She's going to stay the night at Ruth's instead.'

The tears returned, with redoubled intensity. 'Lou, I've ruined everything, haven't I? Our whole relationship – it'll never recover from this, never, ever. We'll be estranged for our entire lives.'

'Mim, there's no way that will happen. She'll grow up, she'll see reason. She'll fall for a movie star or a boy her own age in a week or two, and all this will be history.'

I shovelled briquettes on the meagre fire. I thought there might be a chance of puncturing Mim's black mood by means of a robust injection of commonsense. I was wrong. Nothing

I could say would shift it. Clumsy humour, usually an infallible resource, turned out to be the worst resort of all.

'Listen, at least you're making one person happy. And it's not as if he's getting his rocks off on a National Health therapist and being a drain on the public purse. Look, you'll probably get a gong for voluntary work in the New Year's Honours List.'

Mim gave a wail, and came as close to glaring at me as she had ever come. 'But I can't go on seeing him, it's impossible! I've got to stop him from coming here, it's out of the question, don't you understand, Lou? He can't keep on coming, he can't, I've got to stop him.' She dissolved in a frightening torrent of sobs, her body slumped over the kitchen table.

I put my arm round her shaking shoulders, feeling helpless and inadequate. These were feelings, I could hear Cynthia telling me, secret women's business with which it would do me a power of good to become more acquainted. Our roles should be reversed, I thought. Mim was infinitely better versed than I at looking after lost souls and mending broken hearts. This train of thought led me naturally enough back to Cynthia.

'I hope the old Cyn's okay after last night,' I said cautiously, on the assumption that it might be therapeutic to rekindle Mim's ingrained altruism. It worked, but not entirely as I would have wished. Mim raised her head.

'Yes. Yes. We'd better ring her at work. Can you do it, Lou?' The words emerged thickly, muffled by her hands. I lifted the receiver with reluctance and dialled the number Mim knew off by heart. After many rings the phone was answered by a brisk academic female who made no bones about trying to hide her irritation.

'Cynthia Whicker's not coming in today, again.' I was struck by a rehearsed, satirical quality about her delivery of this sentence. 'She's cancelled her classes.'

'What's the matter with her, did she say?'

'Oh, she didn't need to say. Just the usual.' There was a pause, and then I felt she was unable to resist adding, 'Her *migraine*.' There were pronounced inverted commas around the word.

'Gets it rather a lot, does she? I'm a friend, by the way.'

The woman laughed with what sounded like genuine amusement. 'Are you, then? Well, I expect you are cognisant of her regular – allergic reactions.' She hung up.

I turned to Mim, who was still immersed in her private pain. 'This is very strange, Mim. Migraine must be extremely infectious. First I get it, then you phone in sick with it, and now Cyn. Although I have to say, the chatty educated type I spoke to gave the distinct impression of this being a happenstance with which she was rather tediously familiar.'

Mim blinked at me through swimming eyes. 'You'd better call her at home. Just to make sure.' I wanted to say, make sure of what? Instead I dialled the number Mim recited and pictured the demure ivory phone ringing on Cyn's reproduction Queen Anne bedside table, beside the satin sheets. Eventually I put the receiver down.

'She's not there. Or she is there and definitely doesn't want to speak to me.'

But Mim insisted I try again, and this time the phone was picked up after I had counted fifteen rings. An indeterminate, hoarse grunt issued from the other end.

'Is that you, Cyn? You'll never guess the weird thing that happened today. You and Mim both caught my migraine, and called in sick. Isn't that spooky?'

Cyn gave a groan that managed to convey a strongly negative attitude.

'You don't sound very pleased to hear me.'

'I'm not. Go away and leave me alone.' Her voice was groggy and slurred.

'Are you sure you don't want anything? Some gruel, perhaps? A prairie oyster?'

The expletive in my ear made me momentarily deaf. 'Just get off my back and go and read a comic, or do some colouring in. Or play in a sandpit if all that's too taxing.'

'I'm relieved to hear you're back to normal. Well, I was just checking up. We were concerned.'

'Mim was concerned. You were indifferent.'

'Cyn, that's not the complete and unadulterated truth. Besides being pitiless and masochistic.'

'Where *is* Mim? Why isn't *she* talking to me? Is she all right?'

'Ah, no, not exactly.'

'Let me speak to her.'

I gestured interrogatively at Mim. She shook her head. 'You can't speak to her because she's asleep.'

'But why isn't she all right?'

'Oh, I think she's got the same thing as you. Up to a point.'

'Well, tell her to ring me when she wakes up.'

I put the phone down. 'Mim, since when has Cynthia had a major drinking problem?' Mim put her head in her hands. She seemed disinclined to answer but I pursued the subject. Anything that might take her mind off her own worries seemed well worth pursuing. That it might give rise to more distress did not, at the time, occur to me.

'Is she having treatment for it? Have you suggested she go to AA?' Mim looked dazed.

'They're obviously pretty jolly au fait at the English Department. Her absences have been noticed. That woman was browned off, was my impression. Very browned off indeed.'

Mim's defeated, wordless nod was confirmation. 'If she's not careful Cyn could find herself out on her ear.'

I glanced up at the ceiling. A dispiriting vision of Cyn jobless, penniless, manless and fortyish floated there. Mim was in tears once more, and I guessed she had seen a similar hovering vision. But where my sympathies were largely technical, Mim would be pierced to the heart. It dawned on me at last that I was going nowhere fast in my ham-fisted attempts to cheer her up, and doubtless making things worse. We would both be better off in bed for the rest of the day.

In my toilet bag I found some sleeping pills and the remains of a packet of Valium. I had resorted to these on occasion when in the depths of despair over Sam. Now I made Mim swallow one of each with a glass of warm milk. She had always been uneasy about drugs of any description, regarding them as artificial and chemical. But she took both tablets, rather disturbingly, without a murmur.

My own plans to hunker down under the covers were comprehensively thwarted by the arrival of Stuart not long afterwards. I cursed myself for opening the door. He had rung the bell insistently, and I answered it purely to stop Mim getting out of bed. Stuart stood in the porch with his head thrust forward, carrying my coat and the folder of poster designs. He wore a blue suit with a pink open-necked shirt, and an eager, doglike expression. My face fell so far that he must have seen it, but he appeared oblivious.

'Lou! I stole away from work. I had to see you. You left these.' I let him in with the utmost reluctance, leaving the door open. He came towards me with the clear intention of embracing, and I backed away, tripping over my dressing gown cord.

'You're still in your –'

'Yes, I am. I was asleep when you rang the bell. I know it

was just a routine suicide attempt and you were able to get up in the morning and go to work as if nothing had happened, but it was all a touch novel and exciting for me.'

He looked as if I had slapped him. 'I'm sorry. I just don't seem to be able to do the right thing with you, do I?'

'No, I'm afraid you don't.'

'Well, all that's going to change. From now on.' He took a step forward.

'Stuart, look –'

'You're not going to say you won't see me again. Don't say it, Lou, please, I couldn't bear it. Give me another chance. I promise you it's all over with Gaby, she's out of my life, she has been for years.' He gazed at me beseechingly, his eyes round and moist. 'It's not my fault, really it's not, I've done everything I could, it's just that she's not rational, she's completely – oh, you know the whole terrible –'

To my horror, tears welled in his eyes. I hustled him into the kitchen, where I was gratified to feel the effects of the Aga roaring away. He sat opposite me in Mim's chair, his eyes brimming over. I had an irritating sensation of déjà vu.

'Stuart, listen. It's got nothing to do with the Gaby business –'

'But it must have, you're only saying that, you know you are.'

'I am saying that, yes, but it hasn't, truly.'

'It must have.'

'Please don't go on about it, it hasn't.'

I filled the kettle with water, and saw his eyes alight on the flowers. Shoved callously into the sink instead of arranged carefully and gratefully in a vase. He dragged the back of his hand across his eyes and sniffed.

'You must think I'm a right berk.'

'No, no, not a berk, definitely not that,' I said, unsure of the word's precise etymology.

He attempted a smile. 'I'm not like this usually, really I'm not. I want to be at my best for you, I want to be *worthy* of you.'

'Please don't say things like that, Stuart.'

'You don't understand. I'm in love with you. I've never felt like this before.'

'Isn't that a Gershwin song? You can't be, you hardly know me.'

His intense, adoring gaze was disconcerting. 'I can't be because you're not, you mean. Don't worry, I realise that, I know your feelings for me are not the same as mine for you, not yet. But I'm going to *make* you love me.'

The Four Tops, I was about to say. Or was it Stevie Wonder? Things had come to a head, rather precipitously it seemed, and major brush-off tactics were called for. I removed myself from his orbit and ground some coffee loudly.

'I'm really sorry about this. I should have told you before. I've already got a boyfriend.' I felt extremely silly saying this, and he looked both hurt and unconvinced. I spooned coffee into a pot.

'Come on now, please, Lou, we got all that baggage out of the way when we met. At the party.'

I dredged my memory. What had I told him? I said lamely, 'Maybe I downplayed it a little, you know how it is at parties. The fact is, I'm still in love with Sam.' As I said this, I wondered if it were true, and was instantly and unsettlingly aware that I had never, until now, felt the need to put that question. Sam's magic image, his face, his body, materialised in front of me. I felt confused and suddenly near tears, and poured coffee to distract myself.

'You're on the rebound from the American thing, you don't

have to pretend to me. I know it's a difficult time to think about starting a new relationship, and the last thing I want to do is rush you. We can take as much time as you need.'

I planted a coffee in front him. He turned and encircled my waist with his arms, leaning his head against my stomach. I recoiled as a shudder of dislike ran through me. Feeling he must have sensed it, and hoping this were indeed the case, I said, 'I'm not ready for another relationship and I don't want one.' Especially with you, I wanted to add. 'Look, I know I've behaved badly, but maybe we're quits on that score.'

I looked at him hopefully. His face had turned pink and shiny and there were more tears in the offing. I looked away, hardening my heart. It wasn't difficult. 'I spoke to Sam last night, and he's coming over to see me.' As I said the words, I discovered I wasn't sure I wanted him to come. Not entirely sure, at least.

'That's a good thing. It'll help you settle things in your mind.' He sounded as if he really meant it, and I gave him points for being game. He blew his nose twice and drank some coffee, to my relief. 'But I'm not giving up on you, Lou. You deserve better than a married man who can't make up his mind.'

I cursed myself for stupid, drunken indiscretions. 'By the way, Stuart, since we're getting down to the nuts and bolts, you neglected to confide in me about you and Cynthia.' The 'don't get mad, get even' principle had always appealed to me. He looked pleasingly startled. 'The little fling you both enjoyed? But perhaps you don't recall.'

He had gone bright red. 'Shit, you can really put the boot in, can't you? It was nothing like a fling –'

'A flingette. It would've helped if I'd known. Affairs of the heart being somewhat thin on the ground for Cyn, as you might imagine, the rose-coloured memory of one tends to loom large. She's inclined to want to guard her patch.' I felt a brute for saying this, both to Stuart and Cynthia, but it didn't inhibit me one whit.

For a moment I experienced a vestige of pity for Stuart, whose crimsoned discomfort was glaring. 'I didn't want to . . . it was never my . . . I just sort of couldn't get out of it. It was a ghastly fiasco, if you must know. She virtually, you know, *raped* me in her bloody bedroom.'

The vestige evaporated. 'Spare me the gory details.' I added, carefully pitching my voice midway between concern and light social interest, 'Well, let's get back to last night. Was she – Gaby – was she okay?'

Stuart blew his nose again. 'She pulled through. They pulled her through.' I thought I detected a trace of disappointment somewhere in the terse and weary tone. To my surprise he drained his coffee and stood up. 'I have to get back to the grindstone. No rest for the wicked. I'm sorry I've been such an embarrassment. It won't happen again, I promise you.' He gripped my hand. 'Listen to me, Lou. I want you to lean on me and trust me, to feel you can confide in me and tell me anything. But rest assured I'm not going to stand by and let you dig yourself into a hole like that pea-brained Garrett woman. I'll do anything you want, but not that.'

I pulled my hand away, deeply affronted. 'I think you'd better take the posters, Stuart.' There was no way I wanted a relationship with him, not even a working one.

He shook his head. 'You don't feel like working on them now, but you will. I know you need the money. Don't worry, you won't be beholden to me in any way. You're independent, you're your own woman, I know that. A free spirit. That's what's so attractive about you.'

The Free Spirit was the title of Sam's new play. The play with me in it. I tried to thrust the folder at Stuart but he held his palms up in a jocular gesture of rejection. At the front door he went out, then spun back without warning and gave me an almost frisky little kiss. 'Doesn't it feel good to have cleared the air?'

Having succeeded in getting a variety of feelings off our respective chests, I realised, he thought he had achieved something. I shut the door and leaned against it for a moment, feeling like the leading lady in a bad B-movie. I also felt grubby and rather foolish, and the sick headache was returning at speed.

I had a long penitential shower and washed my hair, and then sat down at the desk in my room. I had the idea that a strong dose of work, a spell of concentrated mental effort, might purge me of some of my transgressions, and I wanted to write a reflective, personal piece about the experience of returning to London after ten years away.

It wasn't to be. I stared at the blank page, in the classic pose of the journalist. It was a position – leaning slightly forward in the chair, elbow on desk, pen poised before the empty, expectant page – that was second nature to me. I was used to holing up in strange places, living out of a suitcase and working off the hoof, setting up the portable typewriter with its converter plug, and switching off from everything except the job at hand. Even the low-grade receding headache was a not unfamiliar part of the scenery.

My mother had named me after a pioneering magazine editor, feminist and mother of a famous Australian writer. I always felt she would have been pleased with my choice of career. It had transported me around the world, and I'd constructed it, I saw clearly now, to carry me far away from my

218

father and stepmother's house that had never been mine. The only house that had ever felt like home to me since my mother's death was this one.

I sat in the silent attic, acutely aware of my surroundings. This house, organically connected to my past, seemed to have a moat around it in which the currents of my present life were surging. I knew they threatened to upset a balance precariously achieved and sweep me off my feet. At the back of my mind, lurking like a shadow in deep water, was Sam. I had been actively avoiding this shadow, closing my mind's eye to it. Now I made a conscious decision to force it to the surface for a moment.

Sam had only been absent from my life for a matter of weeks, but it was long enough to have opened the door a crack towards a cautious future that did not necessarily contain him. Sometimes, most times, that future was a bleak and lonely highway. Once in a while, however, I had seen the gleam of a different road. I was not blind to that tantalising flash of light. Just lately, and only once or twice, it had been crowned with a halo of tiny letters. If I concentrated hard and screwed up my eyes, I could even make out the word they spelled. It was 'freedom'.

11

NOTHING HAD BEEN WRITTEN on the paper, and nothing was much clearer in my mind, but when I floated out of this trance a full hour had passed. I felt light-headed, as if I had emerged from a swoon, and was seized with anxiety about Mim. She was fast asleep, breathing deeply and evenly. I plugged the phone from the kitchen into my room and closed the door.

Tracey Garrett was in the surgery, but rang me back within minutes.

'You gave her what?'

'Valium. And a sleeping pill.'

'Together.'

'Together. But I've taken that particular combination myself before. Several times, actually. When in the throes of severe angst, of the type Mim was exhibiting.'

The doctor's husky chuckle vibrated in my ear. 'Could have done worse, I suppose. Narrowly. But don't let it go to your head. And don't get a taste for home dispensing. I'll call in later and give her the once-over. Might get a chance to say the word that didn't get said last night. As long as our Cynthia's not planning on rewarding you with the sunbeam of her presence again.'

'How right you are.' I filled her in, and was unsurprised to find her well acquainted with Cynthia's problem.

'Known her for years. Couldn't help but notice the permanently bent elbow attached to the shoulder. More to the point is how to get the wretched woman to do something about it. But can't gossip now, patients in the waiting room and no prizes for guessing the lucky lady they're waiting for.'

She hung up. I liked Dr Garrett's nuggety humour and her commonsense. But they hadn't, I reflected, stopped her digging herself into a hole, as Stuart had recently pointed out.

The muffled sound of a door banging downstairs made me jump. Although the winter dusk had already set in it was a still bit early for the children to be home. I sat and listened. There were no more noises, but in my capacity as the sole wakeful custodian of Mim's house I felt obliged to investigate. I picked up the brass table lamp on my desk. It was pitch dark on the landing outside my room, but I left the lights off and tiptoed downstairs, trying to avoid the steps with the worst creaks. The kitchen door was shut, and I had definitely left it open, as we always did, to let the warm air circulate. I paused for a moment then flung it wide, brandishing the lamp.

Gayle, the cleaning student, stood with her back to me, doing something. I felt exceedingly foolish, until she jerked round and I saw what it was she had been doing. Her hands had been in Mim's ancient black handbag, which now clattered to the floor and spilled its contents in a wide arc. Coins spun in every direction from the open purse. I put the lamp on the table. Gayle regarded me with frightened eyes.

'Gayle, what were you doing with Mim's bag?'

'Nothing. I wasn't doing nothing with it, it just fell off.'

'Sit down here with me for a minute.' She pulled a chair out. Stroppy sullenness radiated from her in a tangible force field. I sat down next to her. 'Now listen to me, Gayle. You're not going to get a better employer than Mim, and if you pilfer money from her you're more of a dope than I thought you were.'

Without warning, she burst into tears and scrabbled fruitlessly in her jeans for a handkerchief. Something fluttered out of the right pocket and landed near my feet. It was a five pound note. We reached for it simultaneously and our heads collided with an audible crack.

'You'd better put that back where it came from,' I said in a cold voice. My headache had returned, drawn to its new location like an iron filing to a magnet. Gayle was crying louder than before and holding her head. I passed her a handkerchief, reflecting that my B-movie role seemed to have evolved into something bordering on broad farce. Here I was again, dry-eyed and unmoved, while yet another person sobbed her eyes out in front of me.

'There must be something about me, Gayle,' I said pleasantly. 'I seem to bring on weeping fits in people of both genders, in the kitchen. You're the third one today.'

She snuffled and peered at me over the handkerchief. Her hair had lost its aggressive spikes and the former orange colour had fermented into a pastel shade resembling the rose madder of my childhood paintbox. After a while she stopped sniffing and replaced the note furtively in Mim's purse.

'That's better. Now, how much have you taken altogether? I mean, not counting today.' I remembered bemoaning the fact that the kitty money we kept in a jam jar in the kitchen seemed to have a strange habit of spending itself, and Mim agreeing in a puzzled way that these days she always seemed to have less of the ready around than she thought.

'I haven't taken any –'

'Oh yes you have. We both noticed it. That's why we set this trap. You didn't think there was anyone in the house, but Mim's here too, hiding in her bedroom. She stayed home from work to catch the thief.' I was very firm and stern, and Gayle's lip trembled. 'If you're sensible and upfront with us, we won't tell the cops. This time. But if it ever happens again, you can expect no mercy.'

More and more I felt as if I were performing in a rather bad script. The lines seemed to have a direct connection with a TV police soap, and to emerge unprompted from my mouth. Still, they appeared to impress Gayle. I folded my arms expectantly.

She said in a small voice, 'Only a bit. It was hardly a bit I took. Like, only a few coins, here and there.'

'How come today it was, like, five pounds?'

Her voice shrilled indignantly. 'I never done that before! Honest!' She dragged my pristine white handkerchief across her eyes. Smears and smudges of black mascara gave her the appearance of a woeful clown.

'Gayle, how long have you worked here?'

'More'n a year.'

'Well, Mim obviously feels she can trust you. She leaves her purse around, she gives you a key, she doesn't mind you coming in when she's not here. It's a big responsibility.' Gayle nodded virtuously. 'How's she going to feel now?'

'Are you going to tell her?' The lip wobbled again.

'I think I'll have to tell her. But knowing Mim, she'll want to give you a second chance. But that's all. I won't let her give you a third one.' I got up. 'Now, Gayle, you know Mim too. She always thinks the best of people. That means you. She'd be pretty upset if she thought she couldn't trust you any more.'

'She *can* trust me!'

'Well then, let's put it behind us. We'll pick up all her goodies and from now on we'll make a fresh start. We'll behave as if it never happened. Okay?'

Vigorous nods. We scrabbled together on the floor, packing the usual paraphernalia plus some eccentric Mim-type items, such as an empty cassette box, a tin of cod's roe and a synthetic resin dragon, back in the bag. Looking very relieved, Gayle proffered my sooty handkerchief.

'You can keep that.' At the kitchen door I turned. 'We'll act like it never happened, but we won't forget it did. All right?'

I took the bag upstairs, reckoning that it was only wise to put distance between Gayle and the more tried and true temptations. On the stairs I was overtaken by a whirlwind of blue school serge. Kilburn Old Barn School had recently opted for casual uniforms to avoid fashion disputes. Susanna and Ruth, giggling, flew past me. 'I'm getting my stuff,' Susanna called over her shoulder. 'Going to Ruth's place. I won't be back till Sunday.'

Today was Friday. I plodded in their wake, feeling my age and careworn, and knocked on Susanna's bedroom door.

'Who is it?'

I announced myself and Ruth unlocked the door cautiously. I pushed in unasked, and Susanna stared at me in surprise. She was in the process of removing her school slacks.

'Can't you come back from Ruth's tomorrow?'

'Why?'

'You know why.' Clothes were strewn all over the room. I sat on the edge of the unmade bed, pushing aside a green velvet coat that I might have worn in the sixties. I wondered if it was Mim's.

'I haven't a clue what you're on about. Here, pull.' This last was aimed at Ruth. They embarked on a tug of war, to drag Susanna's trousers off without removing her boots. I watched them as the cuffs slipped out of Ruth's grasp, and Susanna hurtled backwards like a projectile amid peals of mirth.

'Susanna, you know Mim's already organised your birthday dinner. She'll be devastated if you don't show up.'

'You can have it without me.' The trousers were levered off, revealing lacy and very skimpy briefs. I experienced a pang of envy for the flat stomach and lithe adolescent figure.

'Of course we can't, it's your birthday, you're the whole point of it. If you're not there, it doesn't happen.'

'Fine by me.'

I let out a heavy sigh of frustration. Susanna was throwing an assortment of filmy clothes into a duffle bag, following an intimate conference with Ruth on each selection. Most of them looked thoroughly unseasonal, and I felt sure her mother would not approve.

'I'm really, really worried about your mum. I've never seen her how she was today. She didn't go to work, she was in one hell of a bad way. I gave her some pills to make her sleep, and she's been out to it all day.'

'So what if she's upset? *I'm* upset, and it's all due to her.' Susanna seemed to be able to move effortlessly between light badinage with her friend and fiery exchanges with me. Now she turned to Ruth and said something in a voice too low for me to hear. They both snorted, then remembered me and looked only faintly contrite. Susanna pulled on a pair of baggy corduroy jeans.

'Don't mind me,' I said. 'Have fun tonight, just have the grace to make an appearance tomorrow. You *are* the star turn, after all. It's a family thing. Think of Jack and Jake, they'll be terribly disappointed.'

'Won't they just.'

'Perhaps it's no big deal for you, but it means the world to Mim. Quite frankly, she could go to pieces if –'

'So it'll be all *my* fault if she has a nervous breakdown, is that it? That's terrific. That's brilliant. How about Dad, and the divorce, and her having it off with one of my teachers? How about all that stuff? Don't you think that's got anything to do with her losing the plot?'

I thought all that stuff had everything to do with it. It was a very succinct and accurate assessment of cause and effect. 'You're right, of course. It's just that if you and she have a major falling out it could be the last straw.'

'Well, it's too late, baby, cos we've had a major falling out already.' Susanna crammed a plastic folder of cosmetics and a short silky skirt into the bag and tossed it over her shoulder. 'That's the lot, Ruthie, let's go.' They tumbled out of the room. I followed, a torpid sensation of failure in the pit of my stomach.

Susanna looked back at me. 'That loony Cynthia was here again last night, raving on as usual and getting stuck into the booze. Which wouldn't've helped either.'

I had to agree. The girls reached the kitchen before me. When I arrived I saw Gayle wiping down the kitchen table with considerably more animation than she had shown on previous visits. Susanna was rummaging in the kitty jar on the mantelpiece.

'I'm taking a couple of quid. For fares and that.'

Gayle bestowed on me a meaningful glance. I revised my mental estimate of her pickings. There was no doubt the kids also raided the kitty on a regular basis, but it wasn't my place to lecture them. Especially right now.

'Susanna, do please think about tomorrow. It would be very . . .' I sought for the telling word, 'it would be very cruel to stay away.'

Her mouth set in an obdurate line that made her look suddenly older. 'Well, great, I'm glad, because that's exactly what she's been to me. Let's get outta here, Ruthie.'

They surged out of the back door. I wondered if I should have appealed to Ruth. She had said a polite goodbye to me with a nice smile, but there was no doubt her allegiance was very firmly with her friend on this one. She too, I recalled, was heavily stuck on Dave. I felt deeply depressed.

'These are lovely. What d'you want me to do with them?' Gayle was asking me a question. She hauled Stuart's flowers out of the sink. They were still in their crunchy cellophane wrapping and ostentatious pink ribbon.

Chuck them in the bin, I was tempted to say. 'Oh, stick them in a vase. Thanks.'

'Are they from an admirer?'

She was being unusually chatty. Until today I had probably not exchanged more than half a dozen words with her. I found myself wishing for a return to this condition. I grunted.

'I wish someone would send *me* flowers like them.'

'Oh, I expect they will someday.'

'My boyfriend's not the romantic kind. He doesn't see the point of things like flowers.'

She selected one of Mim's jugs, a tall Provençal piece with a shiny green glaze. It was, I saw, exactly the right choice. I watched her arranging the long stems with a surprisingly artistic flair.

'He'd say they just die.'

'What?'

'My boyfriend. He'd say what's the point of wasting money on them, when they just die.'

'If he doesn't see the point, maybe he's not the right boyfriend for you.'

'That's what I'm getting around to thinking. *And* he only wants one thing.'

I recalled Mim telling me something along these lines when I first arrived. 'If he doesn't take any account of what you want, you're probably better off without him, I'd say.'

She deftly repositioned two frothy stems of greenery. 'On the other hand, if I did get another one he'd most likely be the same.'

'Oh, I wouldn't necessarily go that far. There's quite a variety of them out there.'

'But they all want one thing, don't they? That's what my mum says.'

'Well, she's on the button there. But with luck you can find one who wants a few other things as well. To make you happy, for instance.' Her expression suggested that I was dangerously out of touch. 'How old are you, Gayle?'

'Fifteen. Nearly.'

'You do know that your boyfriend could be charged. Fucking's illegal at your age.'

She looked scandalised. I couldn't tell whether this was the result of the notion or my mode of expressing it.

Jake wandered into the kitchen. I hadn't set eyes on him for some days. He cut a big wedge of cheese and stuck it between two slices of the white supermarket bread he favoured.

'Where's Sus?'

'She's gone to stay over at Ruth's place.' I thought I'd better prepare him. 'She said she may not come home for her birthday. Remember we were going to go out for dinner tomorrow?'

'Mmm. Can we go anyway?'

'Well, I'm not sure about that. Your mum might not feel like going, without Susanna.'

'But Dad's coming.' He chewed loudly, giving me unwanted vistas of masticated food. I made a noncommittal noise.

'Have you got a birthday present for your sister?'

'Um.' He considered. 'Yeah, I think Mum got me one. Have you?'

I had bought her a book that had made a lasting impression on me at around her age: *The Diary of Anne Frank*. I'd bought it hoping it might help put her own problems in perspective.

'She doesn't read books, she only reads dumb girls' magazines,' Jake said. I shrugged. A feeling of failure was setting in. I told Gayle she could pick out all the pink carnations and take them home if she liked.

Mim hadn't surfaced by the time Dr Garrett arrived to check on her. She was awake but groggy, and her face still had that dull, listless quality. Her skin looked like putty.

'Has Susanna —?'

'She went to Ruth's,' I said gently. 'She's going to stay there tomorrow. But with any luck she's just making her point, and after that it'll all blow over.'

Tracey Garrett and I had agreed that Susanna was hell-bent on punishing her mother in the most effective way possible, and any further attempts to dissuade her would be futile. Mim showed no inclination to get up. I thought I would leave

Tracey alone with her, hoping the doctor might find a way to deliver our psychologically sound lecture on removing the contentious Dave from her life.

As I retreated, Mim startled me by sitting up in bed. 'Lou – will you ring Jack for me?'

'Ring Jack?'

'The birthday dinner, we'll have to tell him it's all off. And tell him – why. That it's all my fault. Would you mind?' Two fat tears rolled down her cheeks. I looked away, pity for Mim and cold fury at Jack churning my innards.

'Of course I'll speak to him. But Mim –' I looked at Tracey, 'it's *not* all your fault. Please try and see that blame doesn't come into things like this.' I stopped. I wanted to tell her that there was another person prodigiously at fault, at least as much to blame, and that iniquitous cad was her precious Jack. But I knew I could not say this now, or, perhaps, at any time in the future.

I had an inspiration. 'Mim, if it were me in this position instead of you, you'd see it differently. You wouldn't tell *me* it was all my fault, because you wouldn't see it in those terms . . .' I ground to a halt, only too aware that I wasn't getting through. Mim had higher, more exacting standards for herself than for others, that was the trouble. The excuses she was able to wring from the air for other people simply did not apply to her own conduct.

Tracey threw me a consoling grimace. Later she told me wryly she had found it as easy as pie to drop the Dave word. Mim hadn't evinced even the faintest spark of curiosity about how she knew their secret. 'Just lay there passively while I spouted our guff about patient-falling-for-therapist risks. You know, methinks she'd already planned to give him the brush-off herself, amazing though it may seem, and no help needed from you or yours truly.'

'Well, I'll believe it when it happens.' Still, I thought, conceivably this business had been a learning curve for Mim. A more precipitous curve than any of us might have chosen, but perhaps it had enabled her to grow a tender skin, the first stage in producing the type of protective covering the rest of us took for granted. Not that Mim would ever be as thick-skinned as anybody else. Compared with hers, my own self-protective layer was more like a carapace.

Jake mooched up and reminded me that it was Friday. Friday nights were sacrosanct in Mim's house. Everything stopped for Jack's TV show. The fact that Mim was now lying horizontal in bed instead of eagerly switching on the set, hadn't even expressed a desire to see the program, brought home to me the gravity of her condition in a way that nothing else had.

'We'd better tape it for her and Sus,' Jake said. He was keen to watch it himself. I, on the other hand, felt I had had enough of Jack to last me for quite some time.

Motivated primarily by the urge to put off ringing him, and only partly to avoid cooking, I decided to take Jake out for a pizza. His enthusiasm took me by surprise and engendered a guilty pang. Until now, I had tried fairly successfully to ignore him.

I was further enlightened to find that on his own and away from the provocative presence of his sister, he was reasonably engaging company. He told me more about the Special Air Service and its toughening regimen than I needed to know, but once the topic had been introduced I could sit back and let the hair-raising details wash over me. Drinking Chianti from a raffia carafe and munching spicy pepperoni pizza, I felt fleetingly like a student again.

The feeling was abruptly terminated when the sparky young waitress asked me if I or my son would like anything for afters.

We said simultaneously, 'He's not my son,' and 'She's not my mum', and grinned at each other. I was relieved that we were not related in this way, but also disquietingly conscious that I had felt, admittedly for the merest nanosecond, a pinprick of regret.

We both ordered gelato. I watched Jake tucking into a huge dish of four different varieties, his hair flopping over his face like Mim's. He seemed perfectly content, oblivious to the tensions swirling around his home and his mother's distress. Was this really the case? Unsure whether it was even wise to raise the subject, I said experimentally, 'I think your mum's a bit upset about Susanna staying away for her birthday.'

He grunted. I took this to indicate advanced lack of interest, but he was concentrating on piling his spoon with a tower of ice cream that included every flavour on the plate. As he manoeuvred it sideways into his mouth he said, 'She shouldn't of gone with Dave.'

'Well –' I was intrigued to see that he appeared to be taking a moral position, and all at sea as to the type of position I ought to be taking.

Jake added, 'She knew Sus was stuck on him.'

'Mmm. All the same, she didn't mean to hurt Sus.'

'She shouldn't of done it, then.'

That seemed to wrap it up. He started scraping his plate, and I drank the rest of my wine. It all seemed so straightforward, the way Jake spelled it out.

He showed no reaction when we got home to find Mim still in bed and unresponsive, but neither did he object to my suggestion that he take her some soup and toast. I was not looking forward to calling Jack. And after I'd hung up, I wondered if my extreme aversion to the idea had been some kind of premonition.

I was relieved initially when his answering machine clicked on after three rings. Jack's sonorous voice announced: 'This is my all-singing, all-dancing answering machine. Not. It can't do fucking much, but it can take a message. You can forever hold onto your piece, or you can speak now, or both.'

I said, 'Jack, that's a bloody sexist message because I haven't got a piece to hold onto. As you well know. Listen, I'm only ringing you grudgingly and with the utmost reluctance, because Mim is out of action. Susanna's birthday dinner is off tomorrow, on account of she's –'

A woman's voice cut in. 'Lou? That has to be you! It could be no-one else on the planet. I thought you were still in the States!'

It was a mellow, breathy, womanly voice that I hadn't heard for a year or more, and I recognised it instantly. '*Bess!* I thought you and Roland were away on –'

'We were, we were, we've been in Jamaica for a whole gorgeous month, on the most wonderful holiday. We rented *the* most divine villa near Port Antonio. You absolutely have to come next time! Errol Flynn used to stay there, and possibly Somerset Maugham. We only got back yesterday, I'm definitively jet-lagged!'

Cynthia once observed that Bess always spoke in superlatives and exclamation marks. It was quite true, and we had added exaggeration and paradox to the list. We had all, including Cyn, said it with affection. Everyone loved Bess.

'We took the girls out of school. So wicked, but we convinced the Head – so terrifying, she reminds me of Mrs Danvers – that it was going to be molto educational! Lies, lies, all lies! It was hedonism, pure and simple. Not one improving book or cultural pursuit in sight. Just trashy novels, tourist traps, gluttony and sloth. Pure bliss. I put on five pounds. But why am I telling you this when you're here, in the flesh? When can we get together? Let's make a plan!'

We lined up a girls' lunch with Mim and a dinner date to include Roland. Bess said she would consult his diary and ring me back. Roland was a very British stockbroker, handsome, rich and well connected. They lived in Surrey in a Jacobean manor house with live-in help, stables, tennis court and swimming pool. Bess and high style had always, even at university, been irresistibly entwined.

'Well, darling, I'd better love and leave you –'

'Hang on, Bess.' There was something else, I knew, that we hadn't touched on, that we hadn't even skirmished with. That we both had, just possibly, been avoiding. I said casually, 'Is Jack there?' I felt my heart rate go up.

'Not right this minute. Soon – he should be back soon. Don't worry, I'll give him the message.'

'Is Roland with you?'

'Oh no, darling, he never leaves the office till late. Especially after a naughty holiday. All those mountains of boring paperwork to catch up on.'

I swallowed. My mouth was dry. 'Bessie, not to put too fine a point on it or anything, but what are you doing at Jack's?' There was probably an innocent explanation, I told myself. Then I pictured Bess: Jean Harlow hair, creamy skin, hourglass figure with Rubenesque tendencies. With her green eyes and sunny, tropical personality, Bess always appeared the very embodiment of innocence. Which only showed how misleading an embodiment could be.

'Don't be too hard on me, Lou. I know it's absolutely dreadfully sinful.'

My heartbeat raced in my ear. 'Bess. I don't know what to say . . .'

'Don't say anything, darling. Much the best thing. No, you must scold and berate me, I deserve it all. I've descended into a den of iniquity, haven't I? Do you think I'm completely unredeemable, or can I be salvaged?'

'How long has it been going on?' Those wretched song titles again, I thought, clinging around me like cobwebs.

'Rather a long time,' Bess said in a small, little girl's voice. 'Rather a long time, you see.'

'Like, how long?'

'Like, oh, a year.'

'A year.'

'At full strength.'

Something about the way she said the last three words made me suddenly suspicious. 'And at half strength?'

After a long pause, she said with disarming frankness, 'We're not talking just *exclusively* this year, to be brutally honest.'

'Not? Jesus.'

'Yes. There have been bits and pieces for a – for some time. But the vast majority of things have taken place *this* year, if you know what I mean. The *meaningful* bits.'

'Is it serious?' Insofar as anything could ever be serious with Jack, I qualified mentally.

'Serious. Well, you could say it's getting a little bit that way. Hideous, isn't it?'

'It is, rather.' We paused. I seemed to have lost the need to breathe. 'Does Roland know?'

'Only just. I spilled the dreaded beans – or most of them, I left out one or two – on this holiday.'

On this gluttonous, slothful, pure bliss holiday. 'How did he take the news?'

'Not particularly well at all, on the whole.'

'And, does –?' I couldn't bring myself to go on.

'Don't say it. No, she doesn't. Oh God, Lou, what shall we do?'

Her voice quavered, and suddenly we were both on the verge of disintegration. I remembered Susanna's question. She had asked me if I knew her dad's girlfriend, and I had dismissed the idea out of hand. Not only did he indeed turn out to have a girlfriend, but she was one of her mother's and my oldest and dearest friends.

'It's a bit of a bugger, isn't it?' Bess said tremulously.

'Not really. It's more of a holistic, no-holds-barred, everything but the iniquitous kitchen sink bugger.'

'And it might even take in the kitchen sink too. In due course.'

I trusted that the laugh we both dutifully gave sounded hollow to Bess's ears. It certainly did to mine. I wanted to ask Bess who she thought she was kidding. This was Jack, for heaven's sake, with whom she was almost sportively alluding to playing house.

'Bess, we must talk. We must talk urgently, without Mim. Could we meet tonight?'

'Well, that *is* sort of tricky, if you know what I mean. You see, I'm playing truant and I need to go home to the bosom of the famille fairly soon, and Jack's about to –'

'Yes, I get the picture,' I said hastily. We resolved instead to omit Mim from tomorrow's lunch. I decided not to tell Mim that I had spoken to Bess, and to withhold the other piece of news as well. Though well meant, I soon had reason to rue both of these decisions.

The phone rang the moment I put it down, and I picked it up like an automaton. I felt as if I were in a daze, punch-drunk from the weight and import of Bess's tidings. This is not an excuse for what I now did; it is more of an attempt at an explanation. When I made an effort to analyse things later, it was the responsibility of being the sole custodian of this momentous secret that I blamed. It was an onerous responsibility I was over-anxious to share.

'About time too, if I may say so. It always was impossible to get you off the phone when you were in full oratorial flight. Let alone get a word in oneself. Why hasn't Mim rung me?'

The caller was Cynthia, in full peremptory mode and sounding a good deal more coherent than she had earlier in the day. 'Who were you gossiping with, or with whom, if we are to be strictly strict?'

'Bess.'

'Bess? Is she back from her gallivanting? What mischief has she been making?'

'You may well ask.'

'I am asking. Come on, you can't keep these titbits to yourself. Don't be selfish — although I realise that's like asking the cat not to lick the cream.'

When I replayed the conversation, I remembered no break at this point. No prudent pause for thought, not even a hesitation. I just sailed on in.

'Bess is having an affair with Jack.'

I heard Cyn's sharp intake of breath, and then silence. 'Cyn?'

'I heard. Don't hurry me.' Her voice sounded gravelly, and I knew she was struggling with strong emotion. I knew because my own reaction had been a carbon copy. At last she said brokenly, 'Oh, Lord, Lord. Poor, poor Mim. That's why she was confined to bed, I couldn't understand it, I was worried about it all day —'

I cut in, 'Mim doesn't know.'

'*Mim doesn't know?*'

'No. Only me and now you. It's a bit of a relief to get it off my chest, I can tell you.' It was a relief to unload it onto someone else's shoulders, and I felt a physical lightening as I said it. However, it required a radical rearrangement of mind-set to think of Cynthia as a psychological prop. I was momentarily diverted by the process.

Cyn repeated loudly, 'I said, what kind of affair?'

'What kind? Is there more than one?'

'Is it just a fling, Lou, a one-night stand?' The hope was audible in her voice. 'Or – is it not?'

'Not. She says it's been going on for years.'

'For *years*? With *Jack*?'

Cyn's repetitions were beginning to get on my nerves, but I empathised with the sentiment. 'Yes, Bess and Jack, and absolutely full-on for this year. They're contemplating a ménage à deux. I know it sounds beyond the bounds of possibility, for either of them, but there it is.'

'Perhaps that's just it,' Cyn said wonderingly. 'They're so alike – well, only in *that* particular way, it goes without saying. Perhaps each one is attracted by that . . . that *fecklessness* in the other, and feels challenged to tame it.'

'Fecklessness? You mean rampant promiscuity?'

'That's not like you, to be judgemental about another's sexual proclivities. No, I tell a lie, it's entirely like you. It's your own moral turpitude for which you reserve your whole, uncritical armament of approbation.'

'Cyn, your charm is without peer.'

I paused to marvel at the way, even in the throes of a discussion of some solemnity, our latent antipathies insisted on surfacing. The same thing must have crossed Cyn's mind, as she said quickly, 'You say Mim definitely doesn't know?'

'Yes. Why don't you listen?'

'Why didn't you tell her?'

I groaned aloud. 'Cyn, I've had a shitty day. God knows, yesterday was hellish enough, but in some ways I think today transcends it. There was Gayle's stealing, and Susanna's birthday fiasco –'

I bit back the words, but it was too late. Cyn pounced on them, wanting every last detail. I furnished a sketchy account of both events. I could tell she was deeply hurt that she had been omitted from the birthday plans, and told her lamely that it was just a family affair. This only seemed to make matters worse. I knew Mim had always insisted on encouraging Cyn to think of herself as a member of the family, which, indeed, had been one of the long-running conflicts between mother and daughter. It was yet another of the predicaments for which Mim's all-encompassing sweet nature precluded any easy solution.

Cyn wanted to prolong the conversation, to dissect the Bess–Jack axis, to assign guilt and blame, betrayals and, more ominously, duties. If I had been more alert and on the ball I would have picked right up on that. Instead I cut her off ruthlessly. Already I regretted having told her anything, but nowhere near as much as I was soon to regret it.

12

SLEEP WAS STILL A long way off. There were three more phone calls, all for me, all from men, and none of them welcome. I gave them short shrift. One was Stuart, ringing to say he was thinking of me. I told him I was too tired to think of anyone. Particularly you, I added malevolently, but he seemed to take this as my little joke. The second call was from Sam.

'Lou, darling, I've had the worst night of my life. I was picturing you with somebody else and it was gut-wrenching. I felt sick. I *was* sick, I vomited twice. It was the most refined torture I've ever experienced. I was tossing and turning – I had to go and sleep on the couch, in front of the TV. I hardly slept at all. Did you get my message?'

'What?'

'I left a message with him – I *knew* he wouldn't give it to you, the prick. I'm coming over, I can't stand being apart any more. I think I can get there next week. Lou – this guy, this *bastard*, he's a bloody Yank, isn't he? Where did you meet him?'

He thinks it's Dave, I thought. 'Sam, I can't go into any of this right now. I've well and truly had it up to here for today and I'm going to bed.'

'Darling, this is not just anyone, this is me, Sam who loves you, remember? More than anything in the world. Why are you *doing* this? What's going on there?'

I said sharply, 'You went back to your wife, remember?'

'Oh, don't remind me. I push the replay button a thousand times a day. But let's fast-forward to next week –'

'I can't even think of anything like that now, I told you. I'm totally buggered.'

'Who *is* this guy? You're never usually tired like this, you're giving me nightmares. You didn't meet him in New York, did you? When you were with me? Do you – God, I can't bring myself to say this – you don't actually *like* this scumbag?'

The thought of liking Stuart provoked a savage urge to laugh. Before I could respond Sam hurtled on frantically, sounding as if he was hyperventilating. 'Don't answer that, I'd rather not know. I know, I know, it's all my fault if you've got involved with someone else, I *know* that. But I'm leaving Ingrid, I can't stand being separated from you another second. I'm coming over, whatever you say. We'll never be apart again.'

'Sam, please don't do anything irrevocable. I mean it.' I can't believe I'm saying this, I thought. Sam has just said the words that I have longed so desperately and for so long to hear him say, and I am urging discretion. What's more, I am oddly detached, even faintly amused, as if I am an observer at someone else's private melodrama.

Later, in daylight, I knew the reality would hit me and I might see things differently. But that night, alone in Mim's kitchen, I felt more involved in her troubles than my own. Where that was concerned I could see the ironies, only too clearly. In Mim's misfortunes I could find no prospect of light relief.

It occurred to me that I felt towards myself rather as Daria must have felt when she was setting out to compile her various case histories. A little like a classical deity, Aphrodite perhaps, loftily surveying the tangled webs of her subjects' love lives. Or Shakespeare, as he contemplated his poor players strutting and fretting their hour upon the stage. Daria would enjoy being compared with Shakespeare, even more perhaps with Aphrodite. I had a strong compulsion to ring her, to hear her tinkling laugh, but it was too late in the evening. I made a mental note to call her the next day.

As I got up to drag myself off to bed, the telephone shrilled again. The wall clock, a nineteenth century ship's brass that was never wrong, showed midnight advancing at speed, and I was tempted to ignore the bell. Daria's words about the phone, how without it Sam might effectively be on the moon, came back to me. It stopped, then rang again at once. I gave in reluctantly. It was Jack.

'Hallo, daarling.' His voice curled around the word, milking it for all it was worth.

I almost snarled, 'Jack, you're rumbled.'

There was the ghost of a pause, and then a tentative chuckle. In Jack's repertoire of appreciative noises, an encompassing portfolio that ranged from the belly laugh to the ironic grunt, it qualified as sheepish.

'The cat's leapt right out of the bag, matey. Your cover's blown and white-anted and about to topple.'

There was another pause. In any normal conversation with Jack, a hiatus was unusual, even remarkable.

'Is this entirely necessary and rational, darling? Can't we keep it entre nous, just our little secret?'

I was incensed by his tone, veering between the hangdog and the ingratiating. 'Our *grubby* little secret? On your well-worn "what she doesn't know won't hurt her" principle?'

'Well, one hesitates to rock the boat, doesn't one? Unless it becomes absolutely essential.'

'And it isn't?'

He slipped back into character. 'Nothing changes my feelings for you, sweetheart. Say the word, or sing the note, and I will dance to your tune. Not that I dance very well. I perform some other quotidian tasks rather better, or so they tell me.'

I said heavily, 'Jack, why did it have to be Bess?'

'Why do you think, petal? You made me do it.'

'Of all the women you could have chosen.' The shocking sadness of it swept over me like a sandstorm, stinging my face.

'You rejected me. You have to see that Bessie is all your fault.'

'You can stuff that bullshit up your bum.'

'I'll overlook your intemperate schoolgirl language, just this once. I hold no grudges, the door is still open. You can at once assuage your guilt and eliminate the above-mentioned problem. I can be there to pick you up in ten minutes.'

I was in no mood for this gamy humour. It struck me as particularly tasteless, even for Jack. It was also spectacularly disloyal to Bess, an area of thinking I didn't much want to engage with just then. I breathed in deeply.

'Jack, no doubt you're aware of why I called before. Don't even think of showing up for dinner tomorrow, the birthday girl's pulled out and it's all off. Susanna's had a dreadful row with Mim over Dave Benwell, and if you're not feeling fucking ashamed for your despicable part in that, I hope your dick falls off and you get anal fissures before finally expiring with apoplexy.'

I slammed the phone down, then wrenched it off the hook and left it dangling. The cathartic blast of satisfaction I derived from this last intemperate schoolgirl diatribe rapidly dispersed, leaving me with a sour taste in the mouth and a churning stomach that I diagnosed as acute apprehension. I felt anger almost equally apportioned between Bess and Jack, but when I set eyes on Bess the next day the anger fell away.

We had arranged to meet in the city at a smart new place in the Haymarket. It was Bess's suggestion and she was late, as I expected her to be. Bess was invariably late; it was built into her personality and we always said it was genetic.

Mim hadn't made an appearance before I left, sparing me the need to lie about my appointment with Bess. It made a change to have some cause for relief. I felt the day might not abound in consolations. My physical condition had improved, but the unsettled queasiness refused to go away. When Bess arrived, cutting a trajectory through the restaurant like a shooting star, I was rereading the menu, trying to find something I felt like eating.

Resplendent was the word we had commonly used about Bess. It was still apt: tall and voluptuous, narrow waisted, full bosomed, immaculately groomed, she was the epitome of a certain ideal of femininity. If it was a style that was not entirely fashionable, that indeed was somewhat passé, this was neither here nor there with males in general. She glowed, and men, especially the more traditionally masculine variety, gravitated towards Bessie like moths to the candle.

Bess's father was an Australian career diplomat, and she had lived in a number of different countries since childhood. As a fresher she had impressed us with her savoir faire, having a hands-on familiarity with the premier grand crus of Bordeaux and a fount of knowledge about the amatory liaisons of the Bloomsbury Group, as well as the differences between Freud and Jung – something that all these years later I was still hazy about. I remembered her airily defining existentialism and reeling off the composers who comprised Les Six. She told us casually that she had been seduced at the age of fourteen by a French saxophonist, on an ocean liner traversing the Suez Canal.

Whereas I thought of some of us, myself and perhaps Cynthia in particular, as existing in a state of perpetual adolescence, Bess seemed always to have been grown-up and fully formed. She was the one friend I would have described as womanly, and that was as true of her as an undergraduate as it was now, twenty years on. But her culture and her sophistication were worn lightly and easily, like a floaty chiffon scarf and a chic straw hat.

'Oh, Lou, darling!' I stood up and she put her arms, clad smartly in herringbone tweed, around me. I was enveloped in a cloud of tea rose. Again, she had never strayed from this perfume, and it defined her like an olfactory trademark.

'I've been dastardly, haven't I? Will you ever forgive me?'

She gazed at me with her long, curled eyelashes fluttering. Seduced by this appearance, men, and less often women, regularly made the mistake of underestimating Bess. In reality she was one of the most astute people I knew. And unlike Cynthia, her IQ was as high on the emotional as the intellectual table.

We looked at each other and it seemed, to my relief, that we were equally alive to the poignancy of the situation.

'Why did it have to be Jack?'

I had put to him the equivalent question and received a

frivolous reply. Bess took it in the spirit it was offered. She leaned her elbows on the table and laced her ring-laden fingers, her eyes never leaving my face.

'I've asked myself that a hundred thousand times. Why Jack, of all people? There's only one answer I can give you, Lou, and it's the only true one, unlikely as it may seem. We fell in love. Headlong and hopelessly. Well, we plummeted in lust first, and the one thing led to the other. I've always hoped you'd be one of the few people to really understand, because that was how it was with you and Sam.'

I nodded. That was how it was, although for us it seemed there had been no interval between lust and love. 'Except –'

'Except for the loyalty factor. Except that it's Jack and Mim, the friends of our youth, and now all the babies. Susanna and Timmy, I can never get the hang of calling him Jake, can you? and Daisy and Lizzie. Yes, except that it's in the family, aye, and there's the rub.'

And if Ingrid had been the friend of my youth, and if I had known Fergus and Hannah Tinker better, there too might have been the rub. Sam and I were different, I had always told myself. Was this simply a failure of the imagination?

'And Roland,' I reminded her.

'And dear Roland, of course.'

'And except that –' I was unsure how to go on. 'Except that Jack –'

Bess rushed to my rescue. 'Except that Jack's a shocking letch. I know, he's never been what you might call the faithful suburban type. Well, neither have I, if we're talking strict and unadulterated truth. I don't know, Lou, I can't explain it. Maybe you change when you get older. For the first time I feel that I *could* be faithful. If I really had to, if my life depended on it, if you know what I mean!'

Bess's uninhibited laugh and rollicking attitude to life were the assets most prized by her friends. I was glad to see neither had been dulled by time. Jack's seducing zeal came forcibly to mind. I thought: he and Bess were two highly sexed combustion engines set on a collision course. The animal attraction between them was understandable and must have been inevitible. The curiosity was that it had taken so long to ignite.

The waiter, a good-looking young Milanese, arrived and took our orders. Bess engaged him in a flirtatious discussion of the options. I could see he found her, and her coquettish stumbling Italian, distinctly fetching.

I said slowly, 'I can absolutely see how it could have happened. I suppose it's more the – the continuing basis I can't quite . . . well, you know, *Jack*?'

'Oh, I know. He's wholly deplorable, a disgraceful naughty fellow, not at all sensitive and new age. But I'm not sure I want a new age type of man. I've had one a bit, with Roland. Well, not really, but he did have *some* enlightened tendencies. He's an absolute darling, of course, in every way, *except*,' she winked at me significantly, 'the one that matters.'

Roland: affectionate, genial, entertaining, the perfect host. He and Bess had seemed a copybook couple. But Bess always maintained that after the first year or so of marriage they never had any sex. She had claimed this before and after their two daughters, Daisy and Lizzie, were born.

I remembered once sitting in a restaurant with Bess, Cynthia and Mim, when Bessie leant across the table and announced loudly, 'We never have any sex *at all*. Roland just doesn't seem to have any libido, and he won't discuss it.' It was a quiet, subdued restaurant that we had selected specially so we could talk, and Bess had electrified the room.

Cyn, always a stickler for accuracy, promptly objected. 'You must have had sex at least twice. You have two children. Or isn't Roland the father?'

'We did, yes. We actually did have it two times, right out of the blue, and on each occasion I got a bun in the oven. It was quite uncanny.'

In spite of our noisy scepticism and obsessive questioning over the years, Bess never wavered from this story. Both Daisy and Lizzie did indeed take after Roland and were unmistakeably his children, but it became received wisdom that Bess and Roland had a celibate relationship.

Bess had filled in the gaps, as she put it, with keen applicants for the vacant position. She viewed her catchment area with a democratic eye, cutting a clandestine swathe through the village and once scalping the local catholic priest. Another year, extensive renovations to the manor provided a fruitful period, with a crop of Slavic woodworkers and stonemasons.

We used to say that Bess was a walking, talking collage of the S-words: seductive, sultry, sensual, salacious, salivating and, withal, sweet. Her profound sexiness meant that there was never a shortage of applicants, one of the unequal facts of life that inspired Cyn's envy. It was a tribute to Bess's nature that Cyn did not hold this rampant sex appeal against her.

Now Bess leaned towards me again, her voice husky, and I knew some other lubricious revelation was about to come my way. I didn't think I really wanted to hear it.

'We both know Jack too well, Lou, to have any illusions about him. We go back too long. But perhaps you don't know him in a *certain way*, like I do?'

There was a hint of a question. I realised Bess was not entirely confident about Jack's and my libidinous history. I hurried to reassure her.

'No, I don't, absolutely not.'

'You see, Lou, the point is that Jack's *all man*.' Her eyes sparkled. 'The repertoire! The staying power! Whoo hoo! I've never had anything like it in my life, and that's saying something even if I say so myself. It's like being a teenager again. No, much better than that, it's like having the hormones of teenagers and the expertise, the *techniques*,' she peered at me archly, 'of louche characters like us. Do you remember when we were students, how we used to endlessly discuss,' she lowered her voice, 'the ins and outs of *manual dexterity*?'

Both Cynthia and Bess were always willing and eager to discuss intimate matters in considerable detail. This had formed a strong bond between them, Bess functioning as something of an erotic mentor for Cyn, who used the more worldly-wise young woman as a sounding board for her theories. The fact that they were located at opposite ends of the scale of carnal achievement never drove a wedge between them. The student Cynthia had viewed Bess as a romantic, swashbuckling figure, deriving a wistful vicarious pleasure from her conquests. This, I speculated, may now have changed irrevocably.

'He. Is. Quite. Incredible, Lou. Believe me.'

'Wow. Gosh. Well, I suppose he's had a lot of practice.'

Bess gurgled appreciatively. 'He's getting a great deal more now, I can tell you!'

I saw it dawn on her that the tone of the conversation had strayed unbecomingly from its earlier gravitas. She sobered up visibly, and her sea-green eyes met mine with a rueful flicker.

'I shouldn't talk this way about Mim's husband, should I?' She smacked her hand. 'Louie, all I can say in my defence, and it's a pissweak defence, I know, is that their marriage had well and truly done its dash by the time – when we *really* got stuck into it, as it were.'

'When did –?'

'Well, we do have quite a bit of history. He actually tried to get me to leap into bed with him before he and Mim became an item. And – oh dear, this is *very* bad – and afterwards, too, I have a terrible feeling.' She grimaced and squealed. 'Ooh, he's such a rascal and a reprobate, I sometimes forget what a nefarious past he has. Well, present too, but who am I to talk?'

She was laughing gaily again, but I was anxious. '*Did* you?'

'What do you think I am? Not on the eve of their marriage, I have *some* scruples, Lou! And I was mad about that dreadful double bass player at the time. Although it has crossed my mind to wonder what would have happened if I had. Would they have gone ahead with it? Would he and I have got married instead? And if so, where would we be now? I'd have a whole quiverful of kids instead of only two, that's for sure!'

She giggled, in the confidential, conspiratorial way she had, forking risotto into her shiny carmine-coloured mouth with transparent enjoyment. I ate slowly, not tasting the food. Afterwards, I couldn't recall what I had eaten.

Eventually, fortified by pinot grigio, we dragged ourselves around to the matter of Miriam. It was an uncomfortable subject for both of us. I told Bess that assuming she and Jack weren't about to install themselves under the same roof, we should for the time being keep things under wraps. Bess looked mightily relieved.

'Mim's got all this other stuff to deal with. She's got a gargantuan serve on her plate, and she's not coping at all well. *I* know it's splitsville with Jack and has been for ages, *you* know it, even *she* knows it, but it hasn't sunk in yet.' It's probably never going to sink in either, I thought, and saw that Bess was thinking exactly the same thing.

'She needs to regain her strength, get shot of bloody Dave and rebuild the relationship with Susanna. She's not up to anything else right now.'

There was another reason for this speech, a private item on my agenda that I kept from Bess. I was hoping that her dalliance with Jack might be close to running its course. Given the randy track records of the couple in question, I thought this was a more than reasonable assumption. The idea of Jack and Bess becoming a domestic item seemed to me self-evidently preposterous. With any luck, one or other of them would plummet in lust with another candidate next week and Mim need never be the wiser. I was certain that this would be the happiest outcome.

I may as well have saved my breath. The agreement became a historical irrelevance the moment I pushed open the gate of Mim's house and saw a motorcycle blocking the path. I knew whose bike it was and I knew instantly what it meant. The meaning hit me like an ice-pick in the head. I repented my intemperate conversation with Cyn, and cursed the impatient way I had brushed her aside.

I stood in the drive before going in, thinking furiously. Mim, the most loyal of friends, must be deeply wounded by Bess's actions. Except that she wouldn't regard them as a betrayal; she would undoubtedly find some other way of looking at the situation. As hard as I tried, I couldn't think what this might be.

They were in the sitting room drinking in front of the fire. The hi-fi was playing Dionne Warwick's 'Heartbreaker'. I thought that was a bad sign. It was only late afternoon, but bottles of gin and vodka, tonic and orange juice, glasses and an ice bucket in the shape of a top hat were lined up on the mantelpiece.

Both women turned to look at me as I came in. I was glad

to see that Mim was dressed. She was wearing comfort clothes – a misshapen woollen skirt she'd had for years, baggy old Aran sweater and fleecy bootie slippers. It may have been my imagination, but I thought she radiated despair.

Cyn plunged in before I could say anything. 'I know you'll disagree with me, Lou, but I felt I had to let Mim know about Bess and Jack. I expect they thought they were sparing her feelings in keeping it from her. However,' she paused, fixing me with her bulging, unblinking stare, 'I know that if it were me and this had been going on behind my back for years with no-one telling me, I would feel humiliated. Where moral questions are concerned, my rule of thumb, and I've found it stands the test of time, has always been to ask myself: how would *I* like to be treated in the circumstances?'

Cyn aimed this speech at me with a stentorian precision. It had a rehearsed quality, and I guessed she had thought deeply about it and my reaction, and wanted to pre-empt expected objections. There was also a careful emphasis on the beginnings and endings of words, a defiant claim to sobriety that convinced me not a whit. She certainly looked as if she had been up all night. Her hair was more than normally lank and unwashed and her face, heavily scored with black lines around the eyes, looked almost more sickly than Mim's.

Mim came in at the tail end. 'I'm glad she told me, Lou. They – Bessie and Jack – they wouldn't have known how to do it, I can see that. They wouldn't have been *able* to do it themselves.' She was sitting very still, just as she had stood on the stairs. Cyn, on the other hand, was shifting restlessly in her seat, scratching her head and picking at her nails. They were torn raggedly, I noticed.

I said, 'Mim, you do understand that it's only this year that they've been involved?'

'She realises that, thank you, Lou. All the previous times were just peccadilloes that didn't count. Mim knows that Jack always had plenty of casual encounters with other people, and so did Bess, of course, so it wasn't particularly surprising that they coincided now and again.'

Just shut up, Cyn, I thought. I walked over to Mim's chair and hugged her. Her body felt stiff and unyielding, and her cheek against mine was cold. But she gave me a little smile that smote my heart. I poured myself a stiff vodka and tonic.

'I know Bessie would never have started a relationship with Jack unless she thought we, I mean Jack and I, had – until we had . . .' she came to a faltering stop, then rallied and continued tonelessly. 'I needed to have a sign like this, that our marriage is over. I know I've been closing my eyes to it, hanging on to stupid hopes. It's a kind of *Biblical* sign, isn't it, like Gideon when he put the fleece out in the night, and it rained all round it but the wool was dry? And that was the proof he needed that God existed? It *was* Gideon, wasn't it?'

She's rambling, I thought, she's losing it. I looked sideways at Cyn. She carefully avoided my eyes. Her frowning gaze was fixed steadily on Mim, who continued in the same unemotional monotone.

'I've been neglecting everybody in the house, haven't I? And everything's been going to pieces around me, only I've been too preoccupied and self-absorbed to see it. Look at Gayle. It did actually occur to me that she might have been taking money, for a while, but I couldn't bring myself to do anything about it. And then Dave. My own daughter's *teacher*. Twenty-four years old. What was I thinking of? I mean, it's insane behaviour, isn't it? By any standards. I must be temporarily mad. At least I hope it's temporary. No wonder Susanna despises me. No wonder she wanted to go somewhere else for her birthday. Who could blame her? I'd want to too, if I had a mother like me.'

About halfway through this, Mim closed her eyes and started swaying from side to side. Her voice had risen steadily in intensity until the room seemed to vibrate with agitation. It was the longest speech I could ever recollect hearing from Mim, and the most alarming. Before Cyn or I could say anything she had started off again.

'I should have known Jack had somebody else, somebody special. All the signs were there. And of course it would be Bess. He always adored Lou and Bess, and as Lou wasn't here, then it had to be Bessie.'

She was talking about me, I realised, as if I was not present. And as if Cynthia was not there either. Normally, Mim's scrupulous tact would have prevented her singling out Bess and me like this, in case it offended Cyn. Not, I was sure, that Cyn harboured any illusions whatsoever about Jack's feelings. I stole a glance at her. I couldn't tell if she was offended, but she definitely looked worried.

I saw Mim's eyes open abruptly and swivel round the room, as if she had suddenly become aware she was not alone. But she looked straight ahead and not at either of us as she continued, 'It's a relief that it's Bess, and not some unknown person. It means that we can all go on seeing one another in the same old way we always have. There'll just be a small change of – of alignment. It's the best possible outcome, really, when you think about it like that. It keeps everything in the family.'

So this would be Mim's way out, her means of rationalising the situation and letting Bess off the hook. She was trying to convince herself, it was plain. She was nodding and speaking directly to herself, in a sensible no-nonsense tone. *In the family*. The selfsame, telling phrase that Bess had used. Whereas for her it had been a negative, a cause for genuine self-reproach, Mim was resolved to see it as a plus. Bess was fortunate in having no guilt trip unloaded on her head. Ingrid, I guessed, would be nowhere near as selfless. But then, I was not in the family, was I?

I said tentatively, 'I don't know, Mim. They're probably not going to be a permanent part of the landscape.'

I wanted to go further, and cast aspersions on the credentials and staying power of Jack and Bess, but the last thing I wanted was to further upset Mim. My innocuous remark, however, caused Cyn's chin to jut at an ominous angle.

'Well, we can't be sure of that, Lou, and it's better if Mim assumes the worst. As she says, there are certain advantages in the arrangement. Daisy and Lizzie get on well with Susanna and Jake, don't they? So access visits shouldn't be a problem. Assuming that the girls go with Bess after the divorce, that is. Or do you think Roland will want to contest custody?'

This was so far ahead of where we were at that it could have been coming from another planet. I could see Mim start to sway again as she tried to grapple with the implications of horror words like divorce, access and custody. They were words, I was certain, that had never crossed her mind until this moment.

'Let's not get into wild speculation, Cyn, for pete's sake,' I said hastily, but it was too late. The blood drained from Mim's already white face, and she pitched forward. I sprang out of my chair and gripped her by the shoulders.

'Put your head down between your knees and breathe deeply.' Above her bent head I glared at Cyn, who was looking stunned. 'Get water!' I spat at her.

Was it really less than two days before that Stuart had hissed the very same words at me? I had the strange impression of things being circular, a sense not so much of parallel universes but of different patterns of life moving on parallel circuits, and now and again intersecting with an almost mischievous capriciousness.

I thought Mim would be better off back in bed, but my suggestion of a lie-down was rejected. Mim was unusually adamant that she wanted to stay up for the rest of the evening, and touchingly insistent that she derived comfort from our presence.

'You don't have to talk to me,' she said. 'Just having you here in the same room makes me feel a whole lot better.'

Just having Cyn there in the same room made me feel a whole lot worse, generally speaking, but I attempted to douse this feeling for Mim's sake. With a bit of help from me they had both put away enough alcohol for a rugger side, and I thought some rapid sustenance was of the essence. Comfort food, if Mim's haggard mien was any guide. I headed for the kitchen with Cynthia snapping at my heels.

Jake was kicking a ball in the garden with some friends. A single dim light bulb was attached to the garage wall, but from the noise I guessed most of the fun derived from collisions and flying tackles in the dark. The volume of yells and whoops suggested an entire football team, but when they tramped through the kitchen door I saw only two others, both regular visitors, an African boy and a Chinese. The three of them made a pleasing symmetry.

'Aren't we having dinner with Dad?'

'No, not tonight.'

'But why?' This was said in an unappealing whine.

'I told you why yesterday. Because Susanna's not here.' Jake's expression suggested this was a poor travesty of a reason.

'I'm starving. Can we have something to eat?'

I took 'we' to include his friends Billy and Emmanuel, who were looking both hopeful and hungry. A simple dish of Welsh rarebit with grilled bacon and tomatoes for six generated the usual power struggle with Cyn. She wanted me to look after the tea, an operation she made clear was way down in the pecking order. Normally I was happy to let her take over anything to do with manual labour, but now for some reason I was stubbornly reluctant to let her win. I was also of the firm opinion that everyone would be advantaged if Cynthia pottered off home. My tactfully phrased intimation along this line met with a derision that Cyn expressed unhesitatingly.

'I'm not leaving her to *you*. You're completely unsuited to looking after people when they're fragile. Look at you – you can't even make tea properly.'

'Might I take this chummy little opportunity to remind you that Mim nearly keeled over just now, as a result of your monumental tactlessness?'

When she saw that my method involved placing tea bags in cold mugs, Cyn had assumed command of the operation. She warmed the mugs with boiling water and spooned loose leaves into the pot. She added a crocheted tea cosy in the shape of a cockerel and assembled everything on a colourful tin tray adorned with a portrait of a Nigerian military dictator, now deceased.

'I gave Mim this cosy and tray, for her thirtieth birthday,' she said absently. 'Now that's done, I'll let you add the beer to the melted cheese and mustard. But make sure you measure it correctly. Yes, I got them at the local parish fete. St Bartholomew's. They do a very superior fete. It's most important to observe these landmark occasions in people's lives, isn't it?'

She was, I knew, throwing me an oblique but pointed hint that her own landmark birthday, the fortieth, was not far away. We were all approaching this milestone, but Cyn would arrive at it first. In a few days, in fact. The subject had been aired on several occasions since my arrival. Mim and I had promised to give her a party. An unwise promise, I was now thinking.

I ignored the hint and said disingenuously, 'St Bartholomew's, eh? Is that where you regularly worship, Cyn?'

'I don't *go* to church, Lou, don't be ridiculous. Keep stirring that cheese or it'll stick on the bottom. I'm an atheist, like all intelligent, right-thinking people. Your position would be *agnostic*, I expect.'

She pronounced the word as if it was the kind of wishy-washy excuse for a position that someone of my meagre intellectual gifts would adopt. The fact that it was an accurate assessment of my views annoyed me, as it was intended to.

I felt an urgent need to take a break from Cyn's company. 'I'll let you finish off the rarebit. I'm taking the tea in to Mim. She badly needs it.'

'It hasn't brewed yet. It has to stand for three to four minutes. Oh, all right then. Go in and put it down,' Cyn said with slow and exaggerated patience, as if talking to a dementia sufferer, 'and then it will be ready when the rest of the meal is ready. But don't stay there. I need you to butter the toast.'

'The boys can do that.' I made a face at her back. She turned round and saw the last throes of it. 'That's very babyish, as is your wont, and at nearly forty you should have grown out of it.'

She and I were not on speaking terms by the time we all sat down with trays on our laps to watch the tape of Jack's program 'Black and White in Colour'. Mim had seemed pleased to see Emmanuel and Billy, and I was touched when she surreptitiously went into the hall and combed her hair. I was not, however, at all sure whether Jack's show was a wise viewing choice under the circumstances. But Jake was adamant and Mim didn't want to disappoint him. It was also plain that she herself was anxious to see it. For the entire four years the program had been running, she had only ever missed one.

This time he was interviewing a prominent African American actor and stand-up comic whose fiancee had recently left him for another woman. Although this news was already in the public domain, Jack contrived to squeeze out a few fresh and juicy details. The material lent itself to the brand of masochistic humour the young comedian, whose name was Erwin Er, had made his own.

I admired the way Jack was able to commandeer more than his fair share of the laughs, while heading inexorably towards the emotional quicksands. He had started off asking Er about his childhood, moved to first sexual experiences (which marked the commencement of his lifelong difficulties with girls) and advanced to the more recent tribulations.

Having established that Er's previous entanglements with the opposite sex had been prolific but short-lived, Jack proceeded to fish for reasons. They turned out to be many and, if you liked that sort of thing, hilarious: body odour, bad breath, piles, a tendency to break wind at decisive moments. The three boys, I noticed, were rolling around on the floor. But Jack's terrier instincts told him there was something else. I had already guessed what it might be, but was hoping I was wrong.

'So you leave all these gorgeous women – or I should say, they leave you – in the core of their beings, unsatisfied? No staying power, basically?'

'Basically, I guess, none at all. Zilch.'

'Same pattern every time?'

'Sure. The problem in a nutshell.'

'You couldn't quite, shall we say, in the heat of the moments – moments being the operative word – couldn't quite *last the distance*? Couldn't quite *hold on*?' He turned to the studio audience. 'To all the ladies, I mean, you disreputable lot!'

Jack's contorted faces and suggestive eyebrow-raising made his meaning crystal clear to the onlookers, who roared. The jokey-blokey banter that preceded this denouement appeared to have lulled Er into a false sense of security. The camera close-up suggested that he hadn't expected this, although he played up to it manfully.

I had avoided looking at the boys, but could hear Jake in particular chortling extravagantly. I dared not look at Mim either, but Cyn, as ever, gave voice to the unspeakable.

'Does he mean he's a premature *ejaculator*? Is that what Jack's insinuating?' Neither of us answered, but she forged on regardless. 'How do his researchers *do* it? I mean, how do you find *out* that kind of thing about a person? Other than by close personal contact, I mean!'

Mim was next to me and she jerked her head in anguish, but there was more to come. Er's professional aplomb was stretched almost to breaking point as two people who seemed to know him inconveniently well were brought on. They turned out to be from a group therapy class he had attended in Los Angeles, and their testimonies, while judiciously skipping around the nitty-gritty, left no doubt that the comedian's lack of sexual prowess had been a source of trauma.

Halfway through this sequence Mim got up without saying anything and left the room. I waited for a while and then followed, flashing a warning look at Cynthia. I found Mim sitting on the stairs rocking and hugging her knees.

'I can't seem to get away from it, can I? That poor man, so embarrassing, the whole world knowing his secret.'

I hoped she was making the connection between his embarrassment about his secret and Jack's pivotal role in leaking it to the whole world. But I saw after a minute or two that she had another thing altogether on her mind. She was looking up at me with an almost fearful expression.

'I haven't said a word to anyone,' I promised, crossing my fingers.

'Tracey knew about it.' Being Mim, there was not a skerrick of accusation in the flat statement.

'Oh well, she's a doctor.'

'She's not his doctor, though.'

'No? Well, you know the medical profession. They have networks. They hear rumours. No secrets are safe with them.'

I was alarmed to see that this assertion, which I considered fairly unexceptionable, seemed to increase Mim's distress. A gale of laughter issued from the sitting room, overlaid by sustained applause.

'The end of the program,' Mim said. She sighed, a gentle, almost inaudible sigh. The background clapping formed an ironic counterpoint.

'You should go to bed, Mim.'

'Yes.'

She made no move. I sat down next to her on the stairs and hugged her. I saw Cynthia's head come round the door, take in the tête-à-tête and withdraw, leaving behind a gust of injured feeling.

'Susanna'll be back tomorrow, Mim. It's another day. You can both start afresh. Have a talk with her, I mean a really serious, long talk, and explain that you haven't been yourself, and why, but now that's all finished and over with and you want to put it behind you.'

'She'll be fourteen.' Mim's eyes were wide with a kind of sad wonderment.

'That's right. Only fourteen. You've got all the time in the world to put things right between you.' I gave her shoulder a squeeze.

'I'd like her brother to ring and wish her a happy birthday. Is it too late?'

It was just after ten-thirty. 'No, I don't think it's too late. They'll be up carousing, for sure.'

'I would, of course, but I know she won't want to hear my voice. Will you ask Jake for me, please? Would you mind? And see that he does it? I just feel terribly tired all of a sudden.'

I pulled her to her feet. She felt lifeless.

'Of course I will. You go and have a nice relaxing bath.' I watched her slowly climb the stairs. I called, 'Remember, Mim, tomorrow is a brand, spanking new day. The first dawn of the rest of your life!'

I tried to inject the pedestrian words with as much positive, sparkling enthusiasm as I could muster. She turned and gave me a small smile from the top of the stairs. It was too far off to see her eyes, but I knew she was humouring me out of the fondness of her heart.

13

CYNTHIA BLASTED ME WITH an accusing glare when I told her Mim had retired. She had helped herself generously to the port, using a large claret glass, I observed with disapproval. The four of them were watching an American cop show with a lead actor I rather liked.

'Jake, I'm sorry to butt in but your mum wants you to ring your sister before it's too late.' I glanced at the other two kids. 'Shouldn't you both be going home?'

'I've already said that, Lou, but apparently Emmanuel's mother is away and Billy's will be out late and is expecting him to stay the night. There are blow-up mattresses and sleeping bags in Jake's room.' I read Cyn's meaningful look. It said, problem children with no fathers.

Jake groaned and looked blank. 'What do I have to ring her for?'

'It's her birthday, Dumbo.'

'But I'm watching this.'

'Never mind. Your mum thinks it would be a nice idea and so do I. And so does Cyn,' I added sportingly.

'Well, anyhow, I can't ring her.'

'Why ever not?'

'Because I dunno where she is.'

'Jake. She's at Ruth's, remember?'

'But I don't know the number.'

'It's in your mum's address book.' I felt like Cynthia, spelling things out for a moron. 'Come on, it's in the kitchen, where it's always been. I'll take you there. And then you must all go to bed.'

There was a predictable chorus of dissent. Cyn sensed that I had included her. She reacted accordingly. 'In all fairness, Lou, I think we should let them watch the rest of the program.' She was rewarded with sycophantic smiles and nods.

'Only if they help clear up afterwards,' I said. I felt smugly that I had won that little round, at the expense of losing some points with the boys. Jake got to his feet, muttering rebelliously, and shuffled out with me.

Cyn called, 'I'd like to wish Susanna a happy birthday too. Call me when Jake's finished.'

Not on your bossy pestiferous nelly, I thought. In the kitchen I thrust Mim's dog-eared Roladex at Jake, whose body language expressed dumb and passive resistance.

'There. Under W for Webster, Daria and Ruth. And put me on after you've spoken to her, I want to speak to Daria.'

He dialled the number with maddening slowness. His side of the ensuing conversation consisted mainly of negative grunts and head-shaking, and I was quite unprepared for the bombshell that awaited me when he handed over the phone. Daria was already on the line. Her excited voice rang in my ear.

'The boy is saying they are not there, is that right, Louisa?'

'Who do you mean, exactly?'

'The girls, Ruth and Susanna, they are not there in your house?'

'No, they're at your house – your flat –'

'No, no, they are not!'

I was feeling slightly stupefied, a result of drink and tiredness. Daria detected this with her usual acuity.

'Louisa, you are absolutely totally certain they are not there? Is it possible they have entered the house, unseen?'

'Well, I don't – it's possible, I suppose. But why –?'

'Have you personally inspected inside Susanna's room?'

'Ah, no, I haven't personally –'

'Then run off, Louisa, and check it thoroughly, right away. Do not send the boy, go by yourself right now, and come straight back and tell me. I will wait on the telephone. Hurry up!'

I did as I was told, my mind spinning. Susanna's room was empty, but someone had been in and poignantly tidied away all the carelessly strewn clothes. Mim, that someone would have been. Mindful of Daria's instruction to check thoroughly, I found myself on my hands and knees looking under the bed. Before leaving I flung open the cupboard door and scrabbled inside.

'They're not in there, Daria. Nowhere in the room. Definitely.'

'And you are quite sure they are not anywhere else in the house?'

It quickly became plain to me that the girls had given us the slip. They had told Daria they were coming over here for Susanna's birthday dinner. They had told us they were going to stay there. And they had left Daria's at about five in the afternoon, carrying overnight bags.

'We must phone the police immediately! They have

disappeared, all dressed up in short skirts, on the way to your party, between our two houses. Some man has picked them up off the street, and . . .' Daria's voice, always so springy and light-hearted, fell apart.

I sat down on a chair. 'Now hang on, Daria, wait a minute. I don't think that's quite it.'

As rapidly as I could I filled her in about the rift between Susanna and Mim, and the cancellation of the birthday dinner.

'But Susanna is a kind girl, perhaps she has changed her mind? She has decided to forgive and forget, and come back to her mother after all?'

I suspected Daria did not really believe this, but I wondered if her view of Susanna was really so radically different from mine. I said emphatically, 'No, I don't think so. Look, I'm ninety-nine per cent sure she wouldn't have changed her mind. She was furious with Mim, absolutely white-hot livid.'

'But when my Ruth is flying off the handle, she is very soon cooling down, like a bowl of soup –'

'It's not like soup with Susanna at all. She holds grudges. She holds grudges big-time. They've been at loggerheads for days.'

'Then you are thinking they are deliberately telling us a lie about where they are going?'

The shock and hurt in Daria's voice had the effect of altering its timbre. She sounded like another person.

Jake had not said anything to the others and I found them all still slumped and absorbed in front of the TV. For a second I toyed with the idea of keeping the news from Cyn, but she turned on me.

'Why didn't you call me? Why do you always keep everyone to yourself? You knew very well I wanted to speak to Susanna.'

'I didn't call you out of consideration for your welfare, because I wanted to spare you a fruitless journey to the telephone. I didn't call you for the very good reason that she wasn't there.'

'Not there? Where was she, then?'

'We don't know.'

'Don't *know*? What are you saying?' Loud shushing noises came from the boys. Cyn stood up and pursued me into the kitchen. She carried, with a practised and remarkably steady hand, a brimming glass.

I said, 'Swilling our port from wine glasses now, are we?'

'There's plenty left for you, if that's what you're worried about.'

I outlined the situation, with a very bad grace. Cyn grasped its potential seriousness rather more readily than I had. She also insisted on waking Mim immediately.

'Of course we must tell her. It's her *daughter*. Wouldn't *you* like the elementary courtesy of being told if *your* fourteen-year-old daughter had disappeared?' She was halfway up the stairs. I trailed in her wake. She looked over her shoulder. 'No, I expect you'd prefer to leave her to fend for herself in the urban jungle.'

Mim's change of mood amazed me. She seemed instantly to grasp implications that had eluded me, and was out of bed and flinging on clothes before Cyn had finished. Her first decision, predictably, was to ring Jack in case the girls had headed over there. They hadn't, and Jack surprised me, and possibly Mim too, by saying he would come straight over. Mim then drew up a list of Susanna's friends and phoned each one in turn. She managed to contact all but two who were still out at the movies. No-one was prepared to venture an opinion on where the girls might have gone.

Daria arrived halfway through this operation and contributed another name. She and Mim hugged each other. They both displayed a surface calm, but there was an undercurrent of something like panic. Daria looked as if some of her vitality and life-force had drained away.

'This is all so extremely unlike both of these girls,' she kept repeating. I thought that was only half true, at best. The fact that her daughter had deceived her appeared to be almost more upsetting to Daria than the question mark hanging over Ruth's whereabouts.

We reviewed what we knew. The girls had taken overnight things, and were dressed, Daria said, in full party regalia. They had spent some considerable time on hair and makeup. It looked very much as if they knew exactly where they were going.

'Could they have gone to a club, a dance thing, one of those places where kids hang out?' I said, but Mim and Daria considered this was unlikely. One of their friends would have mentioned it, and anyway, they were a bit too young for clubbing. I thought this was dubious in the extreme, and could see that Cyn had the same idea. The mothers, however, were united.

'If they are going to a dance hall, they are not taking their nightdresses and toothbrushes,' Daria said firmly. I caught Cyn's marbly eye.

Although the likelihood was that the girls had headed for a specific destination, both Mim and Daria were clearly anxious to call the police. But as Mim picked up the phone, the front doorbell shrilled. Everyone had the same immediate thought. Accident. Police. The hairs on my neck prickled. We sprang up simultaneously. I remembered Jack was on his way – but Jack still had his own key. This was a subject I had unsuccessfully nagged Mim about.

I reached the door first. Stuart Friend stood there smiling obsequiously, holding a bunch of pink and white carnations. I felt my jaw drop, of its own volition.

'Jesus, Stuart! *Fuck*. What on *earth* do you want?'

He advanced eagerly, but I shook my head and pushed him away.

'I'm sorry, love – I was passing and I saw all your lights on. I couldn't help myself, I just had to see you, I've been thinking about you all day . . .'

He stuttered to a halt as he became aware of the others clustered behind me. Mim and Daria retreated, but Cyn barged forward, elbowing me aside and splashing my shoes with port. Stuart's eyes widened in alarm as he saw her, and he took a step back.

'This is not at all a convenient time for a social call, Stuart,' Cyn hissed. 'We have a family crisis on our hands, and we can't afford to be distracted by irrelevancies. Unless,' she darted a malicious sideways glance at me, 'unless, of course, Lou wants to take you upstairs to her room.'

I didn't dignify this with a response. 'Stuart, I can't see you now.' I seized his arm and shoved him down the path. He pressed himself against me in a way that turned my stomach. 'Listen, I absolutely can't see you at all any more. You mustn't come here again, okay?'

'No, it's not okay.' I could smell whisky on his breath. His voice wobbled. 'Don't say that, I know you don't mean it –'

'I mean it, Stuart. *I fucking mean it!*' Over his shoulder I saw Jack's car swing into the kerb. To my horror Stuart pinioned me with his arms and started kissing me forcibly, jerking my head back. I struggled furiously, kicking him on the shins, but he was considerably stronger than he looked. The carnations crushed against the nape of my neck. His lips were wet with passion, and he smelt sharply of sweat. As his tongue rammed itself into my mouth, I felt the hard knob of his erection.

'Hello, my poppet, does something seem to be the trouble?'

I had never been so pleased to see Jack in my life. He took in my speechless, beseeching gaze and interpolated his beefy forearm between me and Stuart's neck, wrenching him backwards. Stuart made choking noises. I recalled that Jack had boxed for the university, heavyweight division.

'I think we can safely assume the lady doesn't welcome your advances, sonny.' Jack thrust him away as if he were a troublesome insect. Stuart took a few staggering steps, gasping for breath and clutching his neck. I wiped my bruised mouth. The thought that it harboured Stuart's saliva made me nauseous. I found I was trembling.

Jack took the opportunity to give me a big smacking kiss. For once I accepted it with good grace. I leaned into the comforting male roughness of his jacket. He stroked my hair and rubbed my back sensuously. I recalled winding up my most recent conversation with him by expressing the hope that he would be involuntarily castrated and develop painful tears in his rectum. I was relieved that Jack never held grudges.

From behind the safety of the gate Stuart called, 'Lou, if you won't see me again I think I'll kill myself!'

Jack drawled, 'Might be the best way out, old chap. Apparently there are some pain-free methods available these days. Call me if you need a hand.'

He picked up the bunch of tattered flowers and hurled them at Stuart, stems forward javelin-style, stabbing him in the face. Then he picked up my unresisting hand and led me into the house.

Cyn had witnessed this little scenario.

'Perhaps that'll teach you not to steal fruit you've no interest in eating,' she said dourly. 'On the other hand, perhaps it won't teach you a thing.' She turned on her heel. 'Jack, you did the right thing in coming, even though you habitually do the wrong thing. Mim needs your support.'

Jack winked at me. I marvelled at the way Cyn could stash away the booze all day and still perform on cue with a stylish line in invective. Could still, moreover, string more than two words together with lucidity and bite.

Mim greeted Jack with an instant flow of tears. I was pleased to see that he put on a convincing display of solicitude, cuddling her against his chest and kissing the top of her head. Daria and Cyn received an all-purpose frosty smile. Jack hadn't forgotten his character assassination in Daria's book. I watched benignly as he did his creditable impersonation of a loving husband, well aware of Cyn's satirical eye on me. It didn't do to think too many warm and fuzzy thoughts about Jack. I made a conscious effort to redress the balance and remind myself of his less reputable dramatic roles. Particularly the unscrupulous streak he had freely demonstrated on various recent occasions.

I struck the table with the side of my hand, making everyone jump. 'I think I know where they've gone!'

I didn't think – I knew with absolute certainty. I connected significantly with Mim, and saw a reciprocal shadow darken the whites of her eyes. 'Oh. Oh dear. Of course. Dave.'

A stillness fell over the table. In all our minds was the image of Dave Benwell, husky, lithe, oozing buckets of charisma. A sexual magnet to impressionable and virginal young women, among others. And not one to keep his hands in his pockets when there were more interesting places to lay them. I thought: short skirts and skimpy tops. Frilly knickers. I swallowed as the full impact hit me.

Jack cleared his throat. 'Better get on the blower. Check him out.' He avoided my eyes. Mim didn't move. 'Mim?'

When she still did nothing, I said, 'Is his number in the book?'

'The phone's been cut off. They didn't pay the bill.'

'*They*, Miriam?' This was Daria, agitated and on the ball.

'He shares with a friend. Another young man. A musician. A singer in a rock band.'

Daria jumped up. 'A rock band singer? We must go around there, straightaway, and Jack will rescue them.'

This was one area, clearly, where Daria allowed men their uses. I distinctly saw Jack square his brawny shoulders and sit up straight.

'I expect you know where Dave's home is, Mim?' Cyn said in a low, confidential tone. If this was an attempt to be tactful it misfired. Everyone found a pressing need to look away from Mim, who said bravely, 'Yes. I know the address.'

An electric current seemed to galvanise us. In seconds we were pulling on coats and scarves and milling round the front door. There seemed to be rather a lot of us. Always supposing that we found the girls and brought them back, we would need more than one car.

'We'll have to cull this rabble,' Jack was muttering. I could see he was about to count a certain person out, but I felt that I, too, was superfluous to requirements. Mim, however, whispered urgently in my ear, 'No, please come. I need you with me, Lou.'

That left Cyn. The three boys had capitalised on the bonanza of the adults' mysteriously distracted state and were still glued to the TV, this time watching a manifestly unsuitable movie. Through the crack of the door I glimpsed their entranced faces. On the screen a naked girl happily rode a prone male figure.

Cyn was doing up the buttons of her ramshackle raincoat. Mim took her gently by the arm. 'Cyn, darling, I need someone to get those boys to bed. Would you mind awfully?'

Cyn's jaw thrust belligerently in my direction. 'I will if she –' she began, but Jack cut her off. He grabbed Mim and me and shoved us out the door. I didn't look round, but I could feel the guilty heat of Cyn's mortification burning my back.

The route to Dave's house in Cricklewood was mercifully fast and direct, via Kilburn High Road and its extensions, Shoot Up Hill and Cricklewood Broadway. We decided to take two cars, Jack's and Daria's, and travel in convoy. It seemed right that Mim and Jack should be together, so I clambered into Daria's elderly but spotlessly clean VW Beetle, to keep her company.

Daria was subdued for most of the way, occasionally breaking into a torrent of slightly incoherent questions. She was not at all sure the girls would be there, but did I think David was a responsible young man? Had I met his friend the rock band singer?

'Well, I haven't met his friend, but Dave *is* a teacher,' I replied uncertainly. Daria wasn't one to be fooled.

'But he is a particularly good-looking, sexy young teacher, isn't it? Yes, I do remember him now, very clearly indeed, at the co-op party. He was wearing jeans, very *tight* blue jeans, I remember that.'

She lapsed into a reflective silence. The conjunction of young, sexy, particularly good-looking and very tight jeans was, I had to admit, a distinctly unpromising one from a maternal point of view, even if he was a teacher. Rock singer, with its connotations of drugs, loose living and screaming teenage groupies, was even worse.

I jumped a little later when she suddenly said, 'What is its

273

name, that *tight* garment that is worn by the male ballet dancer? On the waist down, showing the bottom and the wedding tackle in full view?'

'Er, tights?'

'Yes, tights, that's correct. Those *tight* blue jeans, one did not need to use much imagination either, not very much at all!'

'Mmm.' I thought it best not to encourage this topic, even though it inspired a brief return to Daria's old gusto. She had one further question: was he famous, Dave's friend the rock band singer?

'I haven't a clue. Well, probably not. I think we'd have heard.'

Ahead of us, Jack's car turned sharply into a dark, silent side road where rundown cars lined the street. He pulled up and came round to Daria's window. It had started to pour with rain.

'We'll double park. Fuck it. We shouldn't be here very long anyhow.'

Daria nodded earnestly. Jack sounded unusually grim and gruff. I felt my stomach knot with apprehension. I couldn't begin to imagine what Mim and Daria might be feeling. Mim was blinking and biting her lip while Daria was humming, not a recognisable tune but an extenuated note that occasionally dropped or lifted an octave. She had done this from time to time in the car, and while I had found it distracting, I hadn't felt I could decently object.

'Shall I wait in the –' I began, but Mim was tugging at my hand. We ducked under the porch. There were two bells on Dave's front door, to the upstairs and downstairs flats. Each was marked with names printed in biro on torn scraps of paper attached to the brick with sticky tape. The problem was that we couldn't decipher them in the gloom. In spite of the late hour Jack would happily have pressed both bells, but Daria was in her car and back in a flash, wet hair swinging, brandishing a torch.

'I am very well equipped for every normal emergency,' she said with artificial brightness. I could only trust that she was not about to be presented with an abnormal emergency with which she might be ill-equipped to deal.

Jack pressed the bell marked Benwell and O'Donnell, which looked like the upper flat. We waited for an expectant moment, then he pressed it again, leaning his ear to the switch.

'Zero decibel rating. Kaput. Defunct.' He pressed the lower bell, Moon, Papadopoulos and V. Popov, Esq., but that achieved a similar result. I squeezed Daria's and Mim's hands. Both felt damp and limp. Jack glanced at Daria. 'Well, nothing for it but brute strength to the wheel.'

Drumming his fists, he unleashed a thunderous hammering on the door. 'Open up! Police!' There were no apparent lights on in the house, and few in the street. Jack paused for a breather, then redoubled his attack. After some time a light came on in the hall and the door yielded cautiously. Jack put his foot out and elbowed his way inside, past a pasty-faced teenager in striped pyjamas and spectacles who stood there, blinking in a bemused fashion. I wondered if he was V. Popov, Papadopoulos or Moon.

'Name!' Jack barked.

'You're never the Bill. Who's asking?' the young man said truculently.

'Who's asking? Father Christmas! Mother Theresa! Who the hell do you think's asking, you blithering idiot?' Jack gripped him by his thin shoulders and shook him. The boy seemed unfazed, staring at Jack's looming visage with the dawn of recognition.

'Hey, aren't you —?'

A guttural female voice shouted from the nearest door off the hall. 'Are you all right, Trevor? What's going on?' A shapeless woman in thick glasses and a floral petticoat squinted out. Behind her a small TV flickered. 'Here, take your filthy hands off of him!' She charged at Jack, who dropped the boy and put his hands up self-protectively.

Daria darted forward. 'It is quite all right, madam, we are not interested in your boy, not in the least, we are harmless people.' The woman gawped myopically from one to the other of us as if we were a perverted band of midlife marauders.

'It's the upstairs tenants we're after,' Jack took over tersely. 'Sorry to discompose you. It's just that it makes it *difficult* for people to discover who's unfortunate enough to be *living* here if you don't *mend* your bloody doorbells.'

Jack had a lifelong habit of always fixing anything the moment it broke, just as he answered all his mail on the day it arrived. He had no patience with any other mode of behaviour, and no comprehension of its pathology.

He marched towards the stairs and the rest of us followed in a mute, obedient line. As I brushed past Trevor I heard him repeating to his presumed mother, 'That's *him*, isn't it, yeah? Him off the TV?' From halfway up I glanced back. Both of them were staring after us as if hypnotised by the beam of Jack's fame.

A flimsy plywood door stood guard over the upstairs flat. Jack rattled it, saw it was secured by the puniest of locks and, before Mim, Daria or I had grasped his intention, put his shoulder to it. The door burst open. There was an audible, shocked gasp from the onlookers on the ground floor. Daria's eyes, I observed, were glinting.

Inside the door were three more stairs. Jack leapt up them,

skidding at the top on some loose, threadbare carpet. Daria was at his heels. Mim and I followed more slowly. My mouth felt strange, and I realised it was because my heart was in it.

Jack bellowed, 'Benwell! O'Donnell!'

A small room on his left was lit by a single bulb hanging from the ceiling. The room was empty, but had manifestly been recently occupied. At the far end was a kitchenette piled with dirty dishes. There were two grubby, sagging couches, a plastic chair and a coffee table covered in scuffed water marks. Bottles filled much of the available space. I counted tequila, vodka, a rather incongruous Pimms and a heap of beers stacked in one corner. Nearly all were empty.

A fetid pall of smoke hung in the air. It was sweet and sickly, and unquestionably dope. There was also a fug of stale beer overlaid by another, more invasive, sour odour. I diagnosed it as vomit. The evidence, inadequately cleaned up, was clearly visible on both sofas.

Jack picked up a saucer of butts – screwed-up, discarded joints – and sniffed them. I felt rather than saw his violent distaste. Though a child of the sixties, he had never embraced much of its ethos and vehemently ridiculed its psychedelic culture. Mim scuttled past him and snatched an object from the arm of the chair. I recognised Susanna's duffle bag. The frothy, girly clothes I'd watched her pack were spilling out of it. Daria was right behind Mim. She bent and picked up a brightly coloured, woven cloth backpack from the floor.

One of them made an inarticulate noise, and for a split second we stood in the crowded, choking room as if transfixed, rather like a quartet of stiff Victorian silhouettes. It's not often in life that you are aware of being on one side of a divide separating ignorance of a potentially momentous thing, and knowledge of it. This, I divined, was one of those times, and it felt like standing on the crest of a dam that was about to be breached by a wall of water.

Then we moved, and Jack slammed the door behind us with such force that I expected to hear the crash of broken glass. There was a dingy bathroom, and two other closed doors facing each other across the narrow passage. Mim made an attempt to grasp Jack's arm but he sprang forward and threw open the nearest one.

I hung back, well behind Mim and Daria, but I caught a graphic picture, a momentary freeze-frame of Dave Benwell in the act of climbing out of the frowsty double bed that took up most of the tiny space. He was wearing nothing but a pair of boxer shorts.

Acting with the hurtling speed that some big and heavy men are capable of, Jack somehow swept him off the bed with one hand and punched him in the face with the other. The full weight of his body, fuelled by rage – and a sliver of guilt? – was behind that right hook. Dave's head smashed face-first against the wall. The whole flat shook with the impact. I glimpsed Dave sliding down the wall into a heap on the ground. Jack snatched up a torn tartan rug from the bed and slung it over him.

A high, agitated cry from Mim and the rasp of Jack's breathing were the only sounds I heard for a moment. I was conscious of feeling sick to the stomach. I found the display of explosive, elemental male violence profoundly shocking. Daria, however, gazed on Jack with a new respect.

There was a muffled, interrogative shout from downstairs. No-one reacted. I became aware of another noise behind Jack: a snoring noise. I heard Mim say, 'She's still wearing her clothes.' At the same time, the other door sprang open and a hiccupping young man in a dashing red nightshirt appeared, rubbing rheumy eyes.

'Mr O'Donnell the unfamous singer, is it? You have kidnapped my Ruth in there?' Daria swept imperiously past him. The young man, very tall and pigeon-chested with dyed scarlet hair, gingery stubble and knobbly knees, looked ashen and semi-comatose. He was obviously having trouble coming to grips with reality, particularly the tooth and claw variety on display here at home.

He was, however, alert enough to take in his friend's prone form, and the blood issuing profusely from his nose. He reeled unsteadily at Jack, fists raised. Jack retaliated by slinging a contemptuous punch that knocked him off his feet. Compared with the punishment unleashed on Dave, this was lightweight stuff. The only advantage his opponent had over Jack just then was youth but, like his flatmate, he was in no condition to capitalise on this precious resource.

He attempted to get up but Jack stamped hard on his shoulder. 'I'm Susanna's father, you dismal excuse for a bloke. And that's her mother.'

'And I am Ruth's mother,' Daria called from the other room. She rushed out. 'She is not conscious. She has been sick in the bucket! What have you done to our girls? What have you given them to eat and drink?'

'And smoke, more to the point,' Jack growled. 'Don't you know that's fucking illegal? She's just turned fourteen years old, you puny little turd. If you've laid a finger on them I'll have you both prosecuted.' He kicked O'Donnell's rear end. His victim groaned and rolled on his back. The bright red shirt rode up, exposing a pink expanse of private parts. Jack jerked it down disgustedly. 'Stupid poofy nightdress.' He wiped his bloodied knuckles on the material.

'My Ruth is still only thirteen!' Daria added in a wail. She rushed to Mim's side, stepping fastidiously around Dave. Susanna lay on her back, her shallow breaths jerking into spasmodic snores. She was still clad, touchingly, in her party finery: spangly top with shoestring straps, and a short swirly skirt. She was covered in a heavy sheen of sweat, her teased hair flattened and sticking to her head. She reeked of vomit.

I felt her pulse. It was rapid, but reassuringly strong. The last of the few times I had smoked cannabis I had mixed it with alcohol. Hours of excruciating, eviscerating retching followed. Even now, years later, the smell of pot made me feel sick. I devoutly hoped that the girls' youthful constitutions were more robust.

Ruth's condition was identical, except that a beach towel had been placed under her head and a bucket on the floor. Its contents filled the room with a powerful pong, in spite of a window open to the street. She, too, was fully dressed, her legs splayed across the bed in daisy-printed tights. Her shoes, dainty purple ballet pumps, had been arranged neatly under the bed. Daria's steady gentle shaking would not bring her round.

Dave was on his feet. Blood still poured from his nose, and he was shivering. The intrusive sound of a car horn floated in from the street.

'Man –' He brushed away the blood repeatedly with the back of his hand. He seemed dazed, flicking his eyes between Mim and Jack and shaking his head. Then he saw O'Donnell, picking himself up off the floor, and the door, hanging from one hinge. 'Man, what *is* all this shit?'

'All this shit?' Jack roared. 'All this *shit* is the consequence of your repellent little soiree with underage children.'

'You outta your mind? I didn't do a thing to them. You

crazy?' He addressed Mim directly. 'I didn't touch Susanna, honest to God, she passed out.'

'She passed out, by the grace of God, *before* you could do a thing to her,' Jack shouted. 'She passed out as a direct result of the filth you and crap-features there were force-feeding her, and then you tucked her up in bed –'

'There was no force-feedin' required,' the gritty but depleted Belfast accent came from O'Donnell, leaning against the wall. He seemed to be making a Herculean effort to stay switched on and upright. 'Believe me, they wanted to smoke. Couldn't get enough of it. And those kids brought along the tequila and skolled it all between 'em.'

There was a note of admiration in his voice and an intake of outraged breath from the rest of us. The car horn became more insistent.

'You let them smoke and drink it all up and you did not attempt to stop them?' Daria wrinkled her nose as if O'Donnell were a slug on a prize bloom.

'Stop them? Oh, God no, that would've really spoilt the fun. No wowserish attitudes allowed in this terminally trendy joint – this is prime, super-hip territory! Just take a look around!' I had never seen Jack so incandescent. 'We're talking kids here. We're talking young kids with fuck-all experience of drink and dope!'

'And if we have not arrived to rescue our girls? What happens then, when they wake up in the morning bright and early and find a young man in the bed?' Daria looked searchingly into the faces of O'Donnell and Dave. Neither seemed prepared to tackle this rhetorical question.

There was a bustle on the stairs. The pugnacious faces of Trevor and his mother appeared around the splintered door. Both carried makeshift weapons, Trevor a bread knife and his mum a door handle. Their readiness to join the fray on their neighbours' behalf ebbed visibly as they gaped at the carnage in front of them.

'What's going on here? There's cars backed up in the street!' It was now possible to distinguish two separate car horns.

'Joe? Dave? Will we get the fuzz? You okay or what?' Trevor's query at least got Jack's attention.

'By all means call the cops if you have a phone that bloody works, and tell 'em we've got a couple of carnal knowledge wannabes here. Who also happen to be proficient in dispensing alcohol and illicit drugs to minors. Go on, lady, move!' as Trevor's mother remained rooted to the spot.

'But we cannot wait until the police are coming unfortunately, madam, as we must take these girls to hospital straightaway.' Daria bustled forward. 'Jack will carry them down,' she targeted Trevor's mum, 'and your nice strong boy will give a helping hand.'

Neither his mother nor Trevor appeared to recognise Daria's positive description of his qualities, but her organising momentum propelled him into action. Still in his pyjamas, he hoisted Ruth outside and deposited her on the back seat of Daria's car. His mum traipsed after them with an air of disbelief. She seemed gobsmacked by the unaccustomed social whirl that had engulfed them both.

As Jack backed past him carrying Susanna's inert body, Dave sprang to life. 'Self-righteous cunt, aren't you, Black? Huh? When did you ever care anything for your daughter? And how about pimping for your wife, fucker?'

I was standing next to Mim. I had kept my mouth shut for the duration of this visit, mainly because I felt I had nothing useful to contribute. Now that I would have liked to contribute something, I was struck dumb. A look of anguish touched

Mim's features. It was an expression I had never seen on her face, and hoped never to see again. Jack made a graphic gesture with his fingers and continued on down.

Dave seemed belatedly to realise what it was he'd said. Seen in close-up next to us, he looked surreal, like a boxer at the end of a punishing round. The rug had dropped to the ground and his face, hands and muscular chest were liberally daubed with blood. He shook his head and glanced quickly away from Mim and me, towards the incriminating room we'd first seen.

'We didn't think we should leave the kids in there. We thought we better put 'em to bed to sleep it off. Guess we shoulda put them in a bed together.' He looked round for O'Donnell who, now the immediate threat had abated, had collapsed back on his own bed. 'But hell, that would've meant bunking up with Joe, and nobody ever told him about showers.'

He sought out Mim, his eyes pleading. 'Mim. Babe. I'm sorry – about this. Things kinda got a bit – but, hey, you know I'd never have touched your daughter.'

Mim raised her head. Her hair was hanging down and dripping from the rain, and I couldn't read her expression. Dave put his hand out and lifted her hair away from her face, very gently. I wanted badly to leave them, but knew my leaving would destroy the moment.

Dave gestured at the staircase, where Jack's presence still hung in the air. 'Forget that. That was just shit talk. He knew I woulda come for you anyway.' He paused. Desperately uncomfortable, I tried to shrink away to nothing. But he went on slowly, seemingly unaware of my presence.

'I guess I know what you want to say, babe. About you and me. We better cool it?'

The inclination of Mim's head was almost imperceptible.

'I thought so. Well,' he took a deep, shaky breath, 'it's been nice knowing you, anyhow. And I mean, helluva nice. You're one great lady, you know that?'

He took her hand and raised it to his lips. I jerked my head away. I found a lump had lodged itself in my cynical throat.

14

I HEARD THE THUDS AND shouting well before Mim and I reached the front door. Trevor and his mum were blocking the open doorway looking out, their faces rapt.

'Excuse us,' I said with as much belligerence as I could muster. They parted grudgingly to let us through, their gaze never wavering from the street. Through a drizzly mist of rain I could see three or four people milling round the cars. A couple of flashbulbs went off, and there were confused sounds of scuffles, footsteps and cursing.

Susanna had been deposited on the back seat of Jack's car. Behind it I saw Daria sitting up, alert and at the ready in her VW. She waved to us skittishly. Behind her, another two cars were banked up in the narrow street.

Jack's engine was running. Mim and I made a dash for it just as two mismatched, wrestling figures reared up in the head-lights. The larger one, who was Jack, shoved the slighter one heavily into the bonnet. Jack stepped backwards, rubbing his hands. His opponent, however, showing rare presence of mind, had contrived to lob his camera to a friend, who shot off down the road.

'Get in!' Jack yelled.

Acting on an intuitive feeling that Mim didn't want to be alone with him just then, I lurched into the front seat next to Jack. Mim squashed in the back alongside Susanna's recumbent form. Jack revved the engine. There were warning shouts, and someone dragged the cameraman off the bonnet. We roared away, closely tailed by Daria.

We had only travelled a hundred metres when Jack swore loudly and slewed to a halt.

'Paparazzo alert!' He leapt out of the car and careered in pursuit of a running figure. In spite of the rain now bucketing down, Daria took this opportunity to rush around to his vacated seat. She said the two backed-up cars had ceased honking their horns considerably when they saw Ruth being carried out of the house by the pyjama'd Trevor. When Jack appeared with Susanna, the driver of the first car had jumped out with a camera.

'He was thinking all his Christmases had come at once! A nice picture for the family album – or perhaps, for the front page of *The Sun*!'

Straining to keep Jack in my sights, I was struck by the incongruous conjunction of everything around me. Here we were in the sluicing rain in Jack's sporty automobile – Susanna semi-conscious in the back, Jack tearing round in a fervour of machismo and Daria chatting animatedly. Was this almost vaudevillian chaos intrinsic to my life in particular, I wondered, or to human existence in general? These events, so disparate to an onlooker, were links nevertheless in a logical and infinite network of chains.

I experienced a moment of piercing metaphysical excitement. It seemed suddenly intoxicating that each life could be defined by its endless permutations – tragic, comic, mundane – all causes and effects of each other, and of other lives, and yet all in their essence unknowable and unpredictable.

This seemed to be a perception, a revelation even, with a mysterious and therapeutic relevance to my own life. I made an effort to imprint and memorise the aura around it as I tuned back in to Daria's excitable frequency. She had utilised the short time before Mim and I came down to summon Dr Garrett. Trevor, whose surname was Moon, and his mum, whose name Daria revealed was Roma Papadopoulos, did indeed possess a working telephone. Mr V. Popov, she added, was their lodger, who worked nights.

'Dr Tracey was fast asleep, but she is dressing up and coming round to your house straightaway,' Daria told Mim. As before, she seemed blithely unaware of the doctor's less than charitable feelings toward her.

The rain drummed on the windscreen. I glimpsed Jack ducking in and out of a row of parked cars. I sensed he was losing heart for the chase.

'Jack and I have discussed this matter,' Daria proceeded briskly. 'We have made up our mind that it is a better idea to keep the girls away from the hospital. The publicity would be a very bad thing indeed for Jack.'

I looked at Mim, but she was quiescent and did not respond. The headlights picked up Jack sloshing towards the car.

'Of course, if Tracey says they must go, well then, too bad, we will hotfoot it to the casualty ward. But both our girls are breathing steadily. With any luck, Tracey will give them a clean bill of health.'

A clean bill of health seemed unduly optimistic, even for

Daria. It did not escape me that she and Jack had made up their mind, in the singular. As he loomed up she threw open the door and exited nimbly, giving his shoulder an approving pat in passing.

'Bastard got away.' His clothes were saturated and he was panting heavily. I hoped he was fitter than he looked. He had had quite a workout.

The return journey was noticeably quiet. Jack was silent for once, and I liked to think that Dave's crude insult had reactivated an extinct or dormant conscience. Or perhaps he had suddenly discovered he had one.

I looked back at Mim at one point, when we were stopped at a traffic light. She sat motionless, hugging herself, with her arms tightly crossed. She was staring down at something. I saw it was her right hand, the one that Dave had kissed. Even in the gloom, I could make out the dark smudge of his blood.

Tracey Garrett was waiting for us in her car outside the house. Why hadn't she gone in, I wondered. Because Cynthia had not answered the doorbell. The reason for this was apparent when we got inside. The sitting room was unusually smoky, and Cynthia lay on the squashiest sofa, legs spread-eagled, in one of her oblivious, snorting sleeps. Jack was volubly incensed to see that she had fallen into insensibility without putting the fireguard in place. Some coals had tumbled out and were smouldering in the hearth.

I picked up the empty port bottle at her elbow. 'She's drunk herself into the usual full-blown stupor.'

Jack added, 'As is her usual full-blown wont. The usual full-blown, *stupid* stupor. You should barricade the portals against her, Mim. She's a living landmine. A pie-eyed parasite, and a walking state of emergency. And, to add non sequitur to injury, there's your argument against open fires in the home, put more efficaciously than I could ever put it.'

It hadn't taken long for Jack's microscopic twinge of conscience to sputter out, I reflected. Here he was striding out on deck again, fully recovered, sails billowing and spinnaker unfurled, while his child reclined insensate in front of him.

Tracey Garrett pronounced the girls fit enough to sleep in their own beds.

'Not that fit is the operative word. They may have vomited up the proceeds, but they're still suffering from alcohol poisoning twinned with marijuana blight. Toxic combination, that one, for the uninitiated. Lucky they're young and strong, instead of old and frail. They'll throw it off. But they're likely to wake up feeling they've been walloped on the noggin by the arse of a Sherman tank.'

We took this in while we got stuck into a surviving bottle of good red from Jack's cellar. As he said, we'd well and truly earned it.

'What should we give them, Dr Tracey, for this sore head, when they wake up?' Daria wanted to know.

Tracey directed her answer at Mim. 'Aspirin. Paracetamol. Any of those reliable old workhorses. However,' she leaned back, 'this is not your friendly family doctor speaking, but should you be minded to employ this opportunity to teach them one of life's little lessons, a spot of delay wouldn't go astray. Let them suffer a bit. In their own best interests, of course.'

We tucked Susanna up safely in bed. She hardly stirred. Then there was the problem of Ruth. Clearly Daria would be incapable of lugging her daughter, slip of a girl though she was, up to their top-floor flat unaided. She wrinkled her brow prettily as she engaged with the complexities of this problem. Jack promptly offered his services. Why not drop them both off in his car? Daria could return tomorrow for hers.

Daria appeared deeply relieved. 'Well, Jack, if you are quite sure. You have certainly carried out the man-size portion of the work today. Jolly well done! You have beaten up the baddies all by yourself, and rescued the maidens!'

Jack puffed out his chest. He obviously lacked any of the problems I found with this generous reading of his contribution. It wasn't that I thought Daria was being mendacious, exactly. Her game plan was too upfront for that. It was more that this was a side of her character I was unexpectedly having a spot of bother with.

My philosophy days at university seemed very far off. I had sallied forth into the world feeling intellectually equipped to trip confidently though the moral maze of life. That confidence had gone out the window, along with a number of other convictions. I had a funny feeling they were gone for good.

Mim sat on the small portion of sofa not occupied by Cynthia. She had tactfully tucked Cyn's legs together and seemed to have retreated into herself. I couldn't tell whether she had even heard Daria's eulogy. Cyn's snores powered on. It occurred to me that she would have been an ally in this ethical minefield I was suddenly treading.

I said goodnight to Daria and Jack at the front door. Jack, with Ruth in his arms, headed for the car with a spring in his step.

'Jack seems to have forgiven you,' I said.

Daria cocked her head. 'For writing all about him, is it? As the plump singer of popular ballads?'

'And a closet queen. There was that too.'

Daria looked slightly chastened. 'Ah, yes. That as well.'

'Lucky he doesn't hold grudges, isn't it?'

'It is very lucky, Louisa. Yes, indeed!' She gave me a delighted smile. There was a winsome and wholly guileless twinkle in her eye.

'Resourceful gal, our Daria,' I remarked to Tracey, who grunted noncommitally. She and I joined forces to pack Mim off to bed. Mim looked inert, drained by the events of the evening.

'And no wonder,' I said. I had stoked the fire and prevailed on Tracey to stay for another drink. Just for fun, I scraped the scummy film off a Dusty Springfield disc. She came on, at full throttle: 'Mama said there'll be days like this, There'll be days like this, My mama said . . .'

'You can always rely on the old Dusty for the pertinent lyric.'

On a coffee table I'd found a note from Cynthia. It read:

'*Your boyfriend (the married one) called from Sydney. He's leaving his wife and children and coming here at the end of the week. He asked if you were out with 'that bloody Yank'. I said you had gone to see an American who was suspected of debauching two underage girls, one of whom was Mim's daughter.*'

I passed the note to Tracey. She read it through and chuckled. 'Well, that's telling it like it is.'

I sprawled out. I felt curiously relaxed, and couldn't understand why. I tried to drum up a more appropriate feeling, such as terror or panic, or perhaps even triumph or rapture, but it was no good. Nothing came. I screwed up the note and tossed it in the fire.

'Sam, his name is. We've been involved for years. He's tried to leave home before but it didn't work.'

'Well,' she clinked my glass, 'here's to it working this time. To Lou and Sam!'

I didn't echo the toast. 'Thanks. But I wish we were toasting you and Nathan instead.'

'Instead? Or as well?'

'God knows. I can't work out what I feel, you see. Or even what I want. I'm a bit on the undecided side. Severely challenged in that area, as a matter of fact.'

'It'll help when you see him.'

'Perhaps it will.'

We sipped our wine in companionable silence, listening to Dusty and the crackle of the fire, and trying to ignore Cyn's rumbling snores. After a while I asked, feeling sufficiently at ease with her to ask it, 'Have you ever felt like that about Nathan?'

'Humph. Can't say I have. Pity, actually. Could use a bit of the old scientific objectivity and scepticism where that gent is concerned.'

'Positively besottedsville? Soul-mate territory?'

'Ain't that the truth.'

'I was like that, for five years, until I came over here and got enmeshed in one thing after another. What do they say? There's nothing like distance for making the heart grow curiously confused.'

'Ha. Probably a lot truer than the original version. Trouble is, I can't get away. Further than the supermarket, that is.'

'You could go to Australia. They're always looking for doctors there, in the outback.' A postcard image of Uluru, Ayers Rock, red, remote and hauntingly beautiful, flashed into my mind.

'Uh huh. What you're not taking into account is that I don't want to go.'

I nodded. I knew exactly what she was saying. I hadn't wanted to go either.

'What if,' I plucked a thought out of the air, 'what if you and Nathan could get together, but only at the expense of losing your kids?'

'You mean, to their esteemed papa?' I nodded. Her eyebrows went up. 'Ugh, nasty one. No kids, no Nathan. No contest.'

'I used to say to Sam, if I had fifteen children I'd leave them, to be with him.'

'Well, you were talking through your hat. Forgive me for pointing out the bleeding obvious, but you didn't have any kids and so,' she leavened the words with a friendly look, 'you had no right to say it.'

I was tempted to point out another inconvenient obstacle, that Sam and Nathan had children too, but I wanted to formulate it so that it sounded less like a Cynthia remark. Tracey, however, pre-empted me.

'Nathan knows he'll lose his kids if we get our act together. Life's not fair, as somebody more famous than us has already noticed.'

'My father always said that. I resented it like mad then, but I have to say it's one aphorism that's stood the test of time.'

A sequence of braying snores drowned this out. Tracey glanced over at Cynthia and shook her head.

'Someone we know's been dealt a ropy hand.'

'A lousy one. But only up to a point. She's her own worst enemy, you know. Jack's right – she *is* a walking state of emergency.' I had been rather taken with this phrase. 'She brings things on herself. Missing work because of drinking, for instance.'

'You mean, because of alcoholism.'

I was slighly taken aback. 'Well, yes. If she loses her job, who'd employ her? I know there's tenure and all that, but they must have ways of getting round it. I spoke to a snooty hireling there who intimated that her comportment was something up with which they would not put, for much longer.'

'Early retirement on health grounds. That's how they get round it.'

'God. How would she exist? She'd get some pension, I suppose.'

'At thirty-nine? Wouldn't get much.'

I was reminded of Cyn's birthday. Some time this week, it must be. I banished the thought.

'No man, and no earthly prospect of one either. I wish I could sool that sap Stuart Friend onto her. They're rather well suited. Insofar as Cyn could be suited to anyone.'

'They're horribly suited, you awful woman, and you know it.'

'Well, you may think that but they fell into the cot once, evidently. Although Stuart insists that he was pushed.'

'Oops! Chivalrous chap, that.' Tracey got up and stretched. 'Better resume my beauty sleep. And return to my slumbering babes. Elder one is nearly Susanna's age – probably get back to find her hosting a bender. Now, where did I put my bag?'

We hunted around for her canvas holdall. It was behind the sofa. As I bent down to retrieve it, it dawned on me that at some point in the recent past Cyn's snores had come to a grinding halt. I snatched a look at her. One bilious eye was open, and glowering into mine.

'Hello there,' I said with a heartiness I did not feel. She closed the eye balefully and turned over. The sofa springs creaked and groaned.

Tracey and I had a whispered exchange on the porch.

'Bugger that, that and that, eh? How much d'you think she heard?'

'Enough.' Tracey Garrett was nothing if not succinct. It was one of her strong points, I thought. From my hazy recall of the drift of our talk, and assessed from Cyn's perspective, I had a nasty feeling I had come off worse than the doctor. Considerably worse, when I thought about it.

'I think I've blown my chances. She'll hate me now.'

'So what's new?' Tracey chucked me under the chin in an avuncular fashion. 'Check on Susanna before you hit the hay.'

I switched off all the lights, hoping Cyn would appreciate my consideration. I found that Mim had cleaned Susanna's face and combed her hair off her forehead. She had removed the party spangles and manoevred her into a nightdress.

In the powder blue baby doll nightie, with her shiny face and hair spread out on the pillow, Susanna looked sweetly innocent. She had even regained a little colour in her cheeks. I envied her youthful resilience, but I also experienced a trace of what I imagined a mother might feel. It was something, I knew, that I had rarely if ever felt before: the kind of concern for another person in which every vestige of self-interest was notable for its absence.

I was exhilarated by this novel feeling. What must it be like, I wondered, there in the room artificially tidied by her mother, to have a daughter? Even my close recent encounters with the mother–daughter relationship at its most fraught could not rid me of the suspicion that there might be aspects of it worth having.

In the morning, when Dr Garrett's prognosis came to pass, I was inclined to revise this opinion. A fourteen-year-old in the throes of a swingeing hangover was not a pretty sight. Disinclined to follow Tracey's advice and hold off, Mim proferred medication at the first sign of distress. It would not stay down, however, and the atmosphere of the house reverberated with misery for the best part of the day. The boys escaped to Hampstead Heath to kick a football. I trusted a soupçon of a lesson was being learned by someone, somewhere.

Cynthia's own thick head, on the other hand, received short shrift. She stayed prostrated on the couch until late in the day, when she thundered up to the bathroom. She then banged into the kitchen, where Mim and I were camped.

We were sitting comfortably by the Aga reading the Sunday papers when Cyn blundered in. She stared interrogatively at each of us in turn. Neither Mim nor I reacted. I could see Cyn champing at the bit. She had never looked, I thought, more drastically down at heel. Her unwashed hair hung in a greasy tangle round her face. She looked unhappy, unhealthy and unwashed.

She pulled up a chair, and I caught an acrid whiff of stale body odour and booze. I turned my head away.

'Off to the shower, are we?' I inquired genially.

She gave me a withering look. 'I assume you got my note?'

I remained impassive. She surveyed me.

'So. The boyfriend's going to leave his wife and family for you. Another feather in your cap – well, more of an Indian headdress now, isn't it? Congratulations! No more lonely nights for Lou. Of course, the wife might have a few from now on, but what the heck, she'll have the children to console her.'

I felt Mim stir beside me. I held up the newspaper and turned the page, obscuring Cynthia. The paper crackled in her face. When she realised I was bent on not responding, she heaved an ostentatious sigh, and waited. The respite was brief.

I jumped as her balled fist smashed into my newspaper with a loud thwack.

'*Well?*'

'Well what?'

'You know what! What happened?'

'When?'

I knew I was being unduly provocative but I couldn't help myself. Radiating exasperation, Cyn rocked violently in her chair. It tipped backwards, and was only saved from crashing to the floor by the edge of the table.

'Last night, of *course*, Lou. I stayed here to put the boys to bed while you all flounced off together, if you recall. Well, what happened? I assume the girls were there, since Susanna's asleep in her room.'

Cyn bristled with hostility towards me, and I could hardly blame her. It was mutual. All the old ill-feeling between us seemed to have coagulated and crashed out into the open. But I saw Mim couldn't face this. Her eyes had closed and her head swayed to one side.

'Yes, the girls were there. They'd been drinking and smoking dope, so we brought them back.' I couldn't resist adding, 'You were dead to the world, by the way, snorting like a sea lion.'

Cyn breathed slowly and deeply through her nose. She clearly wanted more. Much more. She looked hopefully at the top of Mim's head, then spikily at me.

'What do you mean, they were drinking and smoking dope? With David and the rock singer?'

I indicated Mim and put a finger to my lips. Cyn immediately clutched at me and tried to pull me up. We had a brief, inelegant tug of war. Her hand was sweaty and slippery. Finally, to avoid holding it, I let her drag me to my feet.

I closed the kitchen door behind us. Cyn repeated, 'David and the rock singer. What *happened*?'

'It was quite all right, Cyn. The girls were out to it when we got there. Just like you, as a matter of fact. Completely blotto.'

This didn't sound quite all right at all to Cyn, I could see that. She wanted details and embroidery, colour and movement.

'But *where* were they asleep? Had anything happened?'

'What sort of thing did you have in mind?'

I knew I was goading her beyond endurance when she seized me by the shoulders and shook me. This was aggression masquerading as exasperation, and it was barely under control.

'Stop this, Lou, and stop it now! I've got a bad headache. You know perfectly well the sort of thing I mean. Where were they sleeping? Had they been,' she lowered her voice a few decibels, even though we were alone in the sitting room, '*interfered with*, in any way?'

I walked away from her and picked up a book. 'They were asleep in beds. With Dave and Joe. As to the last query, I'm afraid I couldn't say. Although they were still all dressed up in their party frocks.'

There was an expectant pause. I felt Cyn's eyes drilling into my back. When nothing more was forthcoming she said icily, 'I'm getting out of your road. Say goodbye to Mim for me. Tell her I'll ring her tonight. I'll let myself out, don't even think of putting yourself to the trouble.'

When she opened the door Daria was bouncing down the front path, bundled up in an Afghan coat. She looked especially spritely, I thought, as she bestowed beaming smiles on us both.

'Well, well. Ms Louisa and Ms Cynthia! Two strapping

young matrons for the price of one! What an excellent afternoon. I have come to rescue my car, in case you are wondering.'

'There's nothing excellent about this afternoon,' Cyn said repressively. 'It's cold, overcast and about to rain.' She pushed past the diminutive Daria, her raincoat flapping. 'And you can call Lou a matron if you like, in fact it does me good to hear it, but I'd prefer not to be included in the generic term. Strictly speaking it means a married woman, a category into which neither of us falls, but you may be unaware it has taken on other connotations.'

'Suburban connotations of an unflattering, blue-rinse hue,' I added.

We watched Cyn climb clumsily onto her motorbike and dwindle into the leaden landscape, until she evaporated like a puff of smoke. I shivered suddenly. Daria gazed after her.

'Oh, dear me. Our Ms Cynthia is certainly not looking happy.'

'Unlike you, Daria. You're looking distinctly chuffed. I'm afraid Cynthia's only just raised herself from her crapulous bed. She's probably still way over the limit.'

'Ah, then she and I have something in common. Not the crapulous bed or the limit,' she shot me a sly sidelong glance, 'but, I am sorry to say, the very late arising. What a good thing it is Sunday!'

It was tempting to pursue the subject of her evening, but I was inhibited by an unexpected qualm. Instead, I asked after Ruth.

'Ah, that naughty girl is very much better, thank you. Luckily she is not up yet, so one can sneak out!'

Daria's playful expression, and her artless use of the word luckily, reminded me uncannily of Bess.

When Cynthia did call later that evening, I answered the phone. She demanded to speak to Mim and I told her Mim was in the bath.

Cyn sounded drunk and maudlin. 'I want to talk to her. Ask her to call me back. To be sure to call me back.'

'Will do.' But I didn't. I forgot to pass on the message, and took the phone off the hook and went to bed early myself soon afterwards.

Susanna had embraced life with markedly more zest after Cyn's departure. By mutual consent Mim and I made no reference to the events of the previous day. We agreed that these matters should be addressed at some point, but I could tell that Mim's inclination was to position that point in the far distant future.

I thought Susanna seemed slightly chastened by her experience. The behavioural changes that suggested this would have been imperceptible to many, but I knew her well enough to detect them. It would be going overboard, as I said to Bess, to describe her demeanour as remorseful in any way. Still, the habitual resentful sullenness had lifted, and she no longer seized every available opportunity to flaunt her low opinion of her mother.

'Instead she seizes every other available opportunity,' I said. 'Or perhaps every third. But it's an improvement. At least for the moment.'

Susanna went off to school on Monday as usual. The phone started ringing from an early hour and didn't let up until we took it off the hook. I fielded the calls for Mim. Daria was the first up. She asked if we had seen the tabloids. I hurried out to get them. On a normal day, the headlines would have caused me no end of enjoyment.

JACK BLACK IN SCHOOL STOUSH: SIR GETS A NOSE JOB

BEEB'S BLACK BELTS BOLSHIE BEAK

WHAM, BAM, NO THANK YOU, MAN!!

I glanced at one of the stories:

> *The BBC's 'Bonzer Aussie Bloke' Jack Black lived up to his*
> *macho image – and more – late Saturday. The TV tearaway*
> *(pictured above, carrying his daughter) got wind of a late night*
> *social call Susanna, 14, was paying to her favourite teacher's flat*
> *in Cricklewood.*
>
> *During Jack's surprise appearance, his daughter's hunky Phys*
> *Ed teacher, visiting American Dave Benwell, 24, somehow got*
> *his nose broken. Downstairs tenant Mrs Roma Papadopoulos*
> *said a man claiming to be the police had banged at the door after*
> *midnight.*
>
> *'You could have knocked me down with a feather,' says*
> *Roma (pictured below with son Trevor, 16) 'when I saw who*
> *it was. He gave Trevor a real shaking, then went upstairs and*
> *broke the door down!'*
>
> *Jack Black, who was escorted by three women companions . . .*

A grainy, amateurish photo showed a rugged-up figure that
few people would have identified as Jack, carrying an indeterminate bundle. There was a smaller, more recognisable picture
of Trevor and Roma brandishing their weapons.

'Roma and Trevor are the culprits!' declared Daria. 'They
are already talking about money to their editors on the telephone while we are upstairs, no doubt.'

Jack phoned in a lather. He would sue everything that

moved, and then some. He would give the school principal a rocket. As an afterthought he asked after Susanna.

Stuart called. He was plainly agog, but trying to conceal it. Was I all right? Had I been one of Jack's three women companions? I hung up on him before he could get started on his feelings.

After two reporters had called asking for Mim I took the phone off the hook. This was becoming a habit. I had a hunch Sam would be trying to get me, and an equally strong desire not to talk to him. The neutral feeling had been supplanted by a fatalistic attitude. I would deal with whatever happened, I told Mim, when it happened. She was on her way out to work, I was pleased to see, and she looked quite chipper. As Susanna left for school, she had said goodbye to her mother in a manner that could be construed as almost friendly.

Daria and Ruth came over for dinner. The news that Mr Benwell's nose had been broken by Jack Black, Daria chirpily informed Mim and me, had raced all over the school. Ruth and Susanna were basking in their temporary celebrity status. Daria was unsure how much of the circumstantial detail had also circulated.

'But of course, this is now academic. The children can read all about it in the gutter newspapers to their hearts' content. Let us hope their parents only subscribe to the stuffy broadsheets! Anyway, there is no doubt that our strongarm man Jack has emerged from everything quite well.'

She glanced at Mim for confirmation. The three of us were enjoying a pre-dinner drink while the girls prepared the meal in the kitchen. This was Daria's idea. I gathered she thought of it as constituting some kind of reparation. Ruth was a very good cook, her mother reassured us. She would supervise

Susanna who, it was taken for granted, would be worse than useless in the kitchen.

They had manhandled Jake in to do some donkey work. A background of breakdancing music and boisterous screams issued nonstop from the kitchen. At one point Ruth rushed in to inform us that Roma Papadopoulos and Trevor Moon were being interviewed on the telly. She seemed completely unabashed.

Preparations took so long that the pre-dinner drink became a protracted session, and we were very jolly by the time we sat down to pasta and salad, stylishly done. They had cleaned up and decorated the kitchen table with winter branches from the garden. The table napkins folded into swans were, said Ruth grimacing and rolling her eyes, Susanna's main contribution.

Susanna had brought her cassette player into the kitchen. 'We've chosen suitable dinner music from your vintage,' she announced. Our vintage had been pointedly interpreted to mean popular music from the sixties and seventies. It was played more loudly than we might have chosen, but no-one objected. We opened more wine and poured the kids a glass each.

It was rather a vociferous evening with an air of celebration that had a lot to do with a general easing of tension. The two generations were openly relieved to be getting on so well. This led to a lot of silly jokes receiving more appreciation than they warranted.

Mim looked happier than she had since my arrival. The girls' visit to Dave's flat had brought a lot of things to a head and seemed, I thought with cautious optimism, in an odd way to have resolved some of them.

Ruth was particularly animated, directing much of her

conversation at her mother. The unusually close relationship between the two had been founded on communication and trust. Ruth's part in the recent little deception must have shaken it to its foundations. Daria would make light of it to others, but I guessed her own self-esteem and system of values had received a nasty jolt.

The phone rang when Ruth was in the middle of telling us how she had instructed Susanna in the simple art of pasta-draining. She showed a highly developed anecdotal ability. I was nearest to the phone and picked it up reluctantly. The Rolling Stones happened to be blasting out 'It's All Over Now', one of the only songs of theirs I liked. I could hardly make out Cyn's curdled words over the chorus.

'Is that a party you're having?'

'What? Not really.' I was trying to listen to Ruth at the same time. She was describing how she had told Susanna to stand the colander up and tip the pasta into it. Susanna picked up the colander in one hand and held it in the air. When she tilted the saucepan with her other hand the whole lot plummeted into the sink.

Raucous laughter, music and the convivial tinkle of forks on plates competed with Cyn in the background.

'What's going on? Who's there with you?'

Ribbons of fettucine were cascading out of the colander in Ruth's lurid story and hurtling down the plughole as Susanna, screeching, scrabbled ineffectually at the slippery strands. I laughed into the phone.

'Oh, it's only Daria and Ruth over for dinner. And the rest of us. Just family.'

I bit my tongue. Cyn's hurt feelings transmitted themselves down the phone.

'Give me Mim.'

I looked at Mim, flushed and smiling for the first time in weeks. 'She's having dinner, she can ring you back later. Or tomorrow.'

'*No she can't!* She's my friend too! I want her now.'

I took my time. Susanna told a story at Ruth's expense involving cultural studies homework. 'It was supposed to be about different taboos. Like how some people won't eat cows or bacon? And she went and did all this research and wrote this long essay about Francis Bacon!'

'It's Cyn, inevitably,' I told Mim. 'Drunk as a lordess.'

Susanna made a disgusted face. 'Don't talk to her, Mum. Tell her we're busy. Stand up to her.'

I was near enough to hear Mim's quick, affectionate greeting. 'Cyn, dear, it's a bit of a bad time. Sorry about the noise, but we're right in the middle of dinner. Can I call you back?'

'Well done, Mum!' Susanna called loudly. It was the first time I could remember her complimenting her mother. Later it occurred to me that Cyn may well have heard this and other interjections.

The Stones had moved on to 'Ruby Tuesday'. Mim leaned into the receiver. After she hung up she said to me, 'I couldn't quite hear what she was saying. She sounded cross and her voice was a bit muffled, a bit – what's the word?'

'Inebriated?' I suggested.

'Sozzled.'

'Positively plastered!'

'Ludicrously legless!'

'Shockingly stinko!'

'Primitively pissed as a newt!' The children outbid each other, sniggering with hilarity. Certain ironies not lost on us grown-ups seemed regrettably to have passed the girls by.

Susanna and Ruth lifted a homemade chocolate cheesecake out of the fridge and placed it with a flourish on the table. It was greeted with whoops of appreciation.

'Just wait till you try it, you lot.' Susanna passed the knife to Ruth. 'And if it doesn't taste any good, it's Jake's fault for not mixing it properly.'

'And because he stuck his dirty finger in like Jack Horner and licked it!'

I remarked idly to Mim and Daria, 'Cyn was certainly on the miffed side. As well as incomprehensible. She thought we were having a wild party.'

'We are having a party,' Daria corrected me. 'A wild and woolly party for six, with scrumptious cake.'

It was the reiteration of the word party that did it. I looked at Mim as an awful suspicion crept up on me. 'Oh, God! Today's date, everybody. What is it?'

Mim's eyes went blank, and then widened. A look of horror slowly transformed her face. 'Oh, Lou, it's not. Is it? Cyn's fortieth birthday? It can't be. Oh, *no* –'

'It is quite all right, my dear Miriam, don't worry.' Daria gave her wineglass an insouciant twirl. 'We will cheer her up. We will telephone her back right away and sing "Happy birthday, dear Cynthia, happy birthday to you", all together.'

The children groaned in unison. Mim looked stricken.

'That won't work,' I told Daria. 'You see, we were supposed to be giving her a party.'

'We promised,' Mim said miserably.

'But we *are* giving her a party,' Susanna said. 'We just didn't bother to invite her!' She stood up. 'Tarantara! I hereby christen this: absent Cynthia's party!'

The kids chortled. The funny side of it struck Daria and me. The moderately funny side.

'Didn't she say anything at all to you, Mim? It's not like her not to rub it in.'

'She did try to say something, but then she put the phone down. I couldn't quite make it out. And – oh dear. She sounded upset. But I thought it was something about her job.'

'She's probably lost it,' I said airily.

15

THE KNOCK ON THE DOOR came as I was about to leave for Heathrow to meet Sam. The exact sequence is a blur in my mind, but it must have been a day or two after absent Cynthia's party.

I'd finished the article on the housing co-op but I still hadn't spoken to Sam. Instead, a call had reached me from Sam's hyperactive New York agent, Bill Canning.

'Hey hey, Lou Lou, great to have you on the line! Sam's asked me to call you because of the time zones, and he says he's tried over and over and your line's always tied up. Between the two of us, he's pissing himself because he thinks you got wall to wall guys after you!'

The upshot of Bill's call was that Sam was now somewhere over the Atlantic. He'd made a brief stopover in Los Angeles to talk film rights and business with an entrepreneur interested in putting on his New York hit, and he was due in at Heathrow in the afternoon.

Since that early morning phone call I had gone through endless changes of mood and inclination. A whole wardrobe of them, flinging one on and then abandoning it for another colour, another texture. I would meet him; I would ignore his arrival. I was desperate to see him; I would prefer never to set eyes on him again.

I had consulted Mim, Bess, Daria and Tracey. Daria was the only one prepared to come out with a categorically negative imperative.

'You are doing very well, Louisa. Do not spoil everything by starting up the engine again with this man and flogging the dead horse. If it is just some male company you are needing, there are two eager beavers right on your doorstep!'

The eager beavers she had in mind were Jack and Stuart. My snorts, of derision and disgust respectively, provoked a roguish trill of laughter. I accused her of mischief-making, but I concluded afterwards that she was only being true to her principles.

Bess was all for starting the engine up again. 'Just go for it, Louie. He's the love of your life, you've always known that. There's only ever been one course of action when faced with le grand passionay, in my book, and that is to give in. Lie back and enjoy it!'

Mim and Tracey were more equivocal. No doubt remembering our previous conversation, Tracey Garrett was cautious. 'Probably do best to adopt a holding position. Wait for the great man's arrival. Nothing like the real thing for concentrating heart and mind. My guess is, things will pan out all by themselves.'

Mim, who more than anyone had borne the brunt of my existential angst about Sam, suggested I try and tune in to my instincts.

'I think one's subconscious mind can be awfully helpful when one's in a genuine dilemma. It always has a view. But it's a matter of being open and receptive to what it's trying to tell you – and that can be very hard to do.'

'But I know what my subconscious is telling me, Mim, that's the trouble. It's telling me it hasn't a clue.'

'Well, it may seem to be saying that, but maybe you haven't quite dug down far enough, if you know what I mean.'

My face must have shown her I hadn't much faith in what she was saying, and no stomach for the task of digging down. I felt I was taking on Mim's own recent attitude to reality: retreating from it because it was too hard to handle.

But Mim knew about the tortuous workings of my psyche. She startled me by saying, 'Have you ever thought of trying to speak to Ingrid?'

'*In*grid? Never.' This was not quite true. Lately it had occurred to me and, oddly, without the automatic stab of jealousy that her name usually provoked. A sudden thought came to me out of nowhere: Ingrid is a fellow woman. This thought was novel, surprising, and although I didn't really welcome it I couldn't make it go away.

'She wouldn't want to talk to me.' I was sure of that. 'You know, I used to think Ingrid was a monster. But she's not, of course.' There were those words again. I repeated them sagely to Mim. 'She's just a fellow woman.'

Mim nodded. 'You're right. She is.'

In the end I opted to go and meet Sam's plane, as I'd half known I would. I had just rung the airline to check it was on time when it happened. A loud knock on the front door, followed by two rings on the doorbell.

Two smart young police persons, a black male and a white

female, stood on the porch. The woman consulted a piece of paper.

'Are you Miriam Black? Or Louisa Lawson?'

'Miriam's at work. I'm Louisa, yes.'

They produced their identity cards. The man said, 'Police Constable Rahid and this is WPC Ford. May we come in? I'm afraid we've got some rather bad news.'

My first thought was: Stuart. He's gone and done it. Stuart had repeated his threat to kill himself, several more times, and I had laughed it off. It's well known that people who threaten to commit suicide often do, I thought.

I led them into the kitchen. They seemed very ill at ease, and I guessed they hadn't had to break this kind of news to people very often.

'Shall we have a cup of tea?' the young woman suggested nervously. They had a prior arrangement to take it in turns to speak, I decided.

'By all means,' I said. 'I've got to go to the airport and meet someone, though, so we'd better be quick.'

This sounded a bit cavalier, I realised. I said, 'Somebody's had an accident, haven't they?'

They put their elbows on the table, looking serious. Confirming my theory, Constable Rahid said, 'It's a special friend of yours, I'm afraid, Louisa.'

I was reminded of Cynthia's strictures as I jiggled tea bags in three cold mugs. 'Don't worry, I think I sort of guessed. Actually, he's not a special friend. It's Stuart Friend, isn't it?'

The repetition of the word friend gave me a wholly inappropriate urge to laugh. They looked blank.

'No.' This was said firmly in unison. They shook their heads, watching me, I thought, as if I was rather odd. The

WPC said, 'It's not anyone called Stuart. It's not a man at all. It's a woman.'

I stared at them dumbly. 'A woman?'

'It's your friend Cynthia, Louisa.' She read from the piece of paper. 'Cynthia Whicker.'

'What – what's happened to her?'

I was aware of my lips being very dry. WPC Ford picked up a mug of tea and put it in my hand. 'Do you take sugar, love?' I nodded. She added a heaped teaspoon, her eyes on my face.

'I'm afraid she's dead.'

My mind raced giddily. 'But – how? *How* is she dead?'

'She appears to have ended her own life. She did not suffer at all. It was carbon monoxide poisoning, with a hosepipe in the car. Very – well, efficient.'

I felt the blood drain from my face. 'But – but she couldn't. She hasn't got a car. She's only got a motorbike. Are you sure it's her?'

I blinked rapidly. Without warning, tears spurted and coursed down my face. I thought of Mim, Gayle and Stuart, and surely Cyn, who had all wept before me in this kitchen.

The WPC brought out two envelopes and two sheets of paper. They were addressed to me and to Mim. Our names and this address were printed very clearly in Cyn's small, obsessively neat capitals. I tried to suppress it, but heard myself utter a sound that began as a heaving sigh and ended in a sob.

'Do you identify this as Cynthia Whicker's handwriting?'

The WPC passed me a second sheet of paper. It was addressed to whoever found the body, To Whom It May Concern. Cyn had provided a full identification, and directed the police to deliver the two letters to Mim and me.

Cyn had rented a car with a full tank of petrol, and driven

out of London to Epping Forest. She had turned up a narrow track and parked in a picnic ground, where she attached a length of hose to the exhaust pipe and ran it through the driver's window. It was estimated she had parked there with the engine running at about seven in the evening.

She must have thought nobody would go there in winter. But later that night a teenage couple had driven up the track. Cyn's engine was still running, and they could hear music issuing from inside. It was a cassette of the Beatles' 'Help!' that Cyn had chosen to sing her spirit away, and it must have played and rewound itself many times.

There were other cassettes in the car, including Verdi's *Requiem*, Aretha Franklin and Dusty Springfield. And, a very Cyn touch, Ravel's *Pavanne for a Dead Princess*. On the passenger seat next to her were three black party balloons, one champagne glass and an empty bottle of Bollinger. A receipt for a garden hose was in the boot. It was dated Monday, the day after I had last set eyes on Cyn.

The two young constables repeated how sorry they were to have to bring this sad news. The WPC said, 'Cynthia must have been a great friend of yours, then?'

I said automatically, 'No, she wasn't.' I felt a hammer blow to my heart. 'That is – yes. Yes, she was. She was a – great and old friend.'

Even if the harsh, hoarse voice that said these words didn't sound like my own at all, I felt the deep truth of them as I spoke.

Constable Rahid put some questions about Cynthia. Where did she work? Did I know her immediate family? I explained that Cyn was Australian, with no relatives in England.

'We were her family, you see,' I said. 'Well, Miriam was. That's why she left letters for us.'

They asked if she was married, or had a male partner. I said no, rather overemphatically. A glance passed between them.

WPC Ford made a note. 'You and Miriam share this house?'

'Yes. Well, at the moment. It's her house, I only arrived here a few weeks ago.' And yet, I thought, it seems like years.

'So Miriam Black was her *special* friend,' Constable Rahid said delicately. He seemed to be feeling his way. 'Her family. But, er, *you*, Louisa, now live here with Miriam. Am I right in thinking, then, that there was a recent – bust-up, or something similar, between Cynthia and Miriam?'

'Hell no!' Belatedly, I cottoned on. 'No, you're not right at all in thinking that. You've got the wrong end of the stick altogether. Although I can see how you . . .' I slowed down. I could indeed see vividly what they might be thinking. 'You're thinking that Mim and Cyn were in a relationship, I came along and elbowed Cyn out, Cyn was distraught and killed herself. *Or*,' a worse thought struck me, 'or did you perhaps think that I, in a fit of jealous fury . . .?'

I tailed off. This was all too ghastly to contemplate. I stood up distractedly and dragged both hands through my hair. 'Cyn was rampantly – no, *rampagingly* – mad about men. She put them right off, that was the trouble. We're old university friends. Mim's been married for ever, I split up with my boyfriend in New York and I'm crashing here. Mim's house is a refuge from way back. Oh God, you must see . . .'

Both of them stood up too, looking concerned. 'It's all right,' they said in unison. WPC Ford patted my hand. 'It's all right. Cynthia's letters are very thorough, motive-wise, and so is the set-up, method-wise. We have to clarify the relationship aspect, as in any case of sudden death. For the inquest.'

'Will there be an inquest?'

'Oh yes. In any case of unnatural death.'

But we wouldn't have to attend, and this seemed to be an unusually straightforward case. Very open and shut. Meanwhile, Mim had to be told and, they said carefully, the body needed to be formally identified by someone who had known the deceased more than twelve months.

'Perhaps you or Miriam . . .?'

'Not Miriam. She's not very strong at the moment.' I took a deep, calming breath. 'I'll do it.' I thought for a moment. 'Can we break the news to her afterwards? I'd rather be there when you do. She was a lot closer to Cyn than I was.'

In the police car driving to the morgue I filled them in on Mim, in case they had any lingering doubts about our proclivities. They were impressed to hear that she was married to Jack Black. I neglected to mention that Jack was no longer residing in her house, or that he was heavily involved with another of our old friends from university, and I rather regretted saying anything at all when Constable Rahid brought up his recent appearance in the tabloids.

'Is he pressing carnal charges against that teacher?'

I said hurriedly that there was no reason to press charges since nothing had in fact happened, but I could see they were not remotely convinced. I deflected their probing questions about the incident with half of my trained journalistic mind on autopilot.

They probably thought they were doing me a favour by diverting my attention from the point at issue. If that was their purpose, they were unsuccessful. The third quarter of my mind was preoccupied with the prospect of telling Mim. The last quarter was numb. It was inconceivable now to think of going to meet Sam.

At the morgue, all the cinéma-vérité police dramas I had

ever seen provided a template for what was about to happen. All the labyrinthine crime novels I'd ever read led me into the same white-tiled chamber, cold as death, where the body lay on the marble slab, covered by a white sheet. They had even prepared me for the moment someone peeled back that sheet. What they could not quite prepare me for was the moment of truth.

I saw the revealed face, and hesitated. This smooth, serene countenance looked almost unfamiliar to me. Then I realised why; for the first time in my experience, all Cyn's defences were down. She didn't look combative or persecuted; she didn't even look upset. She looked peaceful.

I heard myself say wonderingly, 'Yes. That's Cynthia.'

If I'd been wearing a hat I would have taken it off. I was conscious of my own rude health, my rushing blood and quick breath. The two young PCs stood kindly by me, ready to catch me if I fainted. But my principal feeling was a heightened sense of myself and my surroundings, the impertinence of being uncivilly alive amid this certain evidence of mortality.

I can't recall speaking on the journey to the housing co-op. I sat in the back of the police car, watching buildings, people, streetscapes pass my window, and taking in nothing.

We had to wait for Mim to return from a site inspection. I thought for a while that she would collapse. When the police had driven off after escorting us home, I put a lighted cigarette and a brandy into her ice-cold hands. We sat close together with the cats and a rug over us in front of the fire. I think we were both in shock. We were on the point of opening our letters from Cynthia when I heard the kids slam the back door.

'Shall I?'

I waited for Mim to answer. Finally she nodded. 'If you

think you . . .' Then she shook her head. 'No. It should be me who tells them. If you can help me.'

She called the children in. They were quarrelling as they came through the door, but Mim's drawn and tear-stained face silenced them. I couldn't see my own face, but I guessed it conveyed much the same message.

Mim began haltingly, 'Something very sad's happened, and we must all try to be very brave.' Her voice shook and came to a stop.

The kids looked apprehensive. Susanna asked immediately, 'Is it Dad?'

'No, no. No, it's not your father. But someone you know well has . . . has . . .'

'*Died*, Mum? Who is it?'

Mim seemed oblivious to the tears now streaming down her face like rain. 'It's dear Cynthia.'

'*Cynthia?*' Susanna's face relaxed in a droll grimace. She and Jake exchanged an ironic look. 'Is that all, Mum?'

I had never seen Mim react faster. She leapt up and confronted her children, her whole body quivering.

'Don't ever say anything like that again. To me or anyone else. Cyn is – she *was* . . .' her voice shuddered to a halt, then gathered momentum, 'Cyn has been our darling friend for more than twenty years. You will remember that. You will respect that.'

Susanna and Jake's faces were almost comical in their identical, shocked dismay.

Susanna said quietly, 'I'm really sorry, Mum.'

Her brother nodded. 'Sorry.'

Then, to my absolute astonishment, Susanna moved forward hesitantly and gave Mim a quick kiss on the cheek.

'What happened to her?'

'She killed herself, I think, because she was very unhappy and everything in her life had gone wrong.'

I could see they found this information disturbing. It was obvious that both of them would have liked to ask how Cyn had done it. But, wary of Mim's reaction in a way that was unprecedented for them, they remained silent.

Mim wiped her eyes. 'I'll tell you more about it, but not now. She's written letters to Lou and me, and we have to read them. It won't be easy.'

She sat down. The kids filed out soberly. In the doorway, Susanna turned and said in a small voice, 'Would you like me to make dinner, later?'

'That would be nice.'

'It'll have to be pasta, cos that's the only thing I can do. Sort of. Like the – other night.' Her face changed. I guessed she was remembering that the other night had been Cyn's birthday, and how she had christened it 'absent Cynthia's party'.

She added, looking chastened, 'I'll try not to drop things this time.'

Caught up in the cathartic hilarity of that evening with Daria and Ruth, Mim had forgotten her promise to ring Cynthia back. It occurred to me, but in my animosity towards Cyn I had refrained from reminding Mim until it was too late.

I thought of my last view of Cyn. Daria and I had watched her juddering off, alone on her motorbike, into a blank London mist. There was a vague melancholy about the scene, an atmosphere which I sensed Daria felt too. I had shivered. It seemed in retrospect that the dank air had carried some kind of premonition. Cyn must have gone out the next day and bought the garden hose.

We had watched her until she vanished, swallowed up by an uncaring landscape. Or perhaps, more accurately, it was certain of her friends who had been uncaring, and the landscape was merely indifferent. Cyn's suicide would bestow on me a wrenching legacy. She would leave me lumbered with a great many things, I knew, but the greatest of these would be guilt.

She would leave Mim with a very different inheritance. There would be unexpected side-effects, and I felt sure I had just witnessed one of them. Possibly for the first time in her life, Mim had stood up to her children. She had reprimanded them, and she had done it in a white heat of anger, unhesitatingly and unambiguously. The effect on them had been akin to that of an electric shock.

Mim, too, would feel guilt, but in her case it would be baseless.

Cyn had typed her letter to me. Although the police were withholding the original and this was a photocopy, I could still detect the mistakes which she had painstakingly fixed with corrector ribbon.

The morning of her decision to kill herself, she'd received a letter from the Dean of Arts requesting a meeting to discuss problems arising from her frequent migraines and consequent absences from the English department.

I know what this means. They'll find a way of 'terminating my employment on the grounds of ill health'. I wouldn't get another job. I don't get on well with people, as you of all people know only too well, Lou.

I would have liked to get on better with you, and I regret that our meetings always ended in recriminations. I'm sure you thought I was jealous of your success with men and with friendship. Perhaps I was. Life seems to apportion its gifts without reference to human notions of fairness or accountability. I've always found that hard to accept.

I was always at my best with Mim and Jack and Bess and Roland. Always (and you will have to take this on trust) my funniest and cleverest and most at ease. Although I knew Jack didn't like me, the point was we all reinforced our ideas of ourselves. We were second nature to each other, we recognised each other's leitmotifs and generously indulged them.

That has all gone now, and it's never coming back.

I know I have been a constant worry to Mim, and now that she has so many other problems in her life, problems that are far more significant than me or mine, I do not want to go on being a burden on her. Any role I may have had as her friend and confidante I bequeath to you – although I think you have already pre-empted this bequest. Look after her for me.

Don't blame yourself in any way for this. Not that you would ever do anything as silly as that. I've been thinking about it for a long time, and it's crystal clear to me that things are not going to get any better – in fact, would almost certainly get much worse.

I want to be cremated, not buried. Dispose of my ashes as you and Mim think fit. I doubt if I'll be watching. Unlike you (cf our recent conversation) I don't have any faith in even the outside possibility of an afterlife. Still, keep your hopes up.

I hope life goes on for you in the same sweet way.

Cheers,

Cyn.

I held the single sheet of paper in the palm of my hand. So light and flimsy, yet carrying a weight of context and implication. It was a very Cynthia letter. There were a few barbs here and there, but on the whole I thought she had let me off lightly. Beside me, Mim was gazing at her letter with unseeing eyes. It was three times the length of mine, but she hadn't turned a page for ten minutes or more.

I knew what she was thinking. It wasn't a question of why Cyn had done it, but of why we had failed to anticipate it and forestall her. To that question, I thought, she and I might have very different responses. In retrospect, I saw Cyn's life as having been on a dizzy downward spiral since the Open Dinner. Since *you* came back into her life, a little voice whispered. I rammed the little voice back in its box. It shut up dutifully, but I was fairly sure I hadn't heard the last of it.

'If only we had remembered her birthday,' Mim's voice disintegrated with grief. She would torture herself about this, I knew, for ever. 'If only. Aren't they the two saddest words in the language?'

In the kitchen Susanna and Jake were doing their homework on the table. The ambience was unusually quiet and studious. I set about making tea Cyn's way, with heated pot and tea leaves. I wondered if I was going to think about Cyn every time I made tea from now on. Maybe this would be another of her unexpected legacies.

The children were examining me surreptitiously. Eventually, as I poured boiling water into the teapot, Jake's seething curiosity got the better of him.

'How did she kill herself?'

Susanna must have kicked him under the table, because he glared at her and poked his tongue out. I told them about Cyn's death, keeping it simple. Jake posed a couple of technical questions about hosepipes and exhaust fumes, and then asked, 'How long did it take to work?'

Susanna gave him a dirty look. 'Cut it out! What kind of a question is that?'

'No, it's all right. Well, longish. An hour and a half, perhaps?'

'So if those people that found her had come earlier, she wouldn't've been dead yet. They could've saved her life.'

'Yes, they could.'

He sucked in his cheeks. 'Pretty bad luck, huh?'

'Yep. Sure was.'

There it is in a nutshell, I thought: pretty bad luck. Cyn's death reduced to the roll of the dice. The story of her life. The story of everyone's life. Chance meetings, opportunities taken or missed, advice ignored or acted on, good timing, bad timing. A life going on its own sweet way, and a life going off the rails.

As I was setting the tea tray down next to Mim, the doorbell shrilled with two strong and confident rings. I opened it without a thought. The tall figure standing there in a stylish, full-length leather coat and brown felt hat caused my heart to thud in my chest.

'*Sam?*'

He stood there, surrounded by luggage, absurdly familiar and yet also a stranger. He groaned and opened his arms wide. I fell into them, again without a thought. We kissed, very hard, without drawing breath. I knew that kiss, every permutation and nuance of it, and yet it felt newly minted.

He held me at arm's length, looking at me intensely in the way he always had, and going directly to the crux of the matter.

'Is this the real you? Why didn't you meet me?'

'I couldn't.'

'Why?'

'Oh —' The enormity of telling him stuck in my throat. I felt weak. 'Sam, you can't stay here.' If I was unsure of everything else, I was absolutely sure of this.

He looked as if he had been hit by a thunderbolt. 'What do you mean? Don't you want me here? What is it you're saying?'

'I'm not really saying anything except — you can't *stay* here. Not now. It's just not possible because of what's happened.'

'Why? What's happened?'

Unlike me, Sam never tried to repress his feelings. He allowed whatever he was thinking to write itself on his face without inhibition. Now, I saw his face was haggard with apprehension and doubt. I was still in the doorway, he stood marooned on the porch among his moat of suitcases.

'A friend Mim and I were at university with died yesterday.'

He looked baffled. Clearly he didn't see any necessary connection between this and my incomprehensible attitude.

'You see, we've only just found out. We need to deal with it by ourselves. To, well, grieve in private.' And I'm not ready to deal with the big issue, with why you are here, I thought. Right now I'm into damage control.

'You're throwing me out on my ear because of that? You mean, go to a hotel?'

It made it easier that money was not a problem with Sam. In the last few years of international success he had been rolling in it. And he loved the luxury, impermanence and romance of hotels. As I did. They had played a seminal role in our courtship.

'A hotel, yes. I'm sorry.'

He relaxed slightly and swept me into his arms again. 'Well, maybe that's better anyway. We'll go to the Savoy or the Connaught.' He looked up at the house: 'Somewhere rather more our style.' He whispered in my ear, 'Somewhere with huge beds and fabulous room service, and very good *insulation*. I'm desperate to go to bed with you, I'm starved of it, I can't wait a moment longer.'

'Sam, you don't understand. Our friend killed herself. Committed suicide, out of the blue. Well, kind of out of the blue, anyway. I had to identify her. I can't come with you. I have to stay here with Mim.'

He looked dumbstruck. He didn't understand, not at all, he made that quite clear. I was palming him off on a hotel *on his own*? After he'd flown across the world to be with me? He didn't say it, but the implication was there, in every wounded fibre of his demeanour: I was putting a friend over him.

Although Jack had known him for years, Mim had never met Sam, and this was not the time for introductions. But taxis tended not to cruise down the side streets of Kilburn looking for fares. We would have to ring for a cab.

I said rapidly, 'I'm sorry about this but you're going to have to go right this minute. Wait here in the hall while I phone. Mim's too distraught to meet anyone right now. We can leave the luggage where it is.'

I could see him turning this over in his mind. I realised I could have made a better choice of words.

'So I'm just "anyone" now, am I? Doesn't she know who I am in your life?'

'Of course she knows. Stay right where you are. I'm going to call a cab.'

When I returned Sam was in the sitting room talking to Mim. More accurately, he was chatting and she was scarcely even pretending to listen. Cynthia's letter sat on her lap. Mim's eyes kept darting to it, anguished.

'Minicab'll be here in five minutes,' I told Sam tersely. 'There's a depot just around the corner.'

'How convenient.' He looked pained, and I half expected Mim to reflexively insist on him staying here. She didn't. Mim is growing up, I thought. She's realising that there are limits to good manners, that just occasionally, in the interests of sanity and survival, one must put oneself first. Cyn would have pointed out that I was an exemplary role model for Mim in this regard. As indeed, in any other area involving the exercise of unbridled self-interest.

'Who was this friend who killed herself?' Sam was inquiring sociably.

'Cynthia Whicker,' I said through gritted teeth. 'But –'

'I don't remember her name. You've never mentioned her.'

Just rub it in, I wanted to say. I know, I know, I never gave Cynthia a single thought until I saw her again a few weeks ago. And then after I saw her again I gave her plenty of thoughts, but they were nearly all pejorative.

'What happened? What drove her to it?' He was interested, his writer's instincts on the qui vive.

Mim's head was down and I saw a teardrop fall on Cyn's letter. I grabbed Sam and propelled him from the room.

'Don't just ask imbecile intrusive questions as if it's an ordinary anodyne topic of conversation!' I was almost incoherent. 'You never used to be so insensitive. This is not just any old common or garden nobody falling off the perch or croaking from old age. It's the suicide of her beloved friend, for heaven's sake!'

'Not *your* beloved friend, I see.' Sam was unmoved by my tirade. 'Do I detect a small jarring note there? Spot of bluster, maybe? Could there be a frisson of bad blood, perhaps?'

He knows me too well, I thought peevishly. I had always seen us as soul mates, but for the first time it occurred to me: it's not that we're complementary at all. We're alike.

'I don't want to go into it now, if you don't mind.'

'Aha. I thought it might be a case of the well-known Lou protesteth too much syndrome. If you're ruthlessly insisting on shunting me off to a hotel, you'd better at least let me book one.'

There was a smug gleam in his eyes that reminded me disconcertingly of Cynthia. We were outside the kitchen door, and I realised I was going to have to introduce him to Susanna and Jake.

Within a minute of his having booked a room the three of them were engaged in a discussion about Cynthia. This involved Sam asking questions and the children responding with as much frankness as they felt able to exhibit, given my presence. Susanna kept a careful eye on me, and an undisguisedly inquisitive one on Sam.

His genuine curiosity about them always went down very well with young people. He liked children, found each one fresh and original, and they responded to this novel adult approach with enthusiasm. I found myself wondering what he was like as a father. There was a lavish discomfort in this line of speculation. I had always been evasive about the sensitive subject of his children, both privately and in conversation.

'So what was her attitude to you?' he was asking the kids, elbows on the table. 'What did you dislike about it?'

Susanna looked at me. 'She was always trying to get close to us. It sort of had the opposite effect. I mean, we couldn't be expected to have anything in common with someone like her, could we?'

It was a plea to me. I recognised the guilt, but I wasn't prepared to appease it. She should feel its sting too, I thought. It might do her some good.

'She was always here and she was always drunk!' Jake interrupted. This blithe uncomplicated perspective, I decided, was allowable only on the grounds of his extreme callowness. I could see his sister reach the same conclusion, and resent his privileged reprieve like mad. Well, tough, I thought. Facing the moral music is what growing up should be all about.

Sam's eyes were following this little tableau with amusement. I jumped up.

'Time to go. The cab'll be here.'

Outside he pulled me to him. 'You'll come over tomorrow? Early? For breakfast in bed.'

'Sam, I don't know. I don't think so. I'll try. I'll just have to play it by ear.'

Funeral, I was thinking. Flowers. Will. Wake. We'll have to give Cyn a good send-off. A worthy, rousing send-off.

Mim's mind had been running along the same lines, but before she embarked on them she said to me, 'He's so good-looking, Lou.'

'Yes. He is, isn't he?'

'Byronic, with that long straight nose and all that wild black hair. It was always your type, wasn't it?'

'I suppose it was.'

'He could have stayed here, you know.'

'I know he could. But it's better that he didn't.'

She looked up, her eyes shadowed. 'Are you sure? Even him?'

'Yes, I'm sure. Even him.'

16

CYNTHIA HAD INCLUDED practical details in her letter to Mim. The name of her solicitor, and the information that a copy of her will was in her flat. She had left money, she informed Mim, for a wake. She was anxious that her passing be regarded as a measured and reasonable response, rather than as a tragic aberration. Most of all, she was anxious that Mim should understand that she herself was blameless.

In a poignant echo of Mim's words to her children, Cyn had written to her:

> You have been my dearest friend for over twenty years. No-one could have been truer or more valued, and no-one could have done more for me. I would have already done what I'm now doing a thousand times over, were it not for you. Please never, ever, even for one moment, blame yourself for any aspect of my behaviour, now or previously. I shall be deeply upset if I look down from heaven (or up from the other place) and

catch you feeling guilty or distressed on my account.

Having said that, and knowing you as I do, I also know that it is worse than useless to hope that you will not grieve for me. When you are tempted to, remember this: my happiest moments have been due to you and spent in your house. You have been responsible for sustaining me at the modified level of sanity and sanguineness I may have achieved. And for what I may have achieved on the negative side you are most emphatically not responsible.

I have come to believe that there are some people for whom a limited life span is the right and proper thing. I think I have always known that I am one of those people. There are all kinds of reasons why they (and I shall call them the Type X's) should not feel it incumbent on them to carry on when they feel they have reached an appropriate departure point. I feel I have now reached this point, and there is indeed a sense of appropriateness, of rightness in what I am doing, both for myself and for others. Including you, dearest Mim.

Cyn had handwritten the last part of Mim's letter. She was in the car with the music playing, and in spite of the Bollinger and the gas seeping in, her writing was firm to the end.

I feel very calm and satisfied now, and it may sound strange to you, Mim, but I feel pleased with myself.

Don't grieve, don't mourn. In a very real sense, you see, I am at peace.

With all my love,

Cyn.

In her death, I thought, Cyn has finally achieved a kind of nobility. I saw that peace. It was on her face. I can vouch for it.

'I'd like to have Bessie over,' Mim said when I put the letter down, unable for a moment to speak.

'Bess? Now? Before dinner? Are you sure, Mim?'

'Quite sure. It seems right. It's her tragedy too. And it would be a way of – of breaking the ice. After, you know, what's happened.'

'Well, if you're sure.'

'Yes. I've missed her.'

I rang Bess. She said she would drop whatever she was doing, leave the children with Roland and drive straight over.

'I'll stay the night on the couch. Or in Timmy's bed, if he's in the kennel. Oh, Lou, what a terrible, terrible thing. I should have seen her more, I blame myself. Well, of course I couldn't while we were in Jamaica, but I should have contacted her the minute I got back. Instead of . . . well, *you* know the dreaded thing I was doing instead.'

I remembered that Bess didn't know that Mim knew the nature of the dreaded thing.

'Bess,' I said, thankful I was not being overheard, 'I'm afraid Mim knows too.'

'She *does*? Oh. Oh dear. That's very – *how* does she know? I thought we –'

'Cyn. It was Cyn.'

'Cyn? Oh. Yes, I see. She always made a virtue of *brutal* honesty, didn't she?'

'She did, that's very true.'

'But – are you sure Mim wants to see me, under the circumstances?'

'Quite sure. You know Mim. She's convinced herself it's a good thing, because you and Jack are family.'

'Darling Mim,' said Bess fondly. 'I had a feeling she would understand, and give us her blessing. Didn't you?'

'Well . . . Mmm. I suppose so.'

In the hall I found an envelope pushed under the door. It was addressed to me in small, cramped handwriting. I ripped it open, then tore up the contents into small pieces and chucked them in the fire.

It was from Stuart. He knew that Sam had been and gone, and he wanted to offer me his help in coping with the situation. He also wished to convince me, since he felt I hadn't really taken it in (perhaps I had never experienced this from anyone before?), of his unlimited devotion. I realised with a boiling sense of outrage that he must have been watching the house.

I raced into the street, breathing hard, but there was no sign of him or his car. I felt violated. He must have seen me greet Sam, hung about, and a short time later observed me farewell him.

'That rancid little turd's been spying on me!' I told Mim, then regretted it. She didn't need any more nasty things to think about. As it was, she hardly appeared to register what I'd said.

It was already late, but we held off dinner until Bess arrived, in a cloud of tea rose and mohair. I let Mim answer the door. They came into the kitchen with their arms around each other's waists. Both had shed tears. Bess's nose was pink and shiny where the foundation had rubbed off, and she had streaks of mascara under her eyes. I guessed the children would put this extravagant display of feeling down wholly to its component part: emotion over Cynthia's death.

With some help from Jake, Susanna made a surprisingly good fist of the supper, which was almost identical to that served up two nights before at absent Cynthia's party. Bess, of course, was oblivious to this, but for Mim and me it was a pathetic subtext to what was as mournful a little party as its predecessor had been rollicking. There was no background music from our vintage, there were no napkins folded like swans, and precious few jokes. The quantity of wine put away, however, was much the same.

Having Bess there, with her unquenchable warmth and pizzazz, made a difficult occasion somewhat easier. This was in itself something of a paradox, since her presence, in theory, should have added an additional sticky element to an already distressing situation.

It was a testimony to the length and depth of their friendship, I thought, laid on the line by not one but two major crises, that Mim and Bess behaved towards each other much as they always had: with abundant affection. If I could detect any difference at all it was that each treated the other as if she were an extremely breakable object. At one point Mim looked across the table at me. I knew what she was saying: you see, it's like I said it would be, like it always was.

The three of us stayed up talking long into the night. I think we were equally reluctant to go up to our solitary beds and lie there in the silence, a prey to the night terrors of melancholia and remorse. We put on Bach's St Matthew Passion, Otto Klemperer's version, the very same LP that we had listened to in smoky college rooms with Cynthia, when it was all shiny and new and Mim's proud acquisition. The scratches on the record couldn't mask the sublime sound. There was a little old-fashioned comfort in the fall of our voices against that music and the philosophical flames.

When we eventually retired we had made plans. The cremation might be weeks way, following the inquest. In the interim we all felt we needed to mark Cyn's death with an immediate wake.

Like the trouper she always was, Bess insisted on staying over the next day. She would collect Cyn's will with us, and help organise the gathering. We had already drawn up a list of people to contact. We agreed we should only tell people who had meant something in Cyn's life. It was a piteously small list.

Bess suggested augmenting it with friends from work.

I was dubious. 'Did she have any?'

Mim wasn't sure, but thought Cyn may have mentioned a couple of names. Eventually I was deputised to ring the English Department. Apart from anything else, I was fairly sure that Cyn would have neglected to give them advance warning of her intentions.

I dialled, and got onto the same gruff woman I had spoken to before.

'I'm ringing about Cynthia Whicker,' I began tentatively.

'Oh yes?' The voice conveyed a knowing sarcasm. 'The *migraine* messenger, are we?'

'Well, no, actually we're not –'

'Something else? Severe gastric attack? *Chundering*, is she?'

'No! *Listen* – I'm trying to tell you something!'

'Been carted off to hospital, poor old thing?'

'She's dead, you smug idiot!'

There was a pause. The voice adjusted to a detached impartiality. 'Dead, you say?'

'Yes.'

'So we can safely assume she won't be coming in?'

'I think you can safely assume that.'

'For the foreseeable future?'

'That's right.'

I replaced the receiver. 'That was the most peculiar conversation,' I said to Bess and Mim. 'Do you think all academics are quite mad?'

Soon afterwards we were contacted by two concerned colleagues, but Sam got in first. He demanded to know why I hadn't shown up for breakfast. I told him it was impossible.

'Aren't you forgetting something? I'm in the same country! The same city! Overpaid, oversexed and over here. I was awake *all night* with jet-lag, rattling around all alone on this gorgeous king-size bed, consumed with separation anxiety, and worrying about us.'

This last phrase was delivered with a meaningful emphasis that I chose to overlook.

'Sam, I'm sorry to say this but I'm completely swamped today with all the admin stuff –'

'*Admin* stuff? What on earth are you on about? Are you working as an office temp now?'

'I'm helping to organise a wake, if you recall.'

'But that won't happen for weeks. It's a suicide – there'll have to be an inquest first. Then the funeral. *Then* the wake. Are you trying to avoid me?'

'No! For God's sake –'

'Well, I'm coming over there right now.'

'*No!* Oh, all right then, I'll come to you when we've finished everything.'

'You were never like this before. You never bothered to finish anything. You'd have been halfway through a heart transplant and you'd have pulled out the intravenous drip and come racing barefoot over hot coals to see me, before.'

And that wasn't even the tiniest exaggeration, I thought. I didn't pursue it. I had neither time, nerve nor inclination to go along that road just then. We had sad things to do, and one of the saddest was the retrieval from her flat of Cyn's will.

Mim had a key. As she unlocked the door and we entered the silent apartment, I was besieged with reminders of my one previous visit. I seemed to see Cyn sitting opposite me, taking a huge bite of chocolate cake and licking the icing off her fingers. I had the feeling that even this harmless exercise of hedonism hadn't given her much pleasure. But then, in all probability, neither had my company.

The windows were tightly closed and the flat was over-heated, as before, but now I was conscious of an additional undefined presence in the air. Besides the hot, overstuffed character of the rooms, which made them so oppressive, there was now a strange other quality. After a while I worked out what it was. All these goods and chattels represented the detritus of a life. It had been a comparatively brief one, which in itself is never a cause for rejoicing, and not a life conspicuously well lived. The occupant of this flat had found existence a burden, in the main, and her unhappiness had communicated itself to her possessions.

Cyn's will lay on the purple counterpane. The three of us stood in her boudoir, surrounded by the desolate evidence of wishful thinking. We were hushed, as if we were in a cathedral rather than a would-be pleasure dome. I was hounded by a hallucination of Cynthia, naked and bouncing atop the hapless Stuart on the broad expanse of satin sheets. I wondered if Mim or Bess was haunted by a similar nightmare vision.

'Did Cyn have any other —' I sought for a neutral word, '*romances*? I know about the encounter with Stuart Friend, of course.'

I saw Mim wince, and regretted raising this irreverent subject. But Bess came to my rescue.

'Hardly a thing, poor love. I really did try to push possibilities her way, *gently* and *unobtrusively* of course, but I was hopelessly unsuccessful. There was *one* candidate, wasn't there, Mim, but it must be five or six years ago now. A work colleague too, not from my stable, I couldn't take any credit for him! But it wasn't a great success, I'm afraid. He moved soon after, got another job at a northern university.'

He moved to get away from Cyn's clutches, I thought. 'Did you meet him?'

'Yes, they came for dinner. Just the once. He wasn't an oil painting, it has to be said. A bit on the spotty-swotty side. Roland couldn't abide him, not that he'd ever show it. Horribly into pedantry. He took me to task for confusing pupa and larva, I remember. They're different stages of insect development, evidently. Still, at least he *was* of the male persuasion. Sort of. Although as I told Cyn, I couldn't imagine he was much chop in the cot as he was always fas*tidi*ously washing his hands, and Cyn confirmed that grim hypothesis!'

She glanced hurriedly at Mim and put her arm round Mim's shoulders. Mim burst into tears. But she recovered almost immediately and apologised, wiping her eyes.

'I'm sorry. It's just that – here we are, talking about Cyn as if she were still alive, instead of having killed herself, and we're standing here in her flat, in her *bed*room, amongst all her private things, and I've got her will in my hand . . .'

'You're quite right, Mim. It's disrespectful and I should absolutely know better.' Bess looked up at the ceiling. 'Cyn, darling, if you're watching, forgive all this nonsense. You know we love you to bits. We're so very sorry things didn't work out and you had such a rotten time of it, and we dearly hope you are at peace now.'

Peace, I thought. That word again. A word that had almost certainly never applied to Cyn during her time on this earth, and now seemed an integral part of her leaving it. The free-thinking Bess's impromptu little speech, which only she could have delivered, resounded rather like a prayer. In my mind

Cyn's bedroom was reinventing itself as a shrine, stuffed with the florid and forlorn relics of her aspirations.

We turned away and, by mutual unspoken consent, quickly left. We all felt the need to get out of Cyn's depressing home and read her will in an impersonal environment, and we ended up in a quiet pub near the Barbican. Cyn had been a regular here, and it had a small cosy room off the main bar where, in the early afternoon, we knew we had a good chance of being the only occupants.

'A drink is well and truly the operative word,' Bess announced, 'so I'm buying us a bottle of top drawer French fizz. A cleansing libation at any place and time, and only right and proper today, seeing as it was our dear Cyn's last tipple of choice.'

We popped the cork in unseemly haste and toasted Cyn. The main part of her brief will had been drawn up some years earlier. She had paid off her flat with money inherited from her mother. She left it to Mim, and the contents plus her motorbike to the women's refuge section of the housing co-op. Her mother's jewellery, including an art nouveau necklace, a marcasite watch and several rings, was to be divided up between Bess and Mim, who were her joint executors. Susanna and Jake, Daisy and Lizzie each received small sums of money and specified books from her library. A recent codicil left a hundred pounds to Gayle, Mim's delinquent cleaning student. The remaining money in her bank account was to be blown on the wake.

A further handwritten codicil had been added on the evening before her suicide, and witnessed by a neighbour. It left her collection of vitamins and homeopathic remedies to me.

'I didn't know you and Cyn shared an interest in alternative medicine, Lou,' Bess said ingenuously.

'We didn't. Cyn tried to persuade me to take some pills once, for stress management and suchlike. She said I would find them efficacious.'

'And did you?'

'I stubbornly refused to sample any.'

'Well, as co-executrix I shall personally guarantee their delivery. You can indulge each and every closet hypochondriacal tendency in your armoury!' Bess sounded light-headed as she tossed back a glass. I guessed it was a reaction. I felt much the same myself.

Another effusive note from Stuart was lying on the mat when we returned. He had heard about Cynthia's death, and was profuse with offers of condolences and help. I had an awful suspicion I had glimpsed the rear tyres of his MG burning rubber as we turned into Mim's street.

'What on earth am I going to do about him?'

Bess suggested I utilise my recent contacts in the constabulary.

'Sool the rozzers in blue onto him, Lou. That's what they're for, after all. You've got a good thing going with that dishy young constable, haven't you? I had to do that once. I got my nice village bobby to put the frighteners on someone who wouldn't leave me alone. And jolly effective it was too.'

But Bess in all likelihood had a special thing going with her nice village bobby, I reflected. I wondered if the gentle PC Rahid could be prevailed upon to terrorise Stuart. It seemed unlikely. When Mim was out of the room Bess whispered that Jack was a good man in a scrap. 'And don't forget about Sam, Lou.'

I hadn't forgotten Sam. I was aware that I was now free to go and see him. An invisible gossamer thread was holding me back. With the English Department conversation still fresh in my mind, I asked Bess to ring and tell Sam I'd retired to bed with a severe migraine. Bess had the most ingratiating telephone manner and told the most convincing lies of anyone I knew. Apart from you, Cyn's voice added in my ear.

I listened to Bess's practised charm. Oh yes, she assured Sam, I was awfully upset not to be able to see him tonight. But as he probably knew, once one of these ghastly headaches struck, I was incapacitated for hours. I was dying to see him, and I'd be over as soon as I decently could. In the morning or, she said merrily, in the middle of the night, if the wretched thing went away.

She went on to say how much she was looking forward to seeing him again. Bess, an inveterate traveller, had rendezvoused with Sam and me around the world on various de luxe expeditions, with and without Roland and the girls.

It would be lovely to get together again, even though it was desperately sad that it coincided with such a tragic incident for all of us. Sam hadn't known Cynthia, had he? She had been in some ways a difficult person, but unique and very special. Sam asked a question at this point. Bess answered candidly that yes, there had been the occasional little problem between Lou and Cyn, but there was a deep residue of affection underneath. In fact this was probably why my migraine had come on. It tended to be a reaction to stress, and I was particularly upset by Cynthia's death.

Yes, Bess went on, in answer to another question and without missing a beat or glancing at Mim, Jack was in London. No, he hadn't been especially close to Cynthia in recent years, that was true, but like me he was deeply attached to her underneath. Bess listened attentively at this point and gave a series of brief affirmative responses punctuated by warm gurgling giggles. It hadn't occurred to me until then that Jack had almost certainly told Sam about his affair with Bess. I felt acutely uncomfortable, but if Mim had caught on to what was being said, she showed no emotion.

I thought Bess had laid it on a bit thick, and this was confirmed the next day. I was clinically interested to find that the various forms of paralysis gripping me since Sam's arrival had dissipated during the night. They didn't disperse gradually, like morning fog. Instead, I awoke from a deep sleep to find them vanished. In their place was an uneasy conviction that I could not put this off any longer.

There were serious issues at stake here; I was under no illusion. My future was one, Sam's another, and there were several other people with major interests in the outcome. I tried to shelve these concerns and concentrate, as I had so often done previously, on the here and now. I had always found this surprisingly easy to do, before.

17

I STOOD IN THE PACKED tube next morning hurtling towards the West End. Strap-hanging, suspended in a rocking kind of limbo, I was oblivious to the other passengers. Every now and then I was knocked sideways, and not always figuratively, by a blast of sexual desire. It had been suppressed and buried for what seemed longer than the few weeks I'd been in London, and it exploded inside me with the crude whoosh of a Molotov cocktail.

I felt nostalgic towards this physical passion that had ruled my life, and at the same time detached from it. It was like a well-loved garment that had suddenly turned up after having been given up for lost. I wasn't sure if it would still fit me, or indeed if it was something that I would still wear. Beyond it, in the outer reaches of my consciousness, lurked another thing. This was so vague and formless that it hardly registered as a thought or even a sensation. I was aware of it only as a faint, subliminal buzz of unease, and I put this down to nervous tension.

Sam opened the door and we fell headlong into each other's arms, flinging off our clothes with feverish greed. As he had done before, in so many other hotel rooms in other places, he hung the Do Not Disturb sign on the door and told reception not to put any calls through. We had spent time apart, it was the pattern of the relationship, but never so long or under such circumstances.

But nothing had been forgotten. It seemed as if nothing had changed.

'I was worried that when you finally consented to see me it would be an an anticlimax.' Sam, propped on one elbow, looked into my face.

'You know you're incapable of giving me an anticlimax. Is there an opposite word?'

'The opposite word is climax.'

'Mmm. Right.'

'So why didn't you want to see me?'

'Oh, Sam, let's not talk about it now. I feel like sleeping.' A huge indulgent weariness was consuming me. The flicker of anxiety seemed to have been kicked upstairs, to a remote corner of my mind.

'You didn't have a migraine last night, did you? Bess is a terrible liar. You forget that I direct actors all the time. I can always tell when they're lying.'

'But they lie all the time, that's the nature of acting.'

'You're quite wrong. Lying is the antithesis of acting. Anyway, you can't go to sleep, we're going to lunch.'

'Lunch?' I wasn't sure I could eat lunch. 'Who with?'

'With Jack. At some trendy slap-up joint he knows. Wall-to-wall celebs. You'll love it.'

'*With Jack?*' I sat up. 'I don't want to go and have lunch with Jack. That's the last thing I want to do. I've only just seen

342

you again. I've only just lately found out about him and Bess . . .'

'That's all right. Bess can't make it, she's cooking something for tomorrow.'

'You go and have lunch with Jack, I'll stay here. I'll be here when you get back.'

'Jack won't be pleased. You know he's always fancied you.'

'Phooey. Anyway, he can fill you in on –' I paused, and all the events of the past weeks swirled around me. 'On some of the things that have been going on,' I finished lamely.

On Jack himself and Mim, I thought, and Mim and Dave. Susanna and Dave, Daria and Tracey. On Stuart and Gaby, even on Gayle. And Cynthia, on Cynthia. All these people who had figured in my life, who had been intimately connected with me during the time I'd been separated from Sam, and who were now part of my world.

How could I imagine that Jack, of all people, would tell him about them? But then, how could I tell him myself? Sam knew nothing about this time and these connections, and in that way, in that radical new sense, he knew nothing about me.

'Do I look different to you?' I asked.

'Different? No, you always look the same. Especially after sex. That's the best time for looking. Why do you ask that?'

'Oh, no reason.'

'There's always a reason. Do you *feel* different? About me?' His whole body tensed. 'Is it that guy, that . . .?' He couldn't bring himself to say it.

I stroked his face. 'There's no-one else, I promise. Never has been.' In his relief he looked like a child. 'It's just that a lot's happened since I last saw you. I thought it might have – changed me.'

'No, you're the original genuine article. I've inspected you all over in meticulous detail and I can vouch for it, you're pristine. All these momentous happenings have washed over you without a trace.'

But they haven't, I thought, I'm marked by them. The traces are indelible. You can't see them because they're backstage, behind the scenes. Hidden.

I watched him get dressed, as I had studied him on countless other occasions. Clothes looked very good on Sam, and he took them seriously. Twill trousers, a rust-coloured linen shirt, suede jacket, cashmere scarf. As he put them on he talked at me with his intense, high-energy stream of consciousness.

'We can't stay here in London very long – two or three days at most. The play's booked in for seasons in Germany and Scandinavia, and I want to get back and check how New York's going. You can't leave that lead actor alone or he lapses into Deep South patois. There's talk of LA and Melbourne too. Film scripts. Bright lights, fat city! Easy Street!' He launched into a rousing rendition of 'How You Gonna Keep 'Em Down on the Farm, After They've Seen Paree?'.

I listened, seduced as I invariably was. He hadn't asked me much about my life. I was aware again of something lying in wait, lying lightly, diffidently, at the hinterland of my mind.

He came over to kiss me. 'Oh, to have my own true love in my bed once more. Together again, and never more to be apart.'

He went out whistling. Like me, he had a finely tuned ability to blot things out, to move central moral concerns to the periphery. From there, I knew from experience, they would creep back to haunt him.

I lay in the bed and watched the sunlight dance on the ceiling. There was dappled light outside our second floor window, a thin wintry sun threading through the clouds for the first time in days. I felt sated, all my limbs luxuriously heavy and sleek, in a way that only Sam had ever made me feel. But I couldn't sleep. After a while I got up and wandered around the room.

His familiar possessions were scattered everywhere. The creased leather Gladstone bag in which he kept his portable Olivetti typewriter and notebooks, scripts and research material. His Noel Coward dressing gown. Books and cassettes in piles. I picked up a tape and put it on Sam's portable player. It was Coward himself, singing 'I'll See You Again'. Sam said he often played this when we were apart. I listened. Tears pricked my eyes.

I ran a bath and lay in the deep, hot water, surrounded by bubbles like a forties film star. I thought of the strange epiphany I'd had in Jack's car in the rain – an atheistic epiphany, it must be, in deference to Cynthia. The sudden realisation that all disparate things were linked, that one could predict some things and yet could predict nothing with certainty, because of the infinite web of possibilities, interdependent and unceasing.

I tried to recapture the electric excitement of this revelation. It was not especially profound or obscure, it was embraced by plenty of religions and philosophies. Everyone knew it, to some degree, and yet on another level it was ignored and people lived their lives in a cocoon of oblivion, as if they were autonomous beings at the centre of their own universe. Which on a different level still was a necessary and inevitable way of living.

The single piercing shaft of insight that had so intoxicated me in the car remained elusive. I wondered if it would ever come back. But at the same time I was sure that it had left a residue of itself behind, a nascent spark of enlightenment.

I climbed out of the bath and dried myself with one of the

thick fluffy towels. I had dressed carefully to come to Sam and now, slowly, I put all the clothes back on again. The swinging corduroy skirt that he always liked, the calf-length boots, the wool shirt and antique-buttoned waistcoat. The necklace of tiny freshwater pearls on an intricate old gold chain that Sam had given me. I was feeling slightly sick.

I went in search of something, and found it behind the lamp on the bedside table, on Sam's side of the bed. It was a black and white photograph of his children, and he never travelled without it. The photo was very familiar to me. Hannah and Fergus, very young, eating ice creams. Much of the chocolate ice cream was smeared on their faces. Their mother Ingrid, blonde, youthful and smiling, was in the background, but slightly out of focus. When he met me, Sam liked to say, he had done his dash with blondes. 'Grown out of them,' he would declare, disarmingly.

I thought of the photographs on the dressing table of my bedroom in Mim's house. All of us in our early twenties, thumbing our noses at the vagaries of time and chance. The web of causal connections along which our lives would evolve was already humming and spinning, busily and intricately, but it was invisible and we were unaware. One of those vibrant, posturing youngsters was dead now. A tremor ran through me.

I remembered that we had told reception not to put any calls through, and I cancelled the instruction. Immediately there were three calls for Sam. I rang Mim, who had gone to work. She asked where I was.

'I'm in the hotel room. Sam's having lunch with Jack. Are you all right, Mim?'

'Well,' Mim's voice sounded desolate, 'I suppose it's good to be occupied. I keep thinking about tomorrow.'

'I know. So do I. I'll be glad when it's over.'

'Are *you* all right?'

'So-so.' As I spoke, the immature, amorphous thing that had been lurking at the back of my mind moved forward slightly. My stomach fluttered with disquiet.

'I'll come back tonight, Mim.'

'Oh, Lou, will you?' Mim's voice lightened audibly. 'He won't mind? Are you sure?'

'Quite sure.' I hung up. Sam bounded through the door.

'Anyone call?' It was his invariable greeting. He loved getting messages.

I read them out as he loped over and gave me a lingering kiss. He carried another bunch in his hand. He riffled through them.

'Good lunch?'

'Great lunch. Jack in cracking form. Lasciviously indiscreet, luridly name-dropping. Or should it be the other way round?' He sorted the bits of paper into two piles.

'Didn't take 'em long to track me down, did it? Listen, you don't mind too much if I don't come to that thing tomorrow, do you? Bill Canning's lined up this guy, retail magnate or something, who wants to meet me, mad keen to unload cash registers of loot and invest in plays, apparently. *Just* the kinda guy I like to know!' He sat down and picked up the phone.

I said, trying to keep my voice steady, 'That thing tomorrow's the wake for my old friend.'

He paused, his finger on the dial. 'Yes, I know, but I didn't know her. She doesn't mean anything to me.'

'She meant something to *me*. Shouldn't that mean something to you?'

'Come on, now, don't be a hypocrite. Jack said you couldn't

stand the woman. She was a lush! He told me a scream of a story about the time she laid into him, and you —'

'*Sam!* Shut up! Don't be so bloody —'

He looked amused, and started dialling. 'So bloody what?'

'So bloody callous. *Stop dialling!* And rude and uncaring.'

He turned round. 'Come on, be reasonable. I never even *met* the poor old bat. It's a bit heavy to expect me to go to her wake.'

'*Don't* call her that. She's my age. Younger than *you.*'

'You know I hate those things. It'll be full of people I don't know.'

'And don't want to know?'

'Be fair. I've got a helluva lot to do, and we're leaving in a day or so. What would be the point?'

I stood up, my heart racing. 'The point would be, the point *is*, they're my friends.'

'Exactly. That's my point too.'

I gripped the writing desk, my knuckles white. 'Doesn't it occur to you that I might like you to meet them *because* they're my friends?' I paused for breath. Sam was fiddling with the top of his fountain pen. 'And that this whole business is a pretty harrowing affair, and I might appreciate a bit of support? That I might like you by my side?'

Sam jumped up and crushed me against him.

'Hey, darling, don't get all upset about a small thing like this. If it's so important to you, well of course, I'll try and reschedule some meetings. It's just that I've got so much to do and we're going away in a couple of days.'

I pulled away, shaking my head. 'No.' My heart pounded. 'No what?'

'I'm not. *We're* not.'

'What are you talking about?'

I acknowledged it. The heavy amorphous thing that had been crouching and hiding in the back of my mind moved forward into the light and took possession of me. I broke out in a cold sweat.

'Sam, I can't go with you. I'm not going with you.'

He looked dumbfounded. 'Not going? What d'you mean? Are you saying you want to break *up*? Because of this fucking *wake*?'

'It's not a matter of breaking up, because we haven't been together, have we? Not for weeks. It's not because of the wake. Or Cyn's death. That's got nothing to do with it.'

'Of course it has. It must have. You were fine until I said I might not go. Listen, darling, you're overreacting. You've got yourself in a state about this.'

I shook my head wordlessly.

'What *is* it, then?'

'It's . . . I just can't.' I looked away from his shattered face.

'Don't keep saying that. Don't you love me?'

'Yes.' I didn't hesitate.

'And I love you. Adore you. It's always been there, that *knowledge* between us. So what's the problem?'

Knowledge. That was what it was at the back of my mind, lying doggo. Mim was right. I hadn't wanted to dig down far enough.

'It's this other guy, isn't it?'

I looked into his eyes. 'I give you my word, Sam, there's no-one else.'

'Then it must be the death. This *bloody* suicide.'

'That may be – linked to it. It's mainly other things.'

'I knew I should never have let you go, at New York airport. I knew it. If I hadn't gone back to Ingrid then this would never have happened, would it?'

'Perhaps it wouldn't. I don't know.' I bent and picked up my bag.

'You're not going *now*?' He made an anguished move towards me, his arms wide open.

I shook my head. 'Don't, Sam. Please. I couldn't bear it.'

I ran down two flights of stairs and through the big, opulent lobby. The doorman relaxed his formality and ushered me, with fatherly solicitude, into a taxi ahead of two others.

He leaned over and whispered into my ear, 'There's plenty of other fishes in the sea.'

I was blinded by tears. Later, I would think of these as the first truly grown-up tears I had ever shed.

18

MIM AND I WERE up early, buying flowers. More came in from people like Bess, Daria and Tracey Garrett, and the kitchen and sitting room were full of Gayle's artistic arrangements. Gayle, in a black skirt, white blouse and apron, was on hand to deal with the food and drink. Informed of her little bequest in Cyn's will, she had uttered an incredulous scream.

'That's so lovely of her! I didn't think she knew me that well. Although I s'pose she was here a lot.' A moment afterwards, when Mim had gone upstairs, she said to me, 'Do you think she knew about the –' she rolled her eyes and grimaced, 'the *you* know?'

'Oh, I doubt it,' I said.

Later she rushed up to me as I carried glasses in from the kitchen.

'Your boyfriend's sent a humungous bunch of flowers again! Least I think it's him, cos they're addressed to you. I don't know if we've got enough vases.'

Not fucking Stuart bloody *again*, I said to myself. I thought I'd seen the last of him. But the five dozen long-stemmed red roses were not from Stuart. The card said simply, 'Always, Sam'.

'It wasn't from my boyfriend,' I told Gayle. 'I haven't got one of those any more.'

People started coming through the door and I was borne along by the little tide of our friends, and friends' children. I had to introduce Cyn's two academic colleagues, Maggie and Quentin, who were solid and jolly and didn't know anyone. I had to help Jack with the champagne. After a while, and in the nature of things, the dull ache began to disperse. I took Bess's advice, to absorb it with alcohol, and found it worked well enough.

As Bess said, it was a small wake, but perfectly formed. She brought along Roland as well as the children and I was pleased to see him. The nuances that arrived with them only added to those already floating poignantly round the room. I hadn't seen Daisy and Lizzie for three years. Now they were polite, poised teenagers who, nevertheless, greeted Susanna and Jake with what sounded like wild war cries.

Tracey Garrett turned up with Nathan and her two energetic kids, then Daria and Ruth. We played Cyn's music and tried to cheer ourselves up by drinking too much. The tone quickly became one of rather artificial, hectic gaiety.

'This is just like absent Cynthia's party all over again, isn't it?' Daria said to me. 'And Cynthia is still absent! Oh dear, what a great pity it all is.' She sounded tipsy.

'Do you remember how we watched her ride away on her bike?'

'Oh yes. I remember it very well. There was a bad feeling in the air, a very bad feeling indeed.' Daria shivered theatrically, and pulled her sari around her.

'I felt it too.'

'In fact, Louisa,' Daria added, 'I said to Ruth that very evening, I am afraid Cynthia is going to come to a sticky end, but there is nothing anybody can do about it. Sometimes, you see, I can be surprisingly psychic for my age!'

I was tempted to ask her whether she had any mystical insight into my own future, but decided against it. If I was going to come to a sticky end, I thought, I'd rather not know in advance.

'How *is* Ruth?' The kids had started off with a dutifully mournful demeanour, which dissipated as soon as they were out of our sight. All seven of them were now gathered upstairs in Susanna's room. A series of heavy thumps reverberated overhead as I spoke.

Daria knew what I was referring to. 'Oh, she is very much better. There is even a little improvement on her normal self, as she is anxious to get back into my good books. Plenty of breakfast in bed, I am getting.'

'Susanna's improved a bit, but nothing like to the extent of breakfast in bed. Talking of good books, Daria, how is yours going?' The one, I recollected, about the imminent evolutionary obsolescence of the male sex.

Daria beamed. 'Oh, it is going jolly well, thank you. We are just in the middle of the bit about sperm counts. Those poor unfortunate spermatozoa are on a steep decline, you know, wherever you look.' She twinkled. 'Of course, there is the advantage that smaller numbers of sperms lead to fewer accidents.'

Jack came over with the champagne. 'Can I offer any of you lovely ladies a top-up?'

Daria held out her glass. 'That is an offer I cannot refuse. I would very much like one of your excellent top-ups, Jack. They are always just the thing!'

'Our Daria's grasp of English is getting more colloquial by the day,' I remarked to Tracey.

'And our Jack is doing a sterling job of keeping his options open.' We watched him wave Bess and Roland over and relate a lengthy joke to them and Daria. It ended uproariously. Roland, always generous, laughed as loudly as anyone else.

There was no change in Tracey's position.

'And not likely to be until the dawn of the new millennium. Or beyond. No doubt Daria gave your actions vis-à-vis Sam the royal seal of approval?'

'Oh, she did. I'm exalted in the sisterhood. No longer am I another downtrodden Hope, desperately clutching at a straw man.' I wondered if I had gone too far. Tracey, after all, was still Hope incarnate. She grinned at me reassuringly.

'Is one permitted to ask how you managed to do the unmentionable?'

'Well, I don't even know if it was the right thing to do.' I halted. 'No – that's just what I do know. What I don't know is quite how I did it. Or why, exactly.'

'Humph. Perplexing.'

'Right. It's got something to do with causes. No, effects. Consequences rippling out and drawing other people in . . .'

Tracey passed me a lace handkerchief. It was incongruously dainty in her large hand. I scrubbed at my eyes.

'Daft question. Shouldn't have asked. Well, you're a hard act to follow and that's for sure. Spirit's unwilling *and* the flesh is weak.' We both watched Nathan upend a champagne bottle into Daria's glass. 'Not that winning our Daria's good opinion is number one on the list of priorities.'

'Quite. That was an incidental, rather dubious, benefit.'

'In any event, I imagine the severance process is no bed of

roses.' Her eyes strayed to the big bunch at her elbow. 'Oops, sorry. Bad choice of flora.'

'It's not the happiest time of my life, no.'

'Nothing's irrevocable, of course. Leeward of our demise.'

'*This* is.' I could see she was surprised by my vehemence. It took me by surprise too, but in a different way. At least there was a part of me that had no doubts. Mim would probably say it was the subconscious. My conscious mind, on the other hand, was riddled with them.

The scent of Sam's opulent bouquet mingled with tea rose, and I found Bess at my side. She looked even more spectacular than usual, in a clinging forties-style crepe dress. It was a sober black, as befitted the occasion, but with the subtext of a swooping décolletage. Her aquamarine eyes, outlined in black with thick curled lashes, sparkled with some naughty secret she was dying to impart. I recognised the expression of old.

She put her arm round me affectionately. 'Lou, are you bearing up, darling?'

'Up to a point.'

'This is so strange, isn't it? The thought that we'll never see Cyn again, never have an *argument* with her. Do you think she's here?'

'In the room?'

'I feel her presence, every now and again. She was such an amazing personality, I sort of feel she'll never really go away. You'll scoff, but I often think about what Cyn would say about something I'm doing or saying.'

'Yes. She functions as one's personal moral watchdog.'

Bess was delighted. 'Do you feel that too? That she *reins in* one's worst excesses? She certainly keeps *me* up to scratch! Or tries to, I should say. She has an uphill battle.'

She shook her immaculately waved blonde tresses in a

gesture that successfully caught the eye of each of the small number of men in the room. It was quite unselfconscious. 'She was very influential, wasn't she? In her way. She was the most devastatingly uncompromising person I've ever met.'

'That's right. Her honesty. And willingness to face up to issues. She certainly influenced me.' I'd only just realised this, and it was a shock. It took some coming to terms with. I put it away to think about another time, and raised my glass.

'Let's drink to Cyn. Long may she rein in our worst excesses.'

I remembered the gleam in Bess's eyes. 'Bessie, what did you want to tell me?'

Her eyes opened wide. 'How did you guess?' She dropped her voice. 'Jack and I are on the verge, Lou!'

'Of what? On the verge of *what*?'

'On the verge of moving in together. And do you know, I think it's all Cynthia's fault!'

I felt dazed, and must have looked it. I swilled some champagne.

'You see, Lou, it's all due to Cyn. We might never have reached this point if she hadn't taken the bit between her teeth and told Mim. When she did, that brought it all out in the open. And Mim, being the sweet person she is, accepted it. As you know.'

Uncompromising honesty had its downside, I reflected. Moral issues were never as straightforward as all that. I forced myself to smile at Bess.

'Well, bully for you both.'

'And, Lou,' Bess leaned confidentially closer to me, 'I'm only telling *you* this, definitely not Mim just yet. In any case, apart from anything else, it may not happen . . .'

My mind boggled. 'What? *What* may not?'

'We're going to try for a baby, Lou! I mean, I'm only thirty-nine, and people have babies into their fifties these days. Well into them. I've just been talking to Daria.'

'Daria? Oh god –'

'I thought I might introduce her to Roland. What do you think? Don't worry, I didn't spill the beans, I'm not *that* love-sick and youthfully indiscreet! It was a generalised conversation. You see, she's writing this book –'

'I know all about that book.'

'Well, she has a chapter on late babies. *Very* late. Only, of course, she's writing about babies conceived without direct male input, as it were, and needless to say we do not intend to traverse *that* road!'

Jack came up from behind and brandished champagne. I held out my glass for an urgent refill.

'Good girl,' Jack said approvingly. 'Drink up. Drown your sorrows.' He looked at me as if I were the prototype of a new species. 'Are you pulling through, sweetheart? Weathering the twin storms of death and divorce? Good grief, if we add taxes to the list you'll be in possession of the three certainties of life!'

Over Jack's shoulder I saw Mim and Roland in earnest conversation in the corner.

'I'm fine, thanks. Never been better.'

'I told you to get shot of that schmuck years ago.' He looked complacent. 'It's gratifying to have my advice taken, at long last. Mark my typically wise and prescient words, you'll be a new woman now.'

'Like Mim, huh? Well, I rejected your advice, Jack. I did it all off my own bat.'

'Be ungracious, I don't mind. You're a free agent. Any time you need cheering up, I'm more than happy –'

'Bess told me about your plans. In the areas of relocating and procreating.'

Jack didn't move a muscle. You had, I thought, to admire him. 'Live life to the full, darl. I recommend it unreservedly. I'm doing Sam tomorrow, by the way. Thought I should let you know.'

'On the program? Oh, do you have to?' My stomach felt hollow. 'Well, all I can say is, treat him gently.'

'He's an old mate, it'll be kid gloves territory. What did you expect?' He sounded wounded. 'I thought you might like to make a guest appearance.'

'You thought wrong.'

'Why not? It'd give you a bit of leverage. Help keep me under control.' He grinned.

'No thanks. I'll settle for trusting you. Reluctantly.'

'You're writing the book you always meant to write, aren't you? This'll give you exposure money can't buy. Come on, you know you've always craved it. I'll guarantee you'll be the cynosure of all eyes.'

'No thanks. Bad timing.'

'No inducements?' He gave me what I took to be a significant look.

'No inducements.'

He poured the dregs of the bottle into my glass.

'Jack —' He looked up, with an expectant, wolfish leer. 'Don't mention me. Please?'

'It'll cost you.'

'It'll cost *you*, you bugger!'

I made a fuming mental note to solicit Bess's influence. Mim waved me over. She and Roland had been engaged in a close confab and everyone in the know had given them a wide berth. Roland rose from the sofa in his gentlemanly way.

'Welcome to the refuge of the newly dumped!' he announced in ringing tones. Roland was one the few people I knew who still spoke Received Pronunciation. 'And you're a new dumper, I understand?'

'Well, I can't take sole credit. We both had a fair share of the action.'

'You are too modest.'

'We've been discussing our futures, Lou.' I was relieved to see that apart from looking flushed, Mim seemed quite calm and resigned. 'I expect Bess told you she and Jack are setting up house together.'

'You're both being thoroughly modern and understanding.'

Roland nodded. 'One is wry. But one can't make a stink about it. Must be civilised, after all. Best for the children. Best all round, really.'

Mim said, 'Cyn foresaw this happening. I didn't want to look any further ahead, but she was right, wasn't she? It's better to confront things. They don't go away.'

'It's called taking charge of your destiny and embracing it.'

I had said something like that to Susanna. Sometime, I thought, I must try to convey to Mim that consoling insight, the exhilaration of an unknown future. That almost ecstatic embrace of the unpredictable and uncertain.

Mim sighed. 'Is that what it's called? Well, Cyn did it, I suppose. But I so wish she'd chosen a different destiny to take charge of.'

'As do we all,' said Roland. 'She was a rum bird, in some ways, but a one-off.'

I memorised that, to spread abroad. For Cyn, it was as good an epitaph as any I'd heard.

Neither Mim nor I felt very well in the aftermath of the wake. The following night we watched Jack's program gingerly. He gave Sam a fairly indulgent trot, getting a lot of mileage out of their shared background. Several stories were new to me. The two of them had knocked about together in New York in the early days, and Jack created a romantic, hard-up, quasi La Bohème ambience for their antics. I happened to know that this was largely fantasy.

The closest Mim and I came to cringing was when he questioned Sam about the sources for his plots. Sam agreed that he drew freely on the lives of those around him.

'*Their* love lives. What about your own?'

'Mine is strangely redundant. You see, all my friends know of my professional interest. They generously provide me with more source material than I can handle. As you do yourself, Jack.'

The studio audience laughed. Jack cowered humorously in his chair.

'You mine your friends' love *lives*, but there are also a lot of deaths in your plays.'

'Of course. For the student of choice, dramatisable behaviour, deaths are a rich resource.'

'Take the death out of Shakespeare and you don't have a play?'

'Exactly. And deaths are especially interesting, of course, when they're sudden or unnatural.' Sam leaned back with his hands behind his head.

'Someone I knew of committed suicide recently, and that created a particular train of havoc. It was a catalyst for three separate relationship breakdowns, and that's just the ones *I* know of. I sat down that very night, Jack, and plotted out a whole new play . . .'

Jack changed the subject smoothly. Sam was one of the few people, I thought, who could challenge him on his own terms and outwit him.

We sat quietly at the end, after the kids had gone to bed.

'It's going to be hard for you, Lou,' Mim said at last.

'Hard?'

'To find someone else. He was very special. I can see that.'

'Yes. In his way. But then so was Jack.'

'Yes. In his.' Mim didn't miss a beat. I was pleased with her.

The bright, cold weather held until the day of Cyn's funeral. Our small group clustered in the front pews of the little chapel, conspicuous for our dark glasses and also, I thought, for our relative youth. In the presence of Cyn's simple casket I felt young and vulnerable. Roland, at forty-three, was probably the oldest person there.

Bess confided to me that there was nothing like a funeral for bringing unlikely people together. During the service, and possibly for the last time, Mim and Jack and Bess and Roland appeared in public with their children as two separate families. It didn't last long. Roland had to go back to work, and afterwards Bess and Jack gravitated towards each other.

'They make a toothsome twosome, one must admit,' Tracey observed.

I had to agree. There was something wildly appropriate about them as a couple. They were an unequivocally good fit. Sex pure and simple, I thought with pure and complicated envy. Blazing hormonal harmony. Even in this nebulous atmosphere they were standing close together, brushing against each other, grazing hands. They had found a house in Chelsea, by the river, and were due to move in next day.

Before we sat down for the brief service, the children stood and whispered together. There were five of them, Daisy and Lizzie, and Susanna, Jake and Ruth. Daisy and Lizzie were turned out smartly, like their mother, in tailored coats and skirts and black tights. They wore identical black felt hats that had probably been bought for the occasion.

Beside them, the other three kids looked as if they had called in at a jumble sale on the way through. I knew, however, that they had in fact dressed with unusual care. Susanna wore a long plum-coloured chenille skirt with a frilly cheesecloth blouse and the green velvet coat I had seen lying on her bed. Jake had on his school shirt buttoned up to the neck, one of Jack's discarded seventies ties, khaki serge army trousers that were rolled up at the ankles, and his leather flying jacket lined with greying lambswool. Ruth was wearing a sari, teamed with ripple-soled boots and Daria's Afghan coat.

In deference to Cyn's convictions, we had avoided choosing any music with religious connotations. Instead, the songs that greeted us as we filed in and slowly took our seats were a composite tape from the collection of old cassettes in Mim's sitting room, including 'Leaving on a Jet Plane' and 'I Shall Be Released'.

I thought this may have been a mistake as the words filled the space. They sounded both incongruous and juvenile, but also so nostalgic and bittersweet with their youthful associations that I saw Mim and Bess, shepherding their children ahead of me, struggle to keep their composure.

As I moved to take my seat I was half aware of a flurry behind me. I'd been with Daria, but someone had pushed in front of her. By the time I realised what had happened it was too late and I was halfway along the pew, hemmed in by Cyn's academic friends on my right. On my left, maddeningly, was Stuart. Although I'd refused to see him again he had kept up a bombardment of beseeching phone calls, and letters slid regularly under the door.

Enraged, I tried to shuffle along the seat away from him,

jamming myself against the unresponsive bulk of Cyn's female colleague Maggie, who gave me a chummy, all-girls-together grin. I soon realised that Stuart would move to fill the vacant space. He squashed against me, locking my elbows in. I jumped up with difficulty and tried to get out. There was only one way, and it was blocked by Stuart. He made it subtly but perfectly plain that he was not going to let me pass. I engaged, as unobtrusively as possible, in a graceless little shoving match before I subsided in my seat.

'Why the hell did you come here? Nobody invited you,' I snarled, under cover of 'The Tracks of My Tears'. Whenever I heard any of these songs in the future and Cyn's funeral crossed my mind, I imagined the memory would be contaminated by thoughts of Stuart.

He gave me a sympathetic smile, redolent with understanding and empathy. He leaned against me and whispered, 'I know what you're going through, with Sam and Cynthia. I'm ready to support you in any way you want.'

I closed my eyes against the fleeting thought of Sam. Stuart's hot breath in my ear produced in me something akin to an allergic reaction. My dislike of him had evolved seamlessly, I realised, into loathing.

'I don't want your support in any way, shape or form,' I managed to say. The ceremony began a moment later. At least, I thought, it will be mercifully brief.

Bess, Mim and I had talked about having some kind of eulogy. But it seemed vaguely inappropriate, and in the end we had rejected the idea. Anyone who felt inclined could get up and say a few words afterwards. Instead, we'd searched for some poetry or prose, trawling through Shakespeare's sonnets and Mim's shelves of literary paperbacks. It was extraordinary how each piece we looked at managed to disqualify itself at some point, usually because of some gratuitous religious reference.

We thought of 'Fear no more the heat o' the sun' from 'Cymbeline'. That was fine, until the lines 'All lovers young, all lovers must/Consign to thee, and come to dust.' There must be no reference to lovers, we thought. We were united on that.

It was Jack who provided the key. Mim had insisted on consulting him, and he reeled off a list of predictably unsuitable poems, among them T.S. Eliot's *The Waste Land*, which disallowed itself on the grounds of title alone. However, it sparked a faint memory in me, and I reached for Eliot's *Four Quartets*.

From the first and last of the four poems I cobbled together what we agreed was an extract worthy of Cynthia. It speculated with concepts of time – present, past and future. It had the necessary English Lit. gravitas and intellectual resonance. And it contained sentences of potent and evocative language that had passed into common use. One in particular 'human kind cannot bear very much reality' seemed eerily apposite.

We were fortunate that the minister, a slight, sandy Scot, had a fine timbre to his voice. He read the ringing words better than we could have hoped, with simple emphasis and no histrionics. He came to the end of the chosen passage.

We die with the dying:
See, they depart, and we go with them.
We are born with the dead:
See, they return, and bring us with them.

We watched the doors open and Cyn's coffin slide away and disappear from sight. The music, now haunting and elegiac, was Vaughan Williams' 'The Lark Ascending', the theme of one of Cyn's favourite films.

'Not a dry eye in the house,' Jack said outside. Even his, I noted, looked suspiciously bright. 'Though I must say, picturing the old Cyn as a skylark soaring into the ether was a tough call.'

There had been a silent, emotion-laden interval before everyone filed out. Stuart remained seated, wielding his handkerchief. He stayed in his seat for what seemed an unconscionably long time, and I knew he was obstinately determined to keep me trapped. Maggie and Quentin on my right made restive movements.

'That's poor Stuart Friend, you may remember,' I explained in a carrying whisper. 'He's still holding a torch for Cynthia.' Stuart leapt up as if he'd been seared with a branding iron.

When we finally got outside I said loudly, 'It was good of you to come, Stuart. Why, you're the sole exemplar of Cyn's romantic life. Her only extant *lover*, perhaps.' I had composed this satisfactory little speech while waiting for him to move, and I made sure we were close to Jack. Stuart blushed to the roots of his hair.

Jack didn't let me down. 'Is this the proud keeper of Cynthia's flame?' he boomed. He looked more closely at Stuart. 'You certainly get around, don't you, old chap? Glad to see you didn't bump yourself off as you threatened. You must have been sorely tempted *again*, I imagine,' he lowered his voice, 'after your tragic bereavement.'

Bess made a beeline for Stuart's side. I heard her unleash lavish condolences and ask him, with warm compassion, to tell her *all* about himself and Cyn. Stuart shot me a look of newborn hatred. It warmed the cockles of my heart.

That evening, after the strays and stayers had dispersed, Mim and I sat ruminating in front of the fire. We were both aware, with the potent mixture of melancholy and expectancy which comes with imminent change, that it was the end of a chapter. The room was full of moving shadows, and it felt as if we were not the only ones sitting there.

Mim touched my hand. 'You'll be moving out soon.' It was not a query but a statement.

'Yes. Real life has come back to claim me.'

I had started work on my book. I was a stringer for magazines in Sydney and New York. I'd begun to look for my own place.

'What should we do with Cyn's ashes?' They sat in an urn on the mantelpiece.

'I think we should get rid of them as soon as possible. They make me nervous.' I'd always found the physical reality of someone's remains, reduced to cinders, deeply surreal and uncomfortable.

Mim said, 'Do you know what I'd like to do with them? I'd like to take them to Australia and scatter them in the Blue Mountains, on New Year's Eve.'

'Take the children with you?'

'Oh yes. Sea, light, warmth, wide open spaces. Grandparents. We haven't been back for a long time.'

In my mind I saw the Blue Mountains. That impenetrable range of soaring vertical escarpments, forested with eucalypts, where fine droplets from the leaves hang in the hot air, forming a distant blue haze.

On the fertile plains beyond the mountains lay the town where my family lived. My father and stepmother, and Edward, Henry and Thea. I had grown up hardly knowing them.

'I'll come.'

Mim's face shone as if she had walked into the sun.

'I can see it now,' I said. 'We'll stand up there on Echo

366

Point at dawn and throw them into the void. Into the vast blue bottomless abyss, down, down, way down to the green valley floor.'

It struck again, that swift intoxication. I could see them, the motes, thousands upon thousands of tiny specks, spinning and turning as they caught the light. Some to float away on the early breezes, some to swoop and tumble. Each in its turn to be caught up in another web, and to embark on another journey.

'Listen, Mim . . .' I said.